BEHAVING LIKE ADULTS

ALSO BY ANNA MAXTED

Getting Over It
Running in Heels

ANNA **MAXTED**

ReganBooks

An Imprint of HarperCollins*Publishers*

BEHAVING LIKE **ADULTS**

A NOVEL

HarperCollins books may be purchased for educational,
business, or sales promotional use. For information please
write: Special Markets Department, HarperCollins
Publishers Inc., 10 East 53rd Street, New York, NY 10022.

FIRST EDITION

Designed by Judith Stagnitto Abbate/Abbate Design

Printed on acid-free paper

Library of Congress Cataloging-in-Publication Data
has been applied for.

ISBN 0-06-009667-5

03 04 05 06 07 RRD 10 9 8 7 6 5 4 3 2 1

For Leonie

ACKNOWLEDGMENTS

A huge thank-you to Jonny Geller, Cassie Jones, Sharyn Rosenblum, Carl Raymond, Judith Regan, Deborah Schneider, the brilliant people at ReganBooks, Phil Robinson, Caroline Thompson, Sarah Paul, Anthony Barrow, Mark Curtis, Lorraine Adams, David Sack, John Nathan, Sunil Kapoor, Tiffany Smith (because I forgot to thank her last time), Frank Tallis, Gavin Tranter, Aileen McColgan, Anna Moore, Mary Maxted, Wendy Bristow, Kirsty Fowkes, Andy McKillop, Yvonne and Kate Oliver, Linda Bailey, Anne Bellamy, D.S. Ross Walker, Stephanie, Jeanette King, Andy Robinson, John Perry, and Tracey Moynihan.

CHAPTER 1

Modern women don't believe in love. Believing in love carries roughly the same stigma as halitosis. It's as old-fashioned as going on a diet (as opposed to a detox). It suggests you have no sense of irony, and you like Meg Ryan films. A modern woman cannot accept that Father Christmas is a fraud *and* persist in believing that one sunny day her dark handsome destiny will appear in a puff of Fahrenheit and haul her off to Happy Ever After.

I know all that and yet I *do* believe in love. I apologize. But I can't help it. I presume it's a genetic blip which might also account for my dress sense (too pink).

I just like stuff to be nice. That's even worse. If you wish to maintain even a shred of credibility, you have to be cynical and keep your mouth in a hard straight line even when you find something funny. I'm not stupid. I do know the world is cruel. But I always like to hope that it isn't. I test my *awwww!* count. You proceed through the day, listing every occasion you're prompted to think *awwww!*

You can't cheat and hire a puppy to peep out of a basket. Often, my total is horrific.

When I started the dating agency, Rachel crowed that now I'd see what people were really like. I wouldn't believe the lies they told to get laid! She said this as if I were either a nun or a social retard who believed—despite living in a densely populated part of the planet for twenty-nine years—that seduction was about honing in on the obvious and blurting it. Whereas I'm well aware that if that were the case, the human race would have fizzled out in the Iron Age when Wilma stared at Fred and said, "That's quite a small flint-stone you've got there." Sometimes I think my friends confuse optimism with idiocy.

Of course, unpleasant characters applied. When you launch a dating agency, even if you specify as we did that Girl Meets Boy was for the "young and funky" (which no doubt deterred everyone in both of those categories), you invite weirdos to your door. It's Open Day for Oddballs. It's the Marilyn Manson Fan Club Parents Evening. But overall—despite the nutters, nerds, squares, sociopaths, oafs, half-wits, dummies, brutes, airheads, and deviants gracing our files—the *awwww!* count was immense.

Partly to distinguish ourselves from the Christians with an interest in ornithology and partly to discern if anyone out there possessed a sense of humor (a Good Sense of Humor is a luxury), we asked silly questions on the application form. Even Nige—who'd only agreed to help out because he was between acting jobs and is nosy—agreed that the hoi polloi were far wittier than he'd given them credit for. I particularly warmed to the twenty-seven-year-old man who replied to "Do you have any talents?" with "Probably not."

Girl Meets Boy began as a business, but the people who used it fast melted my heart to a soft, sticky caramel. Also, toward the end of the great fiancé fiasco (not before in case you were wondering), it did occur to me that *I* might find someone. Don't mix business with pleasure? I thought it was a phrase made up by killjoys to stop you from smiling at work. I was trying to enjoy what I'd achieved. I'd achieved so much, everyone said, I should be *so* proud. Oh, absolutely. I'd made sacrifices, but not whole lambs, more the odd chop. I should be happy.

When I'm told I should be happy, I start trying to measure it with a ruler.

Everything is a test. Rachel rings to say that the cab dropped her outside her flat, whereupon she bade farewell to a loud luxurious fart. She then turned and saw her neighbor padding up the path behind her. We howl with laughter. Yes, but is *that* happy? The cat sits on my lap, her purr rumbles through me, and I sigh—that's happy, surely? I visit the art house cinema because I hate Warner Village (Village? It's not a village!), and I feel comforted by the fact that they sell whole-grain flapjacks—even though I wouldn't eat one for a bet. I *watch* myself do this, and I think, That woman, she's smiling. But is she happy?

Self-interrogation is dangerous. Your inner voice pronounces the obvious—"You don't realize you're happy till it's gone"—as if it's your fault for not keeping an eye out, thus making you feel worse than you do already. But you're not to blame. Mostly, happiness doesn't just drop from you like an apple from a tree. It trickles away silently, evaporating over the months and years, until one day you feel a strange hollowness inside. You glance around and it hits you—despite all you own, your great, glorious success, you have nothing.

The good and therefore unreported news is that you can find it again. It might be a bit of a trek. If you haven't the least idea of your destination, the journey takes a little longer. But I'm your fresh-breathed proof. Rachel was right. I *did* discover what people were really like. And yet, after everything that happened, I got happy again. I still believe in love. As I said, I can only apologize. And explain.

When Nige suggested a party to celebrate the success of Girl Meets Boy, I did wonder. I had done well, creating a company from scratch and making it pay. Although any old pinhead can create a company. They make it foolproof at Companies House. For around eighty pounds they hand you over a shrink-wrapped company. All you, the pinhead, have to do is provide the names of the board of directors and their share allocation. I was the director with seventy shares, and in a selfless act my younger sister, Claudia, was secretary with thirty. (This was in lieu of pay for the first month. Nige, however, preferred to resist bribes. That way, he said, he didn't feel "obligated.")

Another twenty quid to Companies House and I could name my baby Girl Meets Boy. Then, the most important part of any business plan, I found a good accountant. And that, give or take a bit of fuss, was it. My accountant did the bore's share of the paperwork, instructing me what I owed the taxman each month via apologetic E-mail. This allowed me to devote myself to my real interest: making Girl Meets Boy a hit.

My strategy was unscientific. I hoped that if I ensured that people had fun, and shelled out for advertising, financial success would follow. And after seven months it did.

So did I really want to tempt Fate and host a party? People *might* have fun, but it wasn't guaranteed. And you have to be pretty pleased with yourself to host a party. The subtext is, "I'm so interesting, I think you should all come to my home and bring wine." And parties are like cakes. They can fall flat for no apparent reason. Also, if you care the least bit about whether your guests are enjoying themselves, you are bound to have a stressed, hassled, fun-free time.

Nige, the arch manipulator, saw me hesitate and cried, "Oh go on! Everyone will have so much fun!"

I looked at his beseeching face and said, "Let's do it."

That's my weakness. I like other people. They interest me. There's hardly anyone you can't learn something from, even if it's "Check in the mirror, front *and* behind, before you go out." Nige wanted cool and exclusive, but I thought we should do the bash Elton John style: invite the world, every member of Girl Meets Boy included. I felt protective toward them, as if they were my kids. Most of them I was fond of. When people trust you, it's hard not to like them, even the annoying ones. This party would be a way of saying thanks.

My only problem was Nick. My ex-fiancé. Our relationship was over, except he hadn't moved out. He was still waiting for his friend

Manjit's girlfriend to clear out her spare room (an excuse so poor I wanted to huddle it in a blanket). The truth was, he wanted me back. I was past being flattered. Nick stayed fixed at that stage of emotional development where you yowl for whichever toy is removed from your grasp. I ended it too amicably for my own good. I feel sheepish about this. I think it's far worse for the "ender" than the "endee." Especially an endee as charming and wily as Nick. He'd guilt-trip me into inviting him to the Girl Meets Boy party, then worry me like a fox all night.

Because of this, I wasn't overjoyed about going on my own. Normally, I wouldn't fret about it. If there's one thing I don't need a man for, it's to attend a party. They're a hindrance every time. But this was different. I wasn't in the right frame of mind to be fighting off Nick the entire evening. I needed a safety barrier. Also, there was something about attending a party for Girl Meets Boy without a partner that bothered me. It felt too puritan. If *I* saw me there alone, I'd be suspicious, like meeting a baker who isn't fat.

As party night loomed, Claudia—I gave her a job when it became obvious that no one else would—tried to encourage me to pick a man off the pile. "Come *on*, Holly," she said, poking the morning's stack of letters with polished fingernails. "It'll be like Cinderella in reverse. Just ring one up and explain who you are. They'll be thrilled. A date with the boss of Girl Meets Yob. Plucked from obscurity to attend your grand ball. The token date. It's the kind of thing that gives blokes a kick. Or—or! or! or! How about this. You could ask Stuart again!"

I choked. Despite my devious plan of skimming off the single cream for myself, after time spent thinking about it I'd gone off the idea. I felt maternal toward these men. Even the thirty-eight-year-olds. Thus, it would not have been healthy to shag them. Plus, I'd had one bad experience, which I'm unwilling to share because it was such a disaster. However, as I've just let slip the disaster's name, I might as well tell you, if only so you see what I was dealing with.

A month before, the PA of a solicitor named Stuart Marshall had E-mailed us, asking for an application form on his behalf. I sent it to her but couldn't resist adding, "Does he make you forge his Christmas cards too?" She replied, "That's the least of it."

Two days later Stuart's details were delivered—by courier—to our office. Stuart's rapacious misuse of company resources gave him an air of benign familiarity. Despite never having set eyes on the guy, I felt I knew him. Claudia was half in love with Stuart already. She fell on that envelope like it was a fifty-pound note.

Nige tweaked Stuart's photograph from her grasp. He arched an eyebrow, drawled, "Whiff of the Channel Five Newsreader," and spun it through the air to me. Well, possibly. Groomed like a racehorse. In blue Speedos. A lot of our clients do that—send us a snap that borders on intimate. Nige finds it "sad and grotesque," but I tend to find it more *awwww!* than *aaaagh!* It's only because they want to be accepted. They want to find someone. They're desperate to prove that they're good enough.

I understand that. It maddens me when I tell someone what I do and they sneer. We're biologically programmed to seek out nurturing relationships and yet, somehow, there are people who assume the attitude that this pursuit is trite. I tell them that those unable to empathize or forge rewarding bonds with others start by pulling the wings off bluebottles and end up breaking into people's homes and dismembering entire families. It usually shuts them up. So I was more sympathetic to Stuart than Nige was. Even when Claudia stuck her feet on the desk and started to dissect Stuart's vision of the perfect woman.

"Jesus Christ, listen to this.

" 'She should have a healthy zest for life'—as opposed to an unhealthy apathy—'she should be secure in herself and her choices'—blimey, he sounds like *you*, Nige!" (Claudia once overheard Nige telling a fellow thespian that he "admired Brad Pitt's choices." Unbelievably, Nige wasn't referring to Gwyneth or Jennifer, but to the genius decisions Brad made when acting. Quite rightly, she's never let him forget it.)

" 'Not needy, but looking to share her passion and vitality'—what an arse!—'ambitious, but probably already sorted careerwise, able to maintain a balance between work and play, prepared to make quality time for her partner and friends, interests of her own but would share a love of good food, wine, company, and exercise. She would enjoy long walks or runs along the beach'—sorry, but who *alive* doesn't enjoy a long sodding walk along the beach?—'and would enjoy riding high when I fly my plane.' Good God, is he for real? What does that mean? Is it some sort of filthy pun? I bet it's not his, I bet he hires it."

"He probably means his toy plane," suggested Nige. "He runs 'round the garden holding it above his head. He wants his perfect woman to watch from the upstairs window."

Agreed, Stuart did sound a little—no a *lot*—much, but I was intrigued. That superlative sense of self-entitlement always starts me wondering about the mother. Not the father, you'll note. Just the mother. I blame her. What a sexist. Shocking. "Go on, Claw."

Claudia grinned. " 'She is ideally at least five foot seven but no taller than five foot nine, physically very active'—well, we all know what *that* means!—'has blond hair'—no, surprise me!—'and aged between twenty-four and twenty-nine. I would hope she has at least one relationship of respectable length behind her and has lived with a former partner. She should live in Zones One or Two'—unbloody-believable—'however, ideally she would not have any baggage (i.e., children or be divorced). She would be a female version of me.' Wow. Holly, you've *got* to go out with him!"

I'd tipped back on my chair to listen, and I nearly fell off it. "What? I'm nothing like that woman! No one is. And you know what I'm like about flying. I panic if the pilot has a weak chin. Anyway, why *me*? What have *I* done?"

I looked beseechingly around our cramped little office—paper everywhere; it seemed to grow from the walls and breed on the floor—hoping for Nige's support. When he pursed his lips, I knew I wasn't going to get it.

"It's what you haven't done," he said. "You need to take action, Holly. Show Nick that it's over. I know you're still fond of each other, but it's not wise, him still lurking 'round the house. You need him to witness that you've moved on to better things. Claw is right. Stuart is just the pissing contest that Nick needs. You needn't tell Stuart who you are. I'll ring him, tell him Girl Meets Yob is giving him a free, er, trial. If we deem an applicant to be, ah, a VIP, we don't put them straight into a speed-dating session. We assign them what we call a 'free-range' date with an elite *counterpart* that's unsupervised and can last as long as they wish. How's that sound?"

"Like bullshit," I said.

Claw started banging her fists on the desk, shouting, "Yes, yes, yes!"

While I am old enough not to be intimidated by two people disagreeing with me, I am also wise enough to know when to save my breath. "I'll think about it," I lied. Well, *I* thought I was lying, but my mind had other ideas. It danced around Stuart the whole day. I want to make this clear, I wasn't attracted to Stuart—I'm not an insane sadomasochist who doesn't know Hitler's CV when she sees it—but Nige was right.

I *was* still fond of Nick, dangerously fond. We'd gone out for five years, most of which were good, great even. And then we'd coasted. We were two parallel lines, always close but never together. Occasionally, we'd have a passionate quarrel during which many promises would be made. But not kept. Nick admitted that he didn't know how to make an effort in a relationship. I was his first, as he put it, Big One. Incidentally, when I say "effort" I don't mean he didn't send enough roses or stud the walls with little love notes (although he didn't). I mean he didn't talk much, wash enough, or seem to take particular pleasure in my company. Don't do me any favors.

But if I had to pinpoint the single factor that drove me to Stuart, it was the Febreze. As Claudia and Nige hummed about me, murmuring, "Go *on,* Holly. Oh *please,* it'll be fun," I thought of Nick, too lazy to shower, spraying his stinky feet with Febreze ("safely eliminates odors on fabrics and kills the bacteria that cause them"). And then a ripple of hard-done-by billowed airily through me and I thought, Ah, why not? What harm can it do?

How long have you got?

CHAPTER 2

thought I was good at reading people. Is there anyone in the world who doesn't think they're good at reading people? I shouldn't have trusted myself. My judgment had already proved faulty with Nick. Why did I presume to know Stuart? The truth is, I'd painted my life into a corner. Instead of freeing me, every choice I'd made hemmed me in. It's a pity to regret, but I did. I needed an escape. And if you're dying in a desert, you'll see hope in air and dust.

I refuse to begin with Stuart, though. He'd love that, if I began with him. The best way to gall people who wish you ill is not to give them space in your head. There's a great putdown in *Casablanca*, where Peter Lorre says to Humphrey Bogart, "You despise me, don't you?" He replies, "Well if I gave you any thought I probably would." I think that's funny. So I'll start with me and Nick.

Five years ago, when I met Nick, he was helping a duck. I was driving through one of the quainter parts of London and I saw this duck waddling along the pavement. A thin young man with a cigarette hanging out his mouth sauntered behind at a respectful distance from madam's tail feathers, ushering her away from the road. Everyone was ignoring them. Londoners are good at this. We can ignore *anything*. That disappoints me. I get a kick when I say hello to the ticket guy at my tube stop and he says, "All right, darlin'," and gives me a high five. It turns my city into a village.

Anyhow, I got the urge to offer the man and the duck a lift. I decided there was no way this guy was a lunatic, as he was helping a duck. So I swerved across the traffic and buzzed down my window. "Excuse me," I said, launching into one of the silliest sentences I've ever spoken, "do you and the duck need a lift anywhere?" Then it struck me that the duck might be his pet. He could be taking her for a walk, and I'd just busybodied in there. In the smarter parts of town you can act like a complete nut and get away with it, so long as you own the matching bag.

I was grateful when the man took the cigarette out of his mouth and smiled. "It's very kind of you," he said, "but I think being in a Golf might scare her. I wouldn't want her getting in, you know, a flap." He giggled at this bad joke, which made me smile. "But you could always leave the car and help me get her back to the pond." I parked on a double yellow and together we directed Jemima toward her pond. We got as far as the Chinese restaurant when, very sensibly, she decided to fly the rest of the way. We returned to a parking ticket.

"You might as well make the most of it," said Nick. "Do you want to get an ice cream?"

Our relationship was not about being adult. Some couples race to become less liberal clones of their parents. Nick's best pal, Manjit, chose Bo, a woman who clamps down on fun like it's illegal. When Nick showed Manjit a new purchase—a shirt with a design of a cat, a cockerel, a donkey, a bird, and a beaver on its back, plus the beautifully embroidered words "Pussy, Cock, Ass, Tit, Beaver"—Manjit said mournfully, "I wouldn't be allowed that." Same when he saw the two electric love hearts dangling from the Golf's rearview mirror. *Tacky.*

I felt sorry for Manjit, although privately I wondered what Bo could actually do to him if he bought a shirt like Nick's. Tear it off his back? Ignore him for a month? Refuse to leave the house with him? Stop hauling him to classical concerts and her school reunions? Manjit, buy the shirt. (He didn't, so I could only presume that in some way he enjoyed the childish relief of relinquishing free will, one of the few advantages of shacking up with a dictator.)

Maybe Nick and I weren't so different after all. We gave each other permission to behave like babies. On the face of it, that was good. In any romantic movie, universal code for "these people are meant to be together" is a shot of the guy sitting opposite the girl in a diner gazing at her adoringly as she stuffs down a burger and talks nonsense with her mouth open, mustard dribbling down her chin. The precise opposite of how a woman eats on a date. The point is: It's okay to act like you're five. You are officially in paradise.

With Nick I acted more like I was five than when I *was* five. I was quite a serious kid. It took me until I met Nick to realize I'd passed up on half my childhood. Nick would say, "Remember the episode of *Fawlty Towers* when Basil attacks the Mini?" I'd blush and say, "No." He'd recall the time he bet Manjit that he could eat three tins of golden syrup. He won the bet, but alas, puffed up and spent three days in the hospital. Or when he and Manjit went exploring on their bikes and found a dead bullet by the stream. High on good citizenship, they'd sped it to the local police station, where officers had to practically stuff their hands in their mouths to keep from laughing.

To me, this was idyllic, a marvelous adventure tale, *Tom Sawyer* meets *The Secret Garden*. My upbringing was fine, nothing wrong with it. Just a little more cautious, conservative. Our TV was black-and-white, toaster-sized, and kept in a cupboard. I was a bookworm. Whereas Nick lived the dream, I read about it. My parents are wonderful people, old-fashioned in their innocence, never expecting much. The first time we went on holiday to Portugal, I remember my father blinking in pleasure because the hotel had a pool. My mother looked cowed at her good fortune. It hurt me to see it in their eyes, What have we done to deserve this?

While they were keen to give us—me, Claudia, and our big sister, Isabella—whatever we wanted, it never occurred to them that we could want more than we were given. Which was books. Visits to stately homes. Museum trips. Two-thousand-piece jigsaws of English country gardens. Love. My parents never wanted more than they were given. My mother would have bitten off her tongue before she complained about anything. Her old friend Leila once gave her a cotton-tissue holder for Christmas. It must have cost 5 pence. A gas station wouldn't dare give it to you free with your petrol. Mum had bought Leila a painting by a local artist she admired.

It was painful to see my mother wriggle to excuse Leila. She didn't give a damn about the meanness, it was the lack of respect that got her. "Well," she said, "money's tight for Leila. And you know Leila, she's a batty old thing." Even though we both knew that "batty" didn't cut it. Unless you're clinically insane you know "tissue holder as gift" is unacceptable. But I kept quiet. It's easier to forgive than to confront. If you've been slapped in the face, you don't need people saying, "Gosh, you've been slapped in the face." "Why didn't she just give you a poo wrapped up in a hankerchief?" cried Nick.

Yea, behold the miracle. My parents adored Nick. He could say and do anything, cheeky as you like. They were in awe, treated him like a prince. That meant a lot. I'm uncool; parental approval matters to me. In fact, *any* parental approval matters to me, probably to the extent of weirdness. Once Nick and I saw a brilliant new band play their first big gig, and the frontman kept saying, in a croak of disbelief, "This is incredible for us, thank you so much for coming." All I could think was, His parents must be so proud. That's my first thought every time I see talented people onstage, Their parents must be so proud. (My second thought is, I wish *I* could do that.)

The mind-set, I suppose, of a woman resisting adulthood. I fell in love with Nick *and* his parents. I cherished the fact that he came from a glamorous family. His mother and father, Lavinia and Michael Mortimer, were a revelation. Rich, sparkly, magical, mysterious, like the parents in *Peter Pan*. They traveled endlessly, collecting art. They campaigned for their favorite charities. They owned a villa in Italy, which they'd renovated from ruin a decade before Umbria became fashionable. They both spoke fluent Italian. I was so bedazzled the first time I went there that when Nick's mother offered me a dish of olives, I went blind with fright. I reached for the brightest item on the plate, and she said kindly, "No, dear, that's a lemon."

Nick's parents indulged him, like we all did. He entertained us. The first two years of our relationship I had a blast. I'd never been naughty—I was content, I hadn't felt the need. But it was liberating, to play. I thought it wild that I had a boyfriend whose job was to dress as Mr. Elephant at children's parties. It endeared me that his small Islington flat was a shrine to grime, and that when his mother visited she would sigh, in her silvery voice, "Oh, *Nick*." *I* didn't comment. If my man chose to live on hygiene's edge, I wouldn't interfere. I was proud of not trying to change him. So very modern of me. Nick and I spent a great many months in his king-size bed screwing, drinking vodka, or both. Only twice was I bitten by a flea.

We bought a cotton candy maker from the Shopping Channel and ate pink cotton candy for breakfast. We got drunk and ran along the road swapping people's doormats and then, because I felt bad about it, we ran along the road swapping them back. We bought twenty squirt bottles of chocolate sauce and had a food fight in the garden until we and the grass were brown. I was thinking to myself, This is what couples do in films. Then Nick stood up and said, "I don't like this. It's like we're covered in poo."

I thought I was a secure person until I met Nick. Then I saw what it was to be heart and soul at peace with yourself. I do believe that people treat you as you present yourself, and Nick presented as a gift from God. Luck followed him around like a puppy. Nick's parents owned a big white boat, and Nick blew it up.

He'd filled it with fuel after a day on the river, turned on the ignition, and *Bang!* The wooden deck splintered under his feet, flames shooting high. He grabbed my hand and we jumped into the Thames. The boat sank. Or as Nick told his father on the phone, "Was lying low in the water." A pipe had come loose and fuel had slopped into the engine. The firefighters said we could have had fifty-foot flames. We were lucky the whole thing didn't explode. Lucky Nick.

It was his idea to buy a house together. I was flattered. I don't mean that in a "Gee, li'l ol' me" kind of way. I mean that I loved Nick so fiercely I wanted to eat him up. If I could have crawled inside his skin I would have. I could almost understand the cannibalistic lust of Jeffrey Dahmer, my desire was so violent. Some nights I'd sob aloud because one day we'd die and then what would I do if we weren't together for eternity? He felt the same about me. "I worship you," he said. "Marry me."

We found a house and bought it with less thought than some people give to buying a newspaper. (Islington flats, even small dirty ones, scrub up well and sell for silly money. Even my non-Islington flat, bought four years earlier when property was affordable, had in those four years earned more than I had.)

It was a riot, flying by the seat of our pants, cheating death. When you live apart and meet for the good times, you can pretty much edit out the worst bits of yourself. The cold slap of joint property ownership put an end to that. Often Nick would lie in bed till midday. He ignored bills, claiming an allergy to paperwork. He left a trail of crap behind him like a snail. I'd considered myself easy-going. Now, to my embarrassment, I found I wasn't.

"Let Nick face the consequences of his actions," bossed my sister Isabella, a psychologist. "If he doesn't water the plants, let them die. He'll learn."

I didn't let the plants die. You don't nurture something, then let it die. Anyhow, I knew they'd die and he wouldn't notice. I consoled myself that Isabella counseled couples on how to argue effectively: be specific in your complaint, employ the pronoun "I," not "you," keep your voice calm and level. When I inquired how *she* argued effectively with her husband, Frank, she replied, "I scream at him."

I screamed at Nick. What next, cutting out recipes? Before I'd been proud that I didn't want to change him. Now that I did, I discovered that I couldn't.

It hit me with a shock that Nick wasn't playing hard before he embarked on forty years of working hard. This was *it* for him. He'd continue to live like a student till he was sixty-five. There was no grand plan, no passion to make a success of his life. His idea of making a success of his life was to live in the moment, be happy. But, I thought, you need *things* to be happy. We didn't set a date for the wedding.

I was ambitious. I wasn't going to end up like my parents— meek, humble, grateful for crumbs. Nick, it struck me, *was* like them in that he accepted whatever happened to him. His fatality bordered on Australian. He had an end-of-the-rainbow approach to finances. He was pleased for me to earn the cash. My career became a sanctuary. At the office I could blank out the rage that pulsed through me when my metal hairpins jabbed my scalp because Nick had absentmindedly picked off their smooth plastic ends. Because he refused to behave even the teeniest bit like an adult, *I* was forced to grow up, and I resented it.

I was an imposter. Do adults think, This book I'm reading

matches my pajamas? Blush when a shop assistant calls them "madam"? Feel heartless when trading in their rusty old car for a shiny new one? Fold a black-and-white-checked dishcloth onto the cat's head and proclaim her Yasser Alleycat? Eat all the chocolate off a Kit Kat first? Lie on the floor and wish they lived on the ceiling? Stroke their childhood toy (not that Fluffy is real, but just in *case*)? Jab a knife into the toaster while it's still on? No? Well, then. I was an adult at work, taking care of others, but I refused to be that at home. Inside, I was still a little girl. Because you're not truly grown up until you're what, fifty?

Our relationship dropped sheer off a cliff. I kept more and more of me to myself. Nick didn't offer to make me coffee, why should I leave him any cherries? He never wrote down my phone messages, why should I tell him he was missing *Larry Sanders*? I was a hypocrite. I had endless goodwill for the world and none for Nick. I'd watch the RSPCA's TV appeal and phone them £500 to repent for the human race. Same for the NSPCC, guilt by association. But I'd spit and boil when Nick begged a fiver. So much for our eternal love. It couldn't survive a broken dishwasher.

Yet when I thought about ending our engagement, I felt panicked, sodden with dread, my insides heavier than I could carry. But then I didn't want to be fifty-eight, married, miserable, and marooned, looking back on a shadow of a life. Girl Meets Boy was a joy for me, but I needed something separate, outside of it. I didn't blame Nick wholesale. He hadn't changed, I had. He was the love of my life. But he was also, undeniably, the catalyst that turned me into a person I didn't much like.

I told him it was over on what must have been the prettiest night of the summer. A fat moon lay low, heavy and golden in the sky. Earlier, the setting sun had tinted the streets and houses pink. I chose to take all this as a cosmic sign: It's not the end of the world. But fuck, it felt like it.

CHAPTER 3

I felt that my resolve might snap like a breadstick. I was always a breath away from begging him to stay. I had to chant in my head, over and over, He doesn't love you enough, you don't love him enough, or I'd weaken. Our families were aghast and distraught, which made it even harder. And when Nick wept, I wanted to wail my remorse at his feet. It would have been easy to be nice to him now. So I focused on his flaws; I magnified them ten times over. He didn't want *me*, he just objected to rejection on principle. I made myself despise him for not having the honesty to walk away.

Scratch what I said earlier about the Febreze leading me to Stuart. I could pretend Nick and his smelly feet drove me to it, to that stupid juvenile plan to humiliate him via some stranger plucked from a pile. I could maintain that Claudia and Nige were so persuasive that I had no choice, but no. Even if my colleague made the call, I made the decision. I'll stand up and say it. It was my fault.

When, two months after I'd told him it was over, Nick discovered I had a date with some guy from Girl Meets Boy, he went bananas. As he slammed the kitchen door again, it occurred to me that our grand plan wasn't foolproof. My date with Stuart Marshall—who'd swallowed the bait, as Nige said, "like a carp biting on a maggot"—was as likely to make Nick want me more as less. I told myself this had nothing to do with me as a person. Nick would battle Stuart over a cardboard box. Which made it easier to tell him just what I thought of his behavior. When you're angry at yourself, there's always the option of taking it out on a loved one.

"Nick," I said, "this doesn't endear you to me. Stop acting like a three-year-old. As of two months ago, it's none of your business who I see. I'm going out with this guy tomorrow, and if you can't deal with that it's your problem. And stop banging doors. You're frightening Emily. Look. Her ears are flattened to the back of her head. And her tail's gone like a toilet brush."

I heard myself make this righteous little speech and knew I'd made the right decision. See? This man turned me into someone I disliked even when we were no longer a couple.

Nick swiveled around from the side, where he was making himself a cheese sandwich, and glanced guiltily at the cat. To be divorcey about it, Emily is technically *his*. He was passing the vet surgery and saw a notice in the window about "the most affectionate" ten-year-old cat who was to be "PTS" (put to sleep) unless she was found a new home, because she had diabetes and her owner "couldn't cope emotionally." Nick yup-yup-yupped the vet's warning about commitment and returned to the flat a hero, with a handful of syringes and a small black fur ball. A month later *I* was giving Emily her insulin injections.

What a bastard, no?

To my surprise, Nick looked meek. "Sorry, darling," he said, sweetly contrite.

I realized he was speaking to the cat. Emily forgave him and arched her back to be stroked. Much as I love her, she sets a terrible example. Nick grinned and glanced at me. "You're right," he said. "I'm being a jerk. I'm sorry. Let me make it up to you. You're seeing this guy, when?"

"Tomorrow. Saturday. Daytime." I hoped I didn't sound defensive.

"Right. Okay. Cool. What you doing?"

"No idea."

I'll say here that office politics bore me to tears, and I think that one of the meanest methods of mental warfare is to cut an employee out of the informational loop. The dawning sense of isolation nibbles away at their confidence, feeds their paranoia, *confirms* it, until they're reduced to a miserable twitching wreck, their superiors' lack of faith becomes a self-fulfilling prophecy, and they resign for fear of being sacked, thus saving the bullies a wad in severance pay. In any hierarchy, it's a practice perpetuated by cowards, and I despise it—like cruelty to animals and waiters—but when the power balance is theoretically equal, I waive my morals.

In other words, I did have a vague idea of what Stuart had planned for our date (a surprise that involved the motorway and glamorous dress, which to me suggested a champagne picnic—how quaint), but I thought if I willfully froze out Nick it would send the right message. I looked him straight in the eye, and he gazed back. He's gaunt, but with a slight puffiness under his brown eyes, which are so dark they're almost black. Once I told him that he reminded me of Johnny Depp's dress sense. It did his ego no good at all. Now I wished I hadn't.

"All right," he said. "How about I make you dinner tonight? You know, to say sorry."

I couldn't think of an excuse fast enough. "Well. Yes. If you want to. You don't have to. Rachel's coming around at some point to lend me a dress." I meant this to sound how it sounded. Threatening. Don't take another step. Back away from your ex-fiancée with your hands up, etcetera. I didn't trust him and he knew it. He chose his reaction with care. "You're taking a risk, aren't you? You don't know where that dress has been. Or worse, you *do* know where it's been. On Rachel. *Urrgh.*"

I didn't want to think about it. Rachel is a dear friend, and I'd say this to her face: She's a foul slob, the finest that Cheltenham Ladies' College has produced. Even Nick (forever shoving his hands down his boxers on the grounds that "it's relaxing, like having a pouch") finds her disregard for hygiene a bit grim. She prefers to wait for the public rest room, as she appreciates a warm toilet seat.

I was about to rub it in by saying, "I don't have anything smart, and *Stuart* said smart," then recalled my vow of silence. So instead I settled for, "What time's dinner?"

I would have been a fool to pass up the offer. Nick is a fabulous chef, when he can be bothered. It was going to be tedious, cooking for myself again. Following a recipe doesn't excite me. It's math with food. (I'd cooked for Nick once during our five-year relationship. Chicken stir-fry. I hadn't cut the chicken up small enough. Nick, choking down a poultry boulder, had said, "I feel like an Alsatian.") At eight-thirtyish, Nick called me to the dining room table. This in itself was hilarious, since for the past four years we'd eaten supper either sitting in silence on the sofa or standing in single file in front of the fridge.

"Smells gorgeous," I said. (No harm in being civil.) "What is it?"

Nick beamed. "It's a Mediterranean peasant soup, *soupe au pistou*, if we're being fancy."

"Mm," I said, like a lamb to the slaughter. "What's in it?"

"Everything. Vermicelli, tomatoes, carrots, you name it." Except he didn't. (The beans, the leeks, the sprouts, the raw garlic, all of which, in my innocence, I found delicious.) The main course was sublime. A colorful plate of roasted vegetables—Jerusalem artichokes, parsnips, asparagus—and a delicious beef curry, crafted from scratch by Nick's "loving hand" with fresh ginger, cloves, cardamon, garlic, chili, cumin, coriander, and turmeric. Dessert was stewed pears with hot chocolate sauce. Nick's behavior was immaculate. He made no snide references to Stuart and when, keen to show that greed couldn't sway my resolve, I asked on the progress of Manjit and Bo's spare room, he gave me a serious answer. Maybe the Stuart plan *would* work. I was impressed.

I only began to be less impressed when Rachel arrived with the dress. I leaned to kiss her and—oh, the irony—she jumped back, crying, "Bloody hell, babes, you smell like Mummy's old Lab! Deal with that breath, it's wilting my hair!" I tested it with cupped hands and nearly passed out. I sped to the bathroom but the damage was done. The reek proved immune to brushing, flossing, and gargling with the sort of evil mouthwash that brings tears to your eyes.

Rachel passed me the dress from a safe, offensive distance ("Ring when you're better, babes"), then left. I checked it over like a guard dog inspecting a poisoned doughnut. It was either breathtakingly postmodern, the essence of cool, or eighties froufrou verging on frumpy. I wasn't hip enough to tell. Dark green sheeny material, sleeveless, bodiced, wide skirt with puffy netting underneath. And a matching bolero jacket. "*You* are going nowhere," I said to the jacket. "I'll tell you that for nothing."

I decided to wear the dress with a bright pink V-neck sweater and Adidas trainers. I had the feeling Stuart would be horrified, which didn't unduly alarm me. Life is not about being reviewed. I was congratulating myself on my inner steel and thanking the Lord for inventing mints when I felt a strange stirring in my gut. My torso seemed to inflate as I stood there. Suddenly, I was uncomfortable, my skin tight and stretched. My abdomen felt like bubble wrap being squeezed but unable to pop. It emitted a bad-tempered growl. I gasped as the breath jolted out of me. The pain was fierce and exact, a lightning strike, as surely as if someone had drawn a line across my stomach and written, Cramp here.

The next seven hours were like a bad chemistry experiment. My breath revolted even Emily, a feline not exactly minty-fresh herself. I farted like a bog of corpses—endlessly; I could have powered a hot-air balloon from London to Colorado—and (the *piss de résistance*) even my urine reeked. Nick had trumped every Bond villain yet by fouling my bladder. You forget asparagus does that to you. It's nasty. Particularly when you look and feel as though you've swallowed a beach ball. As I sat on the throne, groaning at three A.M., Nick called through the door, between gusts of laughter, "Gorgeous, are you getting set for your *date*?"

His inquiries got the response they deserved.

I awoke at 5:37 A.M. slumped on the toilet. It was not an exhilarating moment. Everyone has an ideal self-image. This was a long way from mine. Clutching the towel rack like a bewildered old woman, I tried to lurch to my feet, but my behind was stuck to the seat. I felt like stone, as if I'd fossilized overnight. Slowly, wincing, I peeled myself upright and hobbled to my bed. Lucky for Nick that he now slept in our study. If I'd laid eyes on his snoring form at that moment I'd have surrendered to primeval rage and bitten him.

Time skipped to midmorning, and I drove through the rain in my sleep, still farting. I was aware of a horseshoe-shaped bruise blooming on my buttocks, and I was chewing spearmint gum with ferocity. Stuart had wanted to pick me up from home in his Mercedes Kompressor, but while this would have out-penised Nick good and proper, I'd declined. This was our first encounter—I couldn't call it a date—and I wanted my own transportation (Nige, our intermediary, had reported back that Stuart seemed hurt by this. So I'd compromised. We'd meet in the tube parking lot and he could chauffeur us from there. If it meant that much to him.)

I was so intrigued to see what a fascist looked like in real life, I briefly forgot that I was also under inspection. Then I caught him staring. I wondered how I looked to him. I'm quite a big girl. Rachel says I have a "seventies body." Nick says I have the aura of "I'm Woman, outta my way!" Whatever. I prefer a bit of heft. I feel it's the natural order of things. It pains me to see anyone—kids, teenage girls, old people, greyhounds—that I consider too thin. Peculiar, I know, but I can't help but worry that there's unhappiness behind it. When Nick first got Emily she was a wisp. I'd feed her canned tuna, then pinch her softly like the witch in *Hansel and Gretel* to see if she'd gained weight.

"It does your heart good to see a cat eat," I'd tell Nick, who'd shake his head, laughing. What I meant was, I love to eat, I love to watch any creature eat, to me it's like a celebration of life. But suddenly, crunching on gravel in a ball gown in front of this Viking in yellow shades, I felt odd. My instinct told me that Stuart was the sort who saw it as his duty to inform normal-sized women they were fat and needed to diet. You know, make less of themselves.

"Holly?" he said, a half-smile forming on his geometrically exact face.

"Stuart?" I replied.

His smile went all the way. "You're not at all what I . . . expected. But *very* lovely. I, ah"—he whipped off the shades, revealing blond eyebrows and blue eyes—"goodness, I don't know what to say. I haven't done this before. This is my first time. I'm a blind-date virgin. How about you?"

I didn't want to fib more than I had (which was already quite a lot). As blind dates went, I was an old slapper. All in the name of research, of course. Before I launched Girl Meets Boy I'd tested the services of two established agencies. Both, I'm delighted to report, were ghastly. Stuart needed to know none of this.

"My hymen is intact," I said. Well sorry, but I like a good chauvinist. They're so much fun to bait. To my disappointment and his credit, Stuart resisted the opportunity for fatuous comment ("A little more information than I need, mah-hah-hah!"). Instead, he giggled, raised a yellow eyebrow, and gestured to his silver car. "Shall we?"

He held open the door—"Please! Allow me!"—sweetly formal, like an old-fashioned gentleman. I spotted the hamper squeezed into the joke of a backseat. (Give me a truck over a sports car, any day. It's not my favorite, zooming along horizontal.) "A picnic in the rain," I murmured. "I knew it!"

Stuart laughed. "Good guess. But not quite."

"Oh?"

Stuart glanced side-on at me. "I've arranged something a little more special for us. Let us say"—he looked at me again—"a little more *high flying.*"

Jesusgodno.

"What do you mean?"

I soon found out. To maintain his pilot's license (oh, get a life) Stuart had to fly a certain number of hours per year. He'd had this morning's flight at Northolt booked for ages, so it was no problem to take a guest. His treat. He said this like I might argue. You bet it was his treat. I wasn't about to pay this man to kill me. I tried to be noble and resign myself to the end. This was my due for trying to bait Nick. At the airport we marched from desk to desk. There was a reassuring amount of paperwork. I knew Stuart was aching for me to quiz him about being insane, I mean, a pilot.

I asked him about the safety checks.

"There's one hundred and ten points," he told me. "It takes around an hour. But I once had a plane turned 'round in eighteen minutes. You're just looking at tire pressure, that sort of thing. It'd just come in. But that was at a bigger airport."

Rushing the safety check. Excellent.

I followed him numbly onto the runway. At least, I thought, commercial pilots fly full-time. This guy was on work experience. It wasn't even his plane. He was renting it. When I rent a car, it takes me a day to master the clutch. I spend the first hour leaping about like a kangaroo. And stalling. But that's not such a problem when you're on the *ground.*

"It's pouring," I said hopefully.

"Shit," replied Stuart, frowning skyward.

"What?"

"Water melts the engine."

"Wha—"

"Joke," replied Stuart. "There's my girl."

Our plane had obviously been trundled out of the hangar like a Ford Mondeo out of a shed. I peered at the engineer and tried to assess whether or not he looked alert. I attempted to keep my breathing slow and deep, but I couldn't and panted like a dog. I prayed the cockpit had sick-bag facilities. A large fried breakfast this morning—scrambled egg, sausages, mushrooms, tomatoes, no beans—to settle my stomach already threatened to announce itself as an error.

"It's a Cessna," said Stuart, "twin propeller."

"Right."

"Twin engine, see? Greater stability. In the event of engine failure we've got some power capability. The backup engine gives us some balance control. It enables the plane to still maintain thrust. You're free-falling but, quite simply, you glide the plane down. You have the ability to land it—presuming you've got landing facilities, that is."

"Stuart," I said, keeping my tone jolly. "Please don't say 'free-falling' again."

He laughed, and his eyes crinkled. "I'll keep you safe, Holly. And"—lifting the hamper—"I hate to let a roast chicken go to waste. Hop in, then."

There weren't even steps. I clambered in the little door, and Stuart leaped in behind me. And there we were in Legoland.

"This is . . . cramped."

"Cozy," replied Stuart. I sat dumb in my seat and goggled at the mass of controls. I must have put on my headphones—"the cans" I think Stuart called them—done up my seat belt, watched Stuart flick switches, heard him check in with air traffic control, run through what I should do "in the event of an emergency," but I don't remember much of it. I presume I blanked it out. That safety procedure is just patronizing waffle, anyhow. In the event of an emergency, we all know that it's good-bye world in a big red fireball.

Then Stuart said, "Let's hit it."

What with keeping in the screams and the farts, I had my work cut out. A few of both escaped. Only now do I understand the true meaning of "taking off." Imagine stepping in a lift and jumping up twenty floors. In a jumbo, you feel the power behind you. This was like being pinged from a slingshot. Noise (mostly me, screaming) but no *vroom*. No push. A sick, vertical ascent in a cigar tube. I gripped my seat and focused on not vomiting. I knew if I opened my mouth to scream again, my stomach and its contents would fall out. Nick, I thought, my eyes blind with fear, you can stay forever. Just let me survive.

"Still alive, Holly?" said Stuart eventually.

"Just."

I noticed the plane had *windshield wipers.* How primitive can you get? I was already exhausted with the continuous tension of waiting to die. We were now horizontal but every other second a jolt knocked a gasp out of me. I can only compare it to hurtling a car over the brow of a hill at great speed and feeling your stomach fly. My innards were way behind. All of me trembled so hard I felt that my bones were in danger of rattling out of their sockets. I would have felt safer on a broomstick.

"Stuart. Will it be this turbulent all the time?"

"Chill, Holly. It's just weather. Look at the view. Enjoy it. Relax. The sky is ours—unless that is, we choose to blunder into commercial airspace and knock down a Boeing. Joke. *Joke,* okay? Bet you didn't expect Girl Meets Boy to set you up on a date like this, hey?"

I'm not that keen on the word *hey* as a question. "You're absolutely right. No, I didn't," I replied. I felt bad. Stuart genuinely thought he was giving me a thrill. He was a lot sweeter than his application form. As far as he was concerned, this horror death ride was a laugh. It wasn't his fault I was a nervous flier. Shame on me. This poor man had applied to my agency in good faith, and here I was using him for my own petty purposes—to edge my former fiancé out of the house. If I live, I told myself, I will stop being a coward. I will march up to Nick and say, "Go."

"It's wonderful," I said, glancing out of the window to check the propeller. "But"—it was only fair to tell him as soon as I could—"I feel queasy. I'm not going to be able to eat any roast chicken." Even the idea made me shudder.

Stuart grinned at me. "No problem, Holly. There are other things we can do."

I realized I was ice-cold and my teeth chattered. I like to think the best of people, I really do, but this oily innuendo could only mean one thing. His next sentence was bound to contain the word *joystick*. I can't think of one good reason why, but I laughed.

"Stuart," I said. Shake, rattle, hum, mechanical fault. "If that was a veiled reference to the Mile High Club, you have got to be *kidding* me. I mean that." I stopped. I wasn't going to reel out a list of reasons why not (I don't know you, I don't fancy you, I need you to fly the plane, etcetera). No was it. That, in my view, is enough. But curiosity overcame pride. "I can't believe sex is possible, in *this*. I bet you haven't. Ever."

Stuart laughed. "There are ways and means," he said. "You set the controls, let her ride." He nodded at his lap, a wicked look on his face. "But for a pretty girl you've got a dirty mind, Holly. I wasn't talking about that. I was talking about *this*."

I shrieked shrill and loud as our tin coffin jerked harsh left and tipped in a rush of noise, till the plane lay dead on its side and I could see its flimsy wing sharp above us. "What are you doing," I screamed. "Stop, stop, stop, you're going to kill us!" Normally I'd never speak to anyone like that, not even Nick. "Oh my God, help meeeee!"

We were plummeting, spiraling, a heinous lunatic roller-coaster, toward Earth. My hair stood on end, every follicle prickled, and I had to swallow and swallow to gulp down the saliva, the nausea, the fear. I couldn't even grab the controls. I screeched and Stuart *smiled*. He cried, "Weeeeeeeeee!" I just cried.

"Never," I choked, as he soared upward, "do that again." As it was I could barely speak. "Take me down. Properly. Carefully. Or I'll be sick on you. Or I will have a heart attack from fright and my parents will sue."

"Holly. A spiral is just a bit of fun. It's not dangerous. It's like the natural fall of a paper plane. It's a glider movement, a natural way of swooping. It doesn't even put stress on the plane. I thought you'd find it exhilarating. I'd never put us in danger. It's not like a full three hundred and sixty. I'd never do something as brash as that. That's best left for the circus."

He patted my knee and I wanted to jam a pencil through his hand. "Stuart. You've forfeited your right to preach about responsibility. Back. Down. Now."

The remainder of our flight was conducted in silence. The only talk was with air traffic. Landing was as violent as takeoff, but I was too enraged to scream aloud. The rain was fierce as we touched down, and we got soaked as we crossed the runway, but I was so delirious to be alive I didn't care. Once we were back in Stuart's car, he stuck the heating on high and touched my hand.

"Sorry," he said, "if I scared you. I didn't mean to. I thought you'd enjoy it eventually." His blue eyes looked pained, and I knew he meant it. Giddy with the euphoria of cheating death, I banished the nausea to the back of my throat and sighed. "Forget it. You loon."

Then Rachel's dress—soaked in the downpour—started to dry, giving off, as it did so, the smell of upchucked crayfish. That was it for me. What with the terror, the trauma, the shake it all about, the surprise bonus of eau-de-crayfish puke was more than my guts could handle. I projectile-vomited my fry-up, mostly over the cream interior of Stuart Marshall's Mercedes Kompressor and some over Stuart Marshall himself.

CHAPTER 4

He was actually very kind. I looked at him aghast, straight after I'd finished puking. I'm not sure what shocked me most, the fact that I'd been sick on a stranger and his lovely upholstery or that so much vomit could fly that fast out of my mouth in a horizontal jet. Stuart's face, at that moment, was a study in naked horror. The stench grabbed you by the gut and twisted. By the speed of the pulse throbbing in his neck, I thought he might throw up too. That or punch me.

"My fault," he'd said after a terrible second. "Oh *lordy*, the car!"

Already I felt much better, if a little shaken by "Oh lordy." We both leaped from the Mercedes stink prison, grateful for the fresh sting of the rain. I tore off my soiled pink sweater and Stuart pulled off his vomit-splattered shirt, revealing a tight white T-shirt. Very *Top Gun*. I remembered the blue Speedos. I spat discreetly on the ground before speaking.

"Stuart," I said. "I'm so embarrassed. I will, of course, pay for the car to be cleaned."

I didn't wish to appear excessively contrite, as privately I felt that none of this was really my digestive system's fault. I fumbled for chewing gum, and Stuart held up a hand. I noticed that his hair was curling in the rain. My personal preference is straight hair on a man. I find curly hair less masculine, shame on me. Nick's hair is caramel—halfway between brown and blond—shiny, thick, and *straight*.

"Holly, forget it," replied Stuart. A moderate impression of a smile. "I guess I frightened you up there. As a pilot you reach a certain level of expertise, you get cocky, you forget that what's normal to you isn't to a nonflyer. Don't fret about the Merc. Camille, my PA, will deal with it. I'll ring her now, yes, I know—'weekend'—but she's a saint! She'll send for it to be picked up. We'll get a cab to your little motor, nip home to yours, you'll change, and then I'll take you to a nice restaurant to make up for scaring the hell out of you."

I couldn't quite believe that (a) the man was suggesting food and (b) he wasn't rabid enough to tear my head off. It didn't make sense. He was nothing like the Stuart on his application form. That guy had standards like NASA. This one *adapted*. It was as if he twisted a dimmer switch in his head: FROWN, FADE—SMILE, ON. I didn't think he was a fake (well, no more than any of us are on a first date). I thought he was reasonable. He could admit he was wrong. I liked that. It was a nice change to what I'd been living with for the past five years.

However, Stuart did not feature in my immediate plans, which were to head home alone for a long bath that would be hot enough to turn my skin pink. So despite his curt disappointment, I said a polite good-bye at the airport. Stuart rang my cell phone three times the following afternoon. ("He wants to make good on his investment, babes," said Rachel.) It was my niggling guilt more than Nick's swaggering triumph that drove me to call him back a day later. Stuart didn't seem unpleased to hear from me, if a little piqued that I'd left it twenty-four hours, and we chatted. "Unfortunately," he was off the next morning, a two-week business trip to Bolton. He was "gutted" we couldn't meet that night. Neither I nor the agency had heard from him since.

Despite the unprofessionalism (I shuddered at what he must think of Girl Meets Boy), I'd have left it there. Like every woman who craves respect, I'm a martyr to my career, but there are limits. Sadly, Nige and Claudia, bubbling with evil glee at my misfortune, fostered a communal fondness for the legend of Stuart and wouldn't let the matter drop. And in a way, he *was* the ideal escort for me to take to the Girl Meets Boy party. After the vomit episode there was no danger of an unsolicited pounce. Yet a repeat appearance might convince Nick of our burgeoning love.

Because predictably, despite my bargain with fate at two thousand feet, I hadn't marched up to Nick and said, "Go." Back in the real world it wasn't that simple. Nick hadn't cheated on me. His sins were not tangible enough to give me the moral right to boot him out of *our* house. We had the ultimate in complications, a joint mortgage. Not forgetting that I'd ended our engagement and therefore, perhaps, I should have gone. But Nick had insisted I stay where I was "for now." He'd move to Manjit's. Or so he kept saying, but *when*? My first date with Stuart had given him a jolt. Maybe a second, albeit a month later, would see him off? I had nothing to lose, so I thought. My best hope was to insult Nick out of my life, with Stuart's help.

But you can understand if the prospect of seeing him again didn't exactly thrill me.

I hmmed. Claudia still had her legs on the desk and was staring at me expectantly. Nige was filing his nails.

"If I ask Stuart to the Girl Meets Yob party," I said, "I'll have to tell him who I really am. That I own the agency."

"So?" said Nige, blowing fingernail dust. "What's the big deal? He'll be flattered. It's not like we charged him for his elite date."

"Nige, his elite date cost him about five hundred quid in ground fees and insurance and fuel and steam cleans. He might decide to invoice me. Not that I care about that, it's more the lie."

"What lie?" said Claudia. "Holly, Nige did all the lying. You just turned up. Do me a favor, stop analyzing and ask him to the party. We've got more serious things to worry about. Like what to wear." She swung her elegant legs off the desk and muttered, "It's casual, God help me."

I gave in and invited Stuart.

On the night of the party, Nick skulked about like a vulture waiting for an antelope to kick it. He knew Stuart was picking me up and was itching to answer the door in a proprietorial way. I was far too tired to do anything but let him. Fortunately, I'd had the foresight to explain Nick's status and mental age to Stuart. After a short, shocked silence, he'd been extremely understanding.

Nick's feelings were, I decided, the least of my worries. In the end, Nige had convinced me to hire a room at his club. (The amusing thing about Nige's club was that it was decorated to look about two hundred and fifty years old, yet it had been established for all of seven months. I couldn't see the pin-striped young fogies who lolled in its brown leather sofas without thinking, But, my dear chaps, eight months ago you didn't *have* a club. It makes me ache, how badly we all want to belong.) I still wasn't sure it was the best venue for a party.

"This is a cracking party venue," said Stuart, nodding as we stepped into the cold marble reception. "I like it. Nice choice, Hol. You've got an instinct. That's why you run a successful business."

Out of the corner of my eye, I saw Nick bristle. So there, I thought. Nick's behavior so far that night had been disgraceful. He'd done all he could to cause trouble. He'd begun by asking Stuart to give him a lift to the party—Nick hadn't realized that the performance I planned to enact with Stuart was the only reason I'd invited both of them to the party—and he'd gone on to blurt, accidentally on purpose, that I owned Girl Meets Boy. That was a nerve-shredding moment. Like sticking the last of your rent in a fruit machine and watching your destiny spin. But Stuart had recovered admirably. As I embarked on a speedy damage limitation exercise, his scowl became a smile that spread wide across his face.

"Well, Holly, a powerful woman like you, choosing *me*. I'm chuffed as a rat," he kept saying. "I'm chuffed as a rat."

I prayed that was a good thing.

Stuart, Nick, and I trooped meekly up the wide curling staircase, past a string of stern ancestral portraits—presumably secured last week from Sotheby's—to the top floor. Oh, now this was special. A high-ceilinged room with huge French-shuttered windows, bloodred walls, a stone fireplace in which flickered a real fire, a glass chandelier, gilt mirrors, genteelly battered chaise longues, and grand bowlegged chairs. If it weren't for Missy Elliott grinding out orders from the stereo, I'd have felt bad for not wearing a bustle. Nige and Claw surged from the stately gloom in a joyful wave.

"It's fine. He knows," I mouthed behind Stuart's broad back.

Nige took this as a cue to start talking. "Well, Hollyberry, what do you think? Isn't it *so* fab? Isn't it *gorge*? Roy in the kitchen says we're going to have nibbles coming out of our ears. And there's shedloads of booze, stacks of it. And the bar's through those doors. No one'll want to be the first to arrive, the vile shame of looking too eager, so I reckon we've got one hour max to get off our heads before the proles turn up. No offense, Stuart." All lavishly accessorized with hand movements.

Stuart bobbed his head at the "no offense" comment. I smiled and said, "It's fantastic." Apologies to the community, but the first time I met Nige I thought he was gay. He didn't seem like a heterosexual male, he was so . . . friendly. When I discovered he was straight, I felt cheated. All pizzazz, no action. Then it emerged he was an actor. All right, half forgiven. I worry, though, that Nige thinks the phrase "no offense" excuses him any slander. (Last week, I heard him on the phone telling his bank manager he was "a cunt, no offense.")

Claudia looked Stuart up and down, then Nick. It was hard for my little sis. She and Nick got on brilliantly, until I broke off our engagement. I knew she lost respect for him when he stayed and stayed, but while her support of my decision was hard-line bordering on virulent, I suspected that secretly she pitied his situation and felt rotten acting cool toward him. "Still hoping, Nicky?" she said, not unkindly.

It was verging on awkward, when a clatter on the stairs made us all turn. The door banged open and in clomped Rachel. She wore a red silky shawl flung around her shoulders and was unbothered at five people scrutinizing its stains. Rachel isn't beautiful, but she's very striking, with fine silky hair and large dramatic features that look clumsily put together. She reminds me of a Picasso. No offense.

"The usual suspects," she said to Nige and Claw, adding, *"Mwa, mwa,"* rather than put lip to cheek. Pause. "Nick."

Nick moved his head.

"Rachel," I said hastily, "this is Stuart. Stuart, my friend Rachel."

"Aha. You must be the pilot. The man who scared Holly sick. Not that it matters, babes, that dress has been due a dry-clean since Glyndebourne. How many hours have you flown, Stuart? You must be rather advanced to pull a stunt like that."

"Oh, no," replied Stuart, grinning at his feet. "That's kid stuff."

"What?" barked Rachel—she has no concept of false modesty— "so you're *not* advanced?"

Stuart looked annoyed.

"Who wants a drink?" I said. "Anyone?"

Nige summoned a barman. I wanted to be sober when my prodigies arrived, so I asked for an orange juice. The furor was such that you'd have thought I'd requested the fresh blood of a murdered child at room temperature, no lemon. "An orange juice," I restated as everyone hissed. At least their mindless communal urge to drive me to drink hacked into the awkwardness, and by the time the first guests poked their heads around the door, everyone was well on their way to getting in the mood.

Running a dating agency is like being a nursery-school teacher. You can't be friends with everyone, but you have your favorites. Girl Meets Boy is supposed to be unashamedly elitist, catering for "those who are beautiful, inside and out." That was our unique selling point (excuse me for swearing). But it emerged with our first bag of mail that pretty much everyone thinks they're beautiful inside and out, even people who—to quote Nige—"are very ugly."

It reminded me of those self-help books on confidence, briskly advising you to stare in the mirror every day and chant, "I am amazing." But what if you're *not* amazing?

I couldn't bear it. I didn't know how to reject nonbeautiful people in a way that didn't devastate. I kept sneaking them in. Nige had a fit and accused me of "diluting our appeal." When I replied with a mutinous silence, he tried to make me swear I wouldn't "cross-pollinate." He wanted members to be divided into A's, B's, and C's. At first I thought he meant according to name, but his thinking was more along the lines of *Brave New World*. Trouble is—much as it pains me to admit it—Nige was right. Good-looking people are intolerant of being fixed up with less good-looking people. They'll allow us a small margin of error, which I push to its limit.

Samantha, for example. She crept into the party raw with eczema, in her trademark dungarees. Claudia nudged me. "How the hell does Flaky expect to get a man when she dresses like Andy Pandy?"

I sighed. Every time I see Sam, her vulnerability takes my breath away. She makes it hard for herself. There are men who regard weakness on a par with cockroach infestation. They spot it and get the urge to bash it flat with a sledgehammer. Sam applied to GMB because the love of her life ended their relationship. That was six years ago, and she won't stop talking about him.

"He's the man," she told me sadly, "who's going to ruin my wedding." I didn't say—although I could have—"*What* wedding?"

I was hoping that night to introduce Sam to a new recruit, Bernard. Bernard was rare in that he was a forty-something male who wasn't looking to meet a twenty-two-year-old girl. Sam was thirty-four. For a woman, in dating agency terms, that's past it. You think I'm joking? After a year in this business I know that men would rather meet the devil on a dark night than a thirty-four-year-old woman. To them, thirty-four spells desperate. It means she wants to be married, pop out some kids, *yesterday*. I like men as a gender, but sometimes I could knock their heads together.

Speaking of which, I never got to introduce Sam to Bernard because I was too busy fending off Nick. As you know, Nick has an advantage, he makes me laugh. It kept us together longer than it should. I now realize that his refusal to be serious, while amusing, cut every conversation dead. I'd stop talking to laugh, then lose my train of thought. He'd never encourage me to find it again. If I ever wanted to pursue a discussion to its bitter end, I'd have to bleat, "But anyway, to go back to what I was saying . . ."

But after seven weeks of practiced frostiness, my armor was chink-free. Nick would *not* make me laugh. It helped that my members kept rushing up to me, wanting to chat. Every time Nick embarked on a quip he got cut off. Stuart, though, wasn't acting as possessive as I'd hoped. He tailed me like a shadow, fetching me glass after glass—at some point, the orange turned to alcohol, but it was rude to object—resting a hand gently on my back, showing himself to be the gentleman where Nick was not. But he also seemed nervous, like he didn't want to trespass. He kept glancing uneasily at Nick.

I couldn't blame him—with every fresh drink or touch, Nick twitched with menace. While Stuart's deference was inconvenient, it endeared him to me. I thought it showed sensitivity. I had a burst of affection. "Stuart," I said, curling a finger at him. When he bent his head, I kissed him on the mouth.

Nick flipped.

I felt the breeze as he ran at Stuart and jammed him against the wall. "Stay away from her, all right, you little prick! Stay away from her!" *Boff!* Through bleary eyes, my blearier brain registered that *boff* was the sound of Nick's fist making violent contact with Stuart's mouth. My reflex thought, I'm sorry to say, was: Lucky it's so loud and crowded in here, hardly anyone's noticed. In other words, I was less concerned that Stuart might be missing teeth than that the party wasn't spoiled for my members.

Stuart looked terrified. "Take it easy, mate," he stammered, his shoulders hunched. "Take it easy."

Now I'm the first to pass blame if I can get away with it, but this *was* my fault. Again.

"Nick," I said, grabbing him by the collar. "Jesus!" He shook me off and glared at Stuart. I had the urge to say, "Hang on, soldier, I thought this was about *me?*"

Rachel—she doesn't miss a trick—thundered over. "Babes? You okay?" I rolled my eyes and giggled. Terrible what alcohol does to you, removes your social inhibitions, revealing your more primitive self. *My* more primitive self is a dumb fool.

"I'll deal with the ex," she said quietly. "You take the pilot. Nightmare city."

She frog-marched Nick to a dim corner like a cop dragging an offender away from a crime scene. I turned to Stuart. He was wiping the blood off his mouth with his sleeve.

"I'm so sorry," I said, meaning it.

"That bloke is a fucking nut."

I made a sympathetic face. I mean, what do you say? Yeah, I know. I dated the man for five years. I agreed to marry him. If he *was* a fucking nut, it didn't reflect well on me. But, you know, this was good. Not only did Nick lack the drive to join me in the lovely life I was forging for myself, he had just shown himself to be a thug. He would have held me back. Definitely, definitely, the right decision. All the same, I wasn't comfortable with Stuart bitching about him. That was *my* job.

Stuart must have seen something in my eyes because he shut up. And grinned. His teeth were red.

I giggled. "You look like Dracula."

His smile drooped. He groaned. "I feel dizzy."

I felt terrible. "Stuart"—I had to concentrate not to pronounce it Schtuarch—"Stuart, do you want me to get the club to call you a cab?"

He looked alarmed. "No, no. My car's here."

"But you've been drinking."

"No, I haven't. Honest. Holly, don't look at me like that! It's true, I haven't. If I drive, I don't drink. Ooof." He put a hand to his chin and winced. "But maybe I could do with a chaperone and you could do with a lift. I don't want to tear you away, though. What time is it?"

Bizarrely, this reminded me of when Nick and I were about to catch a flight from New York to L.A. and our pilot sat beside us in the waiting area. Nick doesn't wear a watch and I'd broken mine. I whispered to him, "What's the time on the pilot's watch?" Nick—to whom my fear of flying was, like everything, a joke—glanced at it, turned his voice Hollywood, and boomed in an evil husk, "Time to *die!*"

"It's a quarter to twelve," I told Stuart.

I'd planned to stay till the end, but then it was nearly chucking-out time. No one needed me—all my babies were walking, talking just fine. Their loving mother, however, could barely stand. A lift would be great. It would serve Nick right. And I owed it to Stuart. Poor guy, his jaw was caked in blood.

"If you're getting dizzy spells, I ought to stay with you. But my house is miles out of your way."

He smiled. His teeth were pink. "Listen to yourself, Hol. There's such a thing as being too proud."

Of all the cheek.

"Let's go," I said.

Stuart seemed alert, until we turned into my road, then he zig-zagged the car. I yelped and grabbed the wheel.

"Sorry! Christ, my head, what a weird sensation. All buzzy, like I was floating. I didn't know where I was for a second. Something must have jolted when Nick attacked me. We're okay, though. We're safe."

My heart fluttered out of nowhere. I ignored it. "Look. Pull in here. I'm a minute up the road. Come in, have a glass of water, then you can take a taxi from mine. It's too dangerous to drive."

We weaved along the road together, then I unlocked my door and stood aside to let Stuart into my home. Mean though it was, I felt irritated. I'm past the age where a party is a failure unless you socialize till dawn. Thursday, Friday, Saturday, I enjoy being asleep by midnight. It was one of the few perks of being engaged. And you know what? Compared to some of my friends, that's *late*. Truth was, I was too tired and drunk and old to play geisha to this guy and, while it wasn't his fault, I was annoyed with him for making me.

"Do you want some water, then?" I said, hoping the grudge didn't show in my voice.

"No, Holly," he replied. "I want *you.*"

I felt myself being kissed before I had agreed to it. Stuart's hands were hard everywhere, plucking at my clothes. You don't think a man is that much stronger than you, until he is. My legs and arms felt weak and light, my heart was racing again. This time I didn't ignore it.

"Let's slow down," I said.

"Why? Don't you like me?" He smiled. His teeth were white. Oh, Grandma, what big teeth you have. And suddenly I knew I was in trouble.

CHAPTER 5

It's not as if he leaped on me in an alleyway with a knife. Maybe he misunderstood me. But he had that smile on his face like he didn't want to stop. I tried to pick off his hands; imagine trying to remove a wheel clamp with your fingers. I said, "It's too soon." I thought that was a fair compromise. But he didn't respond, he just kept kissing me, pinchily dragging off my clothes like he hadn't heard. He pushed me flat on the floor, his shoulder pinning down my neck. Then he pried apart my legs with his knee. My hands were at my pelvis, pressing upward with flat palms to keep him off me, but it seemed that he merely brushed them out the way. The fear was so black and thick it was like drowning in tar. I got stiff with panic, breathing in quick little gasps, and he murmured, "Relax, shhhh, relax, enjoy it." But he wouldn't look at me, and then I couldn't speak. It was like my eyesight was a watercolor that had gotten wet. I was seeing in reds and oranges. My vision blurred and ran.

I'd never been treated like that. I lay there like a helpless twit. I had no idea how to defend myself. So I focused elsewhere. I'm a coward when it comes down to it. I don't like to get hurt. I see it in

Emily when she has to get her injection. At first she's all scratch, wriggle, and hiss—not *sssssssss* like a snake, a cat's hiss is more venomous, *hhaaaaaaaaaaaach!* And then survival instinct numbs her and she goes limp. I never liked it when she gave up. I preferred her to bite me; I hated to see the end of hope. Then I did it myself, and I understood her.

Nick says it takes a lot of little burns to understand what a big burn feels like. You learn to be afraid of fire. My problem was, I'd never been burned. I probably should have.

When I was fourteen, I got into a stranger's car, mainly out of laziness. I was going to visit a friend, took the wrong bus, and got lost in suburbia. So I approached some guy coming out of a shop and asked if he knew where this road was. No, but he had a map in his car. Well, I *watched* myself trot down a side street after him, and when he said, "Look, it's only there, I could give you a lift," I heard myself accept. Guess what. He dropped me at my friend's door, and when I thanked him he replied, "No problem, it's my first time in London and I'd hope someone would do the same for me." Yeah, I thought, they won't.

My friend freaked out. Holly, are you mad, and so on. No, merely invincible. I'm highly intelligent, I could tell he was harmless. Believe me, I am alert to danger. I give people the benefit of the doubt, but I'm not suicidal about it. For instance.

One night a few years back, I was on the tube. Two middle-aged men sat opposite me. One looked like he was on drugs, scruffy, crazy, and the other, mean and big. They kept trying to scare me. I'm not kidding, the druggy one leaped out of his seat and screamed "Raaaaaaaaarrrrrrrrrr!" in my face. I jumped halfway to the ceiling and they keeled over laughing. All the potential heroes in the carriage looked away. What was I going to do? Quip, "Aren't you big and brave, picking on *me*"? No way. Fear told me to change cars, and I did.

Afterward I was cross. Why would anyone be like that? How dare they? But I was annoyed with myself, too. I'd run away! Why didn't I stand up for myself? What could they have done to me in a carload of people? Stabbed me and jumped on my head, apparently, but I was spitting that I hadn't fought back, not so much as a squeak. Truth was, I physically couldn't. And I don't mean in the sense that they were bigger than me. I mean that my body plain wouldn't let me. Its every message service was yelling, insistent, *Get out of here now.* I'd obeyed like a robot.

Not this time. I thought I was being sensible. No woman wants to be thought of as hysterical. I knew I didn't want Stuart alone with me in my house, but I forced myself to be mature, rational. My system jangled warning signals but I blocked my ears. You know why? I was too damn polite. It reminds me of an ad, warning against cancer of the bottom or something, that says DON'T DIE OF EMBARRASSMENT. Obviously, the medical establishment is aware that a good half of the population think, What! Let a doctor poke around down there? No way! What if it smelled of poo? Of course I choose to die of embarrassment!

I didn't want to offend Stuart.

He was practically a friend. I didn't want to hurt his feelings by not trusting him. I *like* being decent. It's not very butch, but it makes me feel good inside. If you want to live with yourself you have to uphold at least a few of your own principles. When I bought Rachel a priceless bottle of Decléor face oil for her birthday, I was twitching, I so badly wanted to keep the free tube of antifatigue eye contour gel that came with it, but it felt shoddy, swindling her out of her bonus gift. I hemmed and hawed, nearly gave it to her, and then I kept it. Good grief! Every time I saw it lying unused on the kitchen table, I felt like Judas. The guilt killed me, I had to buy her the aromatic essential balm to restore my faith in myself.

Nick slammed into the house halfway through. Stuart kicked the kitchen door shut. I was too frightened to scream. There were a million thoughts going through my head and nothing at all. It was like I wasn't even there. I was aware of being jolted, of my arms being held above my head, but mostly I was out of myself. When I'm on a plane waiting for it to crash, I dream of elsewhere. I imagine Emily, a warm little black dot, curled up in a ball on our bed. I imagine my mother pottering in the garden, her knees clicking as she bends down. I imagine my father whistling as he polishes his shoes on a newspaper in the kitchen. It keeps the plane in the air, because as long as they're with me nothing bad can happen.

And so I imagined my parents, asleep in their pajamas under their bobbly old eiderdown. I just went to them, slipped out of my body like a ghost; they were so real I could have been hovering over their heads. I thought of Emily, sprawled in the sunshine, *hot;* God, but that cat loves to bake herself like a potato. I thought of me in my tent house when I was small, draping a sheet over a chair and crouching beneath it, all my toys gathered about me like courtiers before a queen. Who'd have thought that little girl would come to this? "I want to be as close to you as I can," whispered Stuart to someone. Then he turned the stereo up. U2. In a way I was glad it was U2. I can't stand their music. It would have been a real bastard had it been Air, or Zero Seven, or any band I really like.

I didn't wish that Nick would come into the kitchen, it was too late to wish for anything. I heard the front door slam again anyway. And then Stuart got off me and said, "I think I'm falling in love with you." I didn't reply. It sounded wrong. "Would you like a cup of tea?" he added. "You should get dressed, you'll get cold on the floor." I shook my head and nodded, but I couldn't look up from the level I was at, which was cat level. You'd think if you were that low you'd be invisible to predators, but you're not. Unless, of course, the predator is wearing a dog trumpet and can only see straight ahead. It's like in films when the goodie is hiding on a ceiling beam and the baddie doesn't spot him. If there's a person hiding on the ceiling, pardon me, but you're *aware* of it.

"I'd better be going," said Stuart, who seemed to be having a conversation entirely with himself. "I'll call you. Bye-bye. I'll see myself out." The way he said it, I nearly replied, "Okay, thanks!"

My hand reached out and turned off the stereo. I realized I wasn't breathing automatically, and I had to sniff and pant to let the air in. I wondered if he had really gone. Claudia is scared of spiders, and when she sees one she vacuums it up, then leaves the vacuum on for three hours in case it tries to crawl out again. I wished there was a version of that for humans. I didn't want to move from where I was. So I stayed on the floor, looking at it, thinking that the little black-and-white tiles were better suited to a bathroom. The dirt and blood showed up too easily. Gray was a better color for a kitchen floor.

I could have sat there till dawn, letting my mind dissolve to nothing, but Emily appeared, rubbed her head against my arm, and said, *"Miaowwww!"*

"Absolutely," I replied, and I stood up to get a tin out of the cupboard. She purred, *prrt-rrr prrt-rrr prrt-rrr,* and it was the friendliest sound I ever heard. She spent two months in a cage at the vet's after her owner gave up on her, and she remains embarrassingly grateful for the smallest attention. It took me a long time to open the tin; my hands were useless and weak, all the strength gone out of them. Emily did a little bunny hop of excitement and nudged against me as I placed the bowl on her mat. I watched as she ate and thought how easy it would be to hurt her. You could break her leg, it would be like snapping a twig. Or kick her so hard in the stomach she'd bleed to death from the inside. I decided I should keep her indoors.

I switched on every light. I smelled like Stuart. I would have a bath. I felt calm. There was some sort of squabble going on in my head, but I refused to be part of it. I double-locked the front door and thought of all the horror films you see where the door is locked and the killer is inside the house. I was being ridiculous. I needed to go to the toilet. I went and it felt like someone was holding a lit match to my skin. But then, fuss fuss fuss, I'd felt sore after sex with Nick before. Sometimes you *need* to fuck fast, even though it looks undignified and you know that you'll sting afterward. It can be quite satisfying, that rawness. A secret reminder of your pleasingly passionate love life.

I wondered where Nick had gone and if he'd come back.

"I think I can have a bath in my own home," I said loudly to the walls, as if they'd voiced disapproval. I turned on the hot tap, and it squeaked as normal. Everything was normal. I didn't want to be in the bathroom while the water ran, because then I couldn't hear anything. So I took off all my clothes in the bedroom. Then I didn't know what to do. I couldn't put on my robe because I didn't want it to touch my skin until I'd had a bath. I wanted to put my clothes in the machine right that minute, but I didn't want to go downstairs naked. I stood, not deciding, until my lungs nearly burst and the bath ran over.

I didn't know why I was being so weird. It was only sex that I didn't want. Big deal. Who hasn't had *that* before? Me, but so what? And, anyhow, maybe, subconsciously, I did want it. I'd asked him out. I'd kissed him on the mouth. I'd given him signals.

"I think I'm falling in love with you." What rapist says *that*?! That "r" word was a disgusting violent word and not a word I wished to use in context with myself. I was a big tough bruiser of a girl, I was not some gossamer victim. It could not be that thing because I allowed it to happen. He was sweet afterward. So I dumped my clothes on the floor and got in the bath. It felt like sulfuric acid, but in a nice way.

I don't know how long I lay in that bath, but the water got cold. So I got out, dried myself, pat pat pat, with a soft towel that rubbed like sandpaper, blow-dried my hair—on, off, on, off, every second so I could hear any creak in the house—made a mental note to buy more soap. Then I put on my pajamas, gathered up my clothes, marched downstairs, booted open the kitchen door, and every nothing noise roared loud in my head. I could hear the clock ticking like a deathwatch beetle, the hum of electricity was so penetrating it tickled my ears and made them itch. The house was alive with activity. I rolled my eyes at myself, stuffed the clothes in the machine, and stuck it on a boil wash.

Then I saw the state of the tiles.

I squirted bleach on the polluted area and scrubbed it with a scouring pad, but you can never clean just a bit of the floor. I always try, then I envisage my sister Issy floating over my head. So I cleaned the whole thing. By the time I finished, the washing machine had ended its cycle. I pulled out my pink cashmere sweater. It was the size of a handkerchief. Really. It was too small to fit a doll. For goodness' sake. I started to huff and puff and pull at the arms. Why? Don't ask. It was like trying to get a mini to grow into a tank. Then I tutted and threw it and all my other sodden clothes in the trash. Why was I getting so uptight? These things happen. Jesus, I'd go to the shop tomorrow, I'd replace the sweater, get a new one. It wasn't a problem. Most damage can be undone.

CHAPTER 6

Triumph!" cried Nige, making me jump when I walked into the office. He was wearing rose-tinted shades, a white shirt, white jeans, and a smug look on his face. Thankfully, he'd drawn the line at white shoes. "Sunshine. Arse. Behold!"

"For the ninetieth time, keep your voice *down*," whispered Claudia, as pale as Nige's outfit. She scowled at a tub of Nurofen. "These pills must be sugar pills."

Nige amended his pitch to a deafening whisper, "Twenty-three messages when I got in, er, at nine fift—"

"You got in at eleven forty-nine, Nigel, like Holly cares. And will you stop. I don't know what you call it, throwing your voice. You're in an eight-by-ten office in front of two people with hangovers, not onstage at the National. Stop rehearsing on me, please."

"Twenty-three messages raving about the party," echoed Nige, in a tone as rich and seductive as warm chocolate. "At *my* club."

He beamed at me, a kid presenting a picture to a parent. I was observing from a great distance, but I cracked a smile. It was cosmetic. Who, I thought, is this person, really? Is he thrilled or is he pretending to be thrilled? He is an actor, his métier (as he'd say) is deceit. Nige can recite "Baa, Baa, Black Sheep" and make it sound like a sonnet. All the world *is* a stage for him. I've watched him when he thinks he's alone. He's like an unread book, inanimate.

He needs an audience to be alive. Which means that everything he says or does is an act. I stopped smiling.

"Success. Hooray. Wonderful. Well done."

Nige sat down, disappointed. I think he expected an ovation.

Claudia looked at me. "So, Tallulah. Quiet today. What happened to you? Jesus Christ."

There was a tennis ball lodged in my throat. "Tallulah? What do you mean?"

"*What?* Don't be coy. It's obvious!"

"Is it?"

My hands were trembling for no reason.

"Nige. Help me out."

Nige embraced his role with the eagerness of a dog falling on a chop. "Holly. We are your dear friends. You have alarmed us. An explanation *silver plate, toot sweet.*"

I felt like a mouse in a corner. I opened my mouth but all it contained was a squeak. Nige was having trouble holding back. Claudia smiled through the pain as he boomed, "Holly Appleton. The prosecution demands to know why, for the first time in twenty-nine years, you are not wearing on your person an item of clothing the color pink!"

In your head, I wondered, do you give a damn?

"There was nothing in the drawer this morning. Okay?"

I know I was being grouchy, but his gaze unsettled me. I felt like a germ under a microscope. You do something once, twice, suddenly it's your trademark. No wonder people rarely change. They try in a tiny way, and their friends and relatives go ballistic, like they've broken a law. It's as if, as long as you remain static, they feel safe. You're less of a threat. Well, that's their problem. That morning, I'd opened my wardrobe and the brown said, "Pick me."

The second after I snapped I felt lousy. I decided there was no real reason for me to be acting the way I was. It was like waiting for your ears to pop. And waiting. Everyone treats you as normal, so you resign yourself to the invisible barrier between you and the rest of the world. You hear your own voice trapped inside your head, and it sounds unfamiliar. Other people sound far away. Normally, I'd be jabbing at my ears with Q-tips, pencils, drumsticks. But that day, I was happy to leave them blocked. A blissful disconnection, like the moment before you fall asleep and dream.

I grinned at Claudia and I made myself grin at Nige. "Brown in deference to the communal migraine, of course. I thought if I wore pink one of you might start fitting."

"Angel child! I don't dare look in the mirror in case my head has actually transformed into a watermelon and my eyes are nasty little black pips. Jesus, Claw, you're right. Why don't these pills work? I've taken at least forty. Oh, boo, I want my mummy!"

"Well," I replied, wanting to make up for my own mean spirit, "could you make do with a doughnut instead?"

"Holly, I didn't know you'd met my mother," replied Nige, making me laugh before I could think about it. I undid the box and ended up eating three, because despite the fact that they were doused in sugar and hemorrhaging jam, the first two doughnuts didn't taste. The third wasn't much better, but I thought I should quit before my heart did.

"The phones are quiet today," I said. That apart, the place was the same as yesterday. I caught Nige glancing at Claudia, his mouth full of doughnut.

"What?"

Claudia giggled.

Nige said, "I turng ga phones aghff because agh our heagachgs."

"Nige! How could you? What if people want to get through? Why didn't you put on the answering machine?"

Nige swallowed the boulder of doughnut lodged in his face. "I couldn't stand to listen to their high, horrid voices. Don't look at me like that, Hol. They'll make it without you for a few hours. They must learn to wipe their own bottoms. This is a dating agency, not a kindergarten. If Sam or anyone needs to speak to you that urgently, they'll try again after lunch. Talking of which. Anyone?"

Silently, I went around the office (or, to be more accurate, spun on my heel) switching the ringer tones back on. I also switched on my computer. I couldn't speak to him. But I was thinking, *I* am the boss, remember, don't you just assume you can take charge. A woman wouldn't. Women are more considerate, they have more humility, a stronger sense of duty. That's why they're better workers. I glanced at Claudia. She was squinting into a vanity mirror trying to pluck a hair out of her chin. Most women. I coughed. She looked up. I raised an eyebrow.

She said, "Got a cough?"

"Claudia, switch on your computer. I want us to get some work done today."

"Of course." She switched on her machine and winced. "Blinded by the light. I need a screen break, it's making me nauseous."

"I think you'll find those two doughnuts you just inhaled are what's making you nauseous, love."

"Nige, you're not funny. I'm getting my eyesight back. Jesus, Hol, now I can see. You look as rough as he does. Hey, and you haven't told us what happened with—"

Some people will do anything to avoid work.

Brrg brrg!

Nige picked up the receiver with a twirl. "Hello, lovely caller, Girl Meets Boy!" After a brief pause, he transferred the call to me, adding loudly, "It's The Great Unwashed."

I glared at him, picked it up. "Rachel?"

"Babes, how *are* you? You must tell Nigel to stop flirting with me. I'm out of his league. I trust you misbehaved with Stuart last night?"

I gripped the phone. "One sec, Rach. Are you two going for lunch, then?"

Nige and Claudia stared at each other in glee. "Yes," said Claudia quickly, wiping the sugar off her mouth. "We'll be at Martha's."

"Not anywhere else?"

Claudia looked at me. "Actually, we thought we'd go to Paris. There's nowhere to eat 'round here."

"What I mean is, stay where I can find you."

I waved them off. They're such babies, I only stop short of handing them a pound each and saying, "Buy yourself some sweets." Then I locked the door.

"Sorry, Rach. So what did you get up to after I left? Did everyone look happy? Did Sam seem okay, the woman in the dungarees? Were people talking to her?"

Rachel laughed a hollow laugh. "Bor-ing! Answer the question, babes. Did you score?"

I'll say one thing about Rachel. She doesn't *hint*. But then, why shouldn't she ask me straight out? I am, after all, in the business of pairing penises and vaginas. (Girl Meets Boy does have platonic facilities, but they tend to be underused.) And why should I be coy? All the weirdness I felt was pure guilt. I'd been in a relationship for five years, of course I was going to feel odd the first time I slept with another man. This unease was down to misplaced loyalty, me dreading that in some way I'd cheated on Nick.

"Yes, I did. Did you?"

"She shoots, she scores! Oh no, babes, we're not talking about *me*. I want a blow-by-blow account. What school did he go to? Was his pecker of a satisfactory girth? Don't bore me with length, length is a red herring. I've no time for it."

When Rachel said that, I fumbled for an answer but I couldn't find one. I giggled, trying to *feel* the giggle, and yes, I nearly felt it. This was more like it. This is what happens when you get laid. Your nosiest friends smash through the boundaries that maturity is meant to bring and ask you cheeky questions they know are none of their business. I'd been with Nick for so long I'd forgotten the routine.

"I've no idea what school he went to, Rach. Hackney comp, for all I know. You're the only person I know who'd ever ask that."

"It's important, babes, it's his pedigree."

A query that would have been more relevant had I slept with an Afghan hound. I was about to say so, but Rachel interrupted: "Ask him next time. Now, about his pecker."

I was a blank.

"I feel quite, quite . . . hurty today, so, so that must mean something."

Rachel cackled. I tried to dig up more information for her, but I couldn't. I had a picture in my head of watching a big man on top of a woman on a kitchen floor. Was that me or did I see it on television? If it's *you*, you're hardly likely to remember yourself from across the room! It must have been on *Casualty* or *E.R.* My brain refused to give me access. Hell knows what I drank last night. I said, "We did it in the kitchen."

"That is *terribly* sexy! I've worked out that it takes the average couple six months to relegate sex to the bedroom, so I bin 'em after five. Well, babes, I'm pleased. I detained Nick for as long as I could. You know, he was desperate to follow you home and kill the moment."

I remembered. "Nick did come in the front door at one point, but I think he heard us and went straight out again. I felt terrible about that. I still do."

"You mustn't. It's not fair of him to make you feel that way. Don't let him spoil this for you. You should be high on the lust hormone—what is it, you remember, the same as whatever's contained in chocolate."

"Cocoa?"

"Don't be facile. Seriously, babes. Don't let him stand in your way. Has he called?"

"Nick?"

"Stuart. Stuart!"

I swallowed. "Not yet, Rach. Do you think that sex with the same person gets better? If it's not that brilliant the first time."

"Now we're getting somewhere. Why, wasn't it?"

"I don't *think* so. He was a bit . . . clumsy."

"Nerves. He was shy! That is *so* sweet. An inconvenience, a huge bore and a waste of your precious time, but *so* sweet."

I nodded. I liked that idea. It made sense. I put down the phone, relieved.

The first time Nick and I had sex it wasn't great. I think we both knew that we'd found each other, that this could be the start of "It." So the other It had to be perfect. As Nick says, a one-night stand is little more than an elaborate wank. If you impress the other person, it's probably because you want to satisfy your ego. It's because you don't care that you can put on a decent show. Because we did care—so we consoled ourselves—our first fuck was appalling.

We kept bumping teeth. Nick's zipper got stuck and I ripped a nail trying to pry it open. And I don't mean boo-hoo, I broke a nail. I'm not a nailsy kind of girl. I mean *ripped*, as in torn away from my bleeding skin. I was just about weeping with pain and frustration.

We finally got there, but tempers were frayed and it was hard to concentrate. I can only explain it by asking you to imagine having sex with Maximus from *Gladiator*. (Not Russell Crowe. Please, what do you take me for?) You'd be so delirious and disbelieving that you and Maximus were actually getting it on, your hour of triumph would be a shambles.

That was me and Nick, the first time. It was supposed to be an erotic ballet, but it felt more like bumper cars. Then I realized I needed the toilet. I tried to ignore it, but it was like he was poking my bladder with a stick. Eventually I had to decide between a toilet break or weeing on him. Which I'm not into. When I sped back from the bathroom, I found Nick's penis asleep. The wretched thing was as limp as if it were lounging by the pool on a sunshine holiday. All attempts at resuscitation were useless. Its owner lay face to the pillow and wouldn't speak or look at me. Call me Sherlock, but I detected resentment.

Frankly, I felt the same way. I'm quite demanding. My belief is, if you say what you want, you have more chance of getting it. I'm not a mind reader, I don't expect men to be. If the word *clitoris* doesn't roll off your tongue, chances are it won't be rolling off his either. I'm not saying I bark orders like a sergeant, rather that I know to show a man what I want instead of forcing him to guess. But with Nick, our connection was such, I'd hoped for telepathy, and I got a crossed line. I felt angry, then I looked at his back, smooth and tanned, and I thought how fragile he was. It's hard for men, being unbreakable.

I wriggled closer, and I said, "Do you remember that chant, at school?"

"No."

"First the worst, second the best."

"No." Muffled into the pillow. Then, "Maybe. Yeah." He rolled over so he was half on his side. "Third the one with the hairy chest."

I pouted. "Ye-es, but maybe we should worry about that when we get to it."

Nick smiled and grabbed me, and we spent a long time proving that second was, indeed, best.

Maybe, I thought, it would be like that with Stuart.

I spent two hours responding to joyful E-mails about the party before Claw and Nige rolled back from lunch, thumping on the locked door and frightening the life out of me. I said I hadn't wanted to be disturbed, then got back to the mail. I love this about our members. They're paying us to provide a service, and yet they're appreciative of the tiniest frills. Well. Most of them are. I was on the last E-mail when Elisabeth Stanton-Browne rang to complain about last week's date night. Elisabeth S-B is high maintenance. And that's an understatement. To describe Elisabeth as "high maintenance" is to refer to the Alps as "hilly."

I didn't mind. I saw her as a challenge. I just hoped there was a man in the world who was good enough. This time she was sour that I'd put her with Martyn for her last date of the evening. I didn't tell her—there was no excusing such stupidity—but *I* thought I was being clever, putting her with Martyn for her last date. I hoped they'd hit it off and go for a drink. This is how it works. We dissect everyone's applications, speak to them on the phone to find out more about them, and then, simply, we match. We meet at a bar every Tuesday and/or Wednesday night—each member attends one night a month—and every person is assigned four dates, each of which lasts twenty-five minutes.

(Originally, we had them lasting fifteen minutes, but it didn't work. The pressure to impress was impossible, like having to justify your existence to an egg timer. Even the sweetest members came across as unbearable. "I earn six figures I scaled Everest with one foot taped to a coffee table my other watch is a Rolex I live in a town house in Chelsea and holiday in Cannes.")

Twenty-five minutes is perfect. Enough time to relax, not enough time to go mad if you loathe someone. After every date, members tick their card, indicating whether they're interested in seeing that respective date again as a friend or as a partner. At the end of the night, Claw, Nige, and I conduct debriefing sessions. Although some members sneak off for debriefing sessions of their own.

To me, debriefing was the most rewarding part of the job—it was when I discovered how wrong or right I'd been in my assessments. If a member was blushing and fluttery about a date, my heart cartwheeled. It was a glorious, vicarious thrill, second only to when people fell in love. We hadn't had a wedding yet, but we had a bunch of lasting relationships and a slew of friendships. That made me proud. *Making* people's lives. As yet, I hadn't made Elisabeth's life.

"That advertising guy, with the shaved head and trendy glasses, Michael—"

"Martyn?"

"Martyn, whatever. He was so straitlaced he could have been a priest. I have to say, Holly, I'm offended that you put me with him. I do have a sense of fun, you know. I do have a zany side. He had *no* side apart from a boring side. We had zero in common, it was painful. Occasionally a word was said that we both related to, and we *clung* to it. Traveling. Clubs. Air hostesses. We *clung* to those words for dear life!"

I was intrigued to hear about her interest in air hostesses but held back from inquiry. I said, "I'm sorry you feel like that, Elisabeth. I did notice there were no ticks on your card and I did want to discuss that with you, but as I remember you had to rush off—"

"I hope you're not suggesting it's my fault. Did anyone put a tick for *me*? Not that I care."

"Yes, actually, you had one friendship tick and one relationship tick"—a lie, but you *never* tell a member that no one's ticked them, it's too hurtful—"but as you know, because you didn't put any corresponding ticks, I can't reveal who."

"Well, I'm not satisfied. I'm paying you, I expect results. What are you going to do about it?"

I could feel Elisabeth's hostility heating my brain. I wanted to soothe her, but Nige was having a showcase conversation with, presumably, another member.

"So," he boomed, his voice filling the small room, "you wouldn't kick him out of bed? Well, only to finish him off on the floor, heh-heh!"

I frowned. Nige was annoying me. You couldn't breathe without him being there. It was invasive, like someone stamping around inside your head.

"Hello? Hello?" *Bash! Bash! Bash!* I realized with a start that

Elisabeth was banging the phone receiver on a hard surface. "Is anyone there? Do I get an answer?"

I rubbed my ear.

"When you ask nicely," I said, and I cut her off. "Yes, *what*, Claudia?"

Claudia had paused from neatening her eyebrows. Her mouth was agape. "Who *was* that?"

"Elisabeth with an 'S' Stanton-Browne with an 'E.' "

"But you were—you were . . ."

"I was rude to her because she was rude to me. When she's recovered her manners, then we'll talk." Fact was, I didn't have the strength to deal with Elisabeth just then. I felt exhausted. I didn't know how to help her. I'd probably ring her later and apologize.

"Flairs for ya."

All heads swiveled greedily toward the door. A guy in a cap and blue overalls was standing there, bored, holding a spectacular bouquet. This thing was out of control: red furry exotic blooms the size of soup bowls, lush green jungle leaves, trailing vines spilling from the cellophane, sleek, slender yellow lilies stiff and haughty, scarlet petals curled to elegant tubes. This was more than flowers. It was a gift from nature, and she was showing off.

I'm not sure that Nige didn't cut off his caller. "Pleasebemine-ohpleasebemine."

Claudia placed her tweezers on the desk.

I stayed where I was. There's something wonderful about being sent a bouquet. The implications are marvelous. This is what you deserve. This is how I think of you. I hoped they were for me.

Nige lunged at the deliveryman, whipped the flowers. He peered at the name on the envelope and snorted. "Bloody hell, *I* organized the venue."

Claudia swallowed. Two to one.

Nige grinned. "Someone likes you, Holly."

Claudia sighed and picked up her tweezers.

I took the bouquet from Nige, placed it gently on a chair, and opened the card.

Sexxxy Holly,
Thanks for a truly special evening.
Big kiss,
Stuart

He'd drawn a smiley face in the "o" of Holly.

"Who? Who? Who?" cried Nige. Claudia flared her nostrils.

I shook my head. "It doesn't say." I smiled. "I'm going to the shops to get a vase and a sweater."

CHAPTER 7

I always think that bad things happen to other people, which reflects well on my capacity for hope and not so well on my sense of compassion. Once, Nick and I booked a romantic weekend (or rather, we booked the weekend and hoped to supply the romance ourselves) on the Isle of Mull. I set the alarm wrong, giving us minus fifty minutes to make the hour journey from our house to Heathrow. Even as I watched 11:39 flick to 11:40 in fluorescent green on the driver's dashboard, I couldn't believe that we would miss our plane. Takeoff time: 11:40. That such a thing would happen to *me* was, literally, unthinkable.

It shows how lucky I'd been so far, my life going so neatly that I expected to get through the whole of it unscathed. But then most people I know are the same. Even Nige, who had a miserable childhood—his mother, unmaternal to say the least, specialized in petty cruelties like cutting his nails so short they bled—believes he's exempt from dying in a car crash because he is *Nige*. When Issy gave birth, she barely blinked at the baby, she was so offended at the pain. Nothing in her experience had prepared her for it. Trauma is for idiots. I suppose optimism is a survival skill.

When I arrived home, the day after party night, with my new pink sweater and saw Manjit's girlfriend's car parked in the drive, my optimism ran away, and I couldn't blame it. Everything about Manjit's girlfriend grates. For a start, her name is Bo—which she once told us is Chinese for "precious." And she is, although not in the way she thinks. (Nick went through a phase of pronouncing it *Boh* to annoy her.) Her car is a green Beetle. You can hear its approach from neighboring counties. It's as much a statement as a shiny red Porsche. She makes me feel guilty, and I don't feel guilty that easily. I suspected I knew why she was here.

I composed my face and unlocked the front door. As I pushed it, *she* pulled it open.

"Hello, Holly, been shopping?"

Already I felt about six years old.

"Yes, I needed a new sweater."

There was a meaningful pause, during which Bo's unconscious screened Third World scenes for my benefit.

Bo, an academic, is paid less than a nurse or a teacher and resents other people earning money. Even nurses and teachers. Even though she has a profitable sideline—she thinks up questions for *University Challenge*. When I launched Girl Meets Boy, the curl of her lip could have rivaled Elvis. You could tell she was dying for the business to go under. She's the sort who feels that if *you* are successful, there's less chance she'll be. When Nick told her the agency had accepted its hundredth member, she raised her thin eyebrows and said, "I'm impressed." She meant, of course, "I'm surprised."

But mainly, I can't forgive her for coming to our house and saying in front of the cat, "Whenever I see an animal charity I walk straight past it." What, I thought, and you're proud of that?

There was a thump above our heads and a bark of laughter. Bo and I glanced at the ceiling as if we expected to see through it. Bo smiled at me, and I felt an uncharacteristic desire to shake her firmly by the throat. She knew I wanted to know what was going on. We smiled thinly at each other, wondering who would crack. I was about to when Nick and Manjit saved me the trouble by lumbering downstairs with the spare futon.

"Beeeee careful, you're scraping the wallpaper!" screeched Bo.

"Sorry," said Manjit. (This is pretty much the only word he ever says to Bo. We went to the theater once, and Nick and I kept count. Twenty-three *sorry*s.) "Hello, Holly. Uh."

When Manjit—who was facing down—said this, Nick—facing up—tried to swivel, tripped, and was nearly crushed by the futon. Manjit laughed.

"Manjit!" said Bo. "He could have hurt himself."

"Sorry," said Manjit. "Uh, how's it going, Hol?"

I smiled at him. Manjit is one of the sweetest men I know. Doubtless he'd been ordered to give me the cold shoulder but couldn't manage it. Manjit finds it very hard to be nasty to people, something others might take advantage of were it not for the fact that he is a black belt in karate. I made him give me a lesson once and he gossiped between chops.

Nick, red-faced, reached the safety of the hall parquet and let go of the futon. He scowled at Manjit, then me. "You locked Emily's cat-flap and she had an accident."

I felt nausea high in my throat. "You haven't let her out, have you?"

Nick's eyes widened at my stupidity. "Of course I let her out, she's an outdoor cat. She was crying to go outside!"

I barged past him, ran through the kitchen, pulled open the back door, and shouted, "Emileee, Emileee." Then I ran back in, grabbed her biscuit box, darted back into the garden, and shook it. "Emileee, Emileee, biiiiiiiscuit!"

Emily, whose acuteness of hearing depends entirely on whether food is imminent, trotted out of the green toward me and curled around my ankles. I scooped her up, shut the door behind us, and poured a small pile of biscuits onto the floor. "Good girl, *good* girl, who's got such lovely furry knickers!"

"Interesting," said Nick. This was mean of him considering he also turns into a loon around Emily. ("Who's Daddy's special whisker kitten?") The great pleasure of sharing your living space with an animal—I prefer not to say "own," it's insulting—is *not* that it enables you to indulge your parental instincts without being answered back. The best thing about a pet is that it allows you to regress to toddlerhood. You speak in a silly voice, you buy yourself a great many brightly colored toys, allegedly for the creature, and its benign presence is a fine excuse to spend many happy hours talking to yourself.

I swung around. "Where's Bo and Manjit?"

"Putting the futon in Bo's car. I'm moving out."

I did think it was sweet that Nick felt the need to tell me this, even in the face of overwhelming evidence. When he's nervous he has this habit of rubbing a hand over his hair and mussing it up so that it covers his eyes. Right then it made me want to cry.

I said, "But the futon won't *fit* in that car. A knife and fork won't fit in that car."

I hoped he'd laugh, but he didn't. He replied, "Then we'll tie it to the roof."

"Right."

"That was pathetic what you did last night, Holly." He looked at the floor and rubbed at an invisible mark with his sneaker toe. "You don't even like that bloke. And you accuse *me* of behaving like a child."

I was unfaithful. That's what I was. It helped to have it spelled out. I shook my head and stared at his feet. I felt a pang at their familiarity. It takes an awful lot to stop loving someone. We'd both pigeon-toed away from the relationship, step-by-step. Every inch, I'd wanted him to drag me back, but he hadn't. I'd found myself dreaming like a teenager. Imagining myself being swept away in his arms, creating desperate situations he'd rescue me from. Not that I needed rescuing, not that I wasn't more than capable of rescuing myself should the need arise, but if *he* did the rescuing it might make him feel useful. Now that I thought about it, I wasn't sure I ever made Nick feel useful.

He swept his hair from his eyes and said, "I don't like to be humiliated."

I nodded vaguely. Maybe I did humiliate him. I was one of those terrible women who wait, tight-jawed, for their partner to finish speaking, then roll their eyes at his friends. But what he said embarrassed me sometimes. And often he'd say the words so slowly, with long pauses in between, like he was barely able to form a sentence. It wasn't that. His brain had jumped to an unconnected thought that was more interesting. His mind was a butterfly, flitting from lilac to daffodil as the mood took it. I found that charming, then I didn't. I'd always be marching ahead, wanting to get somewhere, and he'd be lagging back, enjoying the scenery.

"So I'm out of here. Good-bye, and give my regards to your parents. It was nice knowing you."

"Wait." My hand shot out and grabbed his wrist, and my voice was a silly shrill squeak. What had I been thinking. All my plotting, for *this*? I felt like a city dweller who fantasizes for many years about giving it all up for a fairy-tale cottage near the coast and then does. And realizes she's trapped alone in the middle of nowhere in a cold, damp, crumbling shack with a broken toilet far away from anyone she cares about.

"Nick."

Nick's parents owned a country cottage, but it wasn't a shack. It was fantastic. I think I preferred it to the Italian villa. That villa had a haughty look about it, and I never quite forgave it for the olive/lemon incident, but this cottage was so darling you'd swear it was built by pixies. It was the cottage that Americans think England is made of. Its white-beamed walls seemed to swell in the middle, and its thatched roof sloped almost to the ground, reminding me of a person with a hat pulled down over their ears. Blowsy pink roses rambled around the oak door, and its garden was lush, unruly, and beautiful, teeming with lavender, white lilac, poppies, blackberry bushes, apple and pear trees, around a green lawn.

Some of the happiest days of my life were spent there. Nick's parents love to make a fuss. Any day or occasion that even suggests you might be justified in making a fuss, they make a fuss. On St. David's Day (the family isn't Welsh) Nick's mother decided to bake Eccles cakes. Cooking isn't her forte; they tasted like Play-Doh. Easter, they had us painting eggs, laid by a hen. Well, of course they were laid by a hen, but what I mean is, they were laid by a hen we *knew*. This is sounding worse and worse. But it was wonderful. Then Emily dragged in a hare. It was dead and very bloody. I didn't scream. I had a suspicion that Lavinia, Nick's mother, didn't respect women who screamed. I just about swallowed my tongue instead.

I was glad I did. Nick's father, Michael, picked up Emily in one hand, the hare in the other, deposited both outside the back door, washed his hands in the deep enamel sink, and said, "That's nature for you." Lavinia lit a cigarette in a holder and blew smoke to the ceiling. I nodded and continued painting my egg. And then, a couple of times, we spent Christmas there.

My parents, as with everything, have a sensible attitude toward Christmas. The tradition in our family is that everyone's name goes into a bowl and each person is assigned the task of buying one present, for the person whose name they pick out.

Forgive my capitalism, but I thought it a rotten tradition. (Nearly as bad as Rachel's parents' tradition: The tree is decorated on Christmas Eve and no one is allowed to open their presents until 8:00 P.M. on Christmas Day.) I didn't like receiving only one present, especially if Issy chose it, because then it would be miserably educational. And I loathed giving only one present. I'd go to town and look in Liberty's windows, Selfridges's windows, and I'd see about a million presents that I knew my family would love— *Complete Works of Jane Austen* for my mother, a cable-knit sweater for my father, makeup in gold cases for Issy, a black rubber bustier for Claudia. (She went through a phase of claiming to be a vampire, to the point of having fangs filed. She still has them. They're cute when you get used to them, although my parents never have.) Then I'd have to resist it all and buy a boring old saucepan with a lid because I was only shopping for Mum and a saucepan with a lid was all she knew to ask for.

Nick's parents celebrated with a fury at Christmas. My God! The first December I went to the cottage, Nick bumbled and delayed, so we got stuck in traffic and arrived at 5:00 P.M., three hours late. By the time we crunched into the gravel drive, I was tense.

"Ta da!" cried Nick. I gasped. The apple and pear trees twinkled with tiny lights, and each dinky window of the cottage glowed orange, except for the one that was filled green with the midsection of a great fir tree, studded with red baubles and bows. A fat sprig of mistletoe hung from the porch. I felt like Cinderella stepping from the coach in glass slippers. "See! See why I wanted us to get here in the dark!" We couldn't wait to reach the porch, we kissed in the car.

I squeezed my eyes shut tight and the vision faded. I was back in the kitchen and Nick was going to leave me forever.

"Nick," I said. "You know, I was thinking. And I thought, this is ludicrous, you moving out. It's really okay for you to stay. Really, it is, if that's okay with you."

I could hear myself using too many words, but I couldn't shut up. I felt myself shrinking, all the air fizzing out of me, like a witch evaporating to smoke. The more I said, the weaker I became. I had no dignity but I didn't care. I had to keep him in the house. He wouldn't have to talk to me, do anything, as long as he was there, a warm, safe presence. Now he was leaving, I loved him again. It all came back.

"Are you insane?" Nick was looking at me like I was some kind of nut. There was disgust in his eyes, and it got me right in the chest. "Let me remind you, last night you fucked some guy on our kitchen floor. Do you remember that, or were you too drunk? Nice behavior, Holly, really nice."

He turned and went.

CHAPTER 8

Monday morning in the office I caught Nigel counting my toes. It's a compulsion of his, he has a fear of people having six toes. I've wondered if there's a name for it, extratoephobia or something. Mostly, Claw and I tease him for being weird, but right then I wasn't in the mood. I wanted to tell him to stop looking at me.

"Nigel," I said, curling my feet under my chair, "can you not do that. It's unlikely that I've grown another toe since Friday, when I believe you last checked."

I felt mean as I said it, because despite having no sense of self-awareness, Nige is painfully sensitive. He'll judge everyone else in half a second, but he cannot stand being criticized. His wife, Marylou (they're separated, but it's on-off), once called him a "greedy bastard." Consequently—so legend has it—Nige was "literally unable" to hold up his head. He fled to the toilet and remained there, hunched and gazing at the floor until Marylou chanced to wonder, three hours later, where he was. She had to physically realign his spine, and apologize for two days.

Nige cinched his mouth into a pout. "Holly, Holly, grumpy grumpy! It's only because I care. You know what I think, your blood sugar's low. What you need is a frosted bun. I'll just nip across the road to M—"

Remarkable. I'd known Nige for seven years and worked with him for one, and yet he still hadn't processed the fact that I dislike frosted buns. Our downfall—well, I only say that to sound pious—our *savior* is the bakery-café across the road. It's called Martha's Got Buns, and we'd probably starve to death without it. Their cheesecake—vanilla, crumbly, sweet biscuity base—could take over the world. One bite and nations would submit. Their chocolate croissants—light, feathery, oozy with liquefying chocolate—should be classified as a drug. God didn't create doughnuts, Martha's did. Their frosted buns, however, are vile. Studded with hard pellets of sugar that just about crack your teeth, no icing to speak of, just an unpleasant sheen and a dry tongue-clacking dough containing tiny particles of fruit that might be candied peel but might also be earwax.

"I don't like frosted buns, I've told you before."

"Sweets, you don't know what you're saying. Everyone likes frosted buns, you—"

"Nige. I don't want a frosted bun."

"Sweetheart, you do. You've just forgotten what they taste like. Now you wait here and—"

My heart was pumping at four times its normal speed and my hands were trembling. "Nigel," I said. "Are you deaf, because you don't seem to be able to hear me. In the last twelve months, I must have told you at least four times that I don't like frosted buns. Hear me. I don't like frosted buns, therefore I don't want one. Trust me. I know what I want. *You* do not know what *I* want. Do you understand me when I say that?"

Silence. Then the sound of my sister applauding. "You tell him!"

I blushed. My blood sugar probably was low. But there is something deeply insulting about a person reinterpreting what you say—when you speak perfectly clearly—to suit themselves and their desires. And Nige did suffer from selective deafness. I knew that if I were a casting director, every time I spoke his ears would prick up like a coyote's. People like him choose who and what they wish to hear, and I call that dangerous.

I expected a huff, but to my relief the deaf one skidded across the room, sank to his knees in front of me, and—making full grandiose use of his Las Vegas singing voice—bellowed, "I'm sorreeee, so sorree, please accept my apologeee, ah ha ho ho."

"Please," said Claudia, looking up from *Rolling Stone* magazine. "Less of the Shania Twain. What you so cheerful about?"

Nige got up and tried to brush the dirt off his white jeans. The knees were gray. He beamed. "All I did was sing. And I'm accused of being cheerful! Quite the opposite, *actuellement*. I'm still in recovery from a grotesque and monstrous affront."

Nige paused for effect. Claudia and I made ourselves comfortable.

"Yesterday at three-thirty," began Nige, angling his chin to its best advantage, "I had an appointment with Derek."

Nige said "Derek" in a meaningful tone, as if he were someone Claudia and I were closely acquainted with, possibly related to.

"Who the sod's Derek?"

"*Derek.* My deep-tissue masseur!"

Claudia snorted.

"And the man insulted me. It took every fiber of resolution not to rise from the massage bed and stalk from the room. Plus I'd paid forty quid."

I could stand it no longer. "Right. So what did Derek do?"

"I asked how my shoulders were and he said"—Nige's voice rose to a near scream—" 'There's not much tension in them!' 'Not much tension!' How dare he, him and his hairy fingers! The cheek of him! He knows I live for the verdict, 'You are knotted!' It's a matter of personal pride! It's a badge of honor! For my shoulders not to be knotted . . . it's like, it's like *not* being stressed! In the modern world, if you're not knotted, if you're not stressed, you have no life, you're a nobody!"

"All right, Gielgud, can it," said Claudia. "What is it really?"

His smile rearranged his eyebrows and tweaked the tips of his ears. "I"—Nige stretched this humble vowel into a grandiose three-second syllable—"have an audition on Wednesday for the Courts ad! Yaaaaayyyy!" He jumped in the air, snatched us from our seats, and forced us to gallop around the office with him.

"Nige," I gasped as the three of us lumbered about the main patch of carpet in a small circle, arms around each other's neck. "The Courts ad!" As I said it, I realized I was smiling without effort. And . . . *and.* His hand was draped heavily on my shoulder, and I wasn't bothered. This was a great relief to me. I'd felt funny for the last few days.

The weekend had not been good. I'd missed Nick. The house felt wrong and angry without him. I was hungry, but there was nothing in the fridge, so I ate food you don't normally eat unless there's a famine—a can of refried beans, tinned sardines on pasta, a jar of pickled cucumbers. I didn't feel capable of leaving the premises. When I wasn't eating processed food, I lay in bed, too heavy of heart and limb to move, quaking at every noise. When the phone rang I jumped, but I was too lethargic to answer it. It was all I could do to feed Emily. I sweated a lot but I didn't wash. Maybe I should have.

But we're all allowed an off weekend, aren't we? We don't have to be constantly jetting off to Prague or Barcelona for cultural mini breaks, squeezing every last brisk minute out of our leisure time and making everyone else feel like sloths. By Monday morning I'd grown so still I could have merely stopped breathing. However, I'd pulled myself back from wherever I'd gone to and had a shower, applied makeup, driven to work. Simple actions that required as much effort as pulling a dead fat man uphill on a rope.

So. I needed reassurance that I was fine, and here it was.

Claudia extracted herself from the circle. "Hang on," she said to Nige. "You don't mean that hyper-cheap-furniture ad."

"Oh yes, I do!"

"The one set in a sofa showroom?"

"That's the one."

"With *Sun* women draping themselves over the bargain leather?"

"The very same."

"And men wandering around with blow-dried hair and taupe trousers?"

"My fellow colleagues!"

"Nigel Wilkins, you big tart. I commend you on your lack of class."

I giggled. "What will you have to do at the audition, Nige?"

"Well." Nige dragged his chair into the center of the room, sat down, and crossed his legs. "It's going to be deeply embarrassing. It'll probably be in a warehouse on an industrial estate. I'll be in there for two minutes, in front of a camera and a panel of people who'll require me to make love to a sofa. Or rather, *act* as if I want to make love to the sofa. I'll feel like the most enormous fool. Then I'll have to act like I'm in love with the nest of tables. But, dears, it's money and it's telly, and I want it to be me!"

"You've got to practice, then," I said.

"What!" Nige couldn't believe his luck. "Now?"

Usually, I can't wait to start work. I love the thrill of discovering who's dropped onto the mat, and the kick I get when something they say clicks and I just sense whom to match them with. I even like it when Nige opens what he terms "a communiqué from a desperado" and bellows, "Pass me the tongs!" But right then, I needed to encourage Nige's good mood in the hope it would be catching. And that meant postponing toil.

"One quick rehearsal," I said, "then we should get on." Claudia nodded.

"Okay," said Nige. "I'll have to warm up first, though."

I'd forgotten this bit. I chewed my pen to keep from snickering. Nige tucked his chair under his desk, bounced to center stage, rolled up and down his spine, shook out his ankles. He breathed deep to open up his resonators, ensuring his vocal passage was free so he could connect with his center—"That's your truth," he explained as Claw and I watched, rapt—tried to connect his diaphragm to the roots in his feet—"For more truth"—allowed the sound to travel up through his spine—"Mmm aaaaaaaaah aaaeeeoooo"—took command of all the vowel sounds, limbered up his tongue by attempting to write his name in the air with it—opened up his range by standing on all fours like a cat, meowed "up and down a wall," touching the appropriate body part when he reached the bottom note "to focus the sound," diligently completed his articulation exercises, "Pepperpot pepperpot pepperpot pepperpot! Many men many men many men many men!"

At the end, Claudia and I clapped. Partly to ensure it *was* the end. I offered Nige my chair—we didn't have a sofa in the office, the last thing I needed to do with those two was encourage sloth—and he bowed his thanks. Then he pretended to be in love with it. He did a good job. It was an ugly gray chair, one of those orthopedic contraptions that bullies you into correct posture and spits in the face of style. At one point his lust for that chair was so visceral I looked away. My face screwed up of its own accord.

I told him afterward, "That was very convincing. Wasn't it, Claw?"

"Oh yeah. We'll probably come into the office tomorrow to a family of little chairs."

As it was hard to say if she was being sarcastic, Nige was forced to be satisfied. Of course, another great swathe of the morning was then frittered fetching celebratory cups of coffee and Kit Kats and discussing what makes someone a lead, the Method, and the breed of actor who, if cast as a murderer, felt obliged to run amok first and kill five people. I was enjoying myself, until I looked at the clock and saw that it was midday.

"Right," I said. "That's it. Come on. Work."

Claw and Nige sighed, wiped the crumbs from their mouths, and turned to their desks with regret. So did I. I found it hard to concentrate. I hadn't told them about Nick moving out, not only because it would have meant another bumper round of coffees and Kit Kats. They'd have demanded an explanation, and I didn't want to explain. Unless the words are already formed in your head, neatly packaged like a false alibi, explanations can drag you down paths you don't wish to go. Friends ask bold, poking questions and trick you into analyzing the whys and the hows of your experience.

I'd patted earth over my experience, so I wasn't going to allow anyone to dig it up. Now and then a rotting claw sprang from the cold earth, but I'd stomp it down again. Anything else wasn't in my best interest. I started going through applications. Funny how some women in their midtwenties still write on bunny rabbit notepaper. And I don't mean Miffy or Hello Kitty (a cat, I know) or any childhood character that could scrape by as ironic kitsch. I mean earnestly sketched brown creatures hopping about a painstakingly drawn forest glade. I suppose it's acceptable when you're seven or seventy, but I can't condone it when favored by someone in between. It suggests self-delusion on a grand scale.

That day, I was annoyed by little things. First, the rabbits. Then, two people spelled definitely "definately." Definite, from the word *finite*, for goodness' sake, don't you know anything?

And thirdly, I opened a letter from a guy who wrote that he didn't like people who "picked there nose's." I took his application and scrunched it up and threw it in the trash. Then I got it out again. He was applying for a date with a girl, not to Oxford University to teach English. Then I threw it back in the trash. I'm sorry, but "picked there nose's" was ignorant. He was stupid. No one has to be stupid. Stupidity is laziness. It's a refusal to apply yourself. It shows contempt for the rest of the world, it means you're too complacent to bother employing logic. "Picked there nose's" betrayed a small-mindedness I couldn't tolerate. I bet he hated Jews and blacks.

"Darling, darling, untwist your knickers, he's probably dyslexic," said Nige (any other day the first to cast a stone). "You know the state of the educational system these days. Aw. Look at this. *Do you like dogs?* He's answered, 'Yes. Jack Russells, Westies, Red Setters. Those baggy Japanese ones.' How darling is that? And, Holly, I can't believe you missed this. *What's your greatest asset?* He's written, "My dad's watch"! That's funny, you've got to admit."

I didn't know what to say, so I said, "Has he put an apostrophe after 'dad'?"

"Oh my *dear*." Nige sighed. "You really got out of bed on the wrong side. I think I'll handle this one, if only to shield him from your irrational hatred."

My last word was, "Just don't put him with anyone clever."

I returned to my pile, frowning. I knew Nige and Claw were exchanging glances and stretching their mouths into shocked shapes behind my back. Fine. Let them. Who was next?

I scrolled, unamused, through people's secrets. That day I wasn't myself. I respect our applicants, I feel humbled by the trust they put in me, Nige, and Claw (especially in Nige and Claw). Mostly their quirks go directly to my heart. Our faults are part of what makes us unique. When Nick and I chose the diamond for my engagement ring, I picked an imperfect stone. I think Lavinia, his mother, was secretly appalled, but why would I want a flawless gem, with nothing to distinguish it from any other stone on any other woman's finger in the whole of the Western world?

I promise to do my best by the clients of Girl Meets Boy, I'm a regular Brownie Guide. So what was wrong with me?

"I'm filling in this form because I'm sick of pulling my mates' friends," wrote one twenty-five-year-old. "And I don't want to approach women at bus stops." Marginally endearing, I'd give him that. I read on. *What are your bad habits?* "Thinking it highly amusing to remove my clothes when pissed." I made a noise like a horse with dust in its nose.

"Oi, Holl." Claudia was clutching the phone and jabbing her finger at the receiver. "Gwen Rogers. Reporter. From *London Local News*. Wants to do a piece on us, film a date night. What do you think? Sounds all right, doesn't it? Good publicity."

I was pleased to be distracted. "Yes. I suppose so. Why don't you pass her over?"

I like to give everyone a chance, but I'm wary of the media. It's like a lion bred in captivity. Presents as big-eyed and furry, then you relax and it bites your arm off.

Gwen was very purry. Still, I wondered if Rogers was a nickname. That said, she seemed to be genuine. She liked the idea that we were modern, a club that cool young things (her words, I assure you) could belong to without feeling like losers. She loved that we weren't grimly focused on churning out husbands and wives, that we also catered to those who were interested in making new friends or—self-conscious little snigger—landing a shag, and perhaps it reflected on the difficulty that successful, wealthy, would I say, young men and women, what with their starry high-flying careers, found meeting people *naturally.*

She finished her extremely long sentence and I was still wincing at the word *shag.* I was having second thoughts about that particular option. Sure, it cut down on bullshit, but there was no denying it was a bit brothelly. And that wasn't just me being a prude. Even Claw had reservations. She said she approved of the option "in principle" but hated the way some men rang up wanting to pay for a "shag," adding, "Have you got any blond ones?" I'd heard her reply, "Hang on, I'll see if there's any sitting in the window. No. Might I suggest you try Amsterdam?"

I know this sounds terrible, but somehow it seemed better if they put the request in writing. And before I'm accused of taking sides, it wasn't as if only the men were interested in pure/impure sex. We had a number of women on our books overjoyed to be able to spell out that yes, they only wanted his body. No, really, thank you for the offer of your personality for the next sixty years, but a few hours of horizontal wrestling was enough, really. *See ya.*

I told Gwen that I'd have to check that my clients were happy to be filmed first. If they were I was sure it wouldn't be a problem. I know that TV people think everyone is desperate to get on the box (and most of the time they're right), and I wasn't about to grovel. Gwen started pushing for how soon I'd get back to her. I told her as soon as I could, which, when you think about it, means nothing at all.

I didn't have to inform Nige and Claw what I'd said, as they'd earwigged. Nige offered to call a few of the more exhibitionisty women, and Claudia said she'd get on to the appropriate men. So to speak. I think they could tell I was feeling harassed.

I flicked through the remaining applications in today's pile. *Describe an ideal night out.* "I just hang with the fellas looking for sweet girl attraction."

What?! (That wasn't a question on the form, that was me.) Who, in all seriousness, would *say* something like that? Who did he think he was, John Travolta?

It hit me that I had no way of knowing who these people were. They told me what they liked and I had to believe them. For all I knew, Mr. Hang with the Fellas was a sadistic killer, and I was about to let him loose on Samantha and Elisabeth. (Although, personally, I doubted that any sadistic killer would be a match for Elisabeth, romantic or otherwise.) It wasn't good enough. It was irresponsible. I needed backup. I needed an expert. A professional, qualified in assessing personalities.

I needed my big sister, clinical psychologist and all-round bossy person, Isabella.

CHAPTER 9

I used to have a pathological desire to be friends with the neighbors. They moved in shortly after we did. A neat middle-class couple, he, white-whiskered and benign-looking, and she, prim and well turned out. Very *Daily Mail.* I was shocked and a little hurt when my attempts at friendship were politely but firmly rebuffed. We trotted out of our front doors at the same time one day, and I said, "Hi!" She visibly recoiled. He smiled tightly and said, "Good morning." Once, they accepted a parcel for me, informing me so with a terse note, PACKAGE AT NO. 47. I rang their bell, brimming with hope, and she handed it over with a nod, opening the door a crack.

I asked Nick why our neighbors didn't want to be friends. He looked puzzled. "Why would they *want* to be friends?"

"We're neighbors," I said.

He shook his head. "It's London. Are you *from* London?"

At one point, I got quite obsessed by it. It wasn't like I was after three-course dinners or even coffee mornings, but a chat now and then, a little personal information exchanged, wouldn't that be nice? Maybe it was us. Didn't they like us? Were we too young? Not respectable enough? As far as I was concerned, we were dream neighbors. We didn't play music loud or late, I was always roaring at Nick to turn down the TV, and we confined our screaming rows to those rooms without adjoining walls. I was determined that Next Door would think well of us.

Now, I didn't give a rat's ass.

I marched up the garden path, eyes down. If one of them came out, I would not say hello, or even smile. I'd show them—I'd nod! I'd give her a dose of her own nodding medicine! They could beg me to be friends with them and I'd refuse. Why, they could be the Mansons for all I knew. I couldn't believe that I'd been trying to inveigle my way into their affections. I was older and wiser.

I'd had a grueling day. After my brain wave, I'd stepped outside and rung Issy on my cell phone. She has an office at home and counsels from there. As far as I can tell, she listens to people talk about themselves for fifty minutes, then charges them £90. It's a dream job for her, as she's very nosy. She employs a nanny three mornings a week for her daughter, Eden, age four, and the rest of the time (not that there's *that* much left, as she's at nursery school every afternoon) she looks after Eden herself. I knew she'd love to—and I mean this in the nicest way—escape from the house occasionally.

Within minutes, Issy had agreed to come in for two hours, two days a week, to profile suspect personalities for me. Also, I said she was welcome to bring Eden. We'd play with her, keep her quiet. (Issy's reply: "You have no idea.") I'd skipped back into the office to break the news to Nige and Claw. Nige was cool. As expected, Claw reacted like a rock star on hearing that no minion was available to cut the crusts off her cucumber sandwiches. It was an outrage, a betrayal, the end of the free world as we knew it . . .

A small part of me agreed. I don't know if it's linked to being the eldest child, but Issy runs the gamut of tyranny. Half the time she's imperious, treating us like Blackadder treats Baldrick, the rest of the time, she's sulking because we offended her in our sleep or something. She likes to be the boss, but she also likes to be babied.

The family had the worst time of it when she was pregnant, a period during which she managed to be smug and insecure simultaneously. Her husband wasn't allowed to play Dr. Dre (too aggressive for the fetus) or Dolly Parton ("Jolene" made her weep, as did "You Picked a Fine Time to Leave Me, Lucille"). No person was allowed to blow their nose in her presence (this was after a client honked into a tissue during a session, she'd heard a "clod of bogey come loose," and she'd had to run into the hall and retch). Frank's best friend was banned from their palatial home because he polluted the house with "a male toilet musk." Claw, apparently, said disgusting things (harming the child with her negative vibes), and I was selfish for not sending Emily to a cattery until the baby was ten. Issy refused to watch any film rated higher than a PG—for instance, *The Jackal*—in case the essence of violence crossed the placenta and the baby grew up to be a serial killer.

Still, Issy *was* an excellent psychologist. So she said.

I unlocked my front door, dropped my bag on the floor. Then I stopped. The radio was on. I had not left the radio on this morning, I knew that. Recently addicted to silence, I hadn't turned on the radio for five days. I stopped breathing. A quiet shuffle. Someone. In the kitchen. I swallowed. Gasped for air. My eyes seemed to bulge in my head. Nick. It couldn't be Nick. There'd be more of a trail. My feet didn't want to move, my hand crept to the latch. And then I thought, No.

I disagree with people (burglars, basically) who think burgling is a victimless crime. Rachel was robbed a while ago and they stole her grandmother's jewelry—an ebony and ivory necklace, a diamond brooch, emerald earrings, all antique, but far more precious in sentimental value. The insurance company offered her not quite free rein at H. Samuel.

But it was the violation of her home that devastated her, cruel others penetrating where they had no right, taking what didn't belong to them, what someone else had earned and valued. I gritted my teeth. Whoever this was in my kitchen, *my* home, my sanctuary, his stealing days were over. I tiptoed to my umbrella—oh, it's gorgeous, clear plastic, dome-shaped, with a pink rim and handle—the kind of umbrella I ought to have had when I was four years old. I picked it up, holding it like a spear—*shuffle, clatter*—and crept into the kitchen, my mouth a hard, cold line.

Gloria, my cleaner, squealed and dropped a plate.

"*God*, Gloria, I am so sorry."

Gloria leaned against the cupboard and flapped a hand in front of her face.

"I thought you were a burglar," I added unnecessarily. "I forgot you were coming. I'm so sorry, I would have tidied."

She shook her head. I wondered if she'd actually been struck dumb with fear. This was an unwelcome thought, what with the inevitable lawsuit. "Sit down, I'll make you a cup of tea."

I think I was forming statements that didn't need answers.

Gloria sat down. She's a tiny little thing, and I clean the house before she arrives. I'm not comfortable with the idea of servants. Issy says that's a bourgeois misconception, not understanding that most people, working class or otherwise—if one had to shoe them into a class at all—would rather have *a* job than no job. It's true that Gloria certainly wouldn't thank me for refusing to employ her. She's funding herself through a law degree. Still, every Monday morning before leaving for work, I scrub the bath and toilet, stack the dishwasher, and remove all debris from the floor. All Gloria really has to do is vacuum and spray. She tells me off for it.

This was the first time I'd forgotten. She must have got a fright. Nick had left the spare room in a state.

I switched on the kettle and sat down too. I was panting.

"I think you scared yourself more than me," said Gloria.

I laughed. Not because what she said was funny—it wasn't, it appeared to be true—but because I was relieved not to have stripped her of the use of her voice. "Yeah."

Gloria frowned at me. "You look dead white, like all the blood's gone out of you. You sit. I'll make the tea."

"No, no, Gloria, please—"

"*Sit!*"

Like an obedient dog, I sat.

"Nick's moved out," I said. I felt I owed her an explanation for the elaborate mess in the spare room, and for nearly spearing her through with my pink umbrella. "I'm not used to being in the house by myself."

Gloria turned from the side, a sympathetic look on her face. "He's moved out? For good? But you two, you seemed, I thought . . . Well. What a pity. Leave his voice on the answering machine, though. It's safer. And are your locks good? I'd start setting the alarm at night. And—"

Gloria saw the look on my face and changed track. "So that's why the place is spotless. No wonder you've got thistle knickers, Holly. I am sorry."

I smiled, although I didn't feel like it. If you're paranoid, the last thing you need is other people's paranoia. Or to be called "thistle knickers." Gloria comes out with some odd phrases, most of which she makes up on the spot. As well as training to be a solicitor, she claims to be psychic. She once told me she was exhausted because she'd had hardly any sleep the previous night. I was about to make a facetious comment about a man—*obviously*—when she announced that she'd been woken by angels, calling to her, "Gloria-aaaaa, Gloria-aaaa!"

I'm not good at humoring people. I'd like to, but I can't. I tried to reply in a nonjudgmental tone, "Really? Gosh, how amazing," but my reflex thought was, You're going mad. I managed to compromise with, "Oh." And I knew I *looked* disbelieving. She never mentioned it again. I never saw how the two worlds—legal and spirit—married up in her head. But I don't suppose it matters, as long as she keeps them separate. She's a lovely woman, if a bit volatile. The only person I trust (apart from Nick) to take care of Emily in my absence.

"Why don't you get a friend to sleep over?" said Gloria, placing a mug of tea on the table.

I sat up straighter. "That is a good idea. That's a *really* good idea. I'll ring Rachel."

Gloria smiled. She has a lovely smile. It shuts her eyes completely. That doesn't sound like an asset, but it is. It's wonderful to see someone smile with their whole face. "Sorry about the plate," she said. "I'll replace it."

"Pah," I said. "Don't worry. I've got plates coming out my ears." Gloria giggled.

I took my cup of tea, went into the lounge to ring Rachel. It meant telling her about Nick, but I needed to tell someone. I needed to talk to someone. The sick feeling at the base of my throat wouldn't go away. I was, forgive me for talking like a 1930s paperback detective, uneasy. I knew *something*, yet I didn't know what. As long as I skated along the surface of my composure I was fine. There was more underneath, I knew, but it was dark and cold and deathly, and I refused to go there.

I can only compare it to flying back from Singapore on a jumbo a few years back and reading an article about the Concorde—look, Ma, no fatalities! And I thought, There's going to be an accident. Two months later there was. Unlike Gloria, I have no aspirations to be psychic, so I didn't put it down to that. Nick put it down to me being an atheist flier—I flew but I didn't believe in it. He said I was convinced that every plane would crash because of my poor knowledge of aerodynamics. True. And yet there was more to it than that, a pebble of dread in my gut, lodged there to warn me of what?

"Babes?" said Rachel, picking up after one ring. "I was going to call you. Where are you? Home? Shall I pop 'round? Stay over? Top idea. We'll have a midnight feast. It'll be like school. You provide the food, I'll bring a, uh, torch. Can't wait, I've got *so* much to tell you, I've been a dreadfully bad girl. I'll see you in an hour. Be good till then! *Ciao.*"

Rachel enters a room like Kramer. She doesn't give a damn. She's been known to describe herself as "one of those rich women with a fat bum and a Hermès handbag." I could tell Gloria wasn't impressed. When I introduced them, Rachel's extended hand was limp. Gloria yawned in her face and thundered upstairs. I said to Rachel, "You could have tried to be friendly."

Rachel's nose wrinkled. "Holly. I know you'd like to teach the world to sing. But you shouldn't get too chummy with staff."

"Stop. Now. You're ridiculous. A Victorian throwback."

"True." Rachel smiled at me and swung the Hermès bag onto a chair. She treats herself to a new bag every month. Louis Vuitton. Gucci. Miu Miu. They change in size, shade, and shape. Only the price tag remains a three-zero constant. She tucked her hair behind her ears and unwound a green silk shawl from her neck. She should be ungainly, but she has a feline grace. I think it's a result of her superiority complex. The shawl slithered off her shoulders and my mouth fell open.

"What is *that*?"

Rachel snorted. "That, babes, is what's known in the trade as a love bite. Foul, I know. I wouldn't have thought it was his style, but there you go. Can I help it if I turn men into animals?"

I stuck my cold cup of tea in the microwave. (Another bad habit, caught from Nick. I'm surprised I don't fart to the tune of "God Save the Queen" and hoard copies of *What Hi-Fi?*) I stuck the kettle on for Rachel's Earl Grey. "What man? Who is he? Do I know him? And is that infectious, because it looks like the plague?"

Rachel laughed. I laughed too. Her laugh is infectious, it sounds like a gallon of dirty water being sucked out of a drain. It made the Austrian ambassador giggle, if you can believe that. I'm sure it helps her get work. And before you jump to conclusions, Rachel is a party organizer. If you've ever planned a wedding (I haven't, but I was a bystander to the great calamitous fuss that went into planning Issy's), you'll know that party organizing is the opposite of a breeze. But to Rachel, it's second nature. She knows places and people, she has an instinct for what will work, and when. She is a massive snob about what she calls "nouvy" (nouveau riche) food, and her caterers will never serve you dried-up squidges of orange goo on a soggy biscuit. Cold, poached salmon is outlawed unless requested. As for music, whether you want garage, rock, rap, classical, or karaoke, Rachel is on kissy-kissy terms with whoever's best. Even though I'm not a party person, I love Rachel's parties and so do the glittery crowds who throw and go to glamour-puss events every week.

Rachel inspected the peeling red varnish on her nails. "Actually, you do know him. But I'm sworn to secrecy. For now, anyway. I know, I know, I can't bear it. But he made me promise not to tell. Yet. He's . . . attached."

"What? Girlfriend? Engaged? Married?"

"Married*ish*."

"Whaddya mean, married*ish*? Rachel! He's married!"

"Yes, all right, he is but he doesn't want to be."

"He said that, did he? What else did he say, his wife doesn't understand him?"

"She doesn't, as a matter of fact!"

"Oh come on, Rach."

I couldn't think who it could be. Just about the only married guy I could think of was Issy's husband, Frank, and he adored his wife. Even when she was at her most infuriating, he found Issy charming. He's handsome in what I secretly think is a boring way, very wing commander. Rachel's type. But no. Frank adored his daughter too, always fussing around Eden in public, a doting dad, forever seeing himself through other people's eyes. It couldn't be him.

Anyway, I didn't know why I was acting so pious. I'd just cheated on my fiancé. Ex-fiancé. Except, it wasn't like that. At the time I didn't have a choice. Isn't that what they all say? I hadn't felt right since that night with Stuart. But surely, it was just bad sex. Don't we all feel a bit grim after bad sex? Yes, he'd been mauly and rough and—key *Cosmo* word—*inconsiderate*. And he'd scared me rigid. But that was pretty much it, no? I wasn't sure of anything. I wished I could talk to Rachel. I *would* talk to Rachel. A woman of the world, who better?

"Babes. I will tell you who he is. But not yet. Although I'll say this, he's a demon in the sack. Filthy as buggery. Snah-ha-ha-ha!"

I got the picture, whether I wanted to or not. (And let's not be coy, I wanted to. I'm interested in my friends' sex lives, what they do, how often they do it. I think anyone who isn't is weird.)

"Okay, fine, Rach. I won't ask you. But I don't approve and I'm dying to know and you must tell me as soon as you can. Promise?"

Rachel promised. We sat at the kitchen table, she snapping digestive biscuits in half—personally I require a little more entertainment from my biscuits—me popping Maltesers at speed to try and make them taste. We talked about work for a while, how one particular American socialite (awful, *awful*, to be described as a socialite; worse, surely, than being described as a housewife) had a tantrum because she presumed Rachel would be able to get Prince Edward to attend her fortieth birthday. (Rachel said she *could* have got Prince Edward to attend her fortieth birthday, she just hadn't wanted to ruin it.)

Then, I said, "Rach. Can I ask you something?"

" 'Course, babes, go ahead."

"It's just there's this friend of mine. I know her from the agency. She's seen this guy once or twice. And the last time they went out, and you know, early on in the evening she was quite flirty, kissed him and all that. And, I mean, she'd dressed up and everything. Nothing revealing, but . . . nice—"

Just then, Gloria marched back into the kitchen, and I wondered if I should stop, but it would have seemed odd. So I carried on—

"She made an effort. Anyway, he came back to hers, she didn't invite him, but she sort of did and—"

Rachel interrupted, her eyelids droopy with boredom. "And *he* got the wrong end of the stick and she said no and he got heavy and so she gave in and let him have his wicked way and now she's blaming him because she feels like a whore?"

A Malteser stuck in my throat. "Well, not exactly."

"Well, what then?"

The words were drumming against the inside of my skull and giving me a headache, It wasn't like that, I'm sure it wasn't like that, oh please don't make it like that. But I had no idea how to say what it *was* like.

I tried to whisper so Gloria wouldn't hear, but for some reason—bloody-mindedness, probably—she'd decided that now would be an excellent time to polish the kitchen table.

"It was nastier. She, she really didn't want to. She said that. She tried to get him off her. But it was like he was deaf. He forced her, Rach. She gave in because she had to."

"Babes, if she didn't want to, what was she doing kissing him, glamming herself up, having him back to hers? What's the poor chap *meant* to think? Come on, be fair! She either wants it or she doesn't. She probably said no in a yessy kind of way, and he picked up on that. Gave in because she had to! Why, did he have a gun? She can't change her mind halfway through then cry r— *Fuck!*"

Rachel never finished her sentence, because Gloria gave the table a violent swipe with the duster, knocked over Rachel's cup, and smashed it, spilling scalding hot tea into the speaker's designer-skirted lap. But it didn't matter. I'd got the gist.

CHAPTER 10

When I was a little girl, I believed, like most little girls, that a monster lived under my bed. Needing the toilet in the night was a traumatic event. I'd do my best to banish the urge. I'd squirm and close my eyes and try to fall asleep, but my unconscious was relentless in its determination to get the message from bladder to brain. I'd dream about toilet lines and broken toilets and engaged toilets and *nearly* going but being whisked from the seat at the last second. Then I'd wake, more desperate than ever.

Finally, heart booming, I'd scramble onto my orange bedspread and wobble to my feet. Then I'd take an enormous great leap into the center of the room—as far from spindly grabbing hands as I could launch myself—and race for the door. Afterward I'd repeat the process in reverse, scrambling for the safety of my sheets, sweating.

Well, there I was, twenty-nine years old, and the weekend just gone filled with monsters. The house was crammed with them. It creaked, rattled, shook, and I shook inside it. It was more than just missing Nick. I felt like a mollusk without a shell, soft, weak, and exposed. I racked up a hefty electricity bill. I even dug around the wardrobe and found my old night-light from when I was a kid. It's a china rendition of Sleeping Beauty's castle, dotted with little holes so that when you switch on the bulb, it twinkles like a fairy-tale castle should. I armed myself against evil. Because I knew it existed.

I'm not like some people, so arrogant they don't believe in ghosts. People who make a big noise about not believing in ghosts are asking for trouble. (Which, may I say, doesn't preclude me from being dubious about Gloria's angels. How does she know *what* they are?) Claw and I used to sneak into the school storeroom and play the Ouija board with friends. The more we did it, the more smoothly and fluently the glass moved. We spoke to a girl killed by the IRA. But what freaked me was a spirit that said one of us would have a child, Sarah, with special powers. We all sneered, saying now we knew, we'd *never* call our kids Sarah. It spelled out:

YOU WILL FORGET   SCHOOLGIRL FUN

I never forgot. And that weekend, all my ghosts and monsters had come back to haunt me. They lurked everywhere, under beds and sofas to snatch at my ankles, tapping at windows with bony fingers. It wasn't only the phone ringing—everything unnerved me. When Emily scratched at the door to go out, I nearly leaped from my skin.

When Nick and I first viewed our house, I asked him if he thought it contained any ghouls. The estate agent wouldn't have told me, obviously. I wished Claudia was still in the business. (She was an estate agent for a year but got sick of lying to people. She was sacked for telling buyers, "Don't bother, don't even view it, it's crap.") But Nick walked around and said, "There's nothing here." He has a feel for the aura of a building. I don't. I couldn't even swear to it that *I* have an aura.

I couldn't believe that Nick had been gone just three days. A fine example of an independent woman *I* was. I held a kitchen knife in one hand while I cleaned my teeth. As for the kitchen, I could hardly bear to set foot in it. Still, nothing new there. I was scared of something, but what? I was beginning to suspect that what had occurred with Stuart wasn't good. But I couldn't put a name to it. I'd erased the non-gentlemanly bits, though they had a habit of appearing like old graffiti on a steamed-up window. Had he . . . *taken advantage?*

No. I am a survivor. I am not prey.

So when Rachel said what she said, I wasn't angry with her. Her words made me blush. Yet I didn't wholly associate them with me. It was as if Stuart had done what he did—to? with?—some other girl. Holly (this is the only time I'll talk about myself in the third person) had splintered off from that other girl, like a snake shedding its old skin. Rachel's verdict reassured me. She didn't believe what this other girl had said, and that was fine by me. I didn't want to believe it either. It was so unlikely anyway. Men like Stuart—charming, handsome, clever, intelligent men with careers—didn't do things like that.

My mind refused to let me revisit that night, which was probably very sensible of it, but it also refused to let in much else. What remained was a blurred sense of disappointment. It was like buying a packet of salt and vinegar chips that doesn't contain sufficient flavorings and a wide enough selection of additives to take the skin off the inside of your mouth, and stuffing them in faster and faster, hoping for that delicious soreness kick, knowing it will never come—the feeling of *missing* was similar, but so very much worse.

I looked at Rachel and I wished I had her life. There was certainty in it. Funny, I'd been content with my existence, once. Now it was not positive. This numbness had crept up on me, and to my alarm, I found it comforting. I was a person used to bouncing around wanting to achieve everything; this lethargy was frightening. These last few days I had to fight to get out of bed.

Rachel seemed self-contained and serene, like a contented cat. She was a person who sailed through life. Success came to her, she attracted it. Not like me, I had to work for it. Don't get me wrong, I liked working for it. Until recently. But now, in this slump, I yearned for ease. I was in that state of mind where you buy a lottery ticket because you want everything for nothing. Where you drive through a wealthy area and you look at the mansions and you don't think about people slaving for years to make their fortunes. You think, Lucky, lucky, lucky. I felt that nothing good would ever happen to me again.

Emily chose this moment to weave around my ankles, and I thought about Issy's cool, clinical explanation of why I liked cats. Apparently it was nothing more than what psychologists call "projection." We see our vulnerable selves in these helpless dumb animals (although that's not how I prefer to describe myself or Emily, and I'd also like to think my dental hygiene is a cut above hers). So much for empathy, compassion; no, in the end it was all about *me*, the only reason anyone ever bothered to like anyone. I didn't want to think like Issy, but for the first time in my life I was cursed to see that people *were* obsessed with themselves. It was a feat to get them to listen to you, let alone hear you. Rachel was far too entangled in her own dramas to sense mine.

But oddly, I was almost grateful. Her composed presence, after the corrosive loneliness of the weekend, was soothing. The smell of her Clarins Eau Dynamisante, the confident ring of her smart voice, it was a cocoon around me. She applauded when I said that Nick had finally gone, and when I looked like I wasn't sure I agreed with her, her tone dipped in sympathy. "It's rough on you, babes," she said. "I'm sorry. You loved each other very much."

Hearing this from Rachel made me want to cry. It's hard to bear kindness from someone harsh, because it makes you realize that you must be in a sorry state indeed. I nodded dumbly.

"But, babes, he was holding you back, and you knew that. You weren't happy. Nick is a selfish boy and he'll never change. He has it all on a plate. Why should he? But it's wretched, letting go. You must think that this is short-term pain for long-term gain. And don't forget"—her voice rose to a teasing lilt—"Stuart is waiting in the wings."

I shuddered without even trying. All the same, I appreciated the fact that Rachel didn't interpret what I said (I had enough of that from Issy). It was one of the reasons I liked her. She was immoral and outrageous and opinionated but—though she kept it quiet—she had a kind soul. I should give you an example, or you won't believe me. Well. She once had a spectacular row with Claudia, because Claudia went out with a homeless man and *let him pay.*

Every evening, on the way home from work, Claudia would pass this guy selling *Street News*. She'd always say hello. Some days she'd stop and have a chat. She discovered that the man, in his early thirties, had been an engineer. But after a divorce he'd lost his home and his job. His name was Ted. He was now staying at a hostel. She told him a few horror stories about working as an estate agent, and they laughed. Then Ted asked if she'd like to go to a comedy night with him. Claudia hesitated. Then she thought, If the only reason I'd say no is because this man is homeless, I am shallow and should be ashamed. So she said yes. The comedy night cost £8 for two tickets, and Claudia was aghast when Ted pulled out a tenner. She argued, but he insisted. She decided that to argue further would offend him. But she was so embarrassed, the next evening she took another route home and never saw him again.

"That," Rachel had bellowed across the pub, "is outrageous behavior!" Claudia should have bought "the magazine" but "kept her distance." At a stretch, she could have bought "the poor bloke" a sandwich, but to "lead him on—I mean, would you have *slept* with him?"—was a "dreadful" thing to do. She was appalled that Claudia had "taken his money." Claudia became enraged, comparing Rachel to Margaret Thatcher, Marie Antoinette, and, inexplicably, the Taliban. Claudia said this was typical of Rachel, denying less fortunate people their self-respect, thinking she knew what was best for them, assuming they were stupid—how did she know what kind of sandwich Ted liked? Far better to give him money and let him buy his own sandwich. "He'd spend it on drink," said Rachel. "And anyway, you didn't give him money. You took it from him and then you were so ashamed you ran away. And he *knew* that. You're a hypocrite, babes. Poor bloke."

There was a core of humanity in there somewhere. Even if you had to know what you were looking for. Even if, when Gloria spilled the tea over her lap, it wasn't particularly apparent. I was so busy trying to eliminate the tannin stain on Rachel's skirt, it didn't occur to me to wonder why she was so vehement in assigning blame to "the girl" in my story. Of course, later, I realized that no woman likes to think what happened to the girl could happen to them. The safest, the most reassuring, thing to think is that it must only happen to stupid women who ask for it. That's what I thought too. Which meant I *couldn't* have been.

CHAPTER 11

Considering that the "careers adviser" at my school had only ever heard of three careers (law, accountancy, and the police force), it's a wonder that I ended up doing what I do. It's hard to choose a job that you don't know exists. I fell into it by chance.

Before setting up the agency, I worked for an independent publisher. I started out as tea girl and made enough of a nuisance of myself to end up editing romantic novels. I spent my days with the likes of the Count Von Sarsparillo, his craggy jaw, his dark flashing eyes, his brooding castle in Monte Carlo, his Lamborghini Diablo, his throbbing manhood, his fiery Latin temper, his many kindnesses to small animals and poor people—no wonder that coming home to Nick became a bit of a letdown. There was, for instance, no way Sarsparillo would *ever* wander the house with a pee stain on his jeans. It was doubtful he even peed.

Anyhow, it must have been about two years ago now that Rachel and I were discussing *Summer of the Dark Count.* She said it was tiresome to read about the likes of Von Sarsparillo, because if you ever did meet a count, he was fifty-five and short with a flabby chin and an insufferable personality. Remove the first vowel from *count* to describe him perfectly. Rachel organized parties, and yet *she* found it hard to meet men. None ever turned up alone, they were always superglued to a blonde. She'd exhausted all her friends' friends, and there was no one left. Only fools and drunks approached you at clubs, and frankly, she was no longer prepared to spend her precious leisure time in a hot, cramped basement on the remote chance that Mr. Wonderful would bowl into it and—on the even more remote chance—take a shine to her. What was one meant to do, put an ad in *Men's Health*?

That was when I got the only great idea I've ever got in my life. I squashed it down—I knew nothing about starting a business, and possibly even less about dating. But the idea wouldn't go away. And I kept thinking, Take a risk. If there was one thing I was *not* brought up to do, it was to take risks. My parents are the most cautious people I know. But I told Claudia and Rachel, and they loved it. Rachel, who has more knowledge of the media than I do, suggested we send out a press release announcing the launch of the first twenty-first-century dating agency and await a response.

Rachel helped me write it, then suggested four journalists to send it to. All rang back within two hours. Rachel nearly passed out, then changed her mind and gave me the number for Companies House. "Holly," she said. "Action it. My God, you can't lose. Your initial outlay is going to be about a grand on office rent and stationery. A couple of grand at the most—it's laughable—the press seem happy to do all your publicity for you. You have a winner."

That day seemed a very long time ago.

The next morning—Nick had been gone for five days and counting—I thanked Rachel for staying over and offered to pay to have her tea-stained skirt dry-cleaned. (Gloria hadn't offered.) But my mind was elsewhere. Tonight was Date Night, and we were barely organized. I should have prepared a printed list of every Girl Meets Boy member attending that evening and who we were matching them with. I should have called everyone again to see how they were and check that they were still coming. I should have paid my taxes. I should have spoken to my accountant . . .

I hadn't. I'd been too busy thinking about Nick. Running old tape of our relationship was the only thing that dragged me out of myself. The kind things he did, like letting me warm my cold feet on his thighs in bed at night. Even the warning signs made me smile—me shouting at him to put his plate in the dishwasher, and him saying, "You're horrible. 'Nick! Nick! Nick! Nick!' I'm going to change my name and not tell you!" Now I found this funny. Odd, how I was more lenient in hindsight.

I trudged into the office, assumed a smile for the troops' sake—apparently, you can smile or frown yourself into a good or bad mood if you can be bothered—then smiled for real on seeing Issy. She was sitting at my desk in a blue suit, flicking through the confidential files. Her legs were crossed and she was jangling her left foot. After turning a page, she'd brush her fingers together as if ridding them of dirt. Occasionally, she'd make a note in a large orange notebook. Claudia scowled at me, kept plaiting her hair. Nige was reading *The Stage*.

"Issy," I cried. "Welcome!"

Issy swiveled. "Holly, I'm surprised. What time do you call this?"

Claudia glared at me from behind Issy's back. Then, in case I hadn't got it, scrawled "Told you" on a sheet of white paper and held it up.

I beamed. Issy doesn't frighten me. Her bullying ceased to have an effect when I turned, let's see now, twenty-seven. "Looks like ten past ten, to me," I replied. "Why, what do you make it?"

"Holly," said Issy, rising from the chair so that I couldn't look down on her. "If we're to work together, I need to set a few ground rules. I'm here for two hours, and I expect you to be here for the duration, otherwise it is not an effective use of my time."

"Fine," I said, before she could get up to speed. "Nige, your turn to get in the coffees. We'll have a meeting at half-past."

"Tea for me, Nigel. Lots of milk, no sugar."

"You don't drink tea!" cried Claudia. "You're just saying that to be difficult!"

"Oh, grow up," replied Issy, which is what she always says to Claudia when Claudia is right.

I blocked out the lot of them and riffled through my rough

notes for that evening. Date Nights are a miracle of organization. Even if I *had* rung each member to recheck their availability, I couldn't be sure they'd actually turn up unless I rang them again three minutes before they were actually due. Everyone is so impressive there's no telling if they'll be whisked off to Rome or New York for business at a moment's notice.

Each person is given a card and assigned four twenty-five-minute dates, as I think I've mentioned. That night, we were expecting twenty people. Four of them were on second dates, which means that the previous week they'd both ticked the same box, indicating that they'd like to meet up again and hoped to be more than friends.

Usually it's all I can do to stop myself crying with joy. I feel like a mother hen whose chicks are all grown up. You look at the quiet signs of their delight and you feel it in your heart. On those nights I feel so exhilarated I end up lying awake till four in the morning grinning and—not crying, that's too dramatic—eye-leaking at the ceiling.

But that day I was unmoved. Except that my stomach lurched every time I thought of my women going off into the night with strange men. Although, and I had to remember this, they weren't strange men. They were lovely men, like Bernard. The mainstay of Bernard's letter to Girl Meets Boy was the country cottage he owned in "rural Devon." And the boast that he'd recently taken up cricket. I'd winced, but the next line had torn my heart as if it were a tissue. "I have never," he wrote, "really found that special someone with whom to enjoy life's ups and downs."

"Nige," Claw had said, nodding at me, "Kleenex alert. Holly's got a saddo."

This double indignity had forced me to cease sniveling for two reasons. First, it's humiliating to be read like a picture book, and second, it would have alerted the guards further to the fact that Bernard was—I object to the word *saddo*—not strictly Girl Meets Boy material. He was a little elderly, at forty. Our cutoff line was thirty-eight. But just this once I'd made an exception. I reckoned Sam and Bernard would get on great. He seemed sweet, and he wasn't bad-looking. And his dress sense was hideous, which I felt she could relate to.

Nige booted open the door, balancing four foam cups in a precarious tower stabilized by his chin. The other hand was clutching a greasy paper bag bulging with doughnut shapes. He set down his wares on the desk formerly known as mine but now apparently Issy's and said, "Three coffees, with milk, and one tea, no milk, two sugars?"

"No—" began Issy. Then, "Oh, for . . . give it here."

Claudia took a huge bite of doughnut to stifle her laughter and a splotch of jam flew out and landed on the open page of Issy's orange notebook. Nige and Claudia were on the floor. Issy sighed deeply, ripped out the page, and threw it in the trash. And missed. By the time I'd settled everyone down I knew exactly how Arnie's character felt in *Kindergarten Cop*. (One of my favorite films, if you'll keep that to yourself. "Dere *iss* no bat-room!" being the best line.)

I began the meeting by reeling off the (unchecked) list of candidates and my pairing suggestions.

"On what basis?" Issy barked, after my first couple. Georgina and Mike.

I flapped a folder at her. "Based on what they've said in their application forms, what they've said when we've spoken to them on the phone, and what we've observed on meeting them at previous Date Nights."

Issy nodded, a sharp up-down nod.

I wanted to say, "Look, Issy, if you want more information, say so. Don't nod, then go silent—it feels like manipulation." So I did.

Issy opened her mouth, but Claudia was quicker. "Whoa, whoa, wait a sec—Georgina and *Mike*? When did you decide *that*? Georgina can't go with Mike. They wouldn't get on in a million years. Georgina is a trainee solicitor and a part-time model. She's fun, confident, and she wears those fabulous knee-high boots and pencil skirts, and Mike—"

Nige was nodding. "Mike," he added, "is a sweet guy, but he works in IT for god's sake, *and* he told Claudia last week that he's never eaten an avocado and never intends to, he only likes 'English' food. Won't touch pasta, or pizza. I'm amazed we took him on in the first place, and I bet I know who sneaked him in as well. Georgie is an 'A,' and Mike is a 'C.' If anyone, Mike could go with Sam. But other than her, we're going to find it hard to match him with anyone. If we put him with Georgie, she'll ask for her money back."

I looked at them, amazed. "But Mike is so . . . you said it yourself, Nige, he's so sweet. He's . . . gentle, and nice, and respectful."

Claudia snorted. "Right. And that's just what women want. Sweet and nice and *dull*, Holly!" She opened her mouth so wide I could see to the back of her throat. "Ya-orn! He's dull! He's parochial and boring and he wears plastic shoes. Georgie would spit if we—"

"I'd like to add something to that, if I may," said Issy. "It's a common error to assume that to be successful, both members of a couple have to be the same level of attractiveness. What you should be looking for is balance—"

"Genius, Issy, opposites attract! Did they teach you that in shrink school?"

"Excuse me, Claudia, can I finish what I was saying? Thank you. The gist of what Nigel says is correct, Holly. A woman like Georgina, good-looking, ambitious, we presume, no doubt well traveled, is unlikely to be attracted to a man so—we can deduct from the food preferences—unadventurous, conservative, and unstylish—I'm thinking of the shoes."

Claudia nodded grudgingly.

I felt picked on. "All right," I said. "Forget Georgina for a minute. Elisabeth. Elisabeth"—I smiled at Issy—"Elisabeth Stanton-Browne is hard to please. She hates men who wear marigold gloves and use umbrellas. She wants to meet a third-decan Piscean."

"A truly *terrible* series of dates in the zodiac," offered Nige. "Prone to addiction, depression, tediously sensitive—"

"I thought I might put her with Bernard. They both like sport!" I added as the office erupted.

"Bernard?" shrieked Claudia and Nige in a shrill chorus. "Are you crazy?"

Issy raised a hand. "On what evidence?"

I handed Issy Bernard's letter and Elisabeth's application. Issy scanned them, frowning. "Holly, darling. I see your point but this is a common error. To pair people because they both like sport is not advanced thinking, it's what you'd expect a computer to do. You have to ask *why* they like sport. The whys are truer indicators of compatibility than the whats. And look. Bernard likes cricket because it's not too strenuous, and he enjoys the *Britishness* of it. He likes how the wives make tea, and how civilized it is, and if he can't play he's more than happy to watch. *Traditional* is not the word. As for Elisabeth, she loves skiing, the speed of it, the danger, the glamour of it, the fact that she's good enough—and good-looking enough—to race down a mountain in jeans and a bikini." Issy paused. "Hol. I don't mean to be rude, but seriously, how could you ever think these two would hit it off?"

I looked up. Everyone was staring at me like I'd grown an extra ear. (Nige, like I'd grown an extra toe.) Now I don't mind being disagreed with, but I'd have prefered to delay it beyond the first five minutes of Issy's employment.

"Well, fine, okay," I said, assuming a stern, businesslike expression and resisting the temptation to shout "*I* am the boss!" "It's useful to have your professional opinion, Issy, but this isn't really what I wanted from you. I was hoping you'd help weed out the weirdos, especially the ones who do a good job of disguising themselves." I shuffled my sheets. "This guy, for instance." I shoved Mr. Hang-with-the-Fellas at her. "One of his dislikes," I added, "is poor vaginal hygiene."

I glared around the office, daring people to laugh.

Claudia sucked in her cheeks. "Hol. Admittedly, it'd be crass to mention it to your date over the first coffee. But at least he's honest. Poor vaginal hygiene isn't many people's favorite thing."

I puffed air through my nose. "Well. *Issy* might think it shows an intrinsic dislike of women. His form is peppered with words like *booty*."

Issy looked up. "Have you spoken to him, or met him?"

"No," I said.

Issy sighed. "Darling, he's twenty-two. He's certainly immature, but he's half teasing. Under *What are your greatest assets*, he's written, 'My amazing personality when drunk.' And his other dislike is 'biting toenails in public.' I wouldn't be too harsh."

I must have looked unconvinced, because Issy added, "If you

like, we can call him in for an interview. If he's the meshuggener you think he is, he's bound to let something leak."

"Leak?" said Nige, wrinkling his nose and half his face with it.

Issy half closed her eyes at him like a cat, so I knew he'd said the right thing. She does love to teach people. If she's in a mood you can't hold a conversation with her because she's not interested in a friendly exchange of thoughts and opinions, she's looking to trump you.

"Yes, Nigel," she said. "People who are capable of doing bad things *leak*. They say things in jest which reveal a lot about themselves. And even if they don't, we as human beings are capable of perceiving an enormous amount unconsciously. In the war of evolution we've derived a means of rumbling people who are good at deception. It's a fact that if you film someone who is pretending to be other than they are, if you slow down that film you perceive *microemotions*—for a matter of milliseconds the expression on their face changes. In real life, our minds pick that up. It happens too fast to be seen consciously, but you get a hunch about that person. That's why female intuition can be explained in scientific terms. If you feel uncomfortable but you don't know why, the likelihood is your mental apparatus has picked something up. Unfortunately we're raised to be rational, we see hunches as childish. They're not. They're one of the best defenses we have."

Everyone was silent. Then Nige piped up: "I'm blown away by this microemotion thing. So, what, like this?" He assumed an expression as follows: angelic, angelic, angelic, devil from hell, angelic, angelic, angelic. We all cracked up, even Issy. "More or less," she conceded.

Claudia chewed a nail. "So, what's this guy going to leak, then?"

Issy paused. "What I'm saying is that people are very bad at *not* revealing themselves. They'll say something that isn't socially acceptable, but because it's perceived to be a joke, they get away with it. So, for example, I know of a woman whose new boyfriend joked to her that he'd better go home because she was so sexy that if he didn't leave he'd rape her. She didn't laugh heartily, but nor did she think much of it. Until the next time they met, when he actually attempted it. Fortunately, her flatmate burst in on them."

"Jesus," said Claudia.

"Meeting closed," I said.

Everyone looked startled and peeved. I blanked them out and wondered instead at Claudia's outfit. A gold sleeveless top covered with little gold discs—like disco chain mail—a short denim skirt, and red ankle boots. As the Americans say, go figure.

"Hang on, but what about the fixtures for tonight? Haven't we got to sort out Bernard and Georgina and everyone?"

"This isn't a football game, Nige."

This was unfair of me. Nige takes Girl Meets Boy as seriously as it's possible to take your understudy career.

"Yes, but—"

"Nige," I said, "I don't often do this, but I'm putting my foot down. I have a *hunch* that Georgie and Mike will get on great, and at this late stage I don't want to start messing with the plan. Don't worry. Tonight"—I tried to paint a joyous romantic scene to wipe the scowls off their cross faces—"is going to erupt in a frenzy of sparks. Honestly. It'll be like the Ark."

CHAPTER 12

You were right," said Nige afterward. "It *was* like the Ark. A bloody washout."

I didn't know what to say, so I hummed into my drink. Claudia had been furious; she'd stalked off without a second glance. I was deeply relieved that Issy hadn't been there to see the monumental pig's ear I'd made of the evening. Although I imagined that Claw would recount the scenes for her in language as vivid as a rainbow.

The night had started off well. We met, as we always do, from eight to ten, in the belly of a bar in West London. It's owned by an acquaintance of Rachel's named Seb. Downstairs it's a private club, frequented by posh people. At times, the density of striped shirts is quite dazzling. Girl Meets Boy is cordoned off in a corner, and it's perfect, dimly lit and full of alcoves. Seb is friendly in a professional way—always on autosmile. We certainly buy enough drinks to make it worth his while, and he's not above chatting up some of our blonder members.

As ever, Sam was the first to arrive. To my surprise, she was wearing red-silk bootleg trousers dotted with yellow suns and a lemon-yellow T-shirt. And she'd obviously been to a trendy hairdresser (that, or she'd fallen into a tub of peroxide and been attacked by a wind machine). She was definitely wearing lipstick and mascara. Detectable only by an expert, but there was an overall impression of glossy. "Sam," I said. "You look great!" The words *What happened?* hung in the air. Sam also looked surprised. "Holly," she said. "You did this."

I was aghast. Sam touched my temple. "Are you joking, Holly? I asked you to help me sort out a new image. You even booked the hairdr—sorry, stylist for me. I had it done yesterday."

The memory dumped itself back in my head with a thump. "Of course," I cried. "Idiot me! I must have had a blip."

I must have done, I thought, watching her stride to the bar to be noticed by Seb for the first time. (He's like a dog in that he only sees in certain colors. His vision will not register non-blond.) What had I been thinking? There is something delicious about orchestrating a makeover for a friend who you think doesn't make the most of herself, but I'm not sure it's delicious-good. When Claudia was five, a well-meaning great-aunt, visiting from Devon, bought her a dead doll. At least, that's what Claudia decided, because there was no body, just the *head*. It was human-size and grotesque. Little girls were meant to cut its hair and apply blush to its face, and I'll bet it was thought up by a fifty-year-old man in a suit. Claudia decided the doll had been beheaded by Captain Hook (her frame of reference was limited, but exact) and gave the doll a death-row skinhead, except for one spooky strand. She then made up the face in white foundation and used the red "lipstick" crayon to re-create blood dripping from its eyes and mouth. Then she hung it by the strategic strand of hair to the doorframe of the guest bedroom, bribed me to remove the lightbulbs on the landing, and sat up late waiting to hear our great-aunt scream. It worked too well and my mother had to call the emergency doctor (who, by the way, charged "an arm and a leg").

I felt bad about the heart tremor, but I'm afraid I approved of Claudia's actions on principle. Teaching five-year-old girls that a bare face isn't good enough! When I itch to perform a makeover on women like Sam, I make myself think of that skinhead doll. It reeks of not accepting people for who they are, and that's damaging.

I wondered if the new Sam would appreciate being paired with Mike. What with Georgina, and Sam's babywear-to-babewear transformation, it was his lucky night. Or, at least, that's what it was set up to look like, but I knew it wouldn't happen. Did I say that?

By eight twenty, everyone had arrived. Every week, we spend the first half hour chatting and drinking, so that people relax. Nige flirts with the women, and Claudia and I pander to the men. That night, it was an effort on a par with building a pyramid. I knew Bernard had a crush, or maybe he was indiscriminate, but he kept putting his arm on my shoulder and standing too close. I felt my face turn to granite. I brushed off his arm and stepped back. I think I spotted a microemotion of hurt, but too bad. You *know* what you're doing, I thought. If I had a six-foot boyfriend standing right here, you'd keep your distance.

I'd decided that Sam and Bernard weren't right for each other after all, despite the fact that Sam's eyes kept flickering toward him. He, I noted, when he wasn't pawing me, spent a lot of time gazing at her silk trousers. Possibly, that night, Sam would get some ticks. Previously I'd lied to her, telling her she'd got friendship ticks from the men she'd given relationship ticks, so she wouldn't be disheartened. Maybe that night I wouldn't have to. She looked a different person from the woman who'd once said to me, "I tend to look at a roomful of people, judge them, then be what they want me to be."

I did my best to soothe a new member, Millie, who was keen to reassure me that she had no trouble attracting men. I told her none of the women here had trouble attracting men; the problem was none of them had *time* to attract men. Millie nodded, sighing. She had slightly protruding blue eyes and when she didn't smile (which she didn't) Nige was convinced she looked fishy. "I don't have time to do anything," she said. "I haven't been to the gym for months. Last time I went it cost me seven hundred pounds to have a swim." I waved away her concern. "That's fitness tax," I replied. "It's like having a TV license. You might not use it, but you have to pay anyway." Millie laughed, which made her pretty.

It was time to get to work. Nige and Claw and I sat each of the women down at their own table and brought over their respective dates. Then, for twenty-five minutes, we left them to it. For some reason, Claw and Nige refused to look me in the eye.

Being cold-shouldered gave me the opportunity to peek at the dates. I'd put Sam with Martyn, the guy who according to Elisabeth was so straitlaced he could have been a priest. At first glance, he didn't *look* straitlaced. A shaven head and thick black art-house spectacles. Of course, this was a uniform popular with the—I'm reluctant to say nerd—*earnest person* in disguise. The shaven head was used to hide a receding hairline, and the black spectacles had only recently replaced an owly pair of metal frames. Sam and Martyn must have seen something familiar in each other and resented the reminder, because my straining ear made out the words "Quarter to nine and eighteen seconds."

The others didn't seem to be faring much better. Elisabeth was leaned back in her chair with a face like old milk, ostentatiously inspecting her nails, and Bernard was staring gloomily into his pint. Now and then he'd look around like a dog who'd lost its master. I glanced at Mike and Georgina. Mike was leaning toward Georgie, talking very fast. He laughed at something he'd said and Georgie lifted a hand and wiped her cheek. She had the look of a woman who'd been tricked into attending a live chess match.

Surely Millie was enjoying herself. I'd put her with Xak. Xak (pronounced Zak) was nice to look at, but surprise, he was also nice to the core. Tall, slender, with blue eyes, dirty-blond hair, and adorably shy. He could barely meet your gaze. He worked on the fashion pages of a men's magazine, was twenty-five years old, and had only ever gone out with women who'd asked him. "Models?" I'd said, and he'd laughed. He'd only dated "very plain" (his words) screwed-up women. Here, at last, I thought—the male version of practically every woman I've ever met!

I glanced over. Xak looked petrified. Think a picnicker trapped by a bear. Millie was striking off some sort of list on her fingers. After every strike she'd frown at Xak and he'd nod meekly. I wondered if he was up to a woman who, by her own admission, had recorded every dream she'd ever had since the age of twelve. "What, *all* of them?" I'd said, impressed. She'd replied that dreams were messages from our unconscious that we ignored at our peril. This didn't please me. I have enough trouble keeping up with my E-mails. Crumbs have incapacitated about 40 percent of my keyboard.

Twenty-two minutes into the first date, ground down by beseeching looks from around the room, I gave in and called time. Everyone sprang from their chairs like they were on fire. "This is pathetic," snarled Elisabeth en route to the ladies'. "Thank *God* I have my own resources."

"I'm sorry," I told her. "We'll discuss it later. But I think you're going to get on great with your next date." She didn't. Nor with the one after that, or the one after that. No one did. Two dozen people went home miserable, brooding on the small yet enormous tragedy of having love to give and no one to give it to.

I told Nige there was no accounting for chemistry and it was nobody's fault, and while the look he gave me said different, I wasn't bothered. He didn't understand. I had chosen pairs who wouldn't fall for each other instantly, but it was for the best. People who fancy each other make terrible choices. They're taken in by a wide white smile or the sweet little sigh before speech, and then they pay for that naiveté for the rest of their lives.

You cannot let your genitals make decisions for you. It's evolution's fault, making us want to bonk the whole time. I thought these people would be better off getting to know their dates over time. They'd stand a greater chance of happiness if they weren't in such a rush to swap germs. They might sulk at first, but I was doing them a favor and eventually they'd realize that.

I drove home, my mouth agape in one long yawn. I was that tired, the depth of tiredness where you feel that sleep is a poor answer, you need a three-week coma and a glucose drip to restore your energy levels to capacity. I checked the house from top to bottom to top, fed Emily and paid her a compliment ("Your fur's so shiny and soft it's like you've been polished"—I sense it's part of a cat's required service), imagined what Nick would be doing now, pulled an elaborate face, and fell into bed. Was he thinking of me too? I hoped he also felt friendlier in retrospect.

It was a joy to realize, the next morning, that Nige had his audition and wasn't coming in. Although Claudia is not the sort who needs backup to launch a strike, I was relieved when she rang in "sick." I'd brought some headache pills in anticipation, which I could now save for a special occasion. Just me, then. It wasn't ideal, but then neither was company. Why hadn't Nick rung me? He had about a billion excuses. How was the cat doing? Had he left his cuff links in that silver tin on the bathroom shelf? I missed him. But then, I also missed tripping on the torn linoleum of my parents' kitchen floor when Dad glued it back to the concrete after fifteen years.

You get used to people, things. I wasn't mad about change. Every time there was change due in my life I reckon I stalled it for as long as I could—seven days to two years, depending.

Seven days if it was a food choice. Last year, for one crazy week, Martha decided that custard doughnuts were the new black and abruptly ceased production of the jam ones. I was frozen. I couldn't bring myself to go to Tesco Metro, it would have been like cheating on a wife. But nor could I get around the concept of a doughnut gooey with yellow pus. Need I say, Nige and Claw adapted like a particularly shallow pair of chameleons: "Ooh, *yes*, actually, mm, and long live the cheese fondue while you're about it!" I refused to partake.

On day seven, suffering from severe sugar deficiency, I took a small cross bite. On day eight, Martha decided that fashion was a load of random baloney, cast out the custard interloper, and welcomed back the faithful old jam doughnut. It would have been healthier for me if she had persisted with the pus—I'd have been forced to adapt and move on. The way it worked out, I never learned.

I glanced around the empty office—ludicrous, who did I think was spying on me, Claudia's poster of Kylie Minogue?—then rang Manjit on his cell. He'd think I was calling to snoop on Nick, but he'd be wrong. Manjit was friendly in an unfettered sort of way, which meant that Bo wasn't in the room. I explained why I was calling. I wasn't going to play games. Manjit sounded surprised but pleased. "Cool," he said, "okay." And then, shyly, "I'm pleased you rang, Hol."

I beamed. "Thanks, Manjit, *I'm* pleased I rang. I nearly didn't. Well, when are you free?"

There was a pause. "Um. Well. Now if you like. I've got to meet Bo at two thirty. We're going to a matinee in town, um, that play, you know, the one with the ghost . . ."

"Phantom of the Opera?" It was an effort keeping the shock from my voice. Bo's theatrical taste is painstakingly erudite. Andrew Lloyd Webber was a departure from her intellectual norm.

Manjit giggled. "No! Oh, yeah. *Macbeth.* Any rate. I'm free till then. That gives us an hour, easy, and plenty of time for showers afterward. I'll ring reception and book us a room for, say, twelve, shall I? Wear something light, yeah? You got the address?"

I nodded into the phone. "Got it."

He cut off and I twirled my necklace. I felt nervous. Well, too late to back out now. I glanced at the clock. Time to go home and change, shave my legs and armpits—*pits!* ugh—clean my teeth. My heart was pounding. Silly. This would be *fun.* And if, midtussle, I gleaned some classified droplet of information about my ex-fiancé, what a perfect bonus.

CHAPTER 13

"Come closer," said Manjit, smiling. Christ, what women would do for that smile. "It's all right, Hol. I won't bite you."

I stepped toward him, face red as a poppy. "I'm going to be useless, I know it."

I heard myself say this and squirmed. Since when was I the sort of woman who couldn't speak badly enough of herself? I used to go crazy at Sam for belittling herself. I'd tell her if you can't respect yourself no one else will.

Manjit laughed. "You're gonna be magnificent. I can tell just by looking at you. Have a drink."

I lunged for the bottle, took a large swig, started choking. Manjit sprang forward and patted my back. But softly, so I didn't mind.

"Breathing?" inquired Manjit. "Luverly. Let's get started. First thing, Hol. I'm not going to teach you anything fancy. No Bruce Lee high-kicking martial arts stuff. That's pointless. That's for films. That's not gonna get you anywhere. Any rate, I don't like kicks. They take years to learn, and they don't work. You lose your balance. You need to keep both feet on the ground. The only time you kick someone is if they're on the floor. And if they're on the floor, you shouldn't be wasting your time. And, um, it's slightly illegal. You should be running away. So. We're gonna concentrate on a few simple techniques that work. We're going to repeat 'em and repeat 'em, until they're instinct. And as we practice, you'll find out what feels right, what works for you, yeah?"

I nodded, eyes wide.

"Excellent. Quick word, though. Your best defense? These"— he pointed to my mouth and eyes—"and these." He pointed to my legs, shivering in Lycra shorts. I squeezed my knees together to stop them knocking. For the last ten years I'd been meaning to buy some cool workout trousers, cheekily flared at the ankles. But I hadn't, and my exercise outfit screamed loud as fluorescent orange that I'd last frequented a health club sometime in autumn 1994.

"Let's warm up while we're talking. All right. Roll the shoulders back. Untense. Worst thing, in a fight, is to be tense. Slows you right down. If you want to strike, you have to unclench your muscles before you can move your arm, yeah? Like this, see? Slower. As opposed to this, *whap!*"

I raised my eyebrows.

"Best-case scenario? *No* fight. You're walking down the road, that's not a time to be daydreaming. Not in this day an' age. Me, I mentally classify every geezer walks toward me. White, male, six foot, one hand in pocket—like, *why?* You gotta think, *why* is he walking toward me with one hand in his pocket. Is that how people walk? I don't think so. What's he concealing? A knife? Check, if they've got one hand down by their thigh. To me that says concealed weapon. And thing is, Hol, sounds daft, but if he ain't close up, he can't attack you. Cross the road. He crosses, cross again. Fuck 'im. Don't be embarrassed to make a scene. Scream, dance, act crazy. Whatever he wants off you, he doesn't want trouble. An' another thing. People come up, ask you the time. No *way.* You don't have it. What do you do, telling the time? You bend over, squint at yer wrist—well, bloody 'ell. You give 'em a nice opportunity to snatch yer bag, whip out a knife, whatever. I don't have the time. Yeah, but you got a watch. It's broken. Here's another thing. Someone on the street asks you a question, you *don't have to answer.* They ain't a teacher! This ain't school! Not polite? Bugger that! You're a nice polite girl, Hol, well brought up. But from a safety point of view, that ain't good. That's what they're counting on, yeah?"

I nodded. This knowledge was like a shower of jewels. Diamonds, emeralds, rubies, cascading over me. I wanted to burst into tears with love and gratitude. Men like you, I thought. Bless men like you, kind, decent men, who teach women how to be safe.

"But, Hol," added Manjit. "Someone really wants your bag. Give it to 'em. It's not worth it. Everyday mugger, he'll wave a knife around to scare you, but he doesn't want fifteen years in the nick. Then again, some people are crazy. Do you understand me?"

I nodded.

"All righty, then." Manjit grinned. The gym smelled slightly of mildew. It was a small cool room with mirrored walls and large windows onto a courtyard. I was pleased to be there.

"How is Nick?" I said.

Manjit could have made one of those ooh-*ooh* faces, but he was better than that. He shrugged and rolled his eyes. "Bo caught him putting dirty plates in the dishwasher when it was still half full of clean stuff. You know what he's like. Couldn't be arsed to empty it, was about to switch it on. She was *not* happy."

I hid a smirk.

"He ain't that cheerful either."

I couldn't get the word out fast enough. "Why?"

"It's obvious. I went with him to a kids' party on Sunday and he was *not* in a good mood. It's fancy dress, yeah. Any rate, Nick opens the front door as Mr. Elephant and this snotty little kid done up as a pirate stabs him in the stomach with a plastic sword. I think he winded him. Any rate, there's this tent down the bottom of the garden, and Nick waits till the pirate kid is in it, then he sticks his big scary elephant face in the tent and screams 'Raaaaaaaaaaahhhh!' The kid is hysterical, and crying for its mummy and—in front of the mother, yeah—Nick's going, 'Aw, what's the matter?' The kid was a brat, but what a sod! It's only, what, four? He doesn't care. Every little kid that's annoyed him got the 'Raaaah!' treatment. One of 'em was sick with fright. Or at least, emptied a load of Smarties out of its mouth onto its party dress."

I tried to look severe but couldn't manage it. Several things. Manjit referring to every child, male or female, as "it," and Nick being a bigger baby than all of them.

"But, you know, them—sorry, those mums, they're something else, aren't they? They're like vultures pecking at one another. I mean, on the face of it they're all 'Ooh, how's your little one?' All cooing over one another, but you can see they're gagging to have a pop: 'And how old is he? He's not walking yet? My Amelia, she was walking down the shops, buying pints of milk, and coming back with the right change at four months.' Scary."

I let out the laugh but in a studious way. I was all too aware of Manjit's ability to veer off on a chatty tangent and not return till teatime.

"But, you know, some interesting stuff. Watching those kids fight. Thing is, Hol, most adults fight like those kids. Like they're still at school. Head down, crouched over, arms flailing like a windmill. They don't know how. Even the buff ones. If you want a laugh, watch *Jerry Springer*. And that's good for you. Though I gotta tell you, you think someone's gonna hurt you, hurt them first."

I made a face. Manjit nodded. " 'Sall right, Hol. I'm gonna show you how. And remember, start of a fight, everyone's scared.

He's scared. Everyone has fear. Your attacker is scared. Seriously. The adrenaline starts pumping, there's nothing he can do about it. It's like that kid, emptying its mouth of Smarties. It's the body's reflex, it wants to run away, off-load extra weight. That's why people who're scared puke or wet 'emselves. Or worse. An' go white in the face, it's all the blood, rushing to the legs. Any rate. First thing. Don't punch. Punching's rubbish. You gotta make your hand into a tight ball—it's tiny—you got a good chance of missing your target. And it *hurts* to punch people, trust me. You're better off opening your hand and using the flat fleshy part of your palm."

"The heel of your palm?"

"Yeah, the heel, that's it. Daft, that they couldn't think of a better name for it. Anyway, you hit someone on the nose with the heel of your palm, you'll knock 'em out. Their head goes back and their brain wobbles in their skull like a red jelly. So look. Bring one arm up, in front of your chest and face, yeah, bent at the elbow. Feels odd, doesn't it? But you'll get used to it, right. That's your guard. Nice strong radius, protecting you. And strike, fast, with the other arm, palm out. *Bam!* Beautiful. Don't overextend, don't pull it back first. Aim *beyond* the geezer, yeah? Fast, hard, mean it. And lean into it, support that arm with the force of your body weight, yeah? So you're hitting him with yer whole body. Luverly!"

Manjit slipped his hand into a boxing pad, held it in front of his face, and invited me to hit him. I positioned my feet securely, took my guard, and lunged. Unfortunately, my aim was off and I flew straight past his right ear. "Bother."

"Try again," said Manjit. He peered over the pad. "Still, tonight should cheer him up. I told him he should wear his elephant suit."

I lowered my guard. "Who?"

"Nick."

"What's tonight?"

Manjit frowned. "You know, what'sername, that well-spoken woman with blond hair." I grinned to myself. When I first knew Manjit it was "blond bird this," "posh bird that." Two decades of companionship with Nick, nothing. Three months with Bo and his vocabulary had been spring-cleaned to within an inch of its life.

Then I stopped grinning. "He met her at that Girl Meets Yob party and she gave him her card. Elisabeth something? Double-barrel. You know about that. I thought you knew about that. I thought he might of, *have*, I mean, *have* said something. I mean"—Manjit shifted his feet—"it's all right, though, isn't it? It's over and that, I mean. You ended it."

I nodded. "Absolutely," I said. "It's fine." Then I hit Manjit's pad with the heel of my palm and knocked him flat.

"Beautiful!" He sighed, beaming, from the floor.

I cannot," announced Nige the next morning, "abide Robert Downey Jr. Please hide the paper. I am bored to death of his endless dysfunction."

Claw threw *The Mirror* in the trash. "So the audition went well, did it?"

Nige crossed himself. "One can never tell. But I gave it my all. I have to be satisfied with that."

"And you," I said to Claudia. "You don't look unwell. What was it that kept you at home yesterday?"

My sister bared her fangs. "I had a bug. It might have been brought on by the calamity that was Tuesday night. I was extremely ill, *very* ill. I nearly called an ambulance."

Nearly.

"Was it the kind of ill brought on by excess alcohol?" inquired Nige.

Claudia smiled. "We're not *all* like you, petal," she replied. "Some of us can hold our drink."

Nige wriggled in his seat. "Only through solid years of practice. So did you plan your funeral song? I always do that when I'm ill. Top choice at the moment is 'If I Can Dream'—you know, Elvis. 'If I can dream of a better place—' "

"Yeah?" said Claudia. "That's shit. I'd have 'It's Gonna Be Lonely This Christmas.' "

My voice emerged three octaves squeakier than normal. "Excuse me," I shrilled. "In case you hadn't noticed, this is a business, not a social group. Can we start work, please?"

Claudia and Nigel went quiet. I could see them looking at each other covertly.

"What?"

Finally Claudia spoke. "Holly," she said, "it's a business *and* a social group. And the social part of it is crucial to the success of the business. And, well, this week, it seems to us that you've forgotten that. No one got together on Tuesday, thanks to you. It was bloody embarrassing and a disaster we cannot afford to repeat. The week after next we've got Gwen Rogers and her TV crew filming us—we have got to get it right."

A small shrill elf overtook my voice box. "What are you talking about! How can you *say* that? You know I love this business. I'd do anything for this business! Why do you think I hired Issy?"

Nige cut in: "Good point. At first, sweets, we thought you'd hired Issy to help you pair people with her psychological expertise. But from what we saw the day before yesterday, you hired her to ignore her expensive advice and weed out just about every man that applies—"

"That's not true!"

"Sweets, you refused to accept a perfectly good candidate— what was he, a musician—because under *What's your favorite book and why?* he wrote, 'I don't read books.' Now—"

"Nigel," I said. "You cannot deny that there's something savage about people who don't read books."

Nige sighed. "Hol, I'm not saying it's admirable. Yeah sure, me, I'd want a partner with an extensive library. John Grisham, Jackie Collins, do not pass go; I'd require one Dostoevsky, a Fitzgerald at least, an attempt at Dickens—I'd accept *The Pickwick Papers* up to page nine—an entire Hardy, a whole Austen, one of the Brontës. Not fussed which, but, sweets, that's *me*, I'm a snob, I despise people who play golf, I shudder at those who call dinner 'tea'—"

"Half the country, then."

"Correct, Claw, but happily, this agency does not cater for me, or you, or Holly, and while many, indeed most, of our candidates are well-read, quite a few of them couldn't give a flying eff if the last book their soul mate opened was *Topsy and Tim Go to the Seaside*. And that being the case, it is certainly not for us to judge. To reject, what was his name, Tim, on the grounds that he doesn't like reading is, I'm afraid, unacceptable."

Claudia nodded. "I agree."

I felt picked on. I wouldn't mind but those two are professional layabouts who spend a large portion of the working day discussing such weighty issues as how the seals on plastic soup tubs are so hazardous to open that you expect to rip a nail and how the attempt could quite possibly kill an old person, what sort of patterns you see when you shut your eyes really tight, whether Pringles intensely flavors every sixth crisp to entice you farther down the container, and the invention by a Northamptonshire housewife of an item called "the Stress Towel," discovered when she found that throwing a tea towel over her head signaled to her family that she'd had enough of them.

Behold, the great minds accusing *me* of neglecting my job!

"I am not turning down every man who applies. On Monday I accepted a really lovely guy called, ah, Neil Bottomley—"

"Age fifty-*seven*!" thundered Nige. "With a doctor of philosophy degree in—wait for it—life insurance from the Pacific Western University, California, and who from his picture, taken we see from the computerized date on the back of the shot a decade ago when he still had a thin tufting of hair 'round his ears, before it finally left his head and migrated to inside his ears. Hey, gorgeous twenty-something girlies, check out this mad, bad life insurance salesman we got for you. Ooh, it's your lucky night tonight! Are you insane? This isn't us! We're Girl Meets Boy, not Girl Meets Coffin-dodger. My God! I could finish him off by running up behind him with a chip packet! You carry on this way, you'll kill us, Hol."

"Some women like older men."

"Some women," retorted Nige, "like convicted murderers, and we don't provide those either."

"Well. Look. I don't like some of the things you do."

"Tell me. I'd be glad to address them."

"Tuesday. The nanny. She's been three times but only gets friendship ticks."

"Shannon?" Nige's face was indignant.

"Yes, Shannon. I thought it was out of order of you to tell her she should go to the gym. I thought that was wrong, and disgusting, actually. I'd *never* tell a client to go to the gym."

"You gave Sam a makeover," snapped Claudia.

"Claudia, she asked me to advise her. That's different."

"Hol," said Nige, "Shannon asked me for advice. She wanted me to be honest. And I didn't just tell her to go to the gym. I gave her an entire life-coaching session. I'd told her the month before to relax on her dates because the guys felt like they were being interviewed. I'd told her to stop asking them about their ambitions and possessions and to chat about something like holidays, and then she spent the whole evening grilling them for exact information. Then she was upset because she *still* wasn't getting the shag, sorry, relationship ticks. So I spoke to her on Tuesday and said that it could be partly to do with the way she presented herself, and that maybe she should try to do more alone, go to the gym, to galleries. I wanted to motivate her to do something cultural, develop her personality, make an effort with her looks. She can't be bothered to exercise her body or her brain, what does she expect? It's tough out there, Hol. There are people ten times better looking than her, ten times more interesting. What does she do? She looks after other people's babies. That in itself is not necessarily interesting. She was expecting all these criteria from the blokes but not providing any."

I studied Claudia's footwear. (Pink patent boots with pointy toes, kitten heels, and buckles up to the midcalf.)

"Holly," said my sister, tucking her feet under her chair. "We do mess about, but you do know that Nige and I take our work here very seriously. Last month, may I remind you, the Chocolate Box chain became our sponsors, which, apart from making us all fat, has taken off some of the financial pressure. And who negotiated that deal? I did, with Nige acting as my personal assistant. We care about what happens to this agency. We think it's a brilliant service you've created here, with incredible potential. I love the idea about starting up a gay section, Boy Meets Boy, Girl Meets Girl. We want this to succeed, and we think you have the talent to make it succeed. That's why we're saying these things, not to attack you, but because we believe in you. It's because we respect your judgment—normally—that we *can* be honest with you. If there's anything on your mind stopping you giving the business your full attention, please tell us. We only want to help. We're on your side, Holly."

I swallowed hard. Gave myself a mental shake. Then I sat up straight and looked at both of them dead-on. That caused a fuss in my eye sockets so I settled for gazing first at Claw, then at Nige.

"You're both right," I said, forcing myself not to add "but." I smiled. "And I appreciate"—listen to me, swapped at birth with a Californian—"your honesty. I *have* been preoccupied this week." I paused. They'd expect something. "What with Nick leaving the house, finally."

"Christ, Hol, when? Why didn't you say something?"

I wrinkled my nose. "Last Friday. A week ago tomorrow. Anyway. From now on, I'm back on form. No professors of life insurance, and lots of men who can't read. And even more matching people with who they want to be with."

Nige patted my arm. "Poor angel. No wonder. Dreadfully hard to be pro-smooch when you're at the dog end of a failed relationship. But you'll do it, Hol, I know you will. You're such a softie."

Claudia stood up. "If you'll excuse me. All that earnest niceness and, guah, *relating*. I'm not used to it. It's left a foul taste in my mouth. I need to brush my teeth."

CHAPTER 14

As is normal after an argument between friends, we were all simperingly sweet to one another for a good few days. Claw insisted on organizing my birthday dinner. I was thirty, but I didn't want a fuss. Or rather, I was thirty *and* I didn't want a fuss. But my parents were coming down for it, which meant I couldn't cancel. It's egotistical, summoning friends to a restaurant in *your* honor, then forcing them to pay for the alcoholic excesses of others. There's always a few who don't drink and there's always a few who drink till they're still and green and yet they never offer to cough up extra. They're always too busy coughing up onto the pavement.

Ah well. I'd do what I usually did and pay for everyone's drinks. I find it cuts down on resentment. Costs me the price of a Gucci bag, but then I don't buy Gucci bags and I'm saved from the hell of imagining my dearest friends stamping home muttering, "A hundred quid for one glass of paint stripper *and* I didn't have an appetizer." I wondered if Nick would show. Like he'd dare. With Elisabeth! What a sly, smug . . . But I couldn't blame her. She'd just gone to the Girl Meets Boy party and met a guy. Why should he tell her whom he'd been engaged to, once? It was irrelevant.

I thought this, but I had a hard time believing it.

All the same, I let myself fantasize about Nick's family and birthdays. One thing about his clan, they're always *doing* things, and in a great pack too. Nick doesn't have brothers or sisters, but he has about a million cousins and uncles and aunts, and they're all on fabulous jet-setting terms and they meet up on every occasion to go for clifftop walks and picnics on the beach and sailing excursions—Nick's father in his panama hat—and surfs and Bloody Marys and swims and card games and drinking games. *Drinking games!* My parents have half a glass of sherry and think themselves lush!

On my twenty-sixth birthday, we went to the Hampshire cottage and met up with a great tribe of them. There was a celebratory dinner and Nick's parents got in caterers—friends of friends. Everyone is a friend or a friend of a friend. If they go to see a play, a friend will be starring in it; if they go to a restaurant, a friend will be head chef; if they go to Mauritius, a friend will own the villa. I sat next to a red-faced, white-haired army commander without whose leadership, I suspect, Britain might well have become an extension of Germany. On my other side sat a lord chief justice. He drank till he was purple (he was past the green stage) but was very useful regarding the correct use of cutlery.

I don't mean to gripe, but I don't know *anyone*. Apart from Rachel, I have no connections, no friends of friends. My relatives are decent people, but ordinary with a capital O. My mother's great boast is that she once stood in the same fish line as Jackie Mason. (He bought halibut.) And my father never tires of telling the tale of when he glanced out of his office window and saw Jimmy Connors driving past in a Volkswagen. As for holiday homes, my parents own a caravan. Sorry, recreational vehicle. Admittedly, this was ever so exciting when I was *four*. I delayed telling Nick about Mum and Dad's ownership of a Bedford Autosleeper when we got stuck behind a motor home on the M5 and he cried, "Look at those fools dragging along their stinky mobile toilet!"

Of course, he was a sweetheart when I told him the truth. I waited until we'd overtaken "the fools" and their "mobile toilet," then I said, "Did I tell you my parents are members of the British Caravanning Club?" Nick didn't blink. It was impossible to embarrass him, he was too well-bred. He replied, "I love your parents, Hol. They're two of the most pure-hearted people I've ever met." It was a lovely thing to say. I was stunned. "Thank you," I said. Then I told him about their dream, to own a Peugeot Pilote A Class (approximately ten grand secondhand).

For a while, they'd fantasized about graduating to a Margrove Freeway Demountable on a Nissan Diesel Pickup—a hideous pairing of half a caravan and half a truck, valued at approximately four thousand pounds and containing something entitled a Porta Potti. I think you could detach the Demountable and add a tent, but it was so fearsomely ugly that Issy convinced them not to make the purchase. The Pilote was a good few rungs up the caravanning ladder. It looked like a truck, but, as my mother told me in hushed tones, "It's four-berth, and the model we're looking at has a removable stereo, blow-air central heating, an oven, stove, grill, microwave, a *new* three-way fridge-freezer, a shower, a bike rack, a sun canopy, *and*"—she'd paused in awe—"an electric flushing marine toilet! Can you imagine the luxury!"

I couldn't. Anyway, it turned out to be too expensive. Secretly I was glad. They were knocking on sixty. Why couldn't they treat themselves to a gorgeous hotel in Barbados on the edge of a blue lagoon? Why did they insist on parking their rusty mobile toilet in a muddy field in freezing Norfolk, eating tinned sausages, braving the lashing rain, and scurrying into the woods to wipe their bottoms on leaves each time the toilet became blocked, which it frequently did? The Portugal experience had never been repeated, it had seemed "too extravagant." I hated when they said that, it was like a needle in my heart.

It was hard for me—and my sisters—to accept that our parents *preferred* caravanning and camping to a gorgeous hotel. They found the whole business thrilling. The closest my dad came to gossip was when he revealed that a fellow BCC member knew someone who knew someone who owned a Holiday Rambler. I didn't see the significance until my father showed me a photo of an ill-advised cross between an ambulance and a coach (it reminded me of a dog I once saw, the result of a liaison between a basset hound and an Irish setter). Dad explained that this monster, brand-new, cost £165,000. Good Lord! You could buy an Aston Martin for that and have change left over for a Filet-O-Fish!

"Hol," said Claudia, breaking into my thoughts. Visions of Nick and his loud, unwieldy family vanished and I was back in the office on a dreary Monday morning after another quiet weekend.

"Hol," Claudia repeated. "The restaurant's booked, I thought you'd like to know. And also, Issy's coming in for the meeting at three P.M. about tomorrow's Date Night. Is that all right? I know you're out at lunchtime for your self-defense. God, I should really come with you, but I'm too lazy. I just rely on the pepper spray I smuggled back from New York."

"That's illegal over here, isn't it?" I said.

Claudia grinned. "Oh dear. Oh, and did I say Mum and Dad are hoping to stay with you, if that's okay. I suggested they spoil themselves and get a suite in the Charlotte Street Hotel, well, because *I'd* like to stay there, but of course they wouldn't hear of it. Mad, they can afford it now, what with Granny G popping it. Anyway, they don't want to be a burden, blah-blah, but they're *so* looking forward to seeing us all. Yada yada yada, and not to go to any trouble. I thought you'd be fine with it. I mean, you've got room now. Uh. Sorry."

I smiled. "No prob."

I realized that my parents' financial situation had changed dramatically, what with Granny G popping it—excuse the disrespect, but my mother's mother was not our favorite, thanks to her open dislike of my father (he was working-class, grew up on a council estate, and was therefore not good enough), and Claudia refused to pretend an affection purely because Old Miseryguts was now dead. She'd been a terrifying grandmother, a sour old woman who liked to frighten children, who was forever warning you that if you swallowed an apple pip a tree would grow inside you, if you picked dandelions you'd wet the bed, if you made a face the wind would change . . . She'd scared the life out of me.

But now I realized, thanks to her, if our parents wanted they could purchase the Peugeot Pilote A Class without a second thought. Or even the Holiday Rambler. Granny G was a very rich woman who—despite her family owning half the pig farms in Wiltshire—didn't believe in spending money and would send my mother to bed with no supper if she used more than two sheets of toilet paper per bathroom visit. (I told this to Nick, and his response, predictably, was, "But what if she had diarrhea?")

I glanced at the clock. Ten to one! I'd be late for Manjit. "See you later," I said to Claw and Nige as I sped out the door. Neither one of them had seemed surprised on discovering that I'd started self-defense, and I knew it was because they thought I was doing it to keep up with Nick's activities. The cynicism of some people!

"So," I said after kissing Manjit hello. "How did Elephant Man's date go with Elisabeth?"

Manjit giggled. "Not bad, as it happens. She's not bad-looking, is she? I mean," he corrected, "not as nice as you, Hol. She's a . . . a bit *little* for my tastes. I'm not keen on little people. Kylie Minogue and all that. They freak me out."

I smiled stiffly. "I don't mind little. Thin worries me. Thin people, thin cats. It's the reason I can't go to Greece anymore, too many thin cats. So, how do you know it wasn't bad?"

"Don't ever go to China, Holly. Well, he got in at four A.M., didn't he? Set off the alarm. Bo was not happy. She had a load of work the next day."

"Really." Four in the morning!

"Did you actually ask him how it went?" I added. I couldn't help myself.

"I asked if she put out"—Manjit blushed—"only because it's expected, you know, Hol, not because I was being, um, chauvinistic."

"Of course not, Manjit, you're the perfect gentleman. And what did he say?"

"Um. He said, 'Has Bo got any zinc supplements, I think I depleted my stocks.' "

"That's disgusting."

Disgusting! I repeated in my head. What a baby. I slept with that, that *thing*, and so Nick has to go out and equal the odds! Pathetic. And as for Elisabeth. She, the butter-wouldn't-melt vestal virgin, who responded to our cheeky questions *Describe your ideal fling* and *Describe your ideal shag* with the fairly snitty "Don't do flings, don't do shags." Well, I bet she was rubbish in bed. The sort of woman who gives a man a blow job on his birthday to get a ring on her finger, then never again. And has to think of tiaras and the Harrods bridal department all the while to stop herself gagging, *and* wash out her mouth with Listerine afterward.

I thought these particularly evil thoughts, then felt ashamed. And so what if Elisabeth didn't like giving blow jobs? Not that I had a shred of evidence. It's not a *rational* pastime, is it? Listen to me, I was as bad as a fifteen-year-old boy, calling a girl frigid for refusing to sleep with him. I'm not like that. I've always thought a person's leniency toward others is a direct indicator of their own happiness. Those who judge harshly the behavior and choices of their friends are dissatisfied with *their* lives. It's obvious. So what did that make me?

"So, what are we doing this week?" I said brightly.

"Apart from nattering? I thought we'd go over last week's stuff, refresh your memory. And I'd teach you what to do if someone grabs your wrist. Now, did I tell you about looking your attacker in the face?"

"No."

"Right, well, don't. If you look your attacker in the face, you can't see what he's doing with his arms and legs. And he can make evil faces at you, try and psyche you out, which you don't need. If you look at his chest, then you can see what he's doing with all his limbs, yeah? And it's harder for him to head-butt you. Got it?"

"Yes."

"Good. That was before I forgot. Now. If someone grabs your wrist, the bet is, they'll use the opposite hand to grab your wrist. So left hand to grab your right wrist and vice versa, yeah? So what you got to do is you twist your palm 'round and up on the inside of their arm and grab it, and then crack your other arm down on their elbow. The elbow can only bend one way, yeah? You can either really hurt them, bring your radius—big strong bastard of a bone, remember?—down hard on that elbow, break their arm. Or you can be kinder and use your hand to push on their elbow and force them to the floor. Only thing is, it's got to be fast. Today we'll concentrate on technique, so we'll go slow, but at the end of the day, fast is what we're aiming at. Oh yeah, and you got to know what you're going to do with them once they're on the floor. Because they are *not* going to be happy with you. Do you know what I mean?"

I thought that if I was Manjit I'd be highly tempted to use at least one of these techniques on Bo.

How was the kung fu?" asked Nige politely when I marched into the office. "Should I be scared?"

"Very," I said, and performed a made-up but elaborate high kick I knew he would appreciate.

"Ooh. Move over, Jackie Chan."

I beamed. I was determined to be agreeable. My behavior the previous week had been appalling. And really, there was no need for it. Whatever it was, that *episode*, with, ah, I didn't want to say his name, it was over, done with, forgotten. I'd never liked the saying that people are the sum of their past. It was too prescriptive. I could be whatever I wanted to be. That thing that had happened, it was nothing to do with me, there was no need for it to have an effect—*me*, I was incidental to proceedings. It wasn't personal, it could have been anyone. Therefore, I should shake off this descended darkness, this peculiar tetchiness, and get back to the happy business of playing Cupid.

Even for Elisabeth.

Then again she probably had no further use for Girl Meets Boy. Well. She might. I suspected that Elisabeth didn't plan to toil in an office ten hours a day until she hit sixty and was presented with a carriage clock. Elisabeth had the steel aura of a woman who'd worked herself blue to get into a good school, a top university, and a superior firm. Not because she was career-minded, but purely to add to an already impressive set of credentials for wifehood. Just like a Jane Austen heroine learning to sing and play the pianoforte, all the better to attract the right sort of gentleman.

Nick was certainly a Prince Charming, but a few dates and Elisabeth's businesslike brain would file the fun under "Stage one" and start searching for concrete evidence of providership. At the end of the fourth dinner, she'd dump Nick.

Nick. Nick. Nick. Why did I care what she did with Nick? Why did I still feel such an attachment?

"Issy's here, dearest," said Nige, resting a hand on my shoulder. "Would you like me to grab us some coffees before the meeting starts?"

Meeting?

Nige saw my blank face. "The meeting about tomorrow's Date Night? You called it, Holly."

"Oh! Of course. Sorry. And yes, please, coffee would be lovely." I wondered for just how long we would go on addressing each other like the Queen and Prince Philip (well, one likes to imagine). We were all being so sweet and good to one another, it felt silly and slightly patronizing. Like when you're a child at a party and the entertainer forces you to hold a conversation with a glove puppet. (Incidentally, Nick has never used a glove puppet.)

The meeting was remarkable. We might have been taking part in a communications workshop in California. Intense eye contact. Lashings of listening and letting people finish their point without cutting them short with a yawn or a snort. Lots of "*I* feel this" and "How does everyone else feel?" Many murmurings of "absolutely" and "you are *so* right." One or two exclamations of "what an excellent point." Serious head nodding. Heads bent in humble note-taking. The second the meeting ended, Claudia rushed to her desk drawer, grabbed her toothbrush, and sped, grimacing, to the ladies'. What can I say, I felt her pain.

I also felt exhausted and vaguely anxious. The three of them had—with the utmost courtesy and respect—overriden my every preference. The pairings they'd suggested for tomorrow's Date Night were explosive! We'd be lucky if we didn't have people writhing on the floor in front of us! My God, *anything* could happen. At least three of the men were new. Issy had scoured their application forms, spoken to them at length on the phone, and announced herself satisfied that none of them were lunatics. All the same. My stomach was full of worms.

I'd only refused to budge in *one* instance. Elisabeth. It had been quite a dilemma. Did I place Elisabeth with the candidate most likely to be the love of her life so that she dropped Nick like a dead hedgehog? Or did I punish her trespass with a speed date that would enrage her ego and make her pray for spinsterhood?

Issy had wanted to put Elisabeth with a new guy who had been named Samson by his thoughtless and self-indulgent parents. Fortunately for Samson, he possessed a fine head of hair. He also had engaging brown eyes and was a portfolio manager. He wanted four kids, loved beaches, any book by Charles Bukowski, and his hobby was rowing. Issy thought he and Elisabeth would be a great match. Secretly, so did I.

However.

CHAPTER 15

M̲r. Bottomley?"

"*Dr.* Bottomley."

"Pardon me. I'm Holly Appleton, nice to meet you."

Dr. Neil Bottomley, owner of the philosophy degree in life insurance, stepped into the light of the reception and I fought to keep a neutral face. (It was a more suitable face than the one I wanted to make—that of a teenage girl in a horror cartoon on encountering a decomposing zombie.) Never mind the gray hair, what little there was of it. The teeth, this man had the teeth of a horse. And wrinkles. You could iron out his face and it would be twice the size of a normal person's. He was a bona fide grandpa, dressed in smart grandpa apparel—a cream shirt under a maroon blazer, brown slacks, and leather shoes with plastic soles.

"Tell me, Miss Appleton, do we lurk in reception for a purpose or . . . ?" He raised a bushy badger eyebrow.

I tried not to look shifty. As it happened, we *did* lurk in reception for a purpose. To avoid being seen by any of my clients or colleagues. If Nige or Claw spotted us, I was in trouble.

"Not at all," I replied. "Why don't you get us a table in the café, order yourself a drink, and I'll be with you in a sec."

"I'm teetotal, Miss Appleton, but yes, I can secure us a table, although I look at my watch and I see that that *sec* of yours has already expired."

I smiled and laughed, which I presumed was what was required. Then I fled downstairs to where the real action was taking place. I could tell it was going to be a successful night. There was an animation about it, people seemed to be in a great mood. Nige was holding court to three nodding women—women are so good at listening to men talk—and Claw was bent in discussion with Georgina and Samson. Everyone looked happy.

Where was Elisabeth? On cue, my heart sped up. I'd spoken to her twice, earlier, and she'd sworn she was coming. But what if . . . ? That arrogant madam didn't think she could just . . . Did she? I bet she did. I strode up and tapped Nigel on the back. He looked displeased at being made to stop talking.

"Nige, sorry to interrupt. You haven't seen Elisabeth, have you?"

"Stanton-Browne? Not a sausage."

"Right. Right." *Now* what? "Fine. Look. I might be upstairs for, for most of tonight. I've got stuff to discuss with Sebastian—"

"Seb is over there making cocktails and failing to look like Tom Cruise," said Nige, nodding toward the bar.

"Yes, well, he's joining me later. I'll be in the café doing paper-work till then. You and Claw can take care of things, can't you?"

Nige shrugged. "Whatever."

I scurried back to Dr. Bottomley, simmering. The nerve of Nige, not believing me. I'd lied, but even so. I dialed Elisabeth's cell. It rang—and then it was switched off! She'd recognized my number. She wasn't coming. Which meant *I* was stuck with the doctor of philosophy in life insurance.

Served me right. It was a ludicrous plan. Against the rules. And cruel. It would have been hard to pull off. But I'd have been satisfied even if it had only worked for five minutes before Elisabeth stormed out. Or would I, really? I sighed. Thank heaven she hadn't turned up. I couldn't imagine the scene if I'd said I had someone special for her, that I was so convinced that they were made for each other that I'd bent the rules and secured them a private table in the café, away from the hoi polloi (Elisabeth would have appreciated that phrase), and, guess what, they had the whole evening together!

Shame on me. Poor Dr. Bottomley. He was a pedantic old bore but still. I'd wasted an evening of the man's life—and by the look of him they were in dwindling supply—because of a mean desire to punish the woman who, through no fault of her own, was dating *my* Nick. Not *your* Nick, I corrected myself. I'd become the kind of woman whose problem-pocked relationship is revised as perfect after she's spent three weeks in the real world.

I plodded up to the table, where Dr. Bottomley was smoking a thin cigar. I wasn't sure, right now, that honesty was the best policy. (I mean, when is it ever really?) He smiled without removing the cigar from his mouth. The action reminded me of the Joker. Before I could speak, he was on his feet. "Allow me," he said.

Cigar smoke curled around my ears. I found my coat being removed, and a passing waiter imperiously dispatched to carry it to the cloakroom. He shot Dr. Bottomley an evil look and I prayed he wasn't going to stamp on my coat. It had a pink lining and I was extremely fond of it. I was about to sit down when Dr. Bottomley laid a heavy hand on my shoulder and said again, "Allow me." He pulled out my chair with a flourish. I was about to sink into it when

Dr. Bottomley spun me to face him, grasped both my shoulders, and said, "You seem tense."

I jerked away. My brain did some fast calculations. The memory of his touch burned into my skin. This time I couldn't stop the expression on my face, which was teenage girl in horror cartoon meets great green gang of decomposing zombies. If Dr. Bottomley saw the look, he ignored it. "Now, Miss Appleton. Would you like me to order you a little something from the wine list?"

One impudence treading on another's heels! "I thought you said you didn't drink," I said.

Dr. Bottomley smiled, showing teeth. "Which is another thing from being a wine connoisseur."

Just about every organ in my gut clenched in irritation. The joke of it was, that trotting up the stairs after my exchange with Nige, I'd thought of a woman for him. Despite my reluctance these days to pair up anything more than two shoes, a likely partner for Dr. Bottomley had popped into my head. Really. She was far too old for Girl Meets Boy, much too middle-aged in body and spirit, but I'd kept her on file. The picture she'd sent us said it all. A stern stout figure in a yellow brim hat and pearl earrings, a yellow skirt with matching blouse, belt, and bag, and blue eye shadow. She described herself as "a lady of caliber" whose hobbies were "admiring old buildings" and attending "prestigious social events." I doubted she'd be interested in meeting our crew of twenty- and thirty-something men, who described themselves, variously, as "a dog lover, yes, but I prefer chicken or fish" and "able to play a tune through my nose" and whose hobbies, allegedly, ranged from driving in bus lanes to hacking into the Pentagon.

And even if she was, I doubted they'd be interested in meeting her. But, before the hip-touching incident, she'd bobbed into my head as a viable match for Dr. Bottomley. Now, I'd introduce them over my dead body, and his as well.

"No thank you," I said. "I don't drink alcohol when I'm working, but even if I did, I'm capable of ordering for myself." After a pause I added, "Thank you," then regretted it. *He* was out of line, so why was *I* embarrassed? I decided to be blunt. "Dr. Bottomley," I said, "I'm afraid I have bad news for you. I'd hoped to introduce you to a . . . a woman who applied to Girl Meets Boy, but the truth is, it was to be an off-the-record meeting as it were, and I wasn't going to charge you—as you know the usual joining fee is two hundred pounds—because the fact is, this is an agency that caters specifically for people in their twenties and thirties and so, I'm sorry to say, it isn't suitable for you, and, uh, you aren't suitable for it. My client base requires me to concentrate on, uh"—I searched for a term I thought he'd understand—"youngsters, really, boys and, er, young girls."

Dr. Bottomley reached across the table and patted my hand before I could withdraw it. "I also like to concentrate on young girls!"

At first, I thought I'd misheard. I was speechless. I wiped my hand on my trouser leg. My dearest wish—well, the one that didn't involve the steak knife and a fifteen-year jail sentence—was that I could verbally annihilate him. But I couldn't think of a word to say.

Finally I found my voice—well, *a* voice—and what a thin feeble thing it was too. "The woman I thought I'd found for you has just rung me and she won't be coming. She's got engaged."

It annoyed me that I found it necessary to create an excuse. It was a sign of weakness.

Dr. Bottomley made another grab at my hand, but I was too fast for him. He said, "A pity, but never mind. Now *we* shall spend the remainder of the evening together."

I gritted my teeth. "I really don't think so, I—"

"Miss Appleton, you seem agitated and there is no need. I am simply being sociable, I have no romantic designs on you. I merely ask you to join me for a light meal as a companion, and I think I am owed that much, after being dragged from my home by your so-called dating agency on what appears to be a wild-goose chase."

My great flaw, or one of them, is that when a man tells me things I believe him. Nick was always feeding me ridiculous stories, usually playing on my ignorance of the countryside, in the hope that I'd repeat one in public—"you know that sheep sleep standing up?"—and embarrass myself. Even though Dr. Bottomley's actions belied his words, I believed him. I also had a wild idea that he might "go to the papers." For what exactly, I don't know, but that's what a guilty conscience does to you.

He ordered a smoked tuna sandwich. I ordered a coffee and a steak and chips.

Dr. Bottomley fidgeted when I said "steak and chips." I realized that the albatross around his neck named chivalry meant that he felt obliged to pay for our dinner, but he didn't want to have to cough up more than a tenner. So I scrolled down the wine list and ordered a bottle of their most expensive champagne.

After a heavy silence, Dr. Bottomley asked if I enjoyed my work. I was about to say yes when he embarked on a lengthy tale about *his* work, not his profession, no, plenty of time to fill me in on that later, but his committee work. He was a member of several committees and . . .

I watched his mouth move and thought that he was the worst sort of person to be on a committee, a person who needed power over others to assert his own importance. Just the sort of person you get on committees. I was wondering how to make my escape when I became aware of his great gray face leaning into mine. I gave a small squeal and jumped back. "Fancy it?" said Dr. Bottomley.

"What?" I snapped. He'd bent across the table, his face had felt closer to mine than it was. I told myself to calm down, but I was shaking and sweating.

"I said I recently purchased a new Volvo. A V70. Would you like to come for a drive?"

I was certain his foot caressed my ankle under the table.

A blank in my head again. And then pulsating panic, black fear, the terror of being restrained with an iron grip, hard to breathe, clothes torn, pain shooting through me. It was really happening. It was *me* that this had happened to, it really *was* me. I staggered to my feet, gasping for air. I must have made a sound because everyone in the café turned and stared. Dr. Bottomley rose to his feet, grasped my upper arms, and shook me hard.

"Get off me!" I screamed, and shoved him. Fury suffused his face. I blinked, remembered where I was, and took a deep choking breath. The white walls of the café blurred. I blinked and blinked to get them back to normal.

"Now look here," began Dr. Bottomley in an indignant tone.

"No," I shouted, "*you* look. How *dare* you paw me, how dare you.

I'll have you charged with assault. And how dare you lie to me, say you've no romantic designs, then grope me at every opportunity. I was going to introduce you to a woman, but I'd *hate* for any woman to meet you. You're a disgusting pervert with no respect for anyone."

As I sped from the restaurant, people gaped. Dr. Bottomley stood frozen with horror, the focus of communal disdain. On my way out I noticed that the waiter he'd ordered to carry my coat was totting up the bill with relish. I didn't know what to do. I didn't feel able to waltz into the Girl Meets Boy corner. I didn't want to see anyone. I thought that episode was gone, dead and buried. But it had escaped from its coffin and roared back to life like the killer at the end of a film, vengeful, stronger, worse. I was in *Nightmare on Elm Street*, captive to the horrors of my imagination. I locked myself in the toilet. I closed the seat, laid paper on it, and sat in a ball, eyes fixed and staring. Who knew what I'd see if I closed them? I hugged my knees and rocked gently. I want my mummy, said a five-year-old. Look what you did, chided another voice. Nearly left Elisabeth to the mercy of that creep. Thank God it was you and not her. See, this *is* what happens. You must warn Claudia and Nige immediately.

At some point I unlocked the toilet and rushed into the bar. The Girl Meets Boy corner was bare except for Nige and Claw, clinking their wineglasses in a toast.

"Where is everyone?" I gasped.

Their looks of irritation quickly faded.

"So you tore yourself away from the coffin-dodger, did— *Fuck*, Hol, are you all right?"

"I wouldn't have thought he was your type— Jesus, Holly, you look like you're about to faint. What happened? Sweets, it's twenty past eleven, they all went home ages ago. It was a storming success, if I say so myself. Many *many* matches were made, but, sweetie, angel, what's wrong with you?"

"Stuart," I said, and burst into tears.

CHAPTER 16

I thought I'd puke at the sound of his name in my mouth. Claw had a quick murmured discussion with Nige, then jumped into a taxi with me. She didn't say a word, asked no questions, which was lucky because I was as dumb as a post. She tucked me into bed, fed Emily—"Don't rub your grotesque furred abdomen against my black wool trousers, Cat. Please, ugh, oh, what's the point?"—and slept in the spare room. The next morning she ordered me to stay at home.

"Nige and I will take care of everything for the rest of the week. You're overtired and you need a break. It's been too much for you, what with Nick and now Stuart. I don't know *what* you were doing with Professor Creepy. Well, of course we snuck down and spied on you. What did you expect? I'll expect the gory details when you feel up to it. But don't worry. It's all going to be okay. Now, I want you to stay in bed, eat whole packs of biscuits, drink pints of hot chocolate, put that flea-ridden creature to use as a hot-water bottle, read *Hello,* and watch your video of *The Princess Bride.* You've got to be well enough to attend your birthday party this Friday, do you understand?"

I nodded and shut out the world for three days. Once you've slept and washed and checked the locks and done a few circuits around your house with a knife, gee, well, the time just flies by.

Friday lunchtime, five minutes after I put the phone back on its hook, the world intruded in the form of Rachel, who rang and shrieked, "Happy birthday, babes. I've been trying you all morning. Well, twice. How are you? Claudia says you've had a minibreakdown and that your parents are now staying with her. She didn't sound thrilled. Now, festivities begin at seven thirty, I'm told. Do you know who's coming?"

"Parents. Claw. Nige. Manjit, maybe. Nick, I *doubt*. Sam, one of the girls from the agency. We've sort of become friends. Gloria—"

"Who's Gloria?"

"A friend. She also cleans for me—"

"Oh *God,* Holly. The girl who spilled tea down me. You're such a champagne socialist."

"And you're a revolting snob. Mm, who else. Issy. Frank, Issy's husband."

"He can't make it."

"Who?"

"Frank."

"Oh. How do you know?"

"Claudia said so, silly. How are you getting to the restaurant? Would you like a lift?"

I smiled. "Ooh, that would be nice. Yes, please."

"Good. Can you be ready by seven?"

"Rach, how ugly do you think I am?"

"Funny. What are you going to wear?"

"I don't know yet."

"I could lend you a—"

"Please no, I'll find something."

I put down the phone, leaped out of bed, and foraged through the wardrobe. I *ought* to wear pink, it was my birthday. I felt mean for taking the phone off the hook. M and D (our pet names for Mum and Dad) would have tried ninety times, keen to sing the entire "Happy Birthday" song down the line in a tuneless wail and assure me that if I didn't like my present they'd take it back to John Lewis.

But I'd needed the silence. The memories of Stuart, shoved deep into my subconscious, had sprung from some dark internal attic into broad daylight, stunning me. It had taken me three days to jam them back.

So far, it had been a peaceful birthday. I'd opened all my cards—all six of them. The older you get, the more meager your pile of cards. (On *his* thirtieth, Nige sent himself ten enormous cards, as he'd gotten to know his postman by name and hated the possibility of the man thinking he was unpopular. In fact, Nige devoted so much time and effort into trumpeting the occasion that on the actual day he received thirty-two cards, not including his own.)

Nick hadn't sent me anything. But Claw had hinted of a surprise, so perhaps he'd show up at my dinner. Preferably without Elisabeth. I rang Claudia as I was poking through my underwear drawer, trying to locate some celebratory knickers. No one was going to see them, what did it matter? I couldn't be arsed (if that was a joke, I apologize) to encase my behind in fancy lingerie for me, even if it was the politically correct choice. I chose granny pants.

"Claw?"

"Birthday girl. How you feeling? Happy b-day! Issy rang to say Frank can't make it—work, yawn—but apart from him"—Claudia said "him" in a disparaging tone. She doesn't fully trust Frank, she says he's the kind of man who can wear linen and not look crumpled—"everyone's going to be there. It's going to be a laugh. What? *What?* Oh yeah, hang on, Nige wants a word—"

"Hell-*o*, sweetness, how are you? Many happy returns from the new star of the Courts ad, as seen on TV! Yes, yes, I know, I can barely believe it. I'm a slut, I really shouldn't. It tarnishes my art, it's worse than being an extra. Well, darling, the entire point of acting is to be *noticed*, the entire point of being an extra is *not* to be noticed. If you're pure of soul you refuse to do it, but me, I freely admit to being a tart. It's yet another crime I've committed, but *tant pis*—it's a rich man's world! Now remind me, twenty-nine? Remember, until you're thirty-one, you're not technically in your thirties. Hugely looking forward to tonight. I plan to dress dramatic, a cheap gray suit and yellow shirt *peut-être*, to ease myself into the part. I'm just warning you. So we'll see you at what, seven thirty? Looking forward, big kiss!"

I was thrilled for Nige, although he was plainly going to be insufferable for the next fortnight. It was impossible not to smile after talking to those two. I rang my parents at Claudia's, assured them that my chances of survival were high, then spent a glorious chunk of the afternoon reading *The Glass Lake* by Maeve Binchy. (Like knickers, I believe your reading matter should be chosen for your benefit, not anyone else's. A good book is a friend to be made yours, to be dropped in the bath, smeared with chocolate crumbs, *enjoyed.* The most depressing exercise in the world—apart from real exercise, that is—is skimming the *Observer*'s annual list of pompous people's holiday reading. Why, not a Jackie Collins or John Grisham among them! It's all Kafka, *Beowulf,* and the *Iliad,* untranslated.)

I finally emerged from the pages of Maeve—like disengaging from a warm hug—and strode to the wardrobe. I hold the world record for time spent standing in front of a wardrobe or fridge staring into it. An ice age came and went, and I picked out a shocking-pink halter-neck dress, sixties style. Then I washed my hair, used a curling iron to burn in some bounce, and applied shimmery pale pink lipstick and black-and-white eyeliner. I assessed my reflection. I looked like Panda Barbie, so I wiped it all off and changed into black trousers and a brown shirt.

Rachel rang the bell as I was trying on shoes. When she saw me she screamed.

I jumped. "What!"

Rachel made horrified eyes at my outfit. "You look like the Brownie Guide section of the SS."

I sighed. "I'll change."

Rachel smiled. "Good. Here. Many happy returns." She had a bottle of Taittinger in one hand and a smelly plastic bag in the other, both of which she thrust into my arms. On inspection, the bag contained about a ton of oysters and two greasy tubs, one of foie gras, the other of caviar. Three foods you couldn't *pay* me to eat. I'm a bit of a wimp compared to Rachel. At the height of the Mad Cow crisis, we went to dinner at her favorite place, the Dorchester. I ordered fish. Rachel boomed at the waiter, "I'll have the steak tartare!"

"Rach, this is gorgeous—"

"I know, don't say a word, foie gras, boo-hoo for the goose. But worth it, the taste is bliss on toast!"

I held my tongue. Rachel has a jacket in her wardrobe made from the pelt of, God help me, a snow leopard. Her great-uncle was a furrier. Rach says she no longer wears the jacket, but I don't entirely trust her. Once or twice I've noticed her shoot Emily a look, and I'm relieved she's a splotched cat, not a white Persian. It would only take the party organizing business to dip, and we'd have a Cruella De Vil situation on our hands. We cannot discuss animal welfare; we'd end up not talking. For this reason I've avoided the subject of fox hunting in Rachel's presence for twelve years. I fear that knowledge of her opinion on the issue would mean the necessary termination of our friendship.

I stuck the cruelty/bacteria bag in a remote corner of the fridge, washed my hands, then ran to my bedroom and picked the pink halter neck off the floor. Slowly, I removed the SS outfit and tugged on the dress. I walked out of the room, blanking my reflection.

"Gorgeous, babes. Shall we go?"

I surrendered my fate to Rachel's motoring skills. She drives a car like it's a tractor. Fortunately, in London the traffic jams are such that her refusal to go over thirty miles per hour is less of a hazard. She once drove me to Surrey on the motorway. (It was a houseparty weekend. This intrigues me about posh people, they never tire of spending time together. An evening is never enough, the socializing has to suck up your whole life.) I've never been so petrified. I concluded that Rachel simply couldn't see other road users. She was wearing a blazer and her cell phone was in the left pocket. Every time it rang, she'd take her right hand off the steering wheel to answer it and swerve the car. If she became animated in conversation, she'd forget to press down with her foot and slow to twenty miles per hour. She didn't use signals or side mirrors—perhaps she thought they were common.

On my birthday she seemed hyper and, good friend though she is, I doubted this was in my honor. She was wearing a red wraparound Lycra top and a flared black skirt, the trademark Clarins Eau Dynamisante, and seemed to bubble with excitement. She looked foxy (and no, she wasn't wearing a fur stole) and she didn't stop talking. "So Nigel is going to be on television. What a scream. Lady Sophia was asked to do an ad, you know, for furniture polish. She refused, said they simply didn't pay enough to justify the tackiness of it. I'd have done it like a shot. What are they paying Nigel? I presume the ex-wife will want a cut."

I was about to say that as they weren't yet divorced, Nige's wife didn't have the legal right to demand anything, but Rachel abruptly stopped dead in the middle of the road and the cacophony of horns and screeching brakes took my breath away. "What are you doing?" I croaked.

"Parking."

After seventy reverse, drive, twist wheel, reverse, drive, twist wheel maneuvers, Rachel squeezed the Audi into a space large enough to park a Boeing. I checked my lipstick in the rearview mirror (someone might as well make use of it).

"I feel nervous," I said.

"How sweet you are." Rach smiled. "Good evening, Mr. and Mrs. A., how *are* you both. You look so well. What a beautiful necklace, Mrs. A., I adore turquoise."

My parents, who had obviously spied us loitering on the pavement and been unable to contain themselves a moment longer, stopped short on the porch of the restaurant and beamed shyly at Rachel. That girl, she could charm a cobra out of a basket. My parents were pussycats.

"Thank you, Rachel," stuttered my mother. "You look lovely. So elegant as usual."

"Hello, Rachel," added my father. He coughed and jerked his head toward the Audi. "Nice set of wheels."

The burden of etiquette over, my parents turned to me. "Happy birthday, dear! Are you feeling better? Oh Stanley, she looks pale." I allowed my mother to feel my forehead. My father, standing behind her, winked at me. I smiled at him. Out of nowhere, tears threatened. I glanced down and blinked them away.

"I'm fine, Mum, honestly. I'm feeling much better. I think I had a bit of a cold."

I was speaking her language. She nodded, relieved. "Have you got fresh orange juice at home, dear? I can get you some, it's no trouble. It's better than taking tablets."

I was about to refuse, then realized I was about to deny my mother a great pleasure. "That would be brilliant."

My mother beamed. "Now. We bought you a little something from John Lewis." It's hard to exaggerate the awe with which my parents regard John Lewis, that fuddy-daddy of department stores. Every time they visit, it's like children seeing the ocean for the first time. "It's being delivered on Monday. We can wait in at your house for it, but I've kept the receipt and it can be returned if you don't like it. So if you don't like it, *do* say. But we thought it would go nicely in your living room. I . . . I know Nick took his rug— Oh Stanley, what a fool, now I've ruined the surprise!"

My mother stopped, embarrassed. My father patted her shoulder. "It's all right, Linda." He grinned at me. "The manager let me take a Polaroid, love." He fished in his jacket pocket and handed me a photo. "What do you reckon, Holly, will it do?"

I gaped. Despite the poor quality of the picture, I could see this was an exceptionally beautiful Persian rug, patterned in rich warm oranges and browns, enormous, of superb quality, and horribly expensive. "Mum, Dad, it's fantastic, but—" I stopped. I didn't want to humiliate them. I searched for the right word. "So *extravagant*. It's like a magic carpet. I love it. But are you sure?"

My mother nudged my father, who stammered into speech. "Holly, it's your thirtieth birthday. We're proud of you and we wanted to mark it." He stopped, fished a gray handkerchief out of his trouser pocket, blew his nose. "With an appropriate gift."

A line of a poem came into my head. *Tread softly, because you tread on my dreams.*

Dad coughed and added, "Don't concern yourself with the, uh, anything else. As you know, your nan was kind"—his expression didn't falter—"enough to remember us in her will."

He stopped. I nodded briskly so he didn't feel obliged to elaborate. Claw knows a guy who made out with his mother. In my parents' eyes, discussing money with your offspring is an equally grave offense.

"What wonderful parents you have, Holly," cried Rachel, patently bored of hanging about in the street. "What a glorious gift! Shall we toddle on inside? Everyone's dying to kiss the birthday girl, and I know Claudia can't *wait* for you to see your surprise!"

I hugged Mum and Dad and we allowed Rachel to herd us into the restaurant. Claudia had booked a private basement room. The place was lit with candles and grandly dim, so it was hard to see exactly who was sitting around the table. But the second I walked in there, I knew. The scent of him, I could smell it, like a wolf. The blood drained to my feet. My heart shriveled, a dry leaf crumbling to dust.

Stuart.

He was talking to a woman next to him. She was thin, like a boy, with a short mousy bob. I didn't recognize her. The sight of his golden hair, his slick, scrubbed appearance, I had to fight to breathe. His arm on my neck again, no air, like being dragged by my feet to the bottom of a swamp. Claudia skipped over and I gripped her hand so hard she yelped in pain. She saw my face and erased the smile on hers.

"Chair," I gasped. She grabbed me a chair. I fell into it. I couldn't let go of her hand. I was Dorothy tapping her red slippers, except the one place I *didn't* want to be was home. As long as I held Claudia's hand, I couldn't be in the kitchen, Stuart's heavy body crushing me. People looked over, murmuring. I was pleased that my parents had darted to the far end of the room to greet Issy and hadn't noticed. I dared a glance at Stuart. He was laughing, confident, smug—a fucking party guest at *my* birthday!

Don't show him you're scared, don't show him you're scared. I crossed my legs and squeezed my knees together to stop them shaking quite so hard. I tried to lift the corners of my mouth. "What," I said to Claudia, "is *he* doing here?"

Suddenly, my fearless sister looked terrified. "Holly. I invited him. I spoke to his PA, Camille. That's her over there. He was your surprise. Isn't that what this has all been about, you pining for Stuart . . ." Her voice trailed off. By the time she reached the end of her sentence, it was no longer a question.

I spat, "I *hate* Stuart."

Claudia went white. Oh no. And she'd meant so well. The word *why* was about to form on her lips.

"We had a . . . disagreement," I said quickly. "Don't worry about it. I'm . . . I suppose I'm a bit shocked because I expected . . . Nick."

She received this explanation with a frown and spent the rest of the night glancing suspiciously at me, then Stuart. Still, I noticed her chatting to his PA quite a bit, so she couldn't have been *too* troubled.

As for me, I sat as still and cold as an ice sculpture. Stuart smiled at me once and I looked through him. That he had the audacity to come here! But of course. What perfect proof of his innocence.

He was a larger-than-life guest—or maybe it just seemed so to me. Everywhere I looked, there he was. When he laughed, the noise sucked me in, his mouth getting bigger and bigger and redder and whiter until it swallowed the entire room. He behaved as if it were *his* birthday rather than mine. I didn't behave as if it were my birthday. Whenever someone addressed me, I nodded and laughed without hearing a word and hoped it would do.

I was glad that Nige bounced over and chatted happily for two hours, asking for no more than the odd withering glance from Rachel and the occasional "Oh?" from me. He only paused twice—once, to observe that my father ate dessert like his life depended on it, and again to note that I had the body language of a pretzel. But when I tried to uncross my arms and legs I found that every muscle in my body was frozen. I felt that if I raised my head, it would snap like an icicle. I finally managed it, some time around 11:30, and the goose pimples ran all the way up my neck. My mum and dad, on either side of Stuart, deep in conversation about . . . *what?*

CHAPTER 17

There was a rhyme my mother used to sing to me, "Soldier, Soldier, Won't You Marry Me?" She sang it when she wanted me to finish my boiled egg. I thought it was shocking. This soldier kept saying he couldn't marry the sweet maid because he had no coat to put on. And no hat. And no gloves, no second home in Monaco, etcetera. Honestly, this guy had no end of excuses. So the maid bought him whatever he said he needed. Then in the last verse she proposes for the tenth time, and he says, "Oh no, sweet maid, I cannot marry you, as I have a wife of my own!"

I couldn't believe my mother could sing so jauntily about a

tragedy. That poor maid, she must have been so upset! Why was that soldier so mean, saying things that weren't true? He let her buy him all that stuff when he already had a wife! I was appalled to the depths of my five-year-old soul.

Two and a half decades on, my perspective was different. At five, I felt sorry for the maid because she'd wasted all that time and still didn't have a husband. At twenty-nine, I could appreciate her narrow escape. And yet in one sense the years hadn't changed me. I had a child's faith. My core belief was that people would do right by you.

In survivalist terms, that's not a wise attitude. You don't get antelope in Africa lolling around plains, frolicking by the river's edge for the hell of it. They're not programmed to think, Maybe that alligator lurking in the shallows just wants a chat. Their day is pure business—eat, drink, move on, safety in numbers (cousin Wilberforce is fatter than me, maybe the lion will pick on him). I ought to thank Stuart for stripping me of my naiveté once and for all. At thirty, I finally evolved. I trusted no one.

Over the weekend, despite my most devious efforts, I failed to discover what my parents had discussed with Stuart. They were infuriatingly discreet. Maybe Stuart had let them into some dark secret. Some *other* dark secret. Whatever it was, they weren't repeating a word of it. This is typical of my parents. They hold traditional ideas about what one should talk about with one's children. One time Claw rang my father from university, babbling about a one-night stand. My father—who *never* reproaches us—replied, "I was a virgin when I married your mother and I was quite happy!" and put the phone down.

Even so, it was a blessing to have their company. I invited them to stay on Saturday and Sunday nights, partly to release Claw, but mainly for myself. I'm not sure how I'd have coped alone after Friday. There was an endless crackle in my head, white noise, keeping less-welcome thoughts at bay. And my teeth were clenched hard together. Every so often I'd notice an ache and would have to release the tension by opening my mouth slightly, like a hinge.

Claw and Issy came for tea on Saturday, Issy trailing Eden. Eden is a clever child with something of the Damien about her. On this visit, she drew me a picture to go with a story she'd invented.

(Briefly: Once upon a time there was a land in which all the flowers disappeared. Then the people found out that they were all growing upside down. The flowers were growing upside down in the earth, to smell nice for all the dead people.) Stephen King, eat your heart out. I stuck the drawing on my fridge, but between you and me, I wasn't too happy about it.

Issy's husband, Frank, came too. He was wearing a thin-knit polo-neck sweater, the kind that clings to the contours of your chest. He is honed and toned, and he jolly well should be. He is the sort of man who won't eat chicken skin and spends whole afternoons at the gym. He treats that place like a community center— no joke, he has a group of little fitness friends there and they *train* together. I can't help but think it's a bit girly. Last November they had a fireworks party and he made Issy attend. She said it was the most boring night ever and she was the fattest person there.

Frank also has a narcissistic habit of smoothing the flat of his palm over his chest when he speaks to you. Secretly, Claw and I don't find him—as Nige would say—*sympathique.* Sympathetic, I believe, in English. But he so dotes on Issy, we forgive him his oddities. On Saturday, he showed up with a puffed-out chest, because he'd just surprised her with tickets to the opera. In Verona. I suspect that Issy doesn't give a fig for opera but likes to say she's been. (I've only been once, and I found it spectacular and moving, though if I'm honest, I enjoyed it more in retrospect.) I do think how fortunate that Issy fell in love with a rich man. And then, meanly, I wonder to what extent her falling in love was conditional. She isn't what you'd call a passionate person. When Frank sank to one knee and said, "Will you marry me?" her reply was "In theory, yes."

"Sorry I couldn't make it to your bash, Hol," said Frank, kissing me on both cheeks. "But nobody missed me, so I hear."

"And why exactly *couldn't* you make it, Frank?" asked Claudia. She poked the tip of a vampire tooth with her tongue. She was wearing rose-pink sunglasses, spiky heels, and toted a sausagey handbag too dinky to contain anything larger than a powder puff or a handgun.

Frank blushed. "Work," he replied, clearing his throat. "I had a video conference call with New York and Japan, translators, the whole shebang. It started at nine—ludicrous, I know, on a Friday night, but I think they're nine hours ahead in Tokyo—and I wasn't sure how long it was going to drag on for."

I watched his body language as he rambled on about his dull evening in the office and something didn't feel right. I looked at Issy. She was sharing an almond macaroon with Eden, glancing at her husband as he chattered and smiling in a way that seemed truly peaceful. Hang on, *Issy*, wisdom: Liars are easy to spot because they suffocate you with detail. I was practically choking. But it wasn't only that. Was Saturday a working day in Japan? I felt a surge of triumph and dismay at once. Rach. Having an affair with a married man, she'd said, *Whom I knew*. And she was the one who'd told me that Frank couldn't make it because of work. She'd said Claudia had told her. And she'd left my party early.

After I realized this, I felt jumpy—well, jumpier—it was like the creeping dread you get when you've postponed paperwork for four months and you stop being able to sleep. I couldn't believe it. Had Frank and Rachel even met? Now that I thought about it, of course they had. At Issy's wedding. At a Christmas party organized by Rachel. They were two pretty selfish people, but at heart we're all selfish, so I couldn't hold that against them. Being selfish does not make you a cheat. Anyway, I couldn't believe it of Frank. He *liked* his life. And he knew that if he ever tried anything funny, Issy's legal team would ensure that he ended up a pauper. I didn't want to believe it of Rachel.

Claudia hadn't noticed. She was too busy watching me. I took care to act breezy. I didn't want her to come up with any theories. I wanted to protect her. The truth would hurt too much. I felt the same way about my parents. I can stand a certain amount of pain— I *know* how much I can stand—but it's different when I inflict my pain on those I love. That's harder to bear. Thankfully, I was able to distract Claw with talk of the next Date Night, being filmed by *London Local News*. She and Issy were remarkably excited about it. Me, I couldn't have cared one way or the other.

Both Monday and Tuesday would be sucked up by planning meetings for the wretched thing. I was forced to postpone my self-defense class to Wednesday. I did do one thing for myself, though.

I rang Stuart's PA, Camille, and I told her never to stay late with Stuart in the office. Judging from her cool response, she thought I'd spoken out of turn. I didn't think so. She'd been at my party, we'd met each other socially. It was my duty to warn her. Rage spat, and it was either a nuisance call to Camille or the purchase of a sledgehammer from Sainsbury's Homebase, the smashing of Stuart's skull to a red-and-yellow fragmented pulp and the ruin of the carpet in his lobby.

I tell a lie. Not all of Monday and Tuesday was sucked up by planning meetings. A good third was sucked up by Nige and Claw feasting on the gossip of Friday night.

Camille. Nige worried about the name Camille. It sounded like camel. Claudia disagreed. It was an elegant name, the name of a French film star. What French film star? I meant generically, Nige, you idiot. Nige wanted to know if anyone had noticed that Rachel's number plate was E103 POO. Claw giggled. The fear of buying a car with the number plate POO—or come to that, CAK, or indeed, BUM—had dogged her since childhood. I'd fretted about it too, until I'd actually bought a car and found that, unless you annoy them, they give you a choice.

Ooh, said Nige, and wasn't Bo a sight with a face as long as a horse? Oh, said Claudia, that was normal. Bo was always in a grouch. "She was in a mood with Manjit," I offered, having some inside information on this, "because on Thursday night she dreamed he cheated on her." We all—even me—honked with laughter. Then, inevitably, talk turned to Nige's career. The ad was being shot on Thursday. Claw wanted to know if, when Nige had a love scene with a lady, he ever got "visibly excited." And if he did get a monster stiffy, what happened? Nige smirked. This was plainly a question he'd been asked a few times and therefore had a neat answer. "Before we even kiss, I say to her, 'I apologize if I do, and I apologize if I don't!' "

Then Issy arrived and put an end to merriment. Tuesday night did need a lot of organizing. We had to remind everyone who'd wanted to participate and triple-check that they were coming. "Elisabeth was, well, keen when I last spoke to her," said Nige. "She'd sell her soul to get on cable."

"Hark at you," remarked Claw.

Nige stuck his nose in the air. "Terrestrial. There's a world of difference. You were dealing with her, though, Hol, weren't you? Didn't you have someone for her?"

I looked at my feet, ruffled my notebook. Plan B, find a man for Elisabeth who was so lip-smacking, Nick would be fish-and-chip paper. "Well," I said reluctantly, "I'd prefer it if you rang her. But I have been thinking about Samson."

Nige laughed a dirty laugh. "I'll bet you have, darlin'! No, nice one. I'm happy to deal with her. And what about cute little Xak as her finale?"

He wrote down Samson as Elisabeth's first date and Xak as her last, and I felt peeved.

"What are we going to do about Sam and Bernard? They're booked in for this week," said Claudia.

"We'll do a Wednesday nighter," said Nige quickly, glancing at me.

I frowned. If there was an overlap, we'd have two Date Nights, but it happened rarely. And it wasn't as if the filmed night was over-subscribed. "I don't see why—"

Nige interrupted. "Well, dearest, you must be blind because *we* can all see why. Sam and Bernard are uggers, and that's the plain, pimply old truth. This agency is for beautiful people, that's our Yoo Ess Pee, our *yoo*-nique selling point! It's all right to make the odd ex-ception, and I mean odd, but not when we are being filmed. TV adds ten pounds to your weight—why else do you think I'm down to one doughnut a day—and Bernard is fat. Put him on TV, he'll look like Marlon Brando. We can't have it, we'll get all sorts of mutants ringing up, and none of the sort of people we want to attract."

This silenced me, and I remained quiet for the next twenty minutes as they plotted their showcase matches. Two of the pairs from last week wanted to see each other again, said Claw, so that was easy—guaranteed good publicity. They were all high on sugar and the scent of fame. It felt to me as if the room was one big grin. I wrote down whatever they said, so as to look studious and give my-self a valid excuse for not talking. Only I knew we were playing Rus-sian roulette with people's lives. This bloody film night was going to be a glorious success, and I just felt sick at the thought of it.

. . .

We arrived early at Seb's, as Gwen and her cameraman wanted to inspect the venue before setting up.

Nige and Claw were done up like P. Diddy and Christina Aguilera off to the Proms. Even Issy had made an effort, in a black Joseph trouser suit. I was reminded of an applicant we'd rejected because he'd written: "My ambition is to take a woman to Joseph and dress her from head to foot!" Weird. And the week before, I'd turned down a guy who'd scrawled on his form that he loved kittens but hated cats. What a nut. I hadn't told the others about him, I'd had quite enough of their liberalism.

I could tell Gwen disapproved of what I was wearing. Baggy jeans and a sweatshirt and trainers. You could tell she'd been gearing up for ten million viewers since the age of twelve. She was celebrity thin (I wanted to say "*Please* eat," but knew she'd despise me for it), with a pixie haircut, well-toned calves—I guessed she ran four miles a day before her yoga class—thick expert makeup that would look immaculate on-screen, and a mint-green gypsy top, perfect for TV with its simple neckline, medium hue, and lack of fussiness. Cute, not too serious, considering the fluffiness of the feature.

"Have you got something smarter to wear for camera?" she said bluntly.

"Yes!" cried Claudia, before I could say no. "You're so busy, Hol, I knew you'd forget. I brought this along for you just in case." She displayed a crisply ironed bubblegum-pink shirt between red varnished fingernails. *My* bubblegum pink shirt, pinched over the weekend from the back of *my* wardrobe.

Gwen smiled, a credit to her orthodontist. "Fabby. We'll shoot you above the waist."

I took the shirt from a gloating Claudia and thought, Please do. Preferably in the head.

The cameraman mooched from corner to corner with several tons of black bags and silver cases and spidery tripods, muttering about light. Gwen ran through her interview questions, all of which were predictable. She suggested I apply foundation and blusher, otherwise I'd look "ill."

Meantime, Nige hovered, eventually blurting out, "Sweets, if you don't feel up to it, Gwen is welcome to interview one of us. *Me*, for example. I am a company executive," he added in his best Queen's English.

"I'll be fine," I said.

As my Girl Meets Boy–ites started to arrive, I felt a tweak of pride, despite everything. We *did* have some lovely people. They deserved to find love. I caught Nige nudging Claw as Sam crept in, and Claw glared at me when she spotted Bernard. I didn't know what they were so bothered about. Xak had arrived, a dead ringer for a baby angel, and there was Samson, as fresh-faced and wholesome as a week in Devon. Martyn lowered the beauty count some, but his ordinariness was offset by the trendy shaven head and black art-house specs.

Elisabeth swept in, and the room seemed to hold its breath. She was the kind of woman that men bought champagne for. I couldn't look her in the eye, and she was more than willing to avoid mine. I guessed Nick had told her about us. Still, she plainly didn't like him enough to miss her chance to get on telly. Jesus, the girl was wearing a cat suit. It exposed parts of the body that I would only ever show to another person by accident. Poor Nick.

Georgie strode in, fiercely glam, but, as Nige sighed, "a bit Marbella." He wasn't wrong. For a start, she'd parked her cell phone in her cleavage. Millie followed, furtive, anxious—she had the air of a small squirrel that's just hidden its nuts and is paranoid a big squirrel will find them.

"This is fabby," said Gwen, smiling. I smiled back. *Fabby* was definitely her word. She was all right. I admire people who work hard, on principle, so I had to admire Gwen whether I wanted to or not.

"I'll speak to you at the end of the night, Holly, and I'll speak to a few of your clients now, and then again later, after their dates."

Her word arrangement made it clear she wasn't asking permission. "Fine," I said. I couldn't be bothered to argue. "We'll just do our thing and let you do yours."

I watched her beeline for Elisabeth.

"You *will* be careful what you say to her," said Nige, suddenly at my side.

I tutted. "Of course I will, I'm not an idiot."

Nige grinned. "Looking good so far. I'll bet the camera loves Stanton-Browne. She'll be presenting MTV before we know it." He nodded toward Sam and Bernard, who were propped against the bar, chatting. "Let's only hope she steers clear of Dastardly and Muttley." He glanced at his watch. "Time to rock 'n' roll." He squeezed my hand before trotting off to place everyone with their first dates. "Know what, Hol? We couldn't *pay* for advertising like this. I'm serious, that Gwen is worth her weight in gold."

"What, an ankle chain from Woolworth's?"

"I'm serious. When's this airing? Because we are going to be up to our necks in a lake of gorgeous singles. Gwen over there might look like a sniffy cow, but she's going to double the size of our company." He winked, like a pantomine dame, and said, "Brace yourself. Size matters—and we are on the brink of *big*."

CHAPTER 18

Did I tell you my mother's sister died of a heart attack at age forty-three? Aunt Rose's death shocked everyone—more so than normal, if there *is* a normal—and I think it was because she was such a vibrant person. Nick put it best. "She was right in the middle of life," he said. Aunt Rose, a translator for the UN, was the opposite of my mother in many ways—loud, enthusiastic, energetic, fearless. But they were similar in their kindness and generosity. Aunt Rose cared, and the world could ill afford to lose her.

This was only two years ago, and a few months after the funeral my mother rang to talk about Girl Meets Boy. She'd seen a little advert in her local paper and was terribly excited. We had a jolly chat about how well I was doing and she didn't mention her sister once. "Mum," I said because I couldn't put down the phone on silence. "You know, Nick and I think of Aunt Rose so often."

Her response stunned me. "Of course, dear. It's very sad. She was a great sort of girl. But life is hard, and there's no use going around with a long face. That doesn't do anyone any good. We had her for forty-three happy years, and I'm thankful for that. Yes, it's hard for me, I'm her sister, but it's *far* harder for Uncle Barry. He's had to reconstruct his whole life. And we do have our memories. Uncle Barry showed me a poem he wrote that described Rosy to a T. Why, it was as good as having her stand in front of you!"

Sometimes my mother makes me feel so humble I want to cry. I thought about her attitude for a long time afterward. I thought it was an admirable lesson, to be stoic, bear your woes with a zipped mouth. I believed this for a while before I realized that there's a huge difference between acceptance and repression. Plainly, Claudia and Nige never thought any of this. Their whining after the *London Local News* night went gloriously wrong was apocalyptic.

Everything seemed to be going smoothly (a sign of impending disaster if there ever was one) until, oops, one of our new recruits turned out to be an angry ex-girlfriend of Samson, and she vented her rage at being paired with the rat on camera. They'd dated for two years, she'd had a miscarriage, and he'd blamed her because she'd been drinking tea (two whole cups a day). When she'd cried about it he'd hummed to himself to block out the sound. Also on camera, Samson joked about this and called her a "bit of a sad cow."

"But he seemed so *nice*," moaned Claudia.

Don't they all, I thought. Issy, who'd evaluated him, inspected her Russell & Bromley leather uppers.

That was merely the prelude. The real humdinger occurred when Gwen interviewed Elisabeth at the end of the night. It was supposed to be private, but Nige eavesdropped from behind an armchair. He came away ashen-faced. "She . . . she . . . she *decimated* us!"

At first, I thought we'd just underestimated the stigma of paying to get a date. It was one thing, advertising ourselves as cool and hip, bursting at the seams with gorgeous and clever people. It allowed beautiful women like Elisabeth to kid themselves that they were joining just another elite club, in addition to the Met Bar and Holmes Place. Girl Meets Boy had far more credibility than the traditional agencies, with their humdrum promises of marriage and airbrushed photos of two plain people smiling dumbly in a rapeseed field. But bottom line, we were still a dating agency, and however much Elisabeth wanted her five minutes of fame, she probably didn't want it on the basis that she'd paid a firm two hundred pounds to find her love.

"It was the first time she'd *ever* done anything like this . . . It wasn't her sort of thing at all . . . In fact, she had a boyfriend . . . This was more the kind of thing you did for a laugh, with a group of girlfriends . . . To be honest, the men weren't up to much . . . the women were much prettier . . . The men were nerds . . . This kind of agency is for sad people . . . She'll never do it again . . . It was not a great experience . . . None of the men she'd been matched with were her type . . . nothing in common . . . didn't seem terribly professional . . . didn't seem to think about who they put you with . . . the owner, Holly, once shouted at her when she complained . . . No different from *Dateline* except probably less efficient . . ."

Nige drew breath, sat back. His incredulous expression was tinged with the guilty pleasure of a messenger important enough to deliver fatal news.

"What, she actually *said* all that?" croaked Claw.

Nige pursed his lips. "Every word. And she's still at it, the silly tart!"

We all craned our necks and saw Gwen leaned forward on the edge of her seat, nodding sagely and smiling pixie encouragement. Elisabeth's prim little mouth was moving so fast it was a blur.

"Jesus Christ."

"The two-faced cow. She ought to be horsewhipped!"

"Why would she *do* this?"

"You tell us, you're the blimmin' psychologist."

"Holly, sweets, you're going to have to give a blinding interview. This is what you do. Ignore her questions, have certain points that you want to make, and *make* them. This agency is about people having fun, not about finding husbands and wives. Our clients are beautiful people inside and out—and occasionally their insides are more beautiful than their outs, because while we accept that looks are something, they aren't everything. We offer people four dates a night, and while we *do* take great care to ensure that each pair is compatible, it's not reasonable to expect every one to be a soul mate. *Comprends?*"

"I'll try."

Claw and Nige and Issy exchanged worried glances. As well they might. Gwen was like a shark mistaking a fatty in a wet suit for a baby seal and thinking, Well, this one tastes a bit rubbery, but a meal's a meal. Elisabeth had given her a sniff of a juicy story, and she no longer cared about the truth, the lure of a scandal was irresistible. And maybe I no longer had the energy to defend myself.

Gwen fired accusations at me at the speed of TV lite, and my brain scrambled. I bumbled, stammered, said "You know" a lot. Her questions were so sharp and twisty that I heard myself bleat, "No, we can't be a hundred percent sure we've weeded out every criminal, but my sister"—my *thister!*—"is a psychologist and she helps with our sorting process." I had a nasty feeling that Gwen might edit out half of this sentence, starting from "but."

Nige didn't cry, but only because he was filming for Courts the following day and couldn't risk blighting his moment of glory with puffy eyes. He cared deeply about Girl Meets Boy, but Nige's deep is most people's shallow, no offense. By the time he'd made himself a hot chocolate and completed his beauty routine (I once asked if he used Clinique like every other modern man, and he spat, "Clinique? That stuff is like paint stripper!"), the day's calamitous events would have seeped from his consciousness to make way for the serious business of getting into character.

Claw was pale with fury, and Issy and I had to physically restrain her from punching Elisabeth in the face. My baby sister is unlike most women I know in that she doesn't shirk from a fistfight. "And please don't say anything, you'll only make us look worse," said Issy. True. Claw has a filthy mouth, and when the occasion demands it, even ordinary everyday objects are cunting. This alone has led to a bust-up in which Claw yanked out a great clod of a woman's hair and nearly got sued for it.

I almost enjoyed recounting the tale to Manjit on Wednesday morning.

"You seem chilled about it, though," he said. "Tip your neck from side to side."

Of course I did, I had bigger fish to fry. For instance, the mysterious case of Elisabeth's boyfriend.

"I reckon I know why she did it," announced Manjit, reading my mind. "Oh?" I said—"Oh" being a very plain version of the sound I made, which had more peaks and troughs than the Lake District.

"Yeah," said Manjit. "Turn to your right, bend your right leg, keep the knee above the ankle, stretch your left leg, press gently on that inner thigh. She tried to get heavy with Nick and he was having none of it. Told her exactly what the score was, and she was *not* happy."

My balance is poor at the best of times. I nearly toppled over. "Really? And what *was* the score?"

"You know. One arm across your chest, press the upper arm with the other hand, stretch the muscle. They go out to eat, she snogs the face off him, the second time she sees him she's already telling him he'd look more respectable if he cut his hair."

I suspected that if Manjit didn't keep his regular appointment at Cut and Thrust, Bo would chop off his locks in the middle of the night with a pair of kitchen shears. But tales like this did Manjit good. It made him realize that other men also suffered.

"And he couldn't be doing with it. It was like, three dates, and she's acting like he's her property. Now, you've got a few techniques, you got to decide which of them you feel most comfortable with. The palm strike, the elbow, the knee—I tell you, don't bother going for the groin, it's where it is for a reason, hard to get to. Well, heh, depending on who you are, I mean. Nick's groin was easy enough to get to, eh? Uh, sorry, yeah, a good knee in the thigh, that's going to hurt. Try it on the pad. Beautiful. Did I tell you about a kick to the kneecap? No higher. Best if you can aim it slightly to the side, not with the toe, use the whole of your foot. Hard enough, you'll knock the patella right around! So yeah, he tells her she's a nice girl but he thinks they should call it a day, he's just come out of a heavy relationship, mentions your name and like, he says, she nearly keels over! He thought she knew, but she didn't, and when she finds out, like that, she was—"

"Not happy?"

"Not happy. And when you use any of these techniques, like the palm strike, yeah, best if you shout a command as you do it. That shows them you mean it, really freaks them out. Shout it, like 'Get back!' Really, Hol, scream it, top of your lungs, don't be British about it. Apart from scaring them shitless, it makes you breathe out. It tenses your abs, gives the strike more power. So she goes, 'What, Holly Appleton, from Girl Meets Boy?' And he goes, 'Yeah, I was with her for five years. We lived together, we were engaged and everything. She broke it off.' And she goes, 'When?' and he tells her and he says he's still upset. He says her face went all rubbery and she stormed out the door. So try it, yeah? 'Get back!' "

"So—get back!—he said he was upset?"

"Yeah. Upset. 'I still feel upset,' is what he said."

"When was this?"

"Day before yesterday. I reckon she quite liked him, so I reckon she's a bit put out and she's got it in for you. Saw her chance with the telly people and went for it. That's what I reckon. Bit louder. Try again."

"Manjit," I said. "I think you are, as ever, right. Get baaaaaaack!"

The shame was that when I returned to the office, even though Claudia was in blatant mourning for the agency (all that was missing was a black veil), I found it hard not to smile.

"I don't know what you're so cheerful about. Your firm's going to go under if we're not careful. The accountant just rang saying he's not received this week's checks, *or* last week's. And I've just opened a letter from the bank that informs you that you've reached your overdraft limit on the business. Something to do with a *five-thousand-pound* payment to a company called ADT. What the hell's going on? What's ADT, for fuck's sake?"

"They're a security company," I muttered. "I've had the security on the house updated."

"What! And they charged five fucking grand?"

"It needed a lot of updating. Look, I'll pay it back, okay?"

I expected fireworks, but Claudia merely shook her head and shrugged.

I gave her a second glance and was shocked. Surely this couldn't *all* be because of yesterday? Why hadn't I noticed before? Her nails were bitten so far down, the skin at her fingertips was ragged and bleeding. She had black rings around her eyes and a pinched, miserable look to her. Even her shoes were sober, red ballet flats with gold buckles. Well, sober for her. I wondered if she had suspicions about Stuart, but I guessed she'd forgotten him. Whatever her problem was, the signs pointed to something internal.

"I'm not cheerful," I added. You shouldn't be cheerful, your business could be in serious trouble, I told myself. Bloody overdraft limit. Maybe it *was* a problem. But I couldn't rise to it. Yeah? So? Worse things have happened.

My mind kept darting back to Nick telling Elisabeth where to go, saying he was still upset about the demise of our relationship. Even though it had fueled her resentment and prompted that spiteful speech to our pixie on the scene, Gwen Rogers, it was worth it. To know that despite everything, I could still affect him. Call me contrary, that was important to me. Of course, whatever he'd said to Elisabeth was just an excuse. But he'd told *Manjit* he was "upset." For Nick to locate an unwelcome emotion and actually express it—this was progress.

"Claudia," I said. "You deserve a break. Why don't you take the rest of the day off?"

She didn't need asking twice.

An empty office is never quite silent, there's always an underlying hum. But for the moment it was good enough, and I leaned back in my chair and sighed. When my cell rang I pounced on it in a guilty scramble, as if I'd been sitting in a concert hall.

"Hello?"

"Holly?"

The breath caught in my throat. I felt like an empty glass being slowly filled to the brim with ice water.

"Lovely to see you on Friday, thanks so much for inviting me. It was great to see you again. I've missed you, Holly. I'm sorry we didn't get a chance to talk. The only reason I haven't called is because I've been up to my neck in probate! But that's what you get for doing what your parents tell you and going into law! I hope you liked your present."

It's a measure of the veneration I have for presents that I was able to say to Stuart, "What present?"

There was a pause. Then, "Are you serious? One second." I heard a vague rustling. "I'm appalled. Your present is right here, under my desk! I forgot to bring it. Tell you what, are you in tonight, I'll bring it 'round after wor—"

"No!"

Silence.

"Look, I"—the words fell over themselves in the rush to get out of my mouth—"I'm not in tonight. I mean, look, I'll come to your office, um, is Camille there?"

"She's right outside," replied Stuart. He sounded amused, and my heart scrunched, painfully, like a wrung-out dishcloth. He was *patronizing* me. And what the hell was I doing, agreeing—no, volunteering—to go to his office? If I saw this man in hell it would be too soon. My ever-present fantasy was to blast him to a red mist with a machine gun. I could feel its power in my hands. I could feel its heavy vibration as I aimed it at Stuart and squeezed the trigger. I could feel that gun shaking me like a dog shakes a rat. I could feel the sick pleasure of killing. And yet. It was as if there were a barbed wire entwining my soul, which pulled me gently toward him. In my fuzzy head was the notion that I must face my demon and, if necessary, reenact the . . . scenario. Because this was the only way to undo my terrible impression of events.

"Look, maybe I shouldn't come, I—"

What was wrong with me that I couldn't make an affirmative statement? *Look, maybe?!* Why couldn't I say "I won't be coming, good-bye"? Why was I asking permission?

"Oh, don't be so defensive," said Stuart smoothly, and I couldn't blame him. After all, I'd left the gate open for this. "Do come. We should raise a glass, at least, to my new clients."

I trotted into the trap. "What new clients?"

"Holly. Mr. and Mrs. Stanley Appleton, of course!"

"I'll be at your office in ten minutes, Stuart," I said, and beeped off.

I got a taxi. I didn't trust myself to drive. Oh God. My life made *EastEnders* powerless to soothe (usually, it worked like a charm). What my parents had committed to I shuddered to think. Stuart worked fast. He was like a virus, worming his way into my life, infecting every area. I struggled to identify his tone on the phone. It wasn't just patronizing, it was something else, amused, flirtatious. Jesus. I tried to think, but my head was space dust.

I *was* too defensive. And really, it was time I got a grip on my emotions. That . . . *time* with Stuart wasn't so bad. It couldn't have been what I'd been thinking it was, because if . . . Well, here's the truth—I'm so ashamed I'm almost too embarrassed to say—but while he pinned me down, I held my stomach in. See? That proves it. If a woman is being, you know, she wouldn't hold in her stomach. That makes me feel slightly better, reassures me that overdefensiveness was all it was. Sometimes you can get paranoid about a person, magnify their crimes, turn them into some kind of ogre when they're not.

Another idea drifted in and out of my dandelion head. I should give Stuart a chance. He'd said he liked me. God, he kept going on about it. I should try with Stuart. Imagine, if I let him—no, if I had sex *with* him—again, but this time a proper, two-way thing, and it was nice, enjoyable, if it worked out. Why, even though the concept scared the breath out of me, made me want to rip out my own heart, the consequences were everything.

Normal civilized sex with Stuart would erase the nightmares. It would undo the past and make everything fine again, back to the happy simple way it was before.

CHAPTER 19

As Camille showed me into Stuart's office, she gave me a strange look. Friendly but anxious. I realized I was shaking. I tried to tense, gain control of my body, but I couldn't. I thought, This must be what it feels like to be old. When Camille shut the door behind her, my legs tried to buckle, but I wouldn't let them. *You have to do this. Do it. Only if you do this can you make it right again.* I tottered straight up to Stuart and kissed him, hanging on to the arms of his suit to keep upright.

He stuck his tongue in my mouth and I wanted to vomit. When you think about it, another person's tongue has no business in your mouth. I breathed through my nose so as not to taste it. *I can't do this. Oh God, can't do it, so wrong.* My whole body screamed out. I was the one being shot to death by machine gun, the bullets punching into my soft flesh. *Try, though. Ah, God, anything.* Maybe I was a girl in a film, pretending to collaborate with the enemy to save lives. If I was nice enough, he might release my parents. I didn't know if solicitors held clients to a signed contract, but even if they didn't, I knew Mum and Dad would never break a gentleman's agreement.

Panic smothered me hot and fast. I was an impala being pounced on by a panther, the killer claws peeling the hide off my back in smooth red strips. The rippled strength of my predator forcing me down, my twig legs crumpling, all their running done, the great jaws sinking deep into my soft neck, tearing the life out of me, my dying eyes wide with pain, terror, the strength and blood draining from me as I scrabble, weak, stupid, useless in the dust, sinking, fading, despair . . .

I broke away and sat down fast on the nearest object, a brown sofa, shuddering. Can't do it, screamed a voice in my head, too frightened. Never, never, never could I touch him again, or let him touch me, even with the tiniest tip of one finger. Nothing, nothing in this world could ever make what he did to me normal. Oh, no, no, not better at all, it's all come back. I wanted to sob, deep moaning sobs. I felt an ominous prickling at the corners of my eyes. I'd gouge them out before I cried in front of Stuart. Meanwhile, my heart was in danger of exploding, *splat*, all over my rib cage.

I was reminded of a Bunty Annual I'd had when I was thirteen. The age where I was desperate for a sniff of romance and there was bugger all in Bunty except a cartoon about a kidnapper. Or was he a smuggler? I can't recall, except that he was drawn very handsome and the action took place on the beach. The heroine wore a sleeveless top that had slipped down over one shoulder, revealing a hint of cleavage. The kidnapper had tied her hands behind her back and was trying to force her onto his boat, but he had to make this move seem unsuspicious. "Kiss me," said his speech bubble, "or I will break your arms."

To the thirteen-year-old me, this atrocity was the height of eroticism. What was wrong with me? What blip in my civilized upbringing could have led me to believe that such behavior was sexy? Safe in my pink-carpeted bedroom, I wanted to *be* that heroine! All these years later, clutched by Stuart and feeling a fear so fierce I could hardly see, I realized the extent to which little girls are taught that relinquishing control to a brute is desirable. The truth of this fantasy was so opposite I nearly laughed right there and then.

"Glass of water," I said. Although what I wanted was Valium. Cigarettes. Whiskey.

Stuart smiled and retrieved a mini Perrier bottle from a little white fridge behind his desk. He handed it to me with a glass, still smiling. I was shaking so hard, most of it spilled on his carpet. I didn't even want to know what he was thinking.

"So," I said, crossing my legs and cranking my brittle self into a relaxed position. "Remind me what it is you're doing for my parents?"

Stuart settled himself in the big oak chair behind his desk and ran his hands through his hair. I wanted to run him through with a spike.

"I won't confuse you with legal terminology," he began, "but I specialize in probate, and your parents have inherited an extremely complicated estate. There are shares in various companies that need to be realized and—"

"But they've *got* a lawyer!" As I said this, I wondered if Henry Flaherty, who must be at least ninety-three years old, had passed on or, at least, emigrated to the Cayman Islands.

"I believe, in a remarkable show of bad timing, he retired shortly before your grandmother passed away. He was the firm's only probate chap, so the company wrote to your parents with a few recommendations. Anyhow, your parents were chatting to me on Friday and it became plain they required an adviser to the trustees of the will, to oversee the whole procedure. They wanted someone they knew, rather than a list of unfamiliar names, so when they found out I was a friend of yours and this was my forte . . . Well! Your mother is an executor and, bless, in a bit of a fluster about it."

I gave him a cold look. *Bless.* One of the most patronizing things you can say about anyone. "What exactly needs doing?" I asked.

"Oh, various properties to be sold off, offshore interests. I'll be needing to negotiate with French lawyers, a number of company trust funds, share portfolios, one has to know the best time to realize them for tax reasons. As I say, it's all highly complex."

I nodded coolly, as if it wasn't all gobbledygook. I didn't exactly wish I'd studied harder at school—it's not as if they teach you anything applicable—but I wished I didn't find wills and all the pomposity surrounding them too dull to bother with. I hadn't even written my own will. In the event of my death, Emily would probably be carted off by the state.

"But anyway, enough talking business. How *are* you? Ah, here's your birthday present. Open it now."

It dawned on me that Stuart gave orders in a casual way that made you feel it was rude to disobey him.

"I'll open it later," I said, putting the squashy package in my bag. "So, what's the deal with my parents? Have they signed a contract?"

Stuart shot me a puzzled look. "They're new clients, Holly. I biked them a client care letter enclosing terms of business, as I'm required to do by the Law Society, detailing the basis on which I charge, etcetera, etcetera, and what I've been asked to do. They signed and returned it this morning. And they verified who they are for money-laundering purposes—in case I was inadvertently being paid in drug money!"

Stuart laughed as if to acknowledge that, yes, it was fairly unlikely that my parents would be paying him in drug money. I felt sick. I *always* felt sick these days. It was as if my digestive system had ground to a halt and the food just sat there in my stomach playing cards or something.

"Tell you what, Hol, forget the bubbly—never looks good, boss chugging champers in the office. Tomorrow night I'll take you out for dinner, somewhere nice. I know a great little Italian place. I'll pick you up from home around eight."

Before I could move or speak, he was on the sofa with me—never mind that it never looks good, boss shagging a visitor in the office—pressing me down with his bully body, his lips—thick, rubbery—contaminating the skin on my face, his hands busy with the zip of my skirt. What was it Manjit said? Jab your elbow in his face, neck, stick your fingers in his eyes, and shout, Get back!

I couldn't, I was frozen like an ice pop, a thousand years of self-defense wouldn't help me. In a second, Stuart was off me and straightening his tie. Camille burst in. I coughed, primly, into my hand. The elbow and the command hadn't been necessary. I never knew I could scream so loud.

"She saw a spider," exclaimed Stuart to Camille's startled expression. "You women"—his tone attempted lightheartedness, but he couldn't keep the venom from it—"scared of the littlest insect."

I stood up, brushed myself off. "Quite," I said to Stuart as I strode out.

My bravado lasted exactly forty-five seconds, the time it took me to get out of the building and a good way down the road. My throat felt hot and sore from the scream. I wanted to collapse on the pavement. I could have cried, but I felt too sapped. My legs tingled dangerously and my head swam. When I saw a taxi trundling along the road, I hailed it and crawled in, burbling like an idiot. Then I picked Stuart's birthday package out of my bag as if it were a scorpion and dropped it on the floor of the taxi. It clanked. I ripped open the tissue paper with my foot. A pair of pink furry handcuffs. I didn't howl with fear and rage. I bit my lip and drew blood instead. With cold hands, I rewrapped the "gift." When the taxi dropped me off, I threw the parcel into the trash bin next door. I was in such a rush to run myself a bath that I nearly knocked down Gloria, who was dusting a bookcase in the hall.

"There's nothing for me to do here, Holly," she said as I sped past in a blur. "The place is spotless. You could eat your dinner off the dining room table. I was reduced to sorting out your kitchen cupboards. You gotta stop doing my job for me."

I skidded to a halt. "Sorry."

"And thanks for inviting me on Friday. I liked the geezer I was sat next to—Manjit. His girlfriend had a right face on her, but he was a doll. We had a good chat. I was telling him about my guardian angel, and as it turns out, *he's* had an angelic experience. Different from mine—I mostly hear voices, rich deep voices. He was sitting in his sitting room one night, feeling low—I think he'd torn a ligament—and suddenly the room filled with intense light, *solid* light, like sheet gold. And he felt this touch on his shoulder, like feathers, and he felt comforted, a sense of warmth. Did he ever tell you that?"

I hopped from one foot to the next. "No," I said meanly, "because he knew I'd have laughed him out of town. Manjit lives on a main road. It was probably the flash of a speed camera."

Gloria looked crushed. "But that's *white* light, this was yellow. And how do you explain the feather touch?"

I clenched my teeth. "A breeze. His girlfriend likes the windows open, even in January. Well. I've got to have a bath." As I spoke I could hear my voice waver. I couldn't bear to look at her hurt face.

"You okay, Hol?"

"Bath," I squeaked. I ran one and cried into it. After a few minutes I became aware that I was actually *speaking* as I cried. It turned out to be "How could it happen how could it happen how could it . . . ?" I was too agitated to lean back against the cold porcelain, so I hunched in a ball, pressed the sponge into my face, and howled, "How could he, disgusting, how how owwww?" Eventually, I stopped crying. I remained hunched over the sponge, though. It was a comfortable position. I stayed that way until I heard Gloria yell, "Moff now!"

It was a ridiculous effort, leaving that bath, even though the water was tepid. I didn't have the energy to pull out the plug. I dragged a towel off the door, wrapped myself in it, and slumped to the floor. For the first time I had the urge to tell on Stuart. Shame and denial had kept me silent. But now I finally realized it was all his fucking fault, and I wanted someone to share my outrage. Who would I call? Still not Claudia. She was too volatile. I didn't think I could deal with any dramatics and jumping around. I wanted horror, but I also wanted to be rocked, to have my hair stroked, and to be told, "There, there."

And I knew who I wanted to do it. I wiped my eyes and blew my nose. I was thirsty from all that crying. I wondered how long you have to cry to dehydrate. I drank some apple juice, double-locked the door, and curled up on the sofa with the phone. Emily jumped on my lap, kneading. She has a little white patch of fur around her mouth, as if upon her birth God had decreed, "May your chin always be dipped in cream." I kissed the silken bit of her head between her ears and whispered, "May your chin always be dipped in cream."

Then I rang Nick.

My pulse did its usual, waiting for him to pick up. It was a leap of faith, ringing him like this, but I knew I was doing the right thing. It was not like the old Nick to give a babe the brush-off. The old Nick would have cut his throat before confessing to a third party that an ex-girlfriend had "upset" him. I wasn't thrilled to admit it, but our separation had obviously done him good. He seemed to have grown up a little. Previously, he'd been as rocklike in a crisis as a heap of sand, but *this* would be the occasion he proved he had matured.

"What?"

Then again.

"Nick. It's me, Hol."

"Hol? Oh God, it's you."

His tone had gone from bored to wretched in a split second. My heart shriveled to the size of a pea. I'd overestimated his degree of progress. And his degree of upsetness.

"Nick, if this is a bad time I—"

"It's a very bad time. I saw my"—he paused, spat out the word—"*parents* this morning, Holly. They had some news for me. I'm adopted."

He burst into noisy sobs.

Nick's head was squashed against my bosom—quite painful, but I didn't want to say anything. I just stroked his hair and rocked him. I didn't say "There, there"—when it came to the crunch, "There, there" seemed a silly thing to say. We were in Bo's spare bedroom (frills, swagging, chintz) and Nick was wearing a baseball shirt, faded jeans, and sneakers. He looked about ten. Which I imagine is how he felt. It was agony to see him cry. His face was red and crumpled, and his every sob tore through my own chest. And I thought, with dread, This is what it is to love someone.

"They didn't say," he spluttered, "they didn't tell me, I'm thirty next week and I . . . I don't know who I am. Who am I, Holly, I could be anyone, oh my God, my parents didn't want me, they gave me away, my name, my name could be anything. Clyde . . . Aubrey . . . Cecil . . . Fritz . . . Horace . . . *Tracy* . . . They adopted me when I was *six weeks old,* Holly. They couldn't have kids, that's why I haven't got brothers or sisters, but Jesus, what do I know. I could have ten . . . Christ, for all I know, I'm from *Birmingham*! My real parents, they could be anyone—criminals, drug addicts. My mother could have a club foot and syphilis. I hate them, how could they do this to me, not tell me all this time. My whole life, it's been a lie, fake. I'm not a Mortimer, I'm a stranger, a stranger in my own family. Because . . . because they're *not* my family. I look back and everything is different now. I, I'm no one, I'm alone, alone in the world. I don't know who I am. I'm not Nick. In one second I lost everything that belonged to me . . . my family . . . my whole self . . .

I don't know what time of day I was born, I don't know who I look like, I don't, I don't . . . Oh God, how could they? Shit, shit"—he clenched his fists—"get it together, Nick."

I had no idea what to say. I was appalled. Why hadn't they told him? And why tell him now? Because he was turning thirty? Talk about lame. I'd always thought that Nick's parents were unlike mine in being competent. The world didn't scare them. You could trust Lavinia and Michael to take care of everything, to know what to do in any situation. They were proper grown-ups, well versed in grown-up issues such as tax, conveyancing, dealing with builders, obtaining refunds in shops, not a credit voucher. And now they were revealed as bumbling idiots just like the rest of us.

"Nick," I said. "Your name is not Cecil. It's Nick."

This prompted more blubbering. His eyes were running, his nose was running, his whole face was flooded. I was not being helpful. I tried again.

"Nick. You're still you. You are *not* who your parents are. Of course, it's a massive shock and you are . . . you are in shock. If your . . . your, um, adoptive parents didn't tell you the truth till now, it was only because they were afraid. Because they love you so much—ah, Nick, everyone loves you, you're the most special person. They didn't tell you because they didn't want to risk losing you and, I'm sure, they were scared of hurting you. It must have been so difficult for them—"

"Fuck them."

Anger. Was that good? My counseling skills were plainly a bit rusty. "Wipe your nose on your sleeve," I said à la Florence Nightingale. "I'm going to make you a cup of tea." I scurried downstairs feeling my failure. Tea, tea, refuge of the ineffectual.

I dug out a ceramic mug with a peach-and-black motif—two spiny trees silhouetted against a nuclear sunset. For a person who prided herself on the size of her brain, Bo had rotten taste in kitchenware. Poor Nick, his identity whipped from under him. I shook my head. I jogged upstairs. Nick was sitting on the purple-patterned bedspread, dangling his feet, looking forlorn. He gulped down the tea.

"Mouth like cast iron," I said. "See. Some things never change."

He smiled, put down the mug. "Thanks, Hol," he whispered, "thanks."

The best kind of sex is unplanned, not primped and prepared for. The kind you melt into, where a sudden heat crackles between you from nowhere. Nick reached and stroked the inside of my leg (asking, not telling), filling me with unexpected deep liquid desire (good, healthy). Then we fell on each other (accepting, connected), tugging at each other's clothes (yes, yes, permissible), a silly, wild tangle of arms and legs (me on top, air), him pulling softly at my hair, hungry, mournful (kind, loving), and me, gripping his thin shoulders (different, familiar), pinching the flesh. There was no close enough (erase hard drive, rewrite). We gasped and groaned each other's names (this is what people do). I had goose pimples all over, from lust or . . . something. After, we lay there, sweating, panting, stunned. (I did it. I can do it.) Whew. I'll bet that purple bedspread had never seen such action.

After a long while, Nick rolled over and brushed my hair from my face. His eyelids were still puffed from crying. He lowered his mouth to mine and breathed, "Ah, Holly. I feel like our souls fused."

CHAPTER 20

My head was full of bees. The thoughts buzzed blackly, a thick tangled mess. Nick murmured endearments and I hardly heard them. *Was* that good sex? Yes. It was comforting. Gorgeous, to be with Nick again. No. I hadn't lost myself. I'd acted the part. Too much thinking. A disconnection, observing the action from a wise distance. Impartial, like a war reporter. Control. A squeeze of rage. I'd *done* it, for god's sake. I'd willed myself to want it. I feared that if I'd started shunning sex because of what had happened, I'd never stop. I so desperately wanted everything to be all right. This should have covered what had happened.

Or did it have to be with Stuart? No no no. I'd fix it somehow, but not like that. I felt disgusted with myself. I should have bounced. And look at me. A shred of what I was. *Not*, I hasten to add, that I'd lost any weight. I can't stand these tales of sad, fat women who suffer an extra woeful patch and lose lots of lovely weight because of it—Ooh, surprise! Something *super* came out of it! Look, suddenly now you're all happy and thin! Even if the food choked me, I ate three meals a day, no more, no less. He wasn't going to get me that way.

But in every other way, he'd got me. I'd put myself on trial every day. I ran everything through my head over and over. Something bad had happened, and was it my fault? Back and forth, yes, no. Was I entitled to use that word beginning with *R*? I was caught up in definitions. I had a concept in my head. Didn't you have to be beaten up? There hadn't been violence, just superior strength. And yet, these days I had to force myself to go out. Shopping at Tesco was no longer a chore, it was a grand tour of the seven rings of hell. Now I knew what Nick had been moaning about. I had a terror of crowds. Every Date Night I had to physically force myself not to run from the bar.

That was another thing. I'd loved my job and he'd killed it. Having people touch me. Even a hand on my shoulder. I'd feel my throat close up. The mere *idea* of sex. Anything even vaguely sexual, a poster in the street, and I felt sick. I wanted to shut out that bit of life altogether. Tricky when you run a dating agency. So not wanting to spend every weekday retching, my latest meal hovering malevolently at neck level, I'd cut off. I'd done it when Stuart did what he did. The more you cut off, retreat to a safe place at the back of your head and shut the door, the easier it becomes. Easier than getting upset.

And even then. Once, I had an instance of physical feeling, like being penetrated. A Girl Meets Boy client, female, wearing the scent I'd worn that night. Agent Provocateur eau de parfum. A rather lovely joke, bought for me by Nick. After the thing with Stuart, I'd read the label and it said, "A potent combination of saffron and co-riander with a sensual heart of Moroccan rose oil, jasmine, magno-lia, ylang-ylang, and gardenia in a seductive base of vetiver, amber, and musk." I felt terrible after I read that. Like I'd provoked him.

Nick's arm lay across my chest, too near my neck. I pushed it away roughly. I hated him for not knowing. I hated this for being a big deal, for crowding my head with complications. Why did sex have to feel so important. I needed it to be nothing. Then none of this would matter. But it wasn't like that with Nick. It meant something. It meant that we—ugh, I could hardly bear to think the word—*desired* each other. Oh dear. The wrong side of twenty-nine and I was doomed to see sex through the eyes of a ten-year-old. Gross.

"Will Bo mind if I have a shower?" I said through gritted teeth.

"Yes," replied Nick. "You can use my towel. It's all right," he added, to my look of distrust. "All household towels are washed at sixty degrees, every Wednesday 'without fail, no exceptions.' " He rolled his eyes. "It's like prison. I don't know how Manjit survives. The other day she lined us both up and asked if, after a shower, we stood there yanking out our pubic hair and scattering it over the tiles."

I giggled until I got in the shower, then I sank to the floor and cried and cried. It would probably be easier to tell you about the times I *didn't* cry. At least, when you cry, it's harder to think. It could have been so simple. Nick and I split up. Nick and I grow up. Nick and I get back together. But no, it had to be like this. A sodding great muddle. Jesus, I didn't want him back. He irritated me. He was so blithely unaware of anything. I caught myself. No he wasn't. Of course he wasn't. He'd just had the shock of his pampered life. I stepped from the shower and dried off. The least I could do was to stay with him.

He was asleep when I padded back into the room. Much how I preferred it. Safe. Undemanding. Seeing him there, sleeping, he looked so young. There was a slight fluffiness to him like a nearly grown Labrador puppy. I was reminded of early on in our relation-ship. He'd asked me if water was fattening. No, I'd said. Oh, he replied, but I thought it bloated you. Angel, I said, that's beer. I put on boxer shorts and a T-shirt, got under the covers next to him, and fell asleep too.

"I must say, this is a surprise," shrilled a voice close to my ear.

I started awake with a jump to see Bo bending over the bed, arms folded.

"Bloody hell, Bo. You could have knocked."

I poked Nick with my foot to wake him. He continued to snuffle-snore.

Bo frowned. "It's my house. And it's a house rule. No *bed* guests. Nick knows that."

I stared at her, trying to work out why she was so unpleasant. I'd disliked her on sight. A pale weedy blonde, in the least lovely sense, dreary, droopy, Gwyneth Paltrow at her worst. A bony nose, watery blue eyes. Insipid. And yet, such a fierce domineering personality. She'd stripped down Manjit like a wetted bed, tried her damnedest to shave off his rough edges, to fashion him into her dull, narrow vision of what made a decent man. Thank goodness, she hadn't entirely succeeded.

The first time we met, before we'd even spoken, she'd tried to establish a pecking order. She'd reached out and started to pick cat hairs off my pink cardigan. I was astounded. I'd had Emily two years by then, and in all that time no one, not even Issy, had tried to groom me. Even if I'd left the house looking like a giant fur ball.

"Nick hasn't been well today," I replied. "He needed looking after."

Bo's thin mouth struggled for a moment. "All I can say is that if you were a doctor, you'd have been banned from practicing!"

I laughed rudely at such a wet fart of a put-down. Bo stalked out. Nick woke up, rubbing his eyes. "What?"

I told him, and we giggled and squealed like children. "Young bat!" roared Nick into the covers, his insult safely muffled by acres of thick purple eiderdown. Our giggling stopped, and the corners of Nick's mouth drooped.

"How are you feeling?"

He stared into the middle distance. "Bo's cousin's just had a baby," he said. I nodded. What did this have to do with anything?

"And her mate's pregnant."

I waited.

"They were all here this weekend. Talking about *babies.* 'It's like having your favorite TV program on all day and all night long.' 'It's like being madly in love, every day.' And the pregnant mate, glowing over her stomach, cradling it. And then there's the cousin, sat there with this three-week-old kid. 'Isn't he beautiful, isn't he perfect?' And you know what most babies look like, ugly, like skinned chickens. She was entranced, obsessed, accepting all the compliments at face value, couldn't see we were being kind, couldn't see what it really looked like. I was in there with them for twenty minutes to give Manjit moral support, and she had this stupid glazed look. Didn't take in what the others were saying, just staring in adoration at this red crumpled blob, kissing its scaly head."

I nodded. There had to be a point to this.

"And I see it at the parties too. The mums. Some of them, they've created monsters, and do they see it? No. Their kids are nasty bastards and these women think they're angels."

He stopped. I made a there-you-go face. Nick sighed. It was like all the air was crushed out of him, starting from his toes. "I never thought about it. But now. I think, *My* mother wasn't like that. She had none of the joy that pregnant women had. No cradling her stomach, proudly showing 'round this scan picture of a grainy blob, no taking special vitamins, playing *Swan Lake* to her lump. This woman was doing all that, Hol. Mine didn't. She must have hated me being in there, hoped for a miscarriage. Carried on smoking, drinking, what did she care? Bo's mate, she was talking about her morning sickness like it was a badge of honor. Said in this smug way, 'I don't mind, it's for a good cause.' My mother. If I made her sick, it would have made her hate me even more—"

"Nick, she didn't hate you."

"Don't be ridiculous!" This was snapped, furious. "You don't throw away your own fucking child if you don't hate it!"

"Nick, you don't know the circumstances. Maybe she had no ch—"

"Of course she had a choice! There are *no* circumstances, Holly, *no* circumstances in which I would accept that she was justified in throwing me away! Can you imagine *your* mum, throwing you away because, what, she was eighteen and she was going to have to cut down on fags for the next few years?"

In all honesty, I couldn't.

"It's crap! Any excuse, it's fucking bullshit. This is a welfare state, she could have managed. She made a choice. I hope I fucking ripped her coming out."

I winced. "Nick, that's horrible, you don't mean that."

"Yes, I do." He looked at me through narrowed eyes, then burst out, "Why shouldn't I hurt her? She hurt me!"

"Oh Nick, I can see that, but, you know, maybe she did the best thing for you she could in the circ— I mean, look at who y—"

"No, you look." Said in a hiss. "While all the *other* mothers were hugging their newborn babies to their breasts, feeding them, bonding . . . You know, those first few minutes, hours, days of bonding are crucial to a baby's development—every touch, every look, every whisper. I've not worked with mothers and kids all this time and not picked up stuff. It *means* something. *You* had it, Claudia did, Issy did, Manjit, Nige; don't know about Bo. *I* didn't have it. She probably never even held me once. It must have been, Get this thing out, now take it away, I don't want it. For the first weeks of my life I was fed cow's milk from bottles—"

"Nicky, sweetheart, no one fed you *cow's* milk—"

"No, Holly, that's what formula milk is! I was fed cheap milk from bottles by nursing staff. Strangers. And clothed in a scratchy regulation onesie handed out to rejects by the NHS. And shipped off in the back of a van by authorities to some scuzzy adoption agency. To be *bought*. My very first experience as a human being on this earth was rejection. Rejected by my own parents. And I look about me, see everyone else's doting mummies and daddies. No one else rejected but me. I looked at myself in the mirror before and I felt I didn't know who I was looking at. How do you think I feel?"

I hesitated. "I don't think I'm qualified to say, Nick. It must be incredibly painful." I wondered how long I should pause before saying "but." A few months, possibly.

Nick's shoulders heaved. He looked utterly deflated. I couldn't help myself.

"Nick. This is a terrible, terrible thing for you to learn. I can see how it rearranges your whole world. It's a loss for you, a great loss."

He nodded.

"No one can understand what you're going through. And what

you will go through. It will take a very long time to accept. And adjust. You have a right to feel sorry for yourself."

Was there a less insulting word than *but*?

"Although. Be careful. You don't want to make this harder than it already is. It's hard enough. Maybe it's not wise to let your imagination run wild. It won't do you any good to re-create the first weeks of your life in the worst way possible. I'll bet you were a gorgeous baby. I'll bet you weren't even scaly. I bet the nurses loved you. I truly—and, Nick, I say this from my heart—I truly believe that your mother was sad to give you up. But—and of course you'll wonder about her, and your dad—but it's important to remember that you *do* have what I and Issy and Claw have. You *do* have doting parents. My God, they adore you. I'll bet the first time they saw you, you took their breath away—"

"Oh bullshit, they probably chose me over the kid in the next bed called Winnifred who had a pointed head!"

"Nick. I really don't think it happened like that. Your . . . your now parents wanted you. You were a gift. It must have been amazing. The most precious moments of their lives. I'll bet when they first held you, they felt a *snap* inside their chests, a physical sensation of falling in love—"

"Stop it now." Tears streamed down his face. He wiped them away fast with the back of his hands, and more fell. Maybe it wasn't wise to try to minimize his trauma. I felt this was probably a good time for me to go.

Immersing myself in Nick's problems removed me, a little way, from my own. Made me feel normal. Call me shallow but the first thing I did the next morning was to ring my own parents and invite myself to stay that weekend. Cue, boundless joy. Issy was coming down on Friday night with Eden. They'd have a full house. The more the merrier!

I also thought it would do Nick and I good to have a few days off from each other. Thursday and Friday he rang me three times, and two of those calls lasted several hours. He spat fury and had sore knuckles from punching Bo's flowery walls. I'd realized he wasn't ready to look on the bright side, so I just shut up about it and listened. There was no making it right, so it was selfish of me to try. When he wanted to, he expressed himself beautifully. The words poured out of him. I applauded Bo for having an itemized phone bill.

He hadn't told anyone else, not even Manjit. "I'd like to," he explained, "but Bo makes him tell her *everything*. He'd try to keep it secret, but she'd pry it out of him. She says a hundred percent honesty is crucial in a relationship. Christ, doesn't the witch know anything?"

I enjoyed those conversations, even though I knew I shouldn't. It was exhilarating, Nick inviting me in to share his feelings. He hadn't done it for so long, I'd forgotten how much I'd missed it. I felt privileged, close to him. This was how we should have operated as a couple. Instead, we got lazy, shutting ourselves off. I don't mean to sound pompous, but there can be no intimacy without self-disclosure. It can't be that most of us dry up of things to say about ourselves and the world, but we act like it.

I always feel sad when I see a couple in a restaurant and the woman is just sitting there while the man is having an animated conversation on his cell phone. Or vice versa. It's so disrespectful. Nick and I never got to that stage, but only, I suspect, because I tend to turn off my cell in restaurants. I can do without the glaring hatred of the person at the next table, and Nick's friends are expert at the six-second chat. (Manjit is the exception, but he's been trained to ask if this is a convenient time to speak.)

Now Nick was awash with eloquence. And surprisingly, amid the gush, he asked my opinions. I stopped being nervous of saying the wrong thing because if Nick disagreed, he'd say so straight out. For the first time in years, our conversations were no longer a duel. In the light of new knowledge, he'd revised history. His easy relationship with his fake parents (as he called them) was harshly reinterpreted. They hadn't spoiled him because they loved him, but because they felt guilty about *not* loving him.

I think he wanted me to argue with him. I did. "In one way," I said, "our parents—no, sorry, Nick, I refuse to call the Mortimers your fake parents—are identical. They're proud of us, they adore us, no strings attached. Your parents treat you like a box of jewels. They look at you, I've seen them do it, and it's like they can't believe their luck. The love shines off their faces. They're not demonstrative people. But they can't help it with you. Remember that summer when we . . ."

We talked freely about everything but Wednesday's sex.

CHAPTER 21

Friday afternoon I rang my parents to check that they were still expecting me. I needed to be babied. But I also needed to speak to them about being Stuart's clients. Jesus. That man had a reach like a fucking octopus. He really did manage to spoil everything.

"Tell M and D I'm coming too," said Claudia gloomily from behind a copy of *What Car?* "In fact, I may move to Penge. There's nothing for me here."

I sighed. Even Nige was subdued. Filming of his advert had been a "disaster." He refused to divulge the number of takes. Secretly, I found it hard to believe that such a cheap outfit would permit more than three, even if the actor was as wooden as the nest of tables he was supposed to be selling. Nor did I take seriously Nige's announcement that he had "died a death." I knew he was a good actor. It was false modesty, designed to elicit reassurance and praise.

I couldn't be bothered. I was sick of everyone.

Nick, still ringing me on the hour, was refusing to speak to Michael and Lavinia and torturing himself with thoughts that he hadn't been kissed until he was six weeks old and his real name was Percy.

This was all very well, but *I* was torturing myself with the fact that I'd slept with Nick. One minute I loved him, the next minute I felt disgust and loathing for both of us in equal measure. Now he shared the blame for how I felt. I no longer saw my body as sexual. I wanted to cut myself off from all that messiness and be *pure*, a born-again virgin. Sleeping with Nick had been a potential route to redemption. But no, it was yet another blind alley.

It seemed as if I wasn't the only one with—God, what an ineffectual phrase—"*man* problems." I noted that Frank wasn't joining

Issy and Eden in Penge for the weekend. And, in a suspicious coincidence, Rachel was avoiding me. I hadn't heard from her since my birthday dinner, the entirety of which she'd spent baiting Nige. I hadn't the energy to quiz her on the identity of her mystery man. If it *was* Frank, what would I do? Rachel preferred to dally with other women's men. She'd once told me, "I am phenomenally bad at the task of making the other person feel good in a relationship."

Presumably, this was why she felt safer in a threesome.

I caught myself condemning one of my best friends and felt a twinge of shame. Here I was, committing the very crime I despise in others: presuming a person guilty until proven innocent. Then again, so what? It's true, isn't it? If people have a tiny chance to think the worst of you, they will. This made me relieved that I hadn't told Nick about Stuart. I don't think I could have stood it, if he hadn't believed me.

After what Rachel said, I realized that a lot of people don't think women are trustworthy. Even other women. Their theory is you feel bad because you were an easy lay and the man never called. You're a victim of torture and they think you're telling them something distasteful about your sex life! I thought that, and then I thought, Yes, but these torture victims are *other* women who are properly attacked in less comfortable venues than their own kitchen. I felt defensive for them but didn't include myself in this bracket. What enraged me was that everything everywhere, conscious or unconscious, asleep or awake, seemed to boil down to sex.

I needed to be in a sex-free zone. My parents' house.

"Claudia," I said. "I think we should leave for Penge now to beat the traffic. Can you call Issy and see if she wants a lift?"

Holly, I don't know why you bother sending Issy. You know she always comes back with a load of cr— sh—uninteresting foods. Wait here. *I'll* go."

I creaked the hand brake while Claw dashed into the gas station. It was true, Evian and licorice was not what either of us had in mind for the car journey to Penge. Even Eden looked unimpressed.

Claw returned with four bags of cheese-and-onion Monster Munch, four packs of Hula Hoops, four tubes of fruit-flavored Toffos—"You should have got plain," I said, "they all taste foul apart from the banana flavor"—four bottles of full-fat Coke, a pack of Magdalenas fairy cakes, a pack of milk bottle chews, one roll of Wine Gums, a pack of all-over chocolate Jaffa cakes, and four packs of milk chocolate Aero. "And don't complain, Issy, the air bubbles stop them from being fattening."

Issy glared. "Claudia, are you worried there's going to be a famine? You do know what sugar and additives do to Eden? Were you under the misapprehension that we were driving to Italy? It takes an hour and fifteen minutes. There is food in Penge. This is ridiculous."

"No one with a brain could ever mistake Penge for Italy. You don't have to eat everything, Isabella. I wanted there to be a choice. I thought Eden might like a fairy cake instead of the usual wheat cr—sh— stuff you feed her."

"As you are childless, Claudia, I'll thank you not to tell me how to raise my own daughter."

(All said in a light, breezy tone so that Eden would be less likely to pick up on the animosity. As if. That child is as sharp as a box of hedgehogs.)

"Why don't we play a game?" I said, before the mood deteriorated. "Eden, what would you like to play? I-Spy?"

"No, that's for babies. I want to listen to my tape of 'Peter and the Wolf.' Peter tells lies and the wolf eats him."

I wasn't sure if this was true or Eden's wishful thinking, but I didn't dare argue. I did as I was told and switched on the tape.

Claudia peeled open the roll of Wine Gums. "Bug— Sh— Bother! There's not a single red one in the whole pack! Are they allowed to do that? Isn't it illegal? So unfair. I'll have a black one instead."

There was peace for thirty seconds while she chewed. Then, "Hmph! Weird. These have got a before taste—sort of like envelope glue—*and* an aftertaste. The middle taste's quite nice, though."

"Cordia, will you please be quiet. I can't hear 'Peter and the Wolf.' I missed a bit, Mummy, rewind the tape!"

"No, Eden, *you* be quiet. I'm older than you. I'm a grown-up. I can talk when I want."

Issy turned around busily in her seat. "Claudia. As you seem to be under the curious impression that you're an adult, do you think you could try not to pick a fight with a four-year-old?"

And so on, ad nauseum (I had to stop the car for Eden to vomit seven fairy cakes onto the pavement) until we reached Penge.

Mum was doing her best not to peer down the garden path. Dad was peeling potatoes in the kitchen. I felt myself soften as I walked in. Everything about their house was comforting. From the crooked line of rosebushes on each side of the garden path and its carefully tended square of lawn to the grandfather clock tick-tocking loudly at the end of the hall. The yellow velveteen sofa clashing cheerfully with the orange shag pile in the lounge, my mother's collection of blown-glass animals on the mantelpiece, the white hand-crocheted tablecloth, the sound of local talk radio from the kitchen, the receding smell of fried bacon—theirs was a home to give the editor of *Elle Decoration* a heart attack, but it boasted an aura that few interior-designed properties could: contentment.

"Hello, Granny, I've just been sick. Can I look at the photographs?"

"Oh dear! Were you carsick?"

"No, she was cake-sick," replied Issy, with a sharp glance at Claudia.

"Well, darling, she takes after her mother. I never saw a child with a sweet tooth like yours. You wouldn't leave the table unless we provided pudding. And remember when you nearly missed being a bridesmaid for Cousin Neville because you ate three Mars bars when Leila took you ice-skating, and got a terrible tummy upset? We were a little late to the ceremony because of it. We decided you'd change when we got there in case you had another accident on the way—the bride's mother was in such a tizz she tried to un-dress you in the hall. I seem to recall you kicked her bad leg, but, well, it never did you any harm in the long run."

"Debatable," murmured Issy. My mother was already leading Eden by the hand into her study, an Aladdin's cave of crinkle-edged photographs, ancient yellowed copies of *Women's Realm*, and fusty-smelling storybooks for children of the fifties. Personally, I've looked through *The Monster Book for Girls,* and it's one long riot of racism and sexism. But Eden likes the stiff pages and old-fashioned pictures; happily, the text is too advanced for her. I think if my mother actually *read* some of the stuff she's hoarded since puberty, she'd pale and throw it straight in the trash (or in the recycling unit by the library, at least). My mother's motto is "Live and let live." She has no patience with prejudice.

Claw dropped her bag in the hall and trotted into the kitchen to talk to my father, probably about caravans. Secretly, I think she's his favorite, although he'd die before admitting it. I gazed after her. Her moods seemed to dip and swing, almost by the minute. I supposed I should confront her, ask her straight out what was bothering her, but I was too afraid of the answer. If it was to do with me, I didn't want to know, and if it wasn't, I wasn't sure I was capable of dealing with even one more problem, itty-bitty or not.

Issy had stomped outside to have a smoke in the garden. I hovered in the lounge, knowing that Mum would return in a second to offer cups of tea and a plate of the cakes she liked, dry swirls of pastry stuck together with jam and raisins. Nige would have had a fit. I'd bought a book to read, but I didn't feel like reading it. The brief sense of relaxation was wearing off. I sat down and flicked through a copy of *Gardeners World.* I had no choice—whatever it did to them—and I felt in my heart it would kill them. I had to tell my parents about Stuart.

There was no way they'd break their agreement with him otherwise. They'd see it as a breach of honor. Right. I'd tell them . . . today. Sometime this afternoon Eden would ask if she could play house in the caravan and Issy would be forced to join her. Inevitably, Claudia would receive a call on her cell from one of her many mystery friends (when I thought about it, I knew very little about Claudia's social life) and wander off to a far corner of the house so as not to be overheard. How long would it take to explain, five minutes? They didn't need to hear details.

W ould anyone like some tea and cake?" called my mother on cue. (At any given point in the day, at least one horrible meal is being prepared in their house.) "It'll be in the lounge. And there are Marmite sandwiches if Eden wants," she added as Issy came in from the garden, frowning. Members of my family milled into the lounge like lemmings.

"One can never have too much cake," said Claudia. At least, I think that's what she said; what she *really* said—the sound was muffled—was "Wuf can neger hag koo muk cake."

I allowed my mother to hand me a bone china cup and saucer. No matter how often we say to her, "We grew up here, remember. You don't have to put on a show," she point-blank refuses to serve us a hot beverage in a mug. But I like it, I like the ceremony. I notice she always gives herself the chipped one.

"Stanley, dear, can you bring in the sugar and a coffee for Issy?"

Time passed gently, as the usual conversations progressed along well-trodden routes. Uncle Barry. Leila. Our work. Eden's progress in school.

There were, however, a few interesting departures from the norm. Claudia blurted out, "So when Gran's money comes through, are you going to move to a big house in a nicer area?"

My parents looked startled and embarrassed. My mother said, "All our friends are here, dear. We don't need a bigger space. We're more than happy where we are."

My father added, "It may take quite a while for probate to be granted, Claudia. But while it's wonderful of Granny to have remembered us, we don't feel it would be—I think it might be a little upsetting to your mother if we— We'd rather leave the . . . the proceeds in the hands of our lawyers, at least for now. Until a rainy day."

Claudia shrugged. "What about upgrading the caravan?"

"Claudia!" barked Issy. "You heard what Dad said. Leave it now." Her voice dropped to a low hiss, audible to everyone in the room. "You're making them uncomfortable, it's upsetting for them, you talking about Granny like she was a piggybank!"

An unfortunate metaphor, considering that her wealth was built on pig farms. Claw put down her cup and saucer and snort-laughed elaborately.

"Claudia!" shrieked Issy.

"Oh, pardon me for breathing," muttered Claw, pulling a face. It's amazing how, in the vicinity of our parents, we all regress about twenty years. I guessed I could really set the cat among the pigeons (as my mother would say) by mentioning Stuart. It was galling, how discreet my parents were about their financial affairs. What did they think we'd do, tell all our little friends in the playground?

"And how's Frank. Very busy at work?"

My mother's attempt at changing the subject and the mood didn't entirely work. Issy snapped, "Isn't he always?"

"What's that supposed to mean?" inquired Claw.

"It means," growled Issy, "that I don't know what the hell, er, what the hello is going on with him right now. Eden, go and play in the study. Here, take a sandwich. Don't get crumbs on the carpet."

"Don't worry, Eden, I can Hoover up any mess," said my mother quickly.

Eden exited the lounge with a fistful of sandwiches and an evil look on her face (not that anyone noticed except me). Issy's face crumpled. "He was on the phone the other night, and when I came into the room he put down the receiver quietly but *fast*. And when I asked who it was, he said a work colleague, ringing about a meeting. After he'd gone, I pressed one-four-seven-one, but *he'd* made the call."

My mother's face was a picture—to be precise, a struggle between reality and desire. "Issy, dear, there's nothing untoward about that. He must have forgotten who'd rung who, that's all!" She smiled, relieved to have unraveled the mystery and found it nontoxic.

"Huf," said Issy. "And that's not the only thing. He said he had to go into the office this weekend, but when I rang his direct line, there was no answer."

My mother laughed nervously. "I'm sure there's an innocent explanation, dear. He must have nipped out for a coffee."

"I called him ten times, every ten minutes."

"Well," said my father, "then he must have had a meeting in the meeting room!"

Despite my growing anxiety, I had to put him straight. "Boardroom, Dad," I said. It bothered me, how he lacked even a basic knowledge of business.

My father smiled. Thankfully, he didn't see the correction as a snub, he saw it as helpful. I glanced at Claw. She was staring, tight-jawed, at her tea. I wondered if she also had suspicions about Frank. I shifted gaze to Issy. She sighed, seemed to collect herself. I imagine she'd realized that short of whipping away a black cloak to reveal Frank writhing naked with another woman on my parents' coffee table, there was no convincing my parents that anything in the marital garden was less than rosy. And possibly not even then.

Issy stood up. "Is the caravan key by the door? I think I'll go and play housey with my daughter."

My parents smiled, pacified.

Claw stretched her arms and legs without moving from her chair. "Mum, Dad, is it all right if I have a bath and wash my hair?"

Mum beamed, delighted to be on safe ground again. "Of course, dear. Stanley, is the bubble bath on the side?"

"Yes, Linda."

"Great," said Claw, jumping up. "I'll see you when I see you." The words were jollier than the delivery. We listened to her clump heavily up the stairs. I swallowed. Now was my chance. I cleared my throat. My parents looked at me, hopeful smiles on their faces. I bit my lip.

"I, uh, I wanted to tell you something."

My mother placed her cup and saucer on the table, rested her hands on her knees, and nodded. My father smiled encouragement. They looked old.

Oh God.

I couldn't.

I must.

I sighed. A short, sharp sigh of resolution. Where to begin?

Background. "Mum, Dad. You know that, a couple of months ago, Nick and I broke up."

They nodded, mouths drooping. Save it, I thought.

"Well—"

Deedle deedle doo, do do doooo!

"*Scooby Doo!*" exclaimed my father in a beam of recognition. "Do you hear that, Linda? These days they can do anything, can't they?"

I made a mental note to change my cell ring tone to a tune with more gravitas. The *Scooby Doo* theme was no longer appropriate for me and, frankly, hadn't been for the last two decades. I scrabbled in my bag, where, apparently, the phone had morphed into thin air. Finally it reappeared, and I grabbed it just before it switched to voice mail.

"Sorry, Mum, Dad. Hello?"

"Holly. Where have you *beeeen*?" The voice was whiny, demanding, and made me twitch with irritation. "I've called the house nineteen times. Gloria finally answered. She said you were away, she was cat-sitting. She says when she gave Emily her insulin jab, Emily bit her. Where *are* you?"

"Nick," I said aloud before I could stop myself. My parents glanced at each other. "I'm at Mum and Dad's. What's wrong?"

"Oh. Right." Sulkily. "You could have told me instead of sneaking off like that."

I held my hand over the mouthpiece. "Mum, Dad, sorry. I'll just take this outside."

My parents nodded. They were both grinning. I marched into the garden. "Nick," I said. "I did not 'sneak off.' I just *went*."

"Yeah, without telling me where you were going. I can't believe you abandoned me. I needed to talk." At least one word in every sentence was stretched to peevish self-pitying length. Fury pulsed. How *dare* he? He hadn't changed. He was still a baby, demanding that his needs were met instantly. I was doing him a favor here. We were no longer linked in an official capacity. I had no obligation to him. What kind of blithering fool maintains contact with their ex-fiancé after dumping him? I thought of the sex and shuddered. I'd behaved like a prostitute.

And so had he. Letting me, wanting me to comfort him in this way, as if words weren't enough. He had been utterly selfish, given no consideration as to what I'd wanted. Such a typical male, expecting the woman to serve him, make him feel good. He was another man who never heard what a woman said, only what he wanted her to say. The more I thought about it, the angrier I got, until the mere recollection of his hands on my skin made me want to retch.

"Now that we're back together I'd have thought that y—"

I screwed up my face at the phone in disgust. "We're not *back together*, you . . . you . . . you *idiot!*"

Blip. Dead air.

CHAPTER 22

The journey home was, if possible, more nit-picky than the journey to Penge. The weekend had not fulfilled its promise. Most of us had failed to escape our problems. Issy, who—unbeknownst to Frank—is a social smoker, spent half the trip pretending to puff on sugar cigarettes to confuse her daughter. Eden accepted a fag from the pack and treated us to a fine imitation of "Mummy smoking *real* cigarettes, not sweets."

For a second, Issy looked stricken. Then she laughed and muttered, "What do I care?"

Claudia had remained odd and argumentative until Sunday morning, 10:36, when her cell rang. All I knew was that the person on the end of the line had caused her to blush. She skidded into the hall, conducted a twenty-eight-minute conversation in a seductive growl, then returned to the breakfast table a chirpier person. (Incidentally, she's always sneered at those whose moods swing from hyper-bouncy to near-suicidal according to how their partner is treating them that minute.) The chirpiness still hadn't worn off, and it was beginning to grate.

"The disaster Date Night is being aired this evening, prime time on ITV," I said, hoping to calm her down.

"Yes, well," she replied. "TV isn't an effective form of advertising for us anyway. The audience is too scattered. I'd be more upset if we'd had a bad write-up in *Marie Claire* or *Cosmo*."

It could be arranged. I glanced in the rearview mirror in disbelief. Was there no deflating her? *My* last cell-phone conversation had had the opposite effect. Nick had rung back, a few minutes later, to tell me that he thought it was time we sold the house.

"What else, are you going to sue me for custody of Emily?" I'd replied.

"Don't tempt me."

Pathetic.

I'd stamped back into the lounge, softening my tread as Mum and Dad looked up. I saw their faces, and I knew I couldn't tell them about Stuart. It wasn't only because I knew that they would be mortally wounded, it was also because I felt such deep wrenching shame. So what if he was their solicitor, it's not as if he'd be spending Christmas Day with us. I fed myself this line, then spat it right out again. The idea of that man coming anywhere near my family stoked a fire of hatred so fierce I could have fainted in the heat of it. And yet—I couldn't help it—my shame was fiercer.

Since then, I've reasoned that most people get irate if someone treads on their toe in the tube. That's how much we value our right to be treated with respect. How brittle is our sense of self, that we can feel murderous and violated if a stranger unwittingly squashes our foot. A fraction of how I felt about what Stuart had done to me.

"See you tomorrow," I said, dropping off Claudia with relief. It was ten minutes farther to Issy's, but I couldn't discuss Frank with Eden in the car. Thank goodness.

Gloria, as instructed, had left every single light on in the house. Emily scampered to meet me at the door, meowing. People don't realize cats do that. (Scamper to meet people, I mean, not meow.) There was a message on the answering machine from Nige, inviting himself around to watch the Date Night segment with me. I rang him back to say, Sure, come over. Then I felt jumpy. How long was it since I'd been alone in the house with a man? I knew exactly how long.

Three weeks and two days.

This was *Nige,* for heaven's sake. I was losing all sense of reality. The phone rang again. "Hello?"

"Babes! It's been simply ages, a week at least. I must see you. I'm coming over this minute!"

Rach cut off before I even had time to assume an icy demeanor. I thought about ringing back and declaring, "I prefer not to mix with the likes of my brother-in-law's mistress," but this was patently a ridiculous thing to say. Anyway, her presence would mean that I wasn't alone in the house with a man. Crazy, I know. Indulge me.

Rach had also seen her parents this weekend. For her, this meant a ten-minute trek to Belgravia. Mostly, in London, a tall, skinny town house in a nonscary area will set you back 1.2 million. Those of us who aren't millionaires, who want to live in a house and yet don't wish to move to, say, Penge, therefore squeeze ourselves into a tiny box, crammed between two tiny boxes in a great long line of tiny boxes, each with a puny patch of garden. All for the sake of not wanting to feel suburban.

I couldn't even *dream* what that big, fat, monster, detached, quadruple-fronted house in Belgravia was worth. Whatever, Rachel's parents—Ted and Tod (actually an earl and a countess, a fact their daughter only mentioned to me after two years of friendship)—lived in it. Inside it was like a stately home.

The place was cluttered with *stuff*—busts, paintings, clocks, mirrors, books, maps, porcelain, candlesticks, chandeliers—heirlooms, I supposed. Stiff white, embossed invitations crowded the mantelpiece. "Stiffies," Rachel called them as I tried not to laugh. Tables, chairs, desks, bureaus of antique wood were crammed into every space. The walls were dark red in the lounge, eggshell blue in the dining room. Or maybe the drawing room? the sitting room? the morning room? I get confused. The floors were mostly wood, although some were covered in threadbare red carpet, worn away by dogs' paws. Fresh flowers everywhere, always. It was a testament to formal living gone soft.

It was scruffy, but not as scruffy as the earl and countess. Tod looked weather-beaten, wore no makeup, and dressed like a gardener. But the first time I heard her speak I thought she was putting on an exaggerated posh accent for a joke. I'd never—and some years I listen to the Queen's Speech—heard a person talk so plummily in all my life. She was friendly, with no pretensions (too aristocratic to need them) and a sense of humor full of lewd innuendo. I was impressed and appalled all at once.

Ted was quietly spoken, impeccably polite, a real gentleman. Nothing like the snow leopard–killing great-uncle (dead, fortunately). After a long, distinguished career with the Foreign Office, Ted now spent a lot of time in a place he referred to as "The House." He didn't look like an alcoholic, and I finally plucked up the courage to ask Rachel if "The House" was a posh people's euphemism for the pub (as in "public house"). It was, in retrospect, a foolish question to ask, particularly as Rachel was driving at the time. She laughed so hard she nearly killed us. "No. The House of *Lords,* babes!"

That weekend, a film director, a lord, and a newsreader had joined Ted and Tod for Sunday lunch, and Rach had some tittle-tattle to pass on about various Hollywood marriages, or, as "Steve" had called them, "mergers." Usually I'd suck it up, but I wasn't in the mood. I cut her off mid-yap.

"Tell me another time. Nige is coming. I know you can't stand each other but tough. We're watching the Girl Meets Boy TV thing. It starts in half an hour." I paused and glared at her. "So. Seen your married man lately?"

Rachel smirked. "Married-*ish,* and yes, he was adorable, thank you. We went rowing in Regent's Park and to the V and A. And then we did other things you don't need to know about."

I felt myself go hot. Surely, if it *was* Frank she'd have the decency not to brag in front of me. "I don't want to know," I snapped, although I jolly well did. There was a short silence, broken by the peal of the doorbell. I went to answer it, glad of the interruption, although I doubt Rach would have noticed I was annoyed with her. I was too polite about it. Subtlety washes over her.

"Why's *she* here?"

"I'm Holly's friend. Why are *you* here?"

"I'm Holly's friend and esteemed colleague. I'm also on television. Ha!"

"You know," I said, "maybe I should ring Claw, invite her 'round to keep the peace. I've had a tense weekend and I don't need you two scrapping like dogs."

This threat was probably most terrifying to me. I'd had quite enough of my little sister to last me till Monday. Nige and Rach were silent while I marched to the phone and, in a show of strength, rang Claw. There was no answer, which spoiled the effect. So I put down the receiver and said sternly, "Would anyone like a coffee?"

"Have you any rose pouchong?"

"Rachel," I said, "I don't even know what that is."

"It's a pompous form of tea, darling," said Nige. "Give her a cup of Tetley's. I'll have a glass of white, if you've got. And you have, because I've brought a bottle. Rachel can't have any."

"I don't want any, it looks like paint stripper."

She was obviously desperate for a glass—and I felt like a drink—so we all had some. In a moment of triumph, I discovered a bag of salted peanuts in a cupboard. I poured them into a bowl.

"I imagine this is like being at one of Rachel's parties. All that's missing is a lord in corduroys with buckteeth."

I shrank as far as I could get into the sofa. I was sitting smack-bang-wallop in the firing line.

Rachel laughed. "Nigel, you *dream* of being invited to one of my parties. Now who was I chatting to over canapés last week—ah yes, Sam Mendes. Face it, babes, only through me will you ever get the chance to meet a decent director and be cast in a part that doesn't require you to dress as the back end of an ass."

I knew that Nige was annoyed by this, as he chose to comment instead on the quiz show we were watching. "God, we're an ugly nation."

"Quiet, the program will be on in a sec!" I shouted.

My guests sullenly crunched peanuts for three minutes. "Oh, look, Holly, it's *you!*" squealed Rachel. "How exciting!"

I felt patronized.

"Glad to see Gwen Rogers looks fatter on the box," said Nige. "No doubt that shot of her arse'll send her scurrying for the laxatives."

This was his last cheery comment for a while. We all sat, mouths agape, as Girl Meets Boy was rogered by Rogers. With the help of Ms. Elisabeth Stanton-Browne. Even Rach said nothing.

"She—she made me look like a complete *fool*," I squeaked. "Jesus, I might as well have been wearing a bow tie. Those things— those things she made out I said. She's edited out half of every sentence, I was barely coherent!"

"Never mind about you personally. One goes on TV news, one expects to be made to look a fool. *I* can't believe she made the agency look so bad. It's even worse than we thought. She's made it look as if we stick anyone with anyone, like we don't give a damn. I can't believe this. We should sue her. It's so unprofessional. She's really done us a lot of damage here." Nige looked stricken.

"You don't know that yet," said Rachel.

I glanced at her to see if she was being facetious.

"You never know," she continued. "People may apply out of curiosity."

"Oh, don't be ridiculous," said Nige, but he said it without conviction. I think he was too despondent to be vicious. "All our work, all our hard work, down the sodding toilet." He was working himself up into a frenzy. "We might as well close down. We—"

"Nigel, do be quiet. Can't you see your unnecessary dramatics are upsetting Holly?"

Quickly, I arranged my face to look upset. I wasn't half as gutted as I should have been. The dismay I felt was purely down to vanity, a reaction to being made to look an inarticulate fool in front of an audience of ten million. I wished I could feel more about the plight of the business, but it wasn't there. Nige seemed to have pinched my share of emotion. He sank his head in his hands and sighed. Then, in a high, wavery voice, he gasped, "We are *done* for, I tell you, d—"

"Chin up, babes, it's the Courts ad."

Nige's hands jumped away from his head as if they were electrified, and a great cheesy moon of a grin lit his face. I'm surprised there was room left for his other features. He flopped off the sofa and dropped to his knees on the floor, fists clenched. The advert lasted all of four seconds and was unremarkable. Nige sprang up, clutching his chest. "How was I? How was I? What do you think? Was I convincing? Did you believe in me? I didn't have a double chin, did I? My hands looked natural where they were, didn't they? Oh my sainted aunt, I get paid for this. Ching! Ching! Ching!"

He was such a fraud it was impossible not to smile.

"Your hands were on the ends of your arms, which looked very natural indeed," I said. "And if it wasn't Sunday night, I'd be off to buy a sofa right now."

"What do I think?" barked Rachel, snapping her carpetbag shut for effect. "I'll tell you what *I* think. I think you're quite the most shallow man I've ever met. And believe me, babes, the competition is fraught."

Whatever glory Nige felt, he had the good grace to mute it the following day. All that Claw and I ever heard was the odd "Ching!" Claudia had a long face, but I suspected that while she and Nige were nervous about the future of the business, other sections of their lives were proceeding well enough to soften the blow. It was notable that for the first morning in over a year, there were no inquiries from potential clients. My accountant called my cell twice, but I recognized his number and didn't pick up. When someone rang the office at 11:20, I felt mild curiosity.

"Holly?"

The voice was vaguely familiar.

"It's Bernard. I saw the program last night. I'm awfully sorry."

I smiled. "Aw, Bernard, thank you. But it's all right. I'm sure we'll be fine."

"Hm. Well. Ah. I, ah, thought you might need cheering up, and I, er, wondered if I, ah, could take you out tonight for dinner. I know a French place that's charming. I thought we could have a chat."

It took me a second to recover. "Oh! Bernard! That's very kind of you. But I don't—"

"You'd be doing me *such* a favor, Holly."

Put so sweetly, it was hard to refuse. But could I be bothered to go out for dinner with Bernard? Not really. His crush on me was silly, like a child's crush on a teacher. Yet—and I was more suspicious than most—he was harmless. I was sure of it. He was shy too. He wouldn't so much as pull out a chair for me without considering my feelings first. What else did I have planned? Another fun evening scrubbing myself raw in the bath? Listening to Emily yowl and scrabble at her locked cat flap? Or maybe creeping around the house with my new must-have accessory, the kitchen knife? It would do me good—I could hear Issy saying it—it would do me good to get out.

"Bernard, I'd like that. Tell me where the French place is and I'll meet you there."

This caused dissent, but I insisted. When I parked outside the restaurant at 7:30, he was pacing in front of it. He was dressed smartly for him, a tie under his pullover. I sighed. This man had no idea how to pull chicks. This was either safe or very dangerous. When he saw me, he rushed to the car and hovered on the pavement. I walked toward him, which prompted a bout of head-bobbing. Then, when I didn't lean in any particular direction, he gave up trying to decide which cheek to kiss and shook my hand instead. Perfect.

"I reserved us a table," he stuttered.

"Lovely."

A waiter who looked like Deputy Dawg led us to the center of the room. Bernard and I had the same problem—neither of us looked menacing enough to warrant a good table. This has always bugged me. I'm so unintimidating, people *choose* to sit next to me on trains. The decor was pretty much as I'd expect of a restaurant favored by Bernard. Not cool, not eccentric, not interesting. But the food was delicious. I realized I was starving and had to restrain myself from gobbling my steak.

Bernard cleared his throat. I took a prim sip of water. I prayed he wasn't going to ask me out officially.

"Holly," he began. "I wanted to talk to you. I'm not awfully good at, uh, speaking to women, you see. And when there is someone I like, I don't really know the best way to go about letting her know I'm interested. Which is probably part of why I'm still, ah, unattached. I know I'm fairly new to Girl Meets Boy, and I have met some highly interesting women, but no one who I feel drawn to like, I feel—well, I don't want to speak out of turn, of course—"

"Everything to your satisfaction, sir, madam?" inquired the hangdog waiter. I wanted to jump up and kiss him.

"Perfect, thank you," I replied. "Could you tell me the whereabouts of the, um, ladies' powder room?"

"The toilet, madam? Through the door, past the kitchen, and turn left."

I smiled crossly, snatched up my bag, and fled. Once in the safety of the ladies' powder room/toilet, I ran the cold tap, bathed my wrists, and stared in the mirror. A hollow-eyed ghoul stared back. I wasn't up to this. I just wasn't. I felt like a straw house under attack from the big bad wolf. Why couldn't they all leave me alone? Why didn't even *one* of them have the decency to sense what *I* wanted, instead of barging in like a tank?

I ripped a paper towel out of the machine with a jerk. Then I smoothed my hair, strode into the kitchen, marched out the back door, stomped back to my car, and drove off.

CHAPTER 23

I sped home, hooting the world. There was a moment of clarity, when I looked down on myself, this red-eyed woman staring at the road and not seeing, muttering and laughing to herself about the monster sitting in the French restaurant, and thought, God, what's happened to you? But apart from that, every thought was cheese fondue, a gluey mass that slithered from reach when I tried to grasp it.

I skidded into my road, everything the same. Faded red Ford Escort with the bashed-in passenger door, resting on the curb outside number 28. Ruptured paving stones around the huge oak in front of number 44 and hedge cut in the shape of a chicken. White van parked in the drive of number 57 next to a silver Porsche. Every light lit, every curtain shut tight, number 63. Pink exterior and red door, number 72. It was like Pompeii. You could almost believe that time had stopped a while back and inside their houses people were frozen still, holding their teacups halfway to their lips.

Except. A green Polo with its brake lights on a few meters up from my house. My heart giddied up, it was so easily spooked these days. Stuart had a Merc, calm down. But maybe this was a second car for stalking women. Get it together, Holly. I slowed to a crawl and pulled in on the opposite side of the street. There were two people in the car, heads close. I squinted. Wait a sec, that was Claudia. I breathed an immense sigh. The other person, female, familiar. I needed her to turn her head—there, oh! *Camille.* Stuart's PA. What the—

My first thought was that something had happened to my parents. I leaped out, slammed the door, and raced toward them just as Claw hopped onto the pavement and Camille sped off. She twirled around as she heard my footsteps, her face as red as her knee-high boots.

"Holly! I was just coming to see you—"

"What's wrong, what is it?"

The blush faded until she looked almost white. She compressed her lips and looked straight at me, a laser gaze. Then she said, "I know about Stuart."

It was *my* turn to pale. My mouth fell open and I searched for words. Unless you're an accomplished liar, when someone confronts you with their awareness of the truth, the game is up. I'm hopeless. I ooze guilt. A quicker mind than mine might have snapped back with a clever, evasive response, but I couldn't. Telling fibs is bad enough, but being tricked into telling fibs by a person who is waiting to see if you're dishonest or not is even worse.

"You know about the rape?"

Claudia's reaction couldn't have been more comical if it had been depicted in a cartoon. She did a double take worthy of Scooby Doo, pity there was no "Za-*ikes!*" musical accompaniment.

"What?" Her voice was a croak. "I was talking about stealing clients' funds. *Rape?* Holly, what are you telling me?"

I wanted to curl right into myself like an earwig. "What? What are you talking about, what are *you* telling me? What do you mean, stealing clients' funds?"

"Camille told me, she suspects, well, she more than susp— Fuck that, *rape? Rape?* Holly, oh God, do you . . . Oh God, oh God, you do, don't you, all this time, how you've been, I should have—why didn't I—I had no idea, fuck, why didn't you say, ah Christ, ah Jesus, you mean he—rape? *When?* Jesus, are you all right, oh my God please no, this can't be true, my sister, *rape?* Ah fucking God al—"

I gritted my teeth, shut my eyes, and shook my head. "Okay, stop saying the word now. Stop saying it. It's not as bad as you think. I'm not even sure it *was* that so—"

Claudia gripped my arm so hard I cried out. She softened her grasp instantly. "Sorry, Hol. But you need to tell me what happened. Because I'm going to believe you. Do you understand that? Come on, let's go inside, shall we? Yes, shall we do that? Have you got your key, sweetheart? There it—"

A giggle came from nowhere. "It's all right, Claw, you don't have to speak to me like that. I'm not going to break."

She threw me a look. It said, "I don't believe you." Then she huddled me indoors like she was a minder and I was Michael Jackson. I couldn't meet her eyes, but I knew that she was crying. I don't think crying is infectious—sometimes you see a person cry and you retreat into yourself—but when it's someone you love you want to cry in sympathy. I felt tears prick my eyes.

"Don't cry, Claw. Please don't."

She dropped onto the sofa and started sobbing. "How could he, how could he? The fucking bastard, how did it happen? Oh God, Hol, I don't believe this. How could it happen?"

I patted her shoulder and marched into the kitchen to make her a cup of tea. Short of slapping a person's face and wrapping him or her in a blanket, there's not much else you can do for someone who's had a shock. Which goes to prove we're not quite the advanced civilization we think we are. *My* tears had dried up. I was able to boil the kettle at the crime scene without a shudder. What had she meant about Stuart embezzling client funds? Well. There wasn't that much room for interpretation, so I supposed she meant what she said.

See. You should have told Mum and Dad. I poured the hot water into the mug and jabbed at the tea bag with a spoon. Then I made one for myself, more for solidarity than thirst. I wasn't surprised. Stuart was a very clever man who used his intelligence to take advantage of people. He wanted something, he took it, even if it belonged to someone else. Sex, money, what difference?

When I walked back into the lounge, Claw was sitting upright on the sofa, wiping her eyes. She had a look on her face I wouldn't wish on anyone. She took the tea silently and cleared her throat. "Do you mind telling me this?" she said. "You don't have to if—if it's too traumatic. But you haven't told anyone, have you? And I think you need to."

I made a face. "No, it's fine. I'm happy to tell you. I tried to tell Rachel, but . . ."

Claudia snorted. "I can imagine." She scowled. "I'm listening, Hol."

I curled my legs under me. Emily bobbled into the room, saw Claudia, stopped dead. (Possibly, the screeched refrain "Get that thing away from me!" had, over the last two years, made her wary.) Cautiously, she made her way to me, hopped onto my lap, and started paddling with her paws, all the while staring rudely at Claudia. Claudia stared rudely back but—presumably because of the exceptional circumstances—didn't insult her.

Mostly, I didn't have a problem getting the words out. They'd been racing around my head for so long that they tumbled out, though not always in the right order.

I faltered now and then. Not because the details were horrible (although they were), but because I was embarrassed. Kissing him and expecting him *not* to get the wrong idea? Allowing him into my home late at night? Not knowing how to fight back? Not screaming? (Whoever heard of being too frightened to *scream,* for god's sake?) Not being like a woman in a film who'd have stuck her hand in a half-open drawer, pulled out a knife, and bravely plunged it into her attacker's back?

I stumbled at the points I hadn't done any of these things because I was terrified of Claudia's internal dialogue. "Oh. So Holly didn't bite him, knee him in the groin, pull his hair out, that means she *let* him. And if she let him, well, that doesn't count, then, does it?" I was sure there was a rule somewhere, that "Please, no" wasn't enough, because women say no when they mean yes (not me, or any of my friends, but anyway), that you had to at least infuriate the guy and provoke him to, say, break your nose or crack a rib for it to qualify as rape.

Claudia listened without saying much. If I looked at her to make sure she hadn't fallen asleep, she'd give me a tight nod. If I hesitated for too long, she'd say in a low voice, "Are you all right?" and when I nodded, she'd say, "And can you remember what happened then?"

At one point it felt like Stuart was on top of me and I couldn't breathe. Rape rape rape rape. The word, the deed, blocked for so long, sang and danced in my head, jangled and jingled the entire length of my body, ruling me.

"Inhale into your cupped hands," ordered Claw.

What with this kind of interruption, it took a while, but finally the tale was told. I felt exhausted, shaken, as if I'd run up Everest or—who am I kidding?—the stairs. I wondered if she believed me. (We've all said, "Of course I believe you," to a friend because we don't wish to hurt their feelings, even if we aren't convinced that pixies live at the end of their garden.)

"So what do you think?" I said nervously. "Am I being overdramatic?" I didn't think I was, but I was so confused. I barely knew anymore. I was fully prepared to adjust my belief on the advice of others. "I mean, maybe I—"

"He raped you, Holly."

I assumed a somber expression to match hers. Really? She thought that? Maybe I'd exaggerated.

"You understand, he didn't threaten me with a . . . a hammer, or anything."

Claudia screwed up her eyes like she hadn't heard me correctly. Then she said, in the softest tone, "Hol. You didn't consent to sex with Stuart, so he forced you. That's rape."

"But, you know, in the end, I . . . I let him. I was too scared to fight, I mean, that's not . . ."

"Sweetheart. If someone snatches your bag, whether you fight back or not, that's robbery. If you've got any sense, you *won't* fight back, because you don't want to be robbed *and* killed. Do you get what I'm saying?"

Suddenly, the tears were back in force. I was pretty incomprehensible, even to myself, but through the blubbering, what I was trying to say was "I was scared he'd kill me, I was so scared he'd kill me."

Claw rubbed my back and said, "I know, darling, I know." She made me take a sip of cold tea. I got hiccups immediately. After a long while, she sighed.

"What?" I said.

She sighed again. "I . . . I just wondered, why you didn't feel you could confide in me."

I shrugged. "I was ashamed. I thought it was my fault. I didn't want to make a big issue of it."

Claudia squeaked, "Didn't want to make a *big issue* of it!"

"In a way, Stuart and I were friends. I didn't want this to mess things up."

Claudia looked as though she had an ant nest in her knickers.

"I'd allowed it to happen. I mean, I thought, if I let him do it again, it was wrong the first time, but if the next time it worked out, I thought it would undo what had happened, make it okay. You know, maybe something could come out of it."

Claudia's breath seemed to catch. She shook her head, wordlessly.

"No," I said. "I didn't. I . . . I went to his office—Camille was there. I realized I couldn't. But I still went there. And, well, the more stuff that happens, the harder it is to isolate, to accuse him of anything . . . the more muddled it gets."

Claw took both my hands and tugged a little, encouraging me to look into her eyes. "Hol. I understand what you were trying to do. I can imagine, I can try to imagine, how hard it is to accept that this could happen to you. And God knows, if I were you, I also would have given *anything* to undo it. No one wants to be a victim. No one wants to think of themselves like that. But, sweetheart, it happened, and I'm so sad to say, nothing in the world can undo it. I'm so sorry, Hol. But, you know, I think accepting that he raped you—I know, it's a terrible, harsh word. Accepting it happened, not denying it—if you deny it you're stuck in a circle of guilt and blame. If you accept he raped you, I think it will be easier for you to cope in a—a healthy way, whatever that is. No doubt Issy will have some theory. *If* you want to tell her. And maybe, in time, if you learn to accept it, it'll be easier to move on."

I crossed my eyes to lighten the mood. And also, to express that this was a lot to take in. Being my little sister, she understood me.

She squeezed my hand. "Listen, Hol. Can I ask you something? After—after it happened, did you go to the doctor or a . . . a clinic or anything?"

I shook my head. Claw bit her lip. "I'm just—I wasn't just thinking of evidence. I . . . what if he gave you something, a disease?"

I screwed up my face. "He wore a condom. I mean, I can't remember him . . . him putting it on, but after . . . after when I was clearing up, there was a torn packet." I paused. "That's another thing. What"—I steeled myself—"what rapist is considerate enough to wear a condom?"

Claudia's voice was sharp. "Considerate, bollocks. The rapist who is too fucking clever for his own good. He doesn't want you getting pregnant, does he?"

I picked up a thread. "What do you mean 'evidence'?"

Claudia looked surprised. "Evidence for the police, Holly."

"The *police*?" With effort, I lowered my pitch. "What have they got to do with anything?"

My sister shifted uncomfortably. "Well, you are going to report it, aren't you?"

I nearly laughed. "What, to the *police*? What are they going to do? It was twenty-five days ago. It's my word against his. Who are they going to believe, the senior partner of a law firm or the woman who runs a dating agency and went out with her own client? Mmm, looking good."

Claw's face purpled. "Holly, it shouldn't matter if you were Tallulah Bankhead, what you do for a job has nothing to do with it.

Either you consent or you don't, and if you don't and he has sex with you, then it's rape. I'll say it again and again until it sinks in!"

"Claudia," I said patiently. "Isn't everything these days about image? PR? Spin? The truth is irrelevant, it's what you *seem* to be that counts. And if I seem to be a, a good-time girl"—I cringed—"then who the hell is going to believe that I didn't ask for it? Deserve it? Want it? There's no way I'm adding to my misery by telling the police and having them sneer at me."

Claw shuddered. "Christ, Hol. Where's your faith in human nature. Don't answer that one. But, Jesus, no one *deserves* to be raped. Could any person, any decent person, believe that a woman could do anything that would make her *deserve* to be raped? I mean, even if you were walking naked down a dark road late at night and it happened, yes, you were being reckless, but would people think you *deserved* it then? I mean, if a man walks down a road late at night and gets beaten up by thugs, do people think *he* deserves it? Or is it just women who deserve punishment? Christ almighty, what kind of sick society do we—"

The phone rang.

I jumped up, glad of the excuse. Unfortunately, Emily had also jumped up, and I trod heavily on her paw. The resulting yowl and bolt slowed me down, so Claudia answered.

"Oh, hi . . . Can you speak to me? She's busy right now . . . Right . . . Right . . . Oh, I see . . . Well, look, it was a misunderstanding . . . Tell him I'll call him tomorrow . . . No, tomorrow, I'm busy right now . . . Yes, I'll explain then. Yes, all right, okay, ta, Nige. Yeah, bye."

Claudia replaced the receiver and eyed me gravely.

"What now?" I said. I felt my heart sink, although frankly if it sank any lower I'd excrete it.

"Don't worry, it's nothing. I'll tell you in a sec. But it kind of fits in with my feeling that it would be good for you to report Stuart. Ah! Wait! Hear me out! You know that Nige and I have been worried about you. You might not realize it, but you've been behaving very strangely. I think the trauma has affected you in ways you don't know. It's like you've been numbed. And I'm sure it's self-protection, but it's affected your career, your friendships, everything. Girl Meets Boy is on the brink, I've got to be honest with you. You are seeing everything through a filter, you're viewing everyone and everything in relation to the rape. Everyone is being judged as if they were Stuart. Now, that's entirely understandable, Hol, but it's dangerous."

I suppose I looked dubious, because Claw continued, "That was Nige. Bernard just rang him, very upset."

I blinked. I'd forgotten about Bernard.

"Apparently, he took you out tonight because after two months of membership he *still* hadn't been matched with the only woman he wanted to be matched with—Sam. He took you out to dinner to (a) ask you if you would please, please match him with Sam, because he had a nasty feeling you weren't ever going to and he was too shy to approach her himself, and (b) to ask your advice about what he should say to her on the date to make her like him, because he's had very little experience with women and he didn't want to make a hash of it. Only he didn't get the chance because halfway through his sentence you fled to the ladies' and never came back."

Light slowly dawned. "Oh," I said. "Oh. Well, you see he was going on about there being one woman he liked and so *I* thought—"

Claudia smiled sadly. "I know. That's my point. I think if Stuart had been suffocated at birth, you'd *know* that Bernard wouldn't dream of propositioning a woman who hadn't shown any interest in him. But the rape has made you see all men as various forms of Stuart. You're stirring this trauma around your head like porridge, and it's congealing. As long as you do nothing, there's nowhere for it to go. It's just there, fermenting."

"Poor Bernard."

"Sitting in that restaurant. Nige said he waited an hour for you. He thought you had 'stomach trouble.' "

We both burst out laughing. Then we stopped, and I said, "Claw. Know what? I've made a decision. I'm reporting that bastard Stuart to the police, and may he rot in jail *and* lose his hair clump by clump."

Claudia raised her mug of cold tea and clinked it against mine. "I'll drink to that"—she glanced at its stewed contents—"even though I'd really rather not."

CHAPTER 24

When I was fifteen, an insult employed to disparage one's enemies was "She can't smile, it might crack her face!" Ooh, crushing. But when I woke up the day after talking to Claudia, my lips were so dry and chapped that when I tried to smile it *did* crack my face. Claw had slept in the spare room, and I came downstairs to find her rustling through the kitchen cupboards.

"Bread's in the freezer."

"Duh! How are you?"

I felt a swell of fear. It was a relief, her knowing. But also it made it more real. I had the sense of standing on the edge of a cliff, wondering whether or not to jump.

"Scared. I mean, how do I report it? Dial 911? It seems overdramatic. Or do I walk into the nearest police station?"

"I think we'd be better off going to the local nick. I'll come with you, won't I?"

I looked at my sister. She had the stance of a bulldog and the expression to match. "Of course."

The man at the front desk was scrawling doodles on a pad when we walked in. He seemed thrilled to see us, as if we were long-lost friends. I smiled, wondering what to say.

"Good morning. We'd like to speak to a female police officer," boomed Claw.

He cleared his throat and leaned on the counter with his elbows, hiding the doodle. "I see. And can I ask why?"

I felt Claudia tense beside me. "I need to report a . . . a sexual offense," I said quickly.

"A rape," corrected my sister.

The man coughed, looked down at his pad. "Why don't you make yourselves comfortable"—he waved at a couple of hard plastic chairs—"and I'll ring the CSU. A woman officer will be right with you. Can I get you a cup of tea?" He paused, seemed to remember something, blushed purple, then added, "Actually, I—I'm so sorry. The tea—wait here." He fled.

I smiled at Claw. "We freaked him."

Within minutes, the man reappeared with a thirty-something woman. I'd expected a blue uniform, but she was wearing a burgundy sweater and a black-and-white dogtooth-checked skirt. She had a maternal bosom and a kind face. All the same, she looked as though she could break up a fight in a pub. I decided I wouldn't want to get on the wrong side of her. Her eyebrows were plucked in an I-brook-no-nonsense way.

"Hello, ladies," she said. "I'm Constable Caroline Keats from the CSU. Caroline."

We introduced ourselves. I blurted out, "I'm the one who . . ."

She inclined her head. "Why don't you come with me, Holly? We'll go somewhere private where we can talk properly."

Claw and I followed her meekly up stairs that smelled of bleach. She had solid policewoman's calves. She led us into a small gray office. It contained a desk, a table, and three chairs. It was the kind of place that makes you understand why people have to be paid to come in to work.

"I'd say make yourselves comfortable," said Caroline, wrinkling her nose, "but I'm not sure that's possible. Phew, it's stuffy in here. Do you want me to open a window?"

"I'm fine, thank you," I said. I smiled faintly and sat down. "I'm probably wasting your time."

Caroline regarded me gravely. "All the women say that. It's very rarely the case."

I noticed a notebook on the table and felt even worse.

"It happened ages ago. Three and a half weeks. I don't know why I'm here. It's not like he dragged me off the street. It was in my house, we'd been on a date."

Claudia clenched her fists but kept quiet. Caroline leaned forward. "Holly. It doesn't matter where the assault took place. If he had sex with you and you didn't consent to it, that's rape. And very few rapes are stranger rapes. In most cases, the attacker is a known person, a boyfriend or a colleague. Do you know his name?"

"Stuart," I said. "Stuart Marshall. He's a solicitor." Caroline wrote in her notebook, then placed it on the table.

"First things first," she said. "Tea or coffee?"

"Coffee," I squeaked. "Coffee," echoed Claudia. "Please," we added in chorus. Caroline disappeared and reappeared with mugs and a biscuit tin on a tray. The best of police hospitality, I thought, feeling undeserving. I hoped there were chocolate digestives.

"They always include those glazed pink ones," she said. "Waste of a good biscuit, as far as I'm concerned."

I peered into the tin, pleased to see browns among the pinks.

"Now," said Caroline. "Why don't I explain what we can do for you. Your attack occurred a while back, so it's very unlikely that there's still forensic evidence on you. But we still offer you the choice to see our forensic medical examiner. More for your health than for evidential reasons. She's very gentle."

My heart sank. There *was* no evidence. "He . . . he wore a condom. So . . . and I washed all my clothes in a boil wash." It took me a while to get the words out. "And I've had sex since."

Caroline nodded and scribbled. "Don't worry about that. To be honest, after all this time, it's irrelevant. Ideally, we'd still like you to be examined, Holly, but it's *your* choice. We certainly won't make you do anything you don't want to do. How do you feel about it?"

I nodded, not because I wanted to. "Fine," I lied. At least I'd had a bath.

Caroline smiled a sympathetic smile. "I know it's not pleasant. But we want to do as much as we can. After that, I'd like to sit and talk to you and take a long statement. How does that sound?"

I nodded. "Fine."

"Now tell me, Holly, what do you want us to do with this man?"

I blinked, surprised at the question. Was Stuart's punishment up to *me*?

"Well, I suppose . . . arrest him!"

I blushed at my boldness, but Caroline nodded, a satisfied nod. "I only ask because some women *don't* want us to arrest the man. And if they don't want that, there's not much we can do."

I swallowed. "Would I have to go to court?"

"Not necessarily. If it went to court, you could give evidence via a video link. And if you do go to court, you'll remain anonymous. You do have options."

I sighed.

Caroline smiled. "Tell you what. Why don't I explain what tends to happen? After your examination, we'll sit down—and it doesn't have to be today, it's whenever you prefer—and you can tell me what happened from beginning to end. How you met him, where he lives, details, what happened at the time of the rape, anything you remember like moles, scars, a peculiar smell, a complete description. I'm what they call a chaperone. I'll be with you right through the investigation, and if you remember anything, or want to talk, he contacts you or *anything*, you can call me. What I do then is hand over your statement to the detective investigating the crime, and CID take over. They make checks—they'll check if he has a criminal history, they'll check his address, as they'll need the front and the back covered. Then they arrest him."

Her saying it made it real. "Where will you arrest him? He'll be *so* angry."

"I know what you're saying, Holly. That's why it's important to decide now if you want him arrested."

I thought for a second, then said grimly, "I do."

Caroline nodded. "You're doing the right thing. We'll arrest him at home, either late at night or early morning. If you like, we'll tell you when we arrest him. Then he'll be brought into the station and interviewed by CID."

I felt like crying. "But what if he convinces them he didn't do it?

He's very devious. I mean, he wore a *condom.*" I paused. "I . . . see, I told you, I mean, a real rapist . . ."

Caroline shook her head. Her blond hair was shoulder length but looked to have been heated and dyed too often to swish. "There are some wicked men out there, Holly," she replied, "and they all have their methods. Let's hope he trips up in interview. He'll make out it was consenting and say he was being careful, but the condom could also mean he'd thought it out. Rape is the physical act of sexual intercourse without your consent. He forced himself onto you. And that is rape."

I could see Claudia nodding vigorously out of the corner of my eye.

My throat dried up. "I do still want him arrested. But . . . but what happens after they let him go? He'll want to kill me."

Caroline patted my arm. "If he's bailed there'll be conditions, Holly. We might put conditions on where he travels. He won't be allowed within, say, a mile of your home. He won't be allowed to contact you, and if he does you'll tell us and we'll arrest him immediately."

She made it sound so simple. As if the law could control Stuart.

I met her eyes. "Now, love," she said. "If you're ready and you're sure you want to do this, I'll take you to the examination suite. Now it's not pleasant, but Dr. Atkinson is a love, the best there is. If you've got any questions, do ask."

She led me and Claudia down another corridor and into a room that looked like a lounge belonging to a person with indiscriminate taste. "We'll chat here afterward," said Caroline. "Much nicer." I looked around. It was nice. Very unpolicey. A burgundy carpet, a sofa and easy chairs in shades of peach, and pale pink pastel walls hung with prints of flowers and fields and trees. There was even a stereo. It was softly lit and well aired. I noticed tea and coffee facilities in a corner, and another big tin of biscuits. I was beginning to understand how the Met functioned.

Caroline gestured for Claudia to sit in a comfortable chair and took me through to an adjoining room that looked like it meant business. It contained a doctor's couch, bright lights, white work surfaces, and Dr. Heather Atkinson.

She was right. Dr. Atkinson, a tall, sallow woman with thick black hair and a gentle manner, *was* a love. But even though she told me what she was doing before she did it, and kept checking if it was uncomfortable, the procedure was hateful. I felt I was living someone else's life. Afterward, Dr. Atkinson asked if I wanted to take a shower or bath. I'm not mad on other people's baths at the best of times, but the police had certainly made an effort with theirs—fluffy towels, scented soaps, lotions, and potions—and I did feel better for it. I thought of all the women who must have tried to purify themselves here.

When I returned to what, when they forgot themselves, the police referred to as the rape suite, Caroline was sitting in a hard-backed chair next to a small table and Claudia was hunched in one of the squashier chairs. She was clasping her hands around her knees, and Caroline seemed to be reassuring her. Both of them jumped up when they saw me.

"Are you all right?"

She must have piles of paperwork to get through, and she was treating me like an honored guest! I nodded. The tears threatened to roll if I spoke.

"Are you hungry?" asked Caroline. "Anything you want. Sandwiches, McDonald's, steak and chips—just say. We can't have you answering questions on an empty stomach."

My request of a baked potato with tuna and cheese was granted. Another female police officer delivered it, and when she left the room I burst into tears. Caroline looked concerned but didn't say anything. She nudged the box of tissues on the table toward me. Claudia said, "Steady on, Hol, you haven't *tasted* it yet."

I giggled while sniffing—a move which nearly resulted in a bogey bubble. "I feel so bad, coming here, all this."

"Holly," said Caroline patiently—she seemed to have infinite patience—"you were the victim of a crime, and the man who did it deserves to be inside. I *want* you to be here, I *need* you to tell me. This is what I'm here for. He violated you. He needs catching. You have nothing to feel guilty about. Remember that." She stopped. "You're doing the right thing. It's good to release your feelings. I've seen girls who bottle it up and they're ruined forever. Listen. If you don't feel up to it today, we can wait a few days and take your statement then. You're in control, okay. You're the boss. Do you want to go for a wee?"

I sighed. "No. Today is fine."

She smiled. "Now what about making a start on that potato, it's starting to shrivel."

Claudia, who'd requested a cheese sandwich, bit into it and said, "Nice." I could tell she was trying to be unobtrusive. She hadn't worn her red patent-leather boots. "Hol," she added, "I'm going to give a statement too. It's going to be fine."

I glanced at Caroline to see if she too thought it was going to be fine. Her face was a mask.

I finished my potato and we began my statement. ("This is going to be hard work," warned Caroline, "so if at any time you want to stop, you tell me.") Claudia was ushered off to a less fluffy room to give *her* statement. ("We don't want Claudia being influenced by what you say, Holly. I'd rather she wasn't here if she wants to make a statement, do you see?") At first, I talked and talked—only two panic attacks, not bad, considering—and Caroline listened.

Then she asked me a stream of questions I thought I'd already covered.

When did I first meet Stuart? Describe him. When did it start? How did he behave toward me on the first date? How did he respond when I asked him not to mess about in the plane? Had I ever given any indication that I wanted a relationship? Were there any indications on the evening of the assault? What were my feelings toward him when he first arrived? Were the drinks he bought me normal drinks? Did he drink? Did I feel drunk? Did I feel he tricked me into letting him into the house? What was I wearing?

"A pink top, but it wasn't that low-cut," I said quickly.

Caroline shook her head. "Listen, love. It was a party. You're entitled to wear what you damn well please. I've always said if you've got it, flaunt it. It doesn't matter what you were wearing in *that* sense. I'm asking—well, we ask to find out how exactly the act was committed."

What did you say when he started kissing you? What were his hands doing? What did he do after you said no? Was there any conversation? What were your hands doing?

This particular query started me off on a snivel. "I opened my mouth to scream, but nothing came out. I tried at first to push him, but I was too scared. I couldn't fight him, I didn't know how. I feel like I let him do it," I wailed. I felt my throat beginning to close. I fought it, squeezed the sides of the chair so hard I broke a nail.

"Holly, try to control your breathing," said Caroline. "Slow . . . breathe out for a count of three . . . and in for a count of five. Okay. Owwwwt . . . and iiiiiiin. Good. Perhaps you'd like a sip of water?"

"I feel like I let him do it," I said again, when my windpipe allowed me.

Caroline tutted. "You did *not* let him do it. You didn't want him to kiss you, and if he was a gentleman he would have left immediately. You don't even know if his dizziness was real. You told him to stop kissing you. What did he do next?"

I dabbed my eyes with a tissue. "He sort of pushed me to the floor."

"Well, that in itself is not the action of a normal person."

How exactly did he push you to the floor? Did he try and touch your breasts or any part of your anatomy? Try to remember exactly what happened. Was he talking? Trying to kiss you? Were his legs now pinning you to the ground in any way? What can you remember about him? Was he already aroused? Had he dropped his trousers? Was he wearing underpants? Did you see him put on the condom?

I didn't know that many questions existed, although Caroline took care not to overwhelm me. We had more biscuit breaks than at Girl Meets Boy, which is saying something. When, for the third time, she queried a specific detail about—as she always put it—"the time of the rape," I started to feel odd.

"Feel sick. Do you think I could have another glass of water?" The act of breathing didn't appear to be delivering oxygen to my brain. I felt dizzy, my hearing went, and my vision turned blotchy with yellow and orange light. Even though I was sitting down, I feared I might collapse. I ripped off my cardigan, unbearably hot. It was as if gravity had left my head and it might detach itself from my neck and float off, a highly unpleasant sensation. So *that's* what light-headedness feels like, I realized a second later. Far worse than it sounds.

"Come and lie on the sofa," said Caroline, hauling me there as she spoke with strong hands. She sped over with a glass of water. "Here, lie down, rest your legs up the back. That's it, upside-down, let the blood flow to your head."

The feeling passed after five minutes and I felt foolish. I also felt relieved that with all the physical symptoms I'd had that day, I hadn't flashed back. It had only happened twice and, oh my God, that *feel*-back, when I relived the sensation of that man shoving into me. But never in my life did I want to experience those mind tricks again. It was like my brain was punishing me, sending me back to my worst nightmare for being stupid. Since I'd confided in Claudia, neither the flash- or feel-backs had recurred, but I no longer knew what my subconscious was capable of, what would trigger it to mischief.

"I think that's enough for today," said Caroline, shutting her notebook.

"I'm all right now, really," I insisted.

"I can see you are, but I think *I* need a break. I'm not made of such strong stuff as you are. Would you like to talk again tomorrow? You don't have to come back to the nick—I mean, station. If you prefer, I could come to your house."

"You'd come to my *house*?" I squeaked. I couldn't believe it. I had to say it—I was, after all, my mother's daughter—"You're being so . . . so *thoughtful*. I—I didn't realize the police were like that to ra— People like me."

Caroline smiled tightly. "We didn't used to be and, quite rightly, various agencies kicked up a stink about it. So much so that specific guidelines were issued by the government that have to be strictly adhered to. I say it's a shame that some people have to be *ordered* to be kind. Still, a lot of progress has been made. Anyway, what time is good? Ten-thirty? Very civilized! I'll bring the biscuits, shall I?"

I smiled. "I've always got. Thank you, Caroline. You've been really great."

She put her hand on my arm. "No, Holly, *you've* been great. Look, here's my direct line, give me a call between now and then if you need to. For any reason. Not if your lights fuse, I'm hopeless at DIY—but seriously. If anything bothers you, anything occurs between now and tomorrow morning, I'm on the end of the phone. And if I'm not, someone here can contact me. Okay?"

"It's like having an extra mum," I remarked to Claudia two days later, after emptying my memory of every tiny grain of information about Stuart and myself. By the time Caroline was satisfied with what I'd told her, I was sick of the sound of my own voice and convinced that if I never thought of or heard the name Stuart again, I'd want nothing more out of life. A good thing, surely. It was as if the more grim detail Caroline got down on paper, the less ugliness there was contaminating my head. I shouldn't have felt dirty to begin with, but after giving a statement, I felt cleansed. Weak and more terrified than ever, but cleansed all the same.

CHAPTER 25

The first thing I did on returning to work was to pair up Sam and Bernard. What can I say? I was in the mood for love. I rang Bernard first, apologized, and explained that I'd fled the restaurant because (may God forgive me) I'd had what I thought was an epileptic fit. Before he had time to consider this whippet-thin excuse, I added that I wanted him to formally meet a gorgeous woman the following Tuesday, and would he be available? He pretended to check his diary, then said, "Yes."

Sam also admitted to being free on Tuesday. I decided to give them the last date, so it would be easier for either one to approach the subject of sharing a cab. (It's amazing, at Girl Meets Boy, how often Wimbledon turns out to be en route to Islington.)

The pile of paperwork had grown even taller in my three days of absence, yet it wasn't quite as towering as I'd expected. Fewer checks than normal. I flicked through them, biting my lip. I'd presumed on a bunch of new applications to appease the bank.

"How many new applications have we had this week?"

"Two," said Nige without turning around. He was in a growl because Claudia had refused to tell him about our secret assignment.

My stomach fluttered. Would the bank give me an overdraft extension? The office rent was reasonable, but then again I've been conditioned into thinking that £2.99 for four peaches is reasonable. I also paid Nige and Claw a proper pair-of-princesses wage. Even with the GMBites' regular payments (£50 a month, for which members were introduced to four dates—worked out according to how much one might expect to spend in one evening at a club), at this rate the agency would be out of business within months. I was aghast at how easy it was for a business to fail overnight. I remembered my accountant chirruping, "It's all about cash flow," but only now did I understand what he meant. Jesus. Three and half weeks ago we'd been celebrating its success! I scribbled figures on a scrap of paper and tried to do sums. The calculator refused to be optimistic, so I shoved it and the scrap of paper in a drawer.

I couldn't concentrate for more than three minutes. Swelling in my mind like a great pink bubble of gum was the imminent arrest of Stuart. Claudia did her best to distract me. I did my best too. I thought of how happy Bernard and Sam would be together, and how I was possibly engineering the most important evening of two people's lives. I told myself that I was right to go to the police. I reminded myself of Caroline's approval. I thought of her as a supplement to my mother. Your real parents cannot fulfill every role, so you look for substitutes to fill in the gaps. Or at least I did. My own father was terrified of money. Consequently, I thought of my accountant as a Rent-a-Dad. I worried about his diet (whenever we met for lunch he ate a lot of fatty meat) and hoped he'd keep healthy.

The truth was, Stuart's crime was adult, and yet more than ever, I felt like a child.

I concentrated on organizing Tuesday's dates and anticipated the pleasure of watching Sam and Bernard fall in love (both had guessed whom they were being matched with, and both had rung twice to ask advice on what to wear). Sam had run out of her office at lunchtime and panic-bought a pair of orange trousers and an orange shirt. Further interrogation revealed that she'd also purchased a pair of orange boots. "But you restrained yourself from snapping up the orange hat and gloves?" I said. "Yes," she wailed, "but I've spent one hundred and seventy-eight pounds and I look like a satsuma!" Her excitement made me feel ashamed for not matching them before.

But on the Date Night in question, Stuart was arrested. After Caroline rang to tell me, I had to leave the bar. I couldn't be among people. Now he *knew* what I'd done. Claudia didn't feel right buying me an ice cream, so instead she bought me the grown woman's equivalent—a beauty treatment. I've never had much patience with beauty treatments. Yeah, I want to be beautiful, but I find the actual beautifying process too tedious to bear. To me, a facial is as spirit-sapping as a trip to a lumberyard. Claudia knows this, which is why she treated me (if that's the right word and I'm not sure it is) to a variation.

"The GoodLife Health Center's Alternative Health Assessment. Wow. What is it?"

"I haven't had one, but a friend has and she said it's excellent. It's a complementary medicine clinic. I don't know exactly, but I think they test you for food allergies and recommend you a health plan. I thought it would be good for you, relaxing. You need pampering, girl."

I think what she meant was that my body needed some positive input. She assumed this would do it. (And quite right, for seventy-five quid.) Claw takes an obsessive interest in her own health. Whereas I don't smoke and presume that, granted this favor, my innards will take care of themselves. Claw once went to a clinic and announced she'd cheated on her boyfriend abroad and was scared she'd caught a terminal disease. "And so they gave me every test known to man." Naively, I said, "But you don't *have* a boyfriend. And you haven't been abroad!"

The difference between us is, I don't trouble my body unless it troubles me. Healthwise, I operate on a need-to-know basis. If I'm tired, I put it down to "life" and go to bed early. Claudia taps familydoctor.org into her search engine and investigates the possibility of lupus.

All the same, I looked forward to my appointment as if it were a trip to the seaside. A break, from everything, a little boost. So it was a great shame that, spiritually, the GoodLife Health Assessment proved to be a monstrous error. I sat with an electrical device in my hand while a white-coated woman named Amilie made herself look busy on a computer. Miraculously, after half an hour of drawing a bleeper pen across the screen, Amilie pronounced my fatty tissues, joints, liver, and stomach "stressed" and declared that various other organs—including my heart—were "weakened."

"What?" I croaked. "You're saying I've got a weak heart?"

She smiled, as if this were funny. Her teeth were suspiciously white. "I've been checking the energy levels along your meridians. Your meridians control all the body's biochemical processes. I've used acupressure points along your meridians to measure the energy levels within your organs. High energy reveals that an organ is stressed, low energy reveals that it's weakened."

"Right," I said, not understanding, and feeling too embarrassed to inquire if I had months or weeks.

As if this wasn't enough of a blow, Amilie also discovered that I was missing crucial digestive enzymes. She seemed to hint that it was surprising food didn't emerge from the exit in the exact same form it had been swallowed. She also found me to be intolerant to yeast, tea, red wine, cheddar cheese, lactose, cow's milk, margarine, bananas, oranges, corn, Marmite, lentils, bacon— "But I don't eat bacon."

"That's probably why you're intolerant of it." Hazelnuts, sweet potatoes, artichokes, cabbage, and mushrooms.

I was also deficient in magnesium, germanium, chromium, boron, molybdenum, zinc, vitamin B_{12}, vitamin C—"But I thought you had to be a sailor in the seventeen hundreds to be deficient in vitamin C"—vitamin B_3, vitamin P bioflavonoids, and vitamin B_5 pantothenic acid.

At this wretched point, while convinced she'd made up half those minerals, I wondered whether to dial 999 and scrawl a will on the back of my business card. I considered a boo-hoo but decided

Amilie was far too smug to cry in front of. Her tan was a little too brown, too 1984, for me to trust her entirely as a medical authority. A giggle escaped instead. Amilie looked up from the Personal Diet Recommendations sheet she was laboring over.

When she read it out I didn't listen, as I was too busy fidgeting, but I gave it a cursory glance in the cab home. I was still cross at being guilt-tripped into spending twenty quid on enzymes at the front of the clinic. The Diet Recommendations sheet could be summed up in two words: fat chance. I was to avoid all foods I was intolerant of for four weeks. I was to drink two liters of water and fresh hot lemon daily. I was to eat four fruits daily and three servings of fresh vegetables. Breakfast was to be rye toast, fresh fruit salad, and live yogurt. Lunch was to be a rice salad, a stir-fry with tofu, homemade soup, or fresh grilled fish. Or rice noodles. I should also snack on sunflower and pumpkin seeds. There was to be *no* chocolate.

This is the trouble I have with healthy eating. You have to devote your whole day to it. When you work in Central London, it's not that easy to secure yourself fresh grilled fish for lunch. This diet would only be viable if I moved to the Caribbean. Also, on the rare occasions I have the time and money to eat in a smart restaurant, if ever I try to be goodly and eat fish and vegetables, my stomach starts to rumble within half an hour of returning to the office and I'm forced to make an emergency dash to Martha's. Normal people can't exist on fish and vegetables. We need four roast potatoes and a Mars bar to complete a meal.

But I didn't wish to spit in the face of Claudia's kindness—even if the health assessment had confirmed that I was falling to bits—so I told her I'd enjoyed it. The next six weeks passed in a blur of agitation. The bank announced that if I didn't take control of my finances they'd call in my overdraft. This might have played on my mind, were it not for the fact that I had more imminent concerns: any given moment I expected Stuart to hammer down my door and throttle me. If ever I was in the street—rare—I'd brace myself to be gunned down by a hired hit man. I also thought incessantly about the CPS, imagining a fusty gaggle of gray-haired men and women, poring over my files by candlelight, adjusting their pince-nez.

So when, early one Friday morning, Caroline rang me at home and asked if she could pop around with the investigating DI, the sickness rose to my throat. I had a bath, peered blearily at my face in the mirror—purple eye bags, blotchy skin tone, presumably this was routine when you reached thirty—and dressed in black. Any other color would be tempting fate. *Two* police officers. I opened a fresh pack of biscuits. Then I sat and drummed my fingers on the table, watching the clock tick. Had Emily not brought in a mouse to while away the minutes until the doorbell rang, I'd have dissolved with anxiety.

The second I saw Caroline, I knew it was bad news. Her fiercely blond hair was stiffer than ever, and she wore no makeup. Her face was grave. She'd chosen a longer skirt than normal. The DI, whom she introduced as George, was also in plainclothes. He was friendly but subdued. They still looked like coppers, and I bet all the neighbors were agog. I led them into the lounge as if I were in a dream.

Caroline didn't hesitate. She looked me dead-on and said, "Holly, I am really sorry. The CPS have decided not to prosecute."

I stood up. "Wait a minute." I strode into the kitchen and carried the tray of coffee and biscuits into the lounge. Neither of them took any, so I just served without asking. I was biting my teeth together so hard I'm surprised they didn't crumble in my mouth. Then I said in a dull voice, "So they didn't believe me."

George looked apologetic, like it was his fault. He glanced at Caroline. She said, "Holly. *We* believe you. These people don't know you. It's difficult because after nearly a month there's going to be less forensic evidence than you'd get with a recent rape. At the end of the day it's your word against his." She paused. "But, love, we'd hope that you did feel better for telling us. And if he does it again we'll know, because you were brave enough to come forward and tell us."

I said, "Why didn't they believe me?"

Caroline sighed. "They haven't seen you, they don't know what you're like. I believe you. George believes you. You have to trust us that we dealt with it as thoroughly as we could. But . . . if you haven't got the evidence, you have to rely on someone else's mistakes somewhere else along the line."

I stared ahead at the orange wall. Nick and I had painted this room together. Painted, sex break, painted, sex break. That's the beginning of a relationship for you. We were happy then. Everything he said turned to gold. I felt like a goddess. Even when I peed in the toilet and Nick shouted from the bedroom, "Oi! Who brought that horse in here?" Even then, with my unladylike bladder, I was the most desirable woman in the world. I could do no wrong. I was loved by the one I loved, and there was no greater achievement. How did I get to *this*? I knew Stuart wouldn't slip up.

George coughed and spoke. "Holly, it doesn't necessarily mean the CPS didn't *believe* you, rather that they don't think the balance of evidence is in your favor."

I unfocused on the wall and refocused on George. "So they decided not to waste their money on a court case."

He grimaced. "You did everything you could, Holly. I'm very sorry you've been let down."

Caroline glanced at George and said, "Off the record, Holly— and I'm speaking as a friend, not an officer—we don't rate the CPS. They're not paid enough, they're not given enough time to consider cases. They'll turn up in court and they'll have not even read the papers properly. It's not the first time this has happened. I'm sorry. I hate to be the bearer of bad news."

George remained impassive. He took a bite of ginger biscuit, one of the most boring biscuits there is. I could tell he wished that Caroline had kept her mouth shut about not rating the CPS, and that cheered me slightly. He swallowed and said, "The trouble is, Holly, that Stuart maintained you'd consented, and it was going to be very difficult for you to prove that you didn't consent. *We* know you didn't, we know he's a right nasty bastard, 'scuse my French, but people who don't know you don't. And I know that right now this isn't any consolation—it would have been very traumatic to put yourself through that in court."

I took a gulp of coffee and felt it burn. "So . . . so what happens to Stuart now?"

Caroline's mouth drooped in sympathy. "When the CPS decides to drop a case, the bail conditions no longer apply. But," she added hurriedly, "if he even comes near you, we'll nick him under the harassment act. We'll give him a caution, he'll be arrested. If it happens again you can get an injunction against him."

"And so," I said, in the same dead voice, "does Stuart get to hear about what they decided?"

George replied, "I call him into the station and tell him that all charges have been dropped and no further action is being taken."

"When?"

George looked as if he wanted to sink through the polished walnut floor. "It looks like later this morning."

Caroline cried, "Holly, I'm so sorry. You know we'd give anything for it to be different. Do you want me to give Claudia a ring, see if she can come 'round and be with you?"

"I don't know," I said. It was true. The world was flat, the sky was green. I didn't know anything anymore.

CHAPTER 26

Two days later I got glandular fever. Do not ask me how. It's also known as "the kissing disease," and it's caused by a virus that happens to be a member of the herpes family. As if Fate hadn't kicked enough sand in my face, she was now tipping it over my head with a bucket. (Issy has a client named Mrs. Slapper, the mention of which gave the office a morning of hilarity—"And so, are you a London Slapper or a Manchester Slapper?" But even Mrs. Slapper didn't have to suffer the indignity of a personal association with the herpes family.)

Anyway, I was glad of it. Glandular fever saved me from consciousness. Being conscious proved a waste of time. Any moment I was awake was inescapable hell. I was in shock. I took it personally.

Before, it was one person. Now, it was the world. I couldn't believe they'd do this to me. It had taken me long enough—even Stuart had failed to make me feel like this, but the Crown Prosecution Service had succeeded. For the first time, I felt like a victim. The trauma seeped into me, I was saturated with it. I found myself screaming, "I'll kill them, I'll firebomb their offices, the fucking bastards!" If I wasn't screaming (unwise, with glandular fever), I cried noisily until my eyes were dry and sore.

Slowly, I graduated to a prison of ifs. If this, if only that. If only I'd reported it right after he'd left. If only I hadn't let him in my house in the first place. If only I wasn't such a bungler. What if he does it again, to someone else? What if he's *done* it again? It will be my fault. And the fucking Crown Prosecution Service's, the fucking bastards. I'll firebomb their offices, etcetera . . .

Yes, everyone was trying to train me to not feel responsible for Stuart's actions, but that was easier said than done. I always feel responsible for other people's actions. As if feeling responsible for my own isn't enough of a burden. I felt dreadful, and when your throat is as sore as if you'd swallowed hot coals, you have a temperature of 103, your skin is tinged yellow, lending you a startling resemblance to Marge Simpson, you're sweating obscenely, and your tonsils are swollen to three times their size, you do not require extra helpings of dreadfulness.

The only piece of cheer was that the doctor had told me to avoid sports. Actually, that's a lie. There were a few pieces of cheer. One of the nicest episodes—and this may sound weird—was when Claudia asked Nige to drive us to the doctor. I felt so weak and tired I could barely walk. I fell asleep in the car on the way home and half woke to find Nige carrying me into the house and upstairs to bed, Claudia on his tail. It reminded me of one of the best memories of childhood, when you return from a day out so woozy that your parents wrap you in a blanket like a bug in a leaf and lovingly transport you to the Land of Nod.

Claudia was wonderful. She kept reassuring me that she, Issy, and Nige would take good care of Girl Meets Boy while I rested. Well, she and Issy would. I tried to look grateful and probably failed. Nige had been asked to audition as the understudy of a Hollywood actor who was starring in *Cat on a Hot Tin Roof* in the West End, and his agent thought it was "ninety-nine percent" he'd get the part. Claw expected he'd be overjoyed, but Nige was being snooty. Apparently, you can be *too* good at being an understudy. Your fabulous reputation spreads, you're only ever offered parts as an understudy, and you never step onstage again. Also, he'd asked to view his dressing room and it was the size of a cleaning cupboard, with a view of a redbrick wall and a dead pigeon impaled on a railing. Nige's only chance of glory would be if I came backstage as a "fan," kissed the star on the mouth, and gave him glandular fever.

Secretly, I felt that Girl Meets Boy was doomed (I had made no attempt to pay back my overdraft), and it didn't bother me. Why should it? I wanted to spite the world with a show of indifference. If I didn't care, then no one could hurt me more than they already had. The truth? While the shock wore off, my anger remained white-hot. Problem was, as the virus set in I no longer had the strength to voice it, not even inwardly. To feel anger, let alone act on it, requires energy. Your heart pounds, your blood boils, the thoughts race. Self-pity was a more languid emotion, easier to wallow in. There was a deep and savage wound to the heart, as if the bigger children had picked on me in the playground because I smelled, and when I'd told the teachers, they'd laughed at me and agreed.

I knew Caroline spoke the truth when she said she believed me. But the CPS deciding not to prosecute intensified the pain. They were denying that I'd suffered. It was as if the authorities (and my parents had—wrongly, it seemed—brought me up to respect authority) had sneered at what I'd gone through, dismissed it as unimportant. I was a subject who paid my taxes, and yet my country had decided that I wasn't worth wasting time or money on. Yes, it was Stuart's word against mine, but why wasn't my word deemed as good as his? He'd be laughing at me. He'd got away with it. And they'd let him. Call me naive, I was a white, middle-class girl. I'd *expected* justice.

Claudia understood, even though I didn't say anything. She asked my permission to organize a rota with my mother and Gloria, so that I was never left long in the house alone. Frankly, I didn't give a damn. So what if Stuart decided to break in and kill me for squealing? I toyed with the notion of fetching my favorite knife from the kitchen to fight back, but I had too much of a headache. If he murdered me, at least then he'd go to jail. This time I'd take precautions to ensure a conviction. I'd scratch him, to obtain some under-the-fingernail DNA for whoever it was in London that did Patricia Cornwell's job. And I'd paint "Stuart Marshall did it" on the wall in my own blood. (Or "Stuart M.," depending on how fast I was dying.)

I'd forbidden Claudia to tell anyone, and I was sure she'd kept her word. I was humiliated, and recent events had added to my humiliation. I didn't want to tell my friends because the implication of the CPS deciding not to prosecute was—even though Caroline insisted it wasn't—that I'd been lying. I could do without Rachel and Nige whispering that I must have wanted to punish Stuart for luring me into casual sex. That I was one of those psychotic women who wanted to be a lady and was furious at the man for making her a slut instead, that if I accused him of sexual assault, then I could hang on to my Victorian self-image.

I suppose it was harsh of me to suppose that Nige would think any such thing. There was no danger of him having any opinion on the subject, as he simply wasn't the sort of person who was deeply interested enough in others to suspect anything other than what he'd been told. (Despite his frequent claim, "I *love* other people, that's why I became an actor.") As far as he knew, I had glandular fever, and Claudia asked him to come over to entertain the invalid occasionally. Again, he didn't question it, because he thought of himself as an entertainer. (Or rather, *artiste.*) He just sat at the end of my bed and talked.

"And so this guy actually turned up at the office and said he wanted me to cancel his membership and return his check because he'd seen the news report and as far as he could tell the agency was full of ugly, selfish people. So *I* said, by all means, I'll cancel it, return your check—great, fine by me, there'll be one less ugly, selfish person on our books! Well, I'm sorry. But, darling, good news—*Glamour* might want to do a feature on us. It's not certain, but they might be sending someone down next week. Let's hope we haven't folded by—ah, only joking. Did I tell you about the new girl this Tuesday? The one who'd asked on her membership form not to meet any accountants? Oh, you'd have laughed. Turned up utterly wasted. She was so drunk by date three we had to lift her out of the toilet. I'm half considering calling up some of the rejects we have on our perpetual waiting list. You know that hairy one with a mono-brow and a beard—a *beard* at thirty-two? I mean, is he a tramp? Who's rung us once a week for the last nine months and just *will* not get the message? He turned up at Seb's this week! I'm serious! Came and sat at the bar. I wanted Seb to throw him out, told him to say they had a "no-beard" policy, and believe me, Seb wanted to, but there's enough going on in his toilets that he'd rather not be reported to the cops. So anyway, this creep just *sat* there, ogling our women, and every time there was a break he'd try to buy them a drink. Happily, as he looked like some escapee from the Taliban, he got short shrift . . . Oh look, it's your ghastly friend Rachel . . ."

"Hello, babes, how you doing? Did I hear a prat squeak? Sweetie, I've brought you some caviar and a spoon, only for some reason your bossy little sister wouldn't let me bring it upstairs."

I turned to face the wall, but Rachel stayed regardless, she and Nige talking over each other until Claudia marched in and ejected them. She sat down on the edge of the bed.

"Careful," I croaked. "Emily's under there."

"Ugh," said Claudia. "So unhygienic."

Emily was indeed under the covers. She liked me to sleep on my back, bow-legged, so that she could curl up between my knees. It was a highly uncomfortable habit that had started with Nick. We understood each other about Emily. We always placed her bowl on a sheet of the *Guardian* and if she disliked her food she'd rake at the newspaper, like she raked at her litter tray after making a de-posit. A devastating critique of the catering. We'd hear her rustling and I'd say, "Emily's reading the mewspaper again." Nick would reply, "Yeah, looking for the miaowsic section." I'd add, "She hates their coverage of current a-furrs." Nick would retort, "She prefers the litters page." Silly. But *us*.

We hadn't spoken since Penge. Another reason why it was nice to escape to unconsciousness.

"Listen," said Claw. "Gloria guessed. She found all the leaflets Caroline gave you in the drawer. But! Before you get upset. She, uh, well, she wanted to talk to you. It, uh, happened to a cousin of hers. In different circumstances. She was living in the States. New York. This guy dragged her off the street into a park. After, he tried to slit her throat, but someone came along and he ran off."

With effort, I lifted myself onto my elbows. "Why are you telling me this?" I said.

Claw looked uncomfortable, and not because she was perching on the edge of the bed with half a buttock. "Gloria's cousin got a conviction. But, well, Gloria says that the American police were really unsympathetic—brusque and unsupportive, didn't even examine her in private—and the whole court process was so disgusting that if she'd known what she was going to have to go through, the cousin wouldn't have even reported it. She said she felt like a fish being gutted. Her whole life was twisted 'round by the defense to make her look like a lying tart. She felt like *she* was the one on trial, not her attacker. She said it was like being abused all over again. So Gloria thought—"

"She thought wrong. I'm not interested in other people right now."

This was a lie, of course. I was interested. It was like discovering someone had attended the same (rather horrible) school as you. But if I expressed enthusiasm, Claudia might think I was coming out of my hypersulk and that this terrible news was a comfort to me. I wanted to make it plain that I was inconsolable. This was the only means I had to convey to everyone that my wretchedness was not some transitory emotion that could be jollied away with the thrilling lure of other people's woes. The justice system might not give two hoots, but my misery was serious to *me*. Unlike Gloria, I did *not* have a guardian angel.

Wisely, Claudia suggested I get some sleep and shut the door. She didn't bother me with chat again until a few days later, when the fever began to lift. I could tell my health was improving because I had a sudden hankering. When I was at junior school, I thought all the food they served apart from cabbage was delicious. (And compared with my mother's food, it was.) I loved the roast dinners—

I used to stuff the skinny slices of beef into my Yorkshire pudding and spoon the gravy on top. I drooled over the Rice Krispies syrup cakes, the chocolate brownies with a silvery-baked crust. But my great favorite was cornflake-and-chocolate-goo squares, and this was the craving that dragged me from my slump.

Claw," I said, when she trotted in with my daily mug of spinach soup. (Shop-bought—Claudia and I take after my mother. Mum had offered to cater for the duration of my illness, but added in the same breath, "Although, dear, Dad says you'll recover health much faster if we do a big shop at Tesco instead." As soggy potatoes and Sahara turkey—named by Claw because it was so dry it sucked the moisture from your mouth—were still fresh in my memory from that last stay in Penge, I'd graciously surrendered.) "Claw, remember the cornflake-and-chocolate-goo squares at junior school?"

"Yup."

"I'd die for one of those. I wonder if they still make them. I'd pay you to ring up the kitchen and get the recipe."

Claudia plonked the spinach soup in front of me on its tray. "Now you're taking liberties. Drink this, it's obviously doing you good."

Then she took up her usual position on the edge of the bed and cleared her throat. "And now you're getting better, I wanted to talk to you about something."

"Have you thrown away Rachel's caviar from Wednesday?"

"Straight in the trash."

"Pity, Emily might have liked it. I don't think she's ever tried caviar."

"Holly, that creature licks her own arse and eats flies, but I suspect that even she would draw the line at caviar. That stuff is revolting. The idea, the texture, the taste. Ugh. There's no *need* to eat food like that. It's like people who eat pig's feet. *Why?* What's wrong with a cheese sandwich?"

"So. What did you want to tell me?"

Claw wiggled her foot, a nervous habit. "Okay. Good news, bad news. Stuart is still representing Mum and Dad. I didn't want to tell you before. Camille says it looks as if he's going to brazen it out. He's guessing you haven't told them—or obviously they'd have sacked him immediately."

"Wait. You told *Camille* about what he did?"

"Shit, Hol, I had to. No one else, though."

"Oh great. Great. Brilliant."

"Look, it's okay. You'll see, let me explain. So anyway, we reckon that Stuart thinks that to relinquish Mum and Dad as clients would be like admitting his guilt. Also, Hol, he wants to spite you. He can't believe you reported him. He knows this is the last thing you'd want."

I felt my body cinch itself in, smaller, tenser. "Like he hasn't done enough."

Claudia touched my arm. "Yeah, but wait. He also *needs* to keep representing Mum and Dad."

"Why?"

"Because he's a fucking crook, that's why. Listen to this. Mum and Dad trust him, you know what they're like, anyone in a suit is God. So, three weeks ago, Stuart informed them that he would supervise Granny's house clearance. Camille says Stuart always uses the same valuers, the people who assess how much the assets are worth, to get a valuation for probate. Because you have to pay tax on the estate, yeah? Anyway, Stuart invited Mum and Dad down in a way that made it clear they'd be in the way, so they didn't go. So anyway, it all seems fine. Then, a week or so ago, Camille couldn't find some file, got in a flap, and ended up ransacking random drawers. And she flipped through some papers in an unmarked file. Documents for a property in France. And she wouldn't have thought anything of it, but the name on one of the documents caught her eye. *Mildred Chattersby*."

"But that's Granny's name!"

"Pre-cisely!"

"Wait a sec. How did Camille know that was Granny's name?"

"Oh, well, you see, I'd told her. We were, um, talking about Granny at, ah, your birthday party. So anyway, Camille had been given the list of assets to type up and she knew the—"

"But, Claw, we know about Granny's house in the Dordogne. It's a smelly shack. Mum and Dad know about it—"

"No, Hol, this is a *second* house! Well, not a house, a flat. A huge penthouse apartment in Paris. It seems that Granny bought it about twenty years ago as an investment and rented it out. Mum and Dad didn't know about it, no one did. And Stuart's aware of that because he asked them to give him a rundown of Granny's assets abroad. He must have come across the flat details when he cleared the Wiltshire house. Granny probably kept them under her bed or something. And he's not declared it, it's not on the list that Camille was asked to type up. Camille made a point of asking Stuart if this was the final list and he said yes. That's when she got suspicious."

"But . . . the evidence seems a bit thin. What if it's just a separate file because that's how he does his filing?"

"Then why's it unmarked? And why isn't it included on the final list?"

"So what do you plan to do? Shop Stuart to the police?"

Claudia chose to ignore the sarcastic edge to my voice.

"Uh, we could, but Camille thinks we need to let him go further. She thinks he's embezzled from previous clients, but he's very careful. He only does it rarely and he only defrauds certain types. Camille thinks if we wait a while, Stuart will—oh I don't know how it works—but, well, at some point he gets the grant of probate. Then he'll send it off on behalf of the executors to the French lawyers, and presumably they'll release the cash for the flat or the deeds to whatever account Stuart specifies. And Camille reckons it *won't* be the client account. I mean, we've got to be careful, we're not certain yet, because if we *were* certain that Stuart was a raving crook, then Camille said we could get done if we didn't report it immediately."

My head boggled and I said so.

She grinned and replied, "Holly, Stuart is going *down!*"

I tried not to smile and succeeded. "Claw, I'm glad you're so sure, although I think you should know better by now. I really hope Camille hasn't got it wrong. Are you sure we can trust her? I mean, why's she doing all this detective work on our behalf?"

Claudia grinned again, this time a bashful, blushy sort of grin, and said, "Mm . . . could be because I'm sleeping with her."

CHAPTER 27

G*ah?*"

I instantly realized that, were *I* to announce myself a lesbian, I wouldn't have wished my sister's reaction to be "Gah?" So, quickly, I said, "What, you're *gay?*"

Ingenious. I was no better than Caroline's classmate who spotted her in her police uniform in a police van one Saturday night and said, "Caroline! Are you in the police?" (Caroline told me she'd replied, "No . . . this is for a fancy dress party." She'd patted the side of the van and added, "Thought I'd make an effort.")

Even faster, I added, "That's great!" And even faster, "Sorry. How patronizing. Like the Wimbledon champion congratulating the guy who came second. Sorry. God. I mean, it's great that you, that you've found what you were looking for. It's just that I . . . I had no idea. And you're my *sister!*"

Claudia giggled. "That's exactly why you had no idea."

If I'd had it my own way I'd have sat with my jaw agape for a good four minutes, so a hasty compromise was called for. I wasn't sure if I should give her a congratulatory hug or if that was patronizing too. Then I gave her one anyway, because I could see she was so happy. As I released her, she wiped her eyes.

I paused. "I want to ask loads of questions, but they're probably all grossly ignorant. I don't want to offend you."

Claudia shrugged. "Try."

"Well. How long have you known? I mean, your last boyfriend . . ."

"Seven years ago. Yeah. It was like kissing a girl you don't fancy."

"Jesus. I know nothing about your life!"

Claudia laughed. "It's not wildly different from how you imagined it was five minutes ago. Just substitute the gender. I think I've always known. It wasn't something I had to fight myself about, because this way it just felt right. Infinitely better. Like, 'Okay, *now* I understand!' I was relieved when I knew. It felt normal. But I—well, you never know what your family will think."

I was hurt. "What, even me?"

"Oh, Hol. I should have known you'd be cool with it, but this, it's so much a part of who I am that, well, you want to protect yourself. You're scared of telling the people who matter, because if they had a problem with it, then it would be very difficult. You know, it's like what Nick once said when one of Bo's friends referred to 'the Paki shop.' He said to her, 'I can find no redeeming qualities in a racist.' That's how I feel about homophobia. And racism too, obviously. So there's a lot at stake. I mean, if you don't have a problem, it's not a big deal. It's merely a question of preference."

"So . . . so what made you decide to tell now?"

Claudia inhaled, swelling her chest like a sparrow. A grin spread wide. "I fell in love."

I blinked. "With Camille?"

Claw nodded. "I think she's wonderful."

"Coming from you, she must be."

"Oh, she is. She's brilliant. I totally respect her, she's the cleverest person I know, and very funny. And gorgeous. I feel so lucky to have met her, although . . ."

She stopped, embarrassed. I guessed what she was thinking. Mustn't boast to Holly about my wonderful life when hers is such a godalmighty mess. I gasped, "Oh, no, no, ridiculous!"

She looked down. "I do feel selfish, telling you. It seems so frivolous, with what you're going through."

"Not at all. The opposite. Please. Tell me as much good news as possible, I need to hear it. And love is never frivolous. I mean that. What could be more important than finding love?"

I wondered if I still believed it.

Claudia giggled. "Bo would say 'to be useful in life' or something."

I rolled my eyes. "Yeah, and you know how we all want to be like Bo. What a joy she is, spreading light across the world."

Claudia sighed.

"What?"

"No, nothing."

"Go on, Claw, what?"

"It's just that . . . you've got meaner, Hol. I don't mean that in a bad way. You were probably too nice. You'd never say a bad word against anyone before . . ." She trailed off.

I stared at my duvet cover. Cream, from the Conran Shop. It had looked so serene in *Elle Deco,* in a fashion designer's minimalist home in Notting Hill—all stripped, painted floorboards and antique chandeliers. "Jewelry for the house," she'd called them. I couldn't afford a chandelier that wasn't from BHS—even a tiny one from the architectural salvage company cost four hundred quid—but I was desperate at the time to reignite the spark in our relationship, and surely if I copied something perfect from the Notting Hill house, it would help. I chose the cream duvet and a week later, Nick spilled Ribena on it. I bleached it and it went blotchy. I was doomed to a non–*Elle Deco* life.

"I'm going to throw away this duvet cover and get a new one," I said.

"Okay," replied Claudia.

Claw was good like that. She wasn't the kind of person who insists on a strictly linear conversation, who pounces with a high-pitched "Where did *that* come from?" if you dare to deviate. Nor is she the sort who steams ahead with a gruesome anecdote if you ask her not to. Some people will not be stopped. Claudia was a relaxed conversationalist. Claudia was gay. Weird—not that she was gay, that she was different from how I had supposed her. But then, was she different? No. Her personality hadn't altered. Possibly my mind was clouded over with other things, but I didn't feel as if this was major news. What would change? It wasn't as if my mother was that precious about the Christmas seating plan. (Nick's and Rachel's parents insisted on boy/girl/boy/girl and invited the ghastliest of guests purely to equalize gender.)

"So," I said, such a treat, to get away from myself, "when are you going to tell Mum and Dad? And Issy?"

Claw covered her eyes. "I dread it. I don't know if I ever can."

I squealed. "Are you kidding? I'm sure they'll be happy for you."

I wasn't sure this was true. And again, it sounded patronizing, along the lines of "how *marvelous!*" As if Claudia had no legs and was running the marathon by spinning herself along in a wheelchair.

I tried to offer sense. "Or they might be a little concerned, but only for your sake, because they don't want you to get hurt. Some people are prejudiced. Mum and Dad wouldn't want you to suffer a moment's pain because of it. That's all."

"I don't know. Will it be a neighbor trauma? It will, won't it?"

"I really don't think they'll *tell* the neighbors. Not that they'll try and keep it secret, I don't mean that. They're not big gossips, that's all. Mum will tell Leila."

"Yeah, I can imagine what *she'll* have to say about it. She'll think I have AIDS! No, she'll think I fancy her! I should shave my head and pinch her bottom just to give her a thrill."

I pursed my lips. "I'm not totally sure that would help."

Claudia sighed. "You know what gets me? It's the feeling that if Leila said something snide, Mum wouldn't defend me. Even if she wanted to. She wouldn't dare offend Leila. She'd sort of laugh and say nothing. I couldn't bear that. I'd be so angry. I'd have to stop speaking to her."

She had a look on her face like the insult had actually taken place. I said, "Be calm. Mum and Dad are easygoing. They might find it a bit strange at first, but only because it's outside their experience. Once they get used to it, they'll be fine."

Claudia scowled. "I don't want them to get *used* to it. That implies there's something wrong with it."

"Sorry, but I don't think it does. Don't go in there being chippy. I really don't think it's going to be as bad as you imagine. It's not like they're not going to speak to you."

"No, but I don't want them being funny with me."

"Claw. They're reasonable people. You don't have to be afraid of telling them anything."

My sister gave me a look. "I don't see *you* rushing to confess."

I felt a throb of anger. "It's completely different. You, in essence, are telling them *good* news."

I slumped back on my pillows. My whole life was dreary. I despised my bedroom for its lack of style. It was utterly nonmagazine. I couldn't even read *Living Etc.* without spilling coffee over it. The shame was, I . . . we—Nick and me—we'd loved this house. It wasn't so special, but it appealed to us. We saw it, we knew. It had obviously belonged to an old couple, recently dead. When we viewed it, there was a checked shirt left out to dry on the washing line and an old linen nightdress hanging forlorn in the wardrobe. The paint was cracking and the carpets foul, but I knew it could be our home. That was when I was still imagining a rosy future, children playing in a garden full of apple trees and blackberry bushes.

"Anyway," I added, "I have a reason for not telling them. Didn't you just say that we've got to wait for Stuart to incriminate himself? If I tell Mum and Dad, they'll dismiss him as their solicitor and then he'll have to hand back the papers."

"Not necessarily. Why should he hand back the papers they don't know about? If you decide to tell Mum and Dad tomorrow, I'll be delighted. I had a silly notion that it would be satisfying for you if our family ended up having a hand in sending Stuart to prison. But, really, what does it matter? Camille is going to report him to the Law Society or the police. Whether she does that with or without our help is irrelevant. I just thought it would be nice for you."

My toes curled under the covers. *Nice* for me! What did she think this was? A game? On the principle that I'd feel better if I fed Stuart the parsnip that made him fart in public? I reclined against the headboard in a haughty manner, the opposite of Pollyanna.

"Nothing, Claudia, is *nice* for me," I said. "Please don't use that word. And I choose not to tell M and D for reasons you could never understand. And please remove this spinach soup, I don't want it. I want a cornflake-and-goo square."

Claw stood, tall in her heels. "Whistle for it," she replied, and stomped out. Leaving the spinach soup.

The instant the door shut, I scrambled out of bed and ran after her.

"Wait, come back."

She stopped on the stairs.

I added, "I, um, don't want the conversation to end this way.

I'm honored that you told me. And I wish you and Camille lots of happiness. I'm just . . ."

She ran back. "You're right," she said, rubbing my arm. "I can't understand how it is for you. I'm sorry too. It's just that I hate him to death for what he did to you, and I cannot stand the thought that he won't be punished. Camille was *so* certain, but I suppose she could be mistaken. This whole thing about him being a crook is unlikely. I suppose I'd just like it to be true."

We smiled at each other. A few minutes later I watched from the window as Camille's car juddered to a halt outside the house, and Claudia skipped down the path. I hadn't seen her skip since she was five.

I skipped till, well, a few months ago. Not down Oxford Street. Only in the park, and only for a few steps (Nick always there for backup), but it's surprisingly exhilarating. Adults ought to skip.

I ran a hand through my hair. It was greasy and stuck to my head. You should pull yourself out of this, I thought. It was terrifying that a single incident, and then a follow-up bit of bad news, could puncture me. The glandular fever was nothing more than a symptom.

I'd always thought of myself as tough. I hoped I was kind. But I *knew* I was tough. If I had a goal, I reached it. And if ever my life didn't go to plan, I'd bounce back. You have to. From the dishwasher leaking to being made redundant because your boss doesn't like you, life is full of injustice, and for your own sanity you cannot take it personally. Sure, you can cry in the bath—that's not weak, that's necessary—as long as it doesn't become habit. Often, happiness is a choice. You have to seek it out, whatever happens.

And yet, the morning before, I'd smashed a plate and burst into tears because I'd wanted a cheese and avocado sandwich and all three avocados in the bowl were black. These days, this was the level of problem that felled me. I was like a dandelion spore, captive to the lightest breeze. There was no fight left in me. My business was failing and I couldn't be bothered to save it. It was too much effort to cut my toenails. Any longer, and they'd start to curl. After walking upstairs I'd have to sit on the edge of my bed for five minutes. My pillow was developing a crust.

I thought of Manjit. In his early twenties, Manjit suffered from clinical depression. Nick, trying to be helpful, had suggested that going for a run in the park might help. Wasn't exercise good for depression? No, replied Manjit. Exercise was good if you merely felt a bit low. "If I went for a run in the park," he added, "I'd just be running in the park, depressed."

Seven years later I finally understood what he meant. I could alter location, run away, but my surroundings would change, not me. I picked at the window ledge. The paint was flaky. It was the end of the world. My face crumpled up for a sobbing fit, but I pulled back halfway. I could not let Stuart beat me. Not *him*. I had to erase him from my existence. I could never forgive—why should I?—but I would delete him like a computer error from my life, for *me*. Claw was right. The past was set in stone. But I could act as if I was ready to face the future.

In primary-school assembly, our eccentric (or malicious, I never could decide which) headmaster occasionally made us play the Laughing Game. A hundred five-year-olds began slowly, saying "Ha-ha-ha," and within minutes, the fake jollity would turn into real hysterics. I could never do it. I didn't see what was so funny. It wasn't as if he even did a burp to start us off. But now, I was determined to master the Laughing Game. If I pretended long enough, one day surely it would feel real.

So when the phone rang, I picked it up with a bright "Hello!"

"Holly? Stuart Marshall. I'm suing you for defamation."

He cut off. The blood rushed. I sat down on the floor but it wasn't enough. I had to lie flat out. I felt like I might vomit, and there was a curious deafness in my ears. Why *me*? said that little voice inside all of us that believes evil befalls other people. When you dust yourself off and vow to start again, Fate is meant to cut you a break. That's the universal reward for being plucky. This must be a sign. I was cursed.

Life stank spectacularly.

CHAPTER 28

Having a bad day?" inquired Gloria.

"I'm curled on the floor in the fetal position," I replied. "What do *you* think?"

I glared at her foot, as it was nearest. She always wore sneakers.

"Up to you, but I need to clean."

Feeling foolish, I staggered to my feet. I didn't want to tell her about being sued, because if she told me that my angel would protect me, much as I'd regret it, I was going to have to punch her in the face.

"I felt dizzy," I said. "I'm still recovering from a serious illness."

Gloria looked at me as if she were searching for something. "Would you like a cuppa?"

I dragged out a couple of chairs, screeching them across the floor, while Gloria boiled the kettle. So she wouldn't attempt to make me exhume my demons, I said, "Seen any angels lately?"

She turned from the side, frowning. She had delicate features—a sweet little nose like a doll, large brown eyes with dark lashes, and that wipeout smile—and she dressed like a golfer. Nasty flat shoes and polo necks. Her personality didn't match her looks.

"I hope you're not being sarcastic," she said.

"I'm not, really." I was grateful to be treated so roughly. Like I was normal.

"Good." She paused and took a bite of a chocolate biscuit. "I don't *see* angels. I sense them. And I hear them." She grinned, displaying cocoa teeth. "A few weeks ago I was reading this book. *Crime Classification Manual.* It's mostly about serial killers. They fascinate me."

"Oh!" I spluttered, adjusting expectations of John Grisham. "Not in an I-want-to-marry-you-type way, I hope?"

I hoped she mistook my blush for a fever. One of my most shameful episodes was suggesting to a depressed Manjit that he read a self-help book for men entitled *Male Order*. A perfectly respectable work, but aimed at the guy whose most profound introspection entails catching his reflection in his pint. Manjit had glanced at the cover and said, "I've read some Freud—he was a bit over the top, and Nietzsche—I think he was right about society, and Jung—I mean I take his side against Freud, but I was hoping for . . ." He'd trailed off. I'd blushed at my error of presuming that dialect reflects intelligence.

Gloria shook her head, serious. "The nature of evil," she said. "Mostly, even the most depraved monsters don't think of what they do as evil. They just think they're pursuing their interests."

"What—murder, rape, needlepoint?"

She smiled, in the way people do when they're courtesy-bound to acknowledge your feeble wit, but in a great rush to proceed with disclosure of their own genius. "Anyway. I lost the book. I looked everywhere. Under the bed—I specially remember looking there—in drawers, places I knew it wasn't going to be. Couldn't find it. And then"—a glow lit her features and I feared I knew what was coming—"early one morning, I heard this voice, a tiny but clear-as-crystal voice that said, 'Look under the bed.' I opened my eyes with a snap and there was a feeling of a presence, but as I watched I could sense it fading. I went back to sleep, feeling incredibly peaceful, and when I woke up again, I looked under the bed—"

"And there was the *Crime Classification Manual*," I interrupted, because I didn't think I could bear to hear the punch line spoken in tones of hushed reverence. You'd think with all the death, poverty, cruelty, torture, and misery in the world, angels would have more important tasks to fulfill than to inform Gloria where she'd dropped her storybook. I thought her angel was more likely to be her own memory, or possibly the tooth fairy, who must have a great deal of leisure time these days, what with all the advances in dental care.

"Correct," purred Gloria. She took a great slurp of tea before saying so casually that she was halfway through the sentence before

I caught up, "My cousin never recovered. Six years on, she's still on antidepressants, can't have a relationship. She was seventeen when it happened. It was her first ti—"

I sprang up. "Glor," I said. "This is the trouble with sharing. Your problems become public property. But however much they're picked over by others, they remain *your* problems. If I wanted to discuss it, you'd be one of the first people I'd come to, but I don't. Do you mind?"

Gloria shook her head. "I should've thought. The last thing you need is ear from me." She smiled kindly. Gloria spoke her mind, so plain speaking didn't offend her.

The doorbell rang and I froze. "Don't get it," I croaked. But Gloria was already in the hall. "If it's a blond man in his twenties, don't get it. I'll call the p—"

"It's a woman," bellowed Gloria. "Middle-aged. Glamorous. Posh," she said mockingly. *Powsh.*

I heaved myself up, muttering about Jehovah's Witnesses, and peered through the blind. "Mrs. Mortimer!" I yanked open the door. "Mrs. Mortimer!" I'd always found it hard to call Nick's mother "Lavinia." "Come in, how lovely to see you!"

As I said these words I did a mental run-through of the state of the house. Spotless. Then I realized I was in my pajamas and there was a spinach stain on my crotch. "I'm so sorry for looking like this, I've been unwell. Gloria, could you possibly put the kettle on again, I'll just go and change."

Gloria looked at me, then at Mrs. Mortimer, plainly amused. But Mrs. Mortimer cried, "Please, Holly, you're fine as you are—unless you're cold. It really doesn't matter to me."

But it mattered to me, so I galloped up the stairs and changed. When I galloped back down, Gloria pointed to the lounge and did a quick mime show, pulling her mouth into a droop, curling her hands into fists and rubbing them under her eyes. Mrs. Mortimer was *crying*?

I crept into the lounge. Mrs. Mortimer seemed perfectly composed, legs elegantly crossed, sheer tights—no, stockings, I bet. She wore sleek high shoes, a pencil skirt, white blouse, a smart caramel jacket, and a silk scarf, tied at the neck. Her dark shiny hair was wound into a chignon. But I looked closely and underneath the Estée Lauder face, her dark blue eyes were red and puffy.

"Is it Nick?" I blurted out before I could stop myself.

Her head jerked. "Why, yes. Yes. It *is* Nick."

I dropped on the sofa, a jelly. I must have been jittery, because I was about to mouth the word *dead* when Mrs. Mortimer cried, "Holly, we've made the most terrible mistake, and I'm desperate— I'm sure he's told you—he didn't talk to us for a month and then about two weeks ago he finally agreed to see us, but he's so cold and distant and I don't know what to do, nor does Michael, and we . . . we thought that *you* might be able to help, speak to him, he'd listen to you, he still loves you, of course, and oh! we wouldn't ask but we're at our wits' end, we've caused him such pain—quite, quite the opposite of what we intended—Michael would have come with me, but he's . . . he's too upset, oh Holly, surely *you* see why we didn't tell Nick he was adopted until now?"

I must have a masculine side, I can't bear to see a beautiful woman in distress. More than anything, I wanted to nod my head. After a pause, I shook it.

Mrs. Mortimer put a hand to her mouth. "We didn't want to rock the boat. We thought it would be better for him not to know, to grow up confident, but the last thing he said to me was that his whole life with us had been a deception. I knew this would happen, we should never have told him at all."

I couldn't agree. I took a deep breath—I had never contradicted her before. "But, Mrs. Mortimer. Surely you can see that Nick had a right to know."

She sniffed delicately into a cotton handkerchief. "Lavinia, please. Holly, he was so hurtful. He said it made sense, that he'd always felt different—distant from us. He said he felt like a reject. Of course I said he was special—he *is* special—I said he was special because we *chose* him. And then he said"—she paused and swallowed—"he said, 'Yes, but only after I was *unchosen* by my real mother. So not that special after all.' He was so very angry, Holly. I've never seen him so angry. In fact, I've never seen him so *anything*."

I was silent. This is a terrible thing to say about someone you love, but Nick never struck me as a person who felt deeply. Mrs. Mortimer wasn't entirely right. He was distant from his parents, but only in the sense that even when he was twenty-nine they treated him like a child. But I'd never thought much of it. Very few of my peers had the warm and easygoing friendship that I had with my mum and dad. I'd presumed that Nick's rather more formal attachment to Lavinia and Michael was linked to being an only child and being raised in a more sophisticated household. The higher the class, the cooler the relationship was what I'd presumed. I'd once asked Rachel if she enjoyed spending all her free time in this or that country house with a few friends and a great bunch of strangers. She'd replied, "I grew up in a house full of strangers— Nanny, the housekeeper—I'm used to it."

This made absolute sense to me. There was a ruthlessness about Rachel that seemed to be derived from a rationing of love and the consequent realization that one can only depend on oneself. How close to your parents can you be if they pack you off to boarding school at age five?

Nick's upbringing wasn't quite as rarefied as Rachel's, but from what I could tell, it had similar elements with similar results. Mr. and Mrs. Mortimer had visited Issy with Nick and me four months after Eden was born and could hardly contain their horror. Even when Eden fell asleep, Issy wouldn't put the baby down. She'd barely raised her eyes from her new heart's desire. Lavinia mentioned that Nick had been bottle-fed, and wasn't it super, because you could use the time to cook, make telephone calls, and generally catch up with your chores. Issy had replied that she always maintained eye contact with Eden while breast-feeding—it was essential for healthy development of the self. Hadn't Mrs. Mortimer heard of "mirroring"?

Plainly, Mrs. Mortimer hadn't. In the car home, her only comment was that she had never "pandered" to Nick because she hadn't wanted him to be a "lap baby."

Not that Nick was incapable of love. Throughout our time together, I never doubted he loved me. But I'd presumed that Nick loved on a different level than most people. That was why the vehemence of his emotion when I ended the engagement was such a shock. Certainly, there was an element of wanting what he couldn't have, but it seemed that he'd genuinely loved me more than I'd realized. He just hadn't shown it with the freedom that some people would. And now, *now*, perhaps I could understand why. His first experience was abandonment by the woman who should have adored and protected him the most. Why would you ever trust or dare to love openly after that?

Mrs. Mortimer might say that this was nonsense. Nick hadn't known he was adopted until she'd told him. But—and I'd stake my life on it—Issy would say that, subconsciously or not, of course he'd known. After all, he'd *been* there, hadn't he?

I looked at Mrs. Mortimer and said, "Lavinia, I'll go and see him now."

Yes?" said Nick, when I rang the doorbell. Funny to say it, but for the first time since I'd known him, he looked like his mother's son. He was wearing a shirt and tie, smart trousers, and a blazer, as if he were going for an interview. I preferred his Johnny Depp dress sense, but I wasn't going to mention it. Even his hair was neat. No doubt Bo would think this was her work.

I smiled at him. "Sorry about the last time we spoke. I wanted to see how you were doing."

He gazed at me, suspicious. "You've lost weight. It doesn't suit you."

I nodded at him. "I fully intend to put it all back on again. Anyway, speak for yourself. If you're not careful you'll end up like Bo."

I watched Nick trying not to smile. A source of great amusement to us both was the discovery—Manjit was useless at keeping secrets—that Bo's knees were so bony she had to sleep with a pillow between her legs. Nick had said, "Well, that's her excuse!"

"I suppose we should discuss selling the house," he said finally. "Instruct a devious estate agent, one who isn't like Claudia. Come in."

He made me a noninstant coffee without being asked. And

added milk and two sugars. I looked around Bo's kitchen and wondered how she afforded it. Her taste was chintzy, but expensive. Her home seemed to belong to an older person. Nick tiptoed around it like a much-disciplined bull in a china shop. His blazer hung loose on his shoulders, and I wanted to hug him.

"How you doing, Nicky?"

"Fine," he said. "Badly."

He put the coffee on Bo's pine table, murmured a little "Uh" to himself, and shoved a mat under the mug. It was like observing a tiger in captivity.

"Nick. Why don't we get out of here? Go for a walk?"

His mouth twitched. "If you like."

I drove us to Ally Pally. Alexandra Park, for those of you not familiar with it. Big. Green. Views across London. Not the best views, or the best parts of London, but exhilarating all the same. Nick and I sat on a bench and kicked our feet. I wanted to hold his hand, but I wasn't sure I should, so I didn't. I waited, picking out far-off chimneys and tower blocks full of people going about their lives.

"I want to find my birth mother."

I started. "Really? How do you go about doing that?"

Oh God, I wanted to say, are you sure that's a good idea? I couldn't, of course, say anything of the sort. He would have taken it the wrong way. But this woman had already proved herself unreliable. Nick was not in a fit state to be rejected again.

"You don't think I should."

"Why do you say that?"

"Hol, I can tell."

He drew up his knees and circled them with his arms.

I tried to engage my brain before speaking. "I understand why you want to find her—not knowing who your mother is, it must be like part of your soul is missing. But just be careful, that's all. She might be desperate to see you again—she *should* be—but, well, it's best to have your guard up. Not to go in there expecting a fairy-tale ending."

Nick rested his head on his knees and smiled grimly. "Why not?" he said. "Isn't that how most fairy tales begin? With an abandoned baby? I might turn out to be a prince."

I laughed. "That's not what you said the last time we spoke."

I bent to pick a blade of grass and Nick said, "A dog's probably pissed on that."

I retracted my hand.

"Anyway, Hol, what have you got against happy endings all of a sudden? I thought they were your life's work."

I felt a black doom engulf me. I heard myself say in a voice of ice, "I don't believe in them anymore."

The two of us seesawed off each other. If he was gloomy, I was cheerful. Now it was his turn. He looked at me and grinned his old sloppy smile. "But *you* ended our engagement, Holly."

I ignored the teasing tone.

"Nick, believe me. It wasn't that."

He frowned. "What was it, then?"

I told him. And as I did, I started to wonder why the hell I hadn't told him before.

CHAPTER 29

I've never seen a person physically fine yet in so much pain. One moment he'd rock in agony, the next he'd moan like an animal. Then he'd spring from the bench, pace in no particular direction, dig his fists into his eyes, and say, "Ah, Christ. Jesus Christ." I found myself in the peculiar position of having to comfort *him*. Tears streamed as he gasped, "I'm so sorry, Hol. I let you down. I'll kill him for you. I'll fucking do him, he'll die, the bastard. He'll pay for this, I swear it."

I stroked his hair, and he cried in my lap, hugging my hips and muttering, "Oh, Holly. Holly, how could it?"

"Don't, Nick, you'll make me cry too," I said. I wasn't going to say "It's all right," because it wasn't. "It's a nice idea in theory, but I don't really want you going to prison for killing Stuart."

He sat up suddenly, white-faced. "It's my fault. If it weren't for me, you wouldn't have—"

"Nick, don't be ridiculous."

He shook his head. His face crumpled again, but he clenched his teeth and gained control. "I'm sorry," he said in a strangulated voice. "*You* should be the one making a scene, not me. I don't mean to steal your grief. I—God, Holly—what you mean to me, I just—" He clutched the portion of shirt over his heart. "The pain, I wish I could take it from you. Ah God, I should have been there, to protect you, to think . . . I heard you with him, in the kitchen, and I thought . . . I'm so stupid, I thought . . . Ah, Hol, I wish I could take your pain—" His voice cracked.

I felt a corresponding pang in my own chest. "Thank you. I know you do."

I understood what he meant, because sometimes I felt his misery as if it were my own. Although that means something wonderful, it's not entirely practical. You feel twice as much love but you end up feeling twice as much hurt, and it can bounce back, to and fro, forever. I was well aware of this as we sat there—that while baring my soul to Nick gave me some sort of peace, it had equal potential to give me some sort of hell. I didn't want to sit here for the rest of the day regurgitating. I felt I'd rather get Caroline to fax him my statement.

Anyhow, Issy says that despite Oprah and Jerry Springer, merely talking about a trauma is not always healthy. Talking is only worthwhile if, at the same time, you're *processing* the horror, coming to terms with it. If not you merely nurture it until it becomes larger, like a tumor in your head, and lodges there, no longer your past but your hideous present. I certainly hadn't "come to terms" with it, a phrase surely conceived by an idiot. I'd made some mental progress through talking to Caroline (about three inches). But now, thanks to the CPS, I was back to—not square one—square two, maybe.

And it wasn't as if I was short of new problems. I was wondering if I should tell Nick about Claudia and Camille's suspicions of Stuart and their little plan, when he grasped my hands.

"Hol," he said. "I'm being selfish. Tell me, tell me what *you* want. What can I do to help you?"

I smiled into his eyes. It's rare that you hear a man admit to being selfish. I felt I should reward him for good behavior. "There is one tiny thing." I explained about Stuart threatening to sue me.

Nick didn't have the sort of face that turns purple, but if he'd been a puce sort of guy, at that moment he'd have gone blueberry. "*What?*" he roared. He quickly lowered his voice. "You should tell Caroline immediately," he said. "But you know what? Like he'd *dare*. This is bullshit, Holly. He's trying to terrorize you. If he sues, he draws attention to himself and what he's done. I really don't think you have to worry about this. It would be an insane move on his part. If he persists, tell him you welcome the action. Tell him you can't wait to tell everyone what he did, that you'll enjoy it. If you want, I'll ring him. Or better still, I'll consult Dad."

Michael Mortimer was a senior partner at a blue-chip London law firm, Mortimer Valancourt. They even sounded like avenging knights. Stuart's little outfit was a joke in comparison.

I blinked. "I thought you were barely speaking to him."

Nick's face was a scowl. "I think this is slightly more important than my little sulk, don't you?"

I struggled to speak. Unless I was hallucinating, here was a new Nick rising from the ashes—strong, supportive, selfless. A smart woman would have given him encouragement for good behavior. I was about to fling his kindness back in his face.

"Actually, Nick, don't ask Michael. It's very . . . big of you, but right now, I don't feel comfortable with the idea of him knowing. I haven't even told M and D. But don't worry. I *will* ring Caroline. And anyway you're right. Of course Stuart doesn't want to sue me. He'd be mad."

Despite these brave/stupid (is there a difference?) words, I had a fantasy vision of Stuart facing the might of Michael Mortimer in court and being crushed to a dust. The fear of what Stuart was capable of still burned, but at least now I had the mental ammunition to fight it.

This realization made my stomach rumble.

Nick looked like he might argue, then didn't. "Food?" he said instead.

I smiled my gratitude. "Good idea. Where shall we go?"

Except for spinach soup, my cupboard was bare, and as I knew that Bo was given to such pronouncements as "We don't eat butter in this house," there was no point going to her place.

As it was Nick, I didn't bother garnishing the first thought that came into my head. "Somewhere where people are kind to us."

This ruled out about half the restaurants in London. The last time I'd booked a table for 7:00 P.M. on a Thursday, at a former favorite of mine, they'd demanded back the table at 8:30. And after the waiters had hung about like a brood of vampires, snatching our plates while we were still chewing, service charge had been added to the bill, which was dumped on the table unrequested. This was BS—Before Stuart—so I'd paid up and sighed. "Well, it *is* Thursday night." I'd dissuaded Claudia from making a scene. (She managed to dawdle spitefully over her cappuccino until 9:20 and had to be satisfied with that.)

"*I* know a place," said Nick. "Cantina Italia. It's a little place in Islington. Smoky. Hard chairs. But *so* friendly. And the food is likketyspishous."

"Is that good?"

"A cross between lick your lips and delicious."

"Let's go!"

I drove, squeaking at Nick to give me directions at every turn. (He never does unless forced, mistakenly believing that because he knows the route, I should too.) To be fair, apart from that, he's the ideal passenger. He doesn't bark orders like, say, Issy does. ("Careful that car! Pay attention! Watch that cyclist! Signal, signal! Slow down, you're speeding! Mind that pedestrian! Brake! Don't jolt! Progressive braking!") Sometimes you'd smash headlong into a Winnebago just to shut her up.

Cantina Italia was exactly what the doctor ordered. (The benefits of red wine, etcetera.) A long, thin restaurant, with a reassuring gaggle of middle-aged Italians feasting on pasta and garlic bread at the kitchen end. The smiley waitress sat us near the door in a quiet corner. It had been a while since I'd sat opposite Nick in a restaurant, alone. Toward the end of our relationship, a lethargy had overcome us. We would go out to dinner, but only with the safety net of friends. They were the buffer zone—their presence ensured that Nick and I would make an effort, rather than sit there dumbly. And they were also the entertainment, as Nick and I no longer had the energy to try to enchant each other.

"Been a while," said Nick, reading my mind.

Feeling shy all of a sudden, I straightened my knife and fork on the table. "Can you remember our first date?" I asked, giggling.

Nick rolled his eyes and shook his head. This meant, yes, I do remember it. I only wish I didn't. Our first *proper* date—not counting the ice cream after the duck episode—was at a cheap, plasticky Central London chain restaurant. We'd sat outside, coughing into the traffic. Nick had been so keen to impress me but at the same time communicate that he was cool that out of all the sumptuous, sophisticated, softly lit gourmet venues in the capital, this grubby bar-café, with its tasteless, overpriced, pseudo-French food, had been his top choice. But we were high on love, and the stale brioche could have been plastic for all we cared.

"Remember the roses?"

Nick beamed. "The best thirty-seven quid I ever spent."

A man with a bucket of red roses—the scourge of courting couples everywhere—had galloped toward our table and yodeled, "A rose for the lady?"

Nick had bought thirty-seven roses, the entire contents of the bucket. And the fact that every single one had drooped brown in death the following morning didn't matter. The thought was everything. And if only both of us could have stuck by that principle for more than three years, we might have made it work.

I squirmed happily and flapped the menu at him. "What are you going to have?"

Nick chose seafood spaghetti, and I chose the homemade gnocchi with tomato sauce and mozzarella. We also shared a plate of garlic bread—a pizza in disguise. And I had an arugula salad. I always overorder in nice restaurants; it's my squirrel-stuffing-nuts-for-the-winter gene. We talked about Bo and Manjit for a while, why

Bo seemed to have dashed straight from her teens to middle age. Even the house she lived in looked from the outside like a fifty-something's home—flat, drab, and suburban. And the previous week she'd snapped at Nick for querying her obsession with the weather forecast ("I don't know why you bother, Bo, all you need to know is that it's going to be raining for the rest of our lives!").

We didn't approach serious conversation until dessert—not normally a great time to approach serious conversation because you can never quite concentrate, a fine dessert demands your full attention. But even though my crème brûlée was exquisite, Nick won the battle with what he had to say.

"You know, I said I wanted to find my real mother before, and you said you weren't sure it was a good idea. I . . . wasn't being entirely straight with you. I've already started looking. I started looking about a week after Lavinia and Michael told me the truth. And I think I've found her."

I swallowed a great crunchy chunk of caramel without tasting it. "What! Already? Oh my God! No, no, great idea! How? Who is she? Have you seen her? What about your father?"

Nick ran his hands through his hair and mussed it. As he talked, he repeated the gesture until his hair stood on end. I preferred it that way. "No. I haven't seen her yet," he said. "But I know where she lives. It was a shock, that Pamela found her so soon. Oh yeah, I thought it would take months. *I* didn't trace her personally, I found this woman, Pamela Fidgett, who runs her own agency. I partly chose her because I like her name. There's a few agencies, and most of them charge thousands. But she was different. Less bureaucratic. She had long gray hair, like a good witch, and she kept dropping things off her desk. But she knew what she was doing, I could tell. She cared. There were loads of thank-you cards pinned about the place. She said that as she traced, she tended to build up a picture of the mother. For instance, there'd be a file on me from the adoption agency, with notes from the hospital, how much interest she'd shown in me after the birth, letters from her, if she'd ever written. Pamela says nothing ever got passed on in those days, so that by the time I got to meet my mother, I'd be a little prepared for what kind of person she was, how she might react toward me.

Also, Pamela charges by the hour, and most of her tracings cost between one-fifty to two hundred and fifty pounds."

"God," I spluttered, "that's *nothing*!" Nothing, I meant, for a whole new family. I was in awe. "You're so matter-of-fact about it, Nick. I so admire that. It's an incredible amount to take in." As I spoke, I was aware of a softer, more benign attitude toward him. For the last three or so years there'd been a sharpness to our conversations, no courtesy, no frills, no gentility, if such allowances still existed in the twenty-first century. "So, how did she trace her?"

Nick grimaced. "It's not as if I have a choice. Inside, I *am* in a state. There's so much to wonder about. You can be very bitter. I still haven't got my head around it. But Pamela has been great. She's almost like a counselor. She's very wise in the ways of human nature, if that doesn't sound too Brothers Grimm. She had a lot to say about why some adoptive parents don't tell their children they're adopted. Remind me, I'll tell you about that. Oh yeah, so how did she trace her.

"Five weeks ago, I found Pamela on the Net, rang her, and she said that before she could do anything, I had to find my birth certificate. And she said I could do that by going to the local Family Records Center. They make you have this thing called a Section fifty-one counseling session. You know, 'Why now, are you prepared for the consequences, etcetera, etcetera.' And then—"

"What sort of consequences?"

Nick, who was talking very fast at this point, looked mildly irritated at the interruption. "The obvious, like, if I was illegitimate, which Pamela says I probably was, and my mother had since married and not told her husband, if that was the case she might not want to know me." He gabbled the words as if to gloss over such a remote possibility. "So anyway, there's this excruciating wait, but two weeks ago I finally get the birth certificate and that has my real, well, the name that my *blood* mother gave me on it. And her name on it too."

I clamped my hand over my mouth and another great blob of crème brûlée was lost forever.

"I'll tell *you*," he added. "But don't you tell anyone."

I swore silence, and he beckoned me to lean over the table,

then whispered in my ear. I felt a shivery thrill as if he were sharing the password to the end of the rainbow.

"Nick, that's a beautiful name. And hers too, it sounds lovely. Although I've always thought 'Nicholas Mortimer' was a fantastic name. Very noble."

He shrugged, as if not wanting to commit. "Easy come, easy go," he said. He paused. "I wonder who she named me after."

There had been more bureaucracy, but at every stage of her search, Pamela had kept Nick informed. Several factors made detection easier. Nick's blood mother had a fairly unusual name, hadn't moved far from the area in which she'd given birth, and she hadn't divorced. Pamela had no trouble finding her marriage certificate. Nick hadn't wanted Pamela to write to his mother. (If he *had* given permission, she'd have penned a cryptic letter: "I have a client who is trying to trace someone he knew in *[date of Nick's birth]*. His name is *[whatever she'd named him]*. If you would like to contact him, this is the number to call.")

Instead, Pamela had given Nick the woman's address and dug up the local newspaper coverage of her wedding.

I stared at him. "You have a picture of your mother?"

He nodded. Then, carefully, he pushed our glasses of wine and water to one side of the table and took an envelope out of his jacket pocket, the one over his heart. Together, we pored over the grainy photograph. "That's her," said Nick unnecessarily, as there was only one person in the picture in a big white dress. "What do you think? Do you think I look like her?"

I badly wanted to say yes, but the truth was, there was little resemblance. This woman had dark straight hair, curled into a wave at the bottom, and a round face. She was a lot plainer than her son. She looked happy and smiley, as you'd hope on her wedding day, but I couldn't help but think of her as cruel. You caused my boyfriend a lot of heartache, I thought, staring at her. You should have been more careful, you selfish, thoughtless woman. Then I realized that had she been more careful, there would have been no Nick.

I squinted. "It's hard to tell, but I think you have similar shape of mouth. And there's maybe something in the eyes."

"I look nothing like her."

I found his hand and held it. "Perhaps you look more like your dad. But really, Nick, you look like *you.*"

He looked down at the table. "She only lives ten minutes from Mum and—Lavinia and Michael," he said without raising his head. "I could go and sit outside her house and spy on her, like, *now.*"

I felt a flutter of fear. If this woman hurt him again, caused him even one more second's pain, I'd scratch her eyes out, kill her as soon as look at her. "If you want, I'll come with you. I mean, I don't even have to look, I'll hide my eyes if you don't want me to see her. But maybe you should have someone with you."

Nick smiled. "Thanks, Hol. I don't think tonight is the night. I should be taking care of you, if anything. But, well, if I do decide on a stakeout, I'll call you. You can provide the doughnuts and coffee. And I won't make you hide your eyes. I don't *think* she'll turn you into a pillar of salt."

I grinned and lifted my glass to take a sip of wine.

Nick lifted his and clinked it against mine. "To your recovery, Holly, and a life full of joy, love, and wonder. To the future."

CHAPTER 30

Nick insisted on paying for dinner. Not so long ago, I would have considered a response along the lines of "Blue moon, is it?" But the bitter resentment fueling the last months of our engagement had dissolved. (See what breaking up does for your relationship?) I was also touched by the fact that since the Stuart revelations, Nick wasn't treating me any differently. I *felt* different, but he was treating me like the old me—with a little more respect even—and this made it easier to behave like the old me.

Claudia had been an angel, but the dynamic between us had changed for the worse. She was patient, polite, even patronizing—alarmingly unlike herself—so I was reminded of the delicate state I was in the entire time she was with me. I felt like an idiot child who couldn't look after herself and had to be watched. I suppose that it was hard for women to accept what had happened to me, because then they'd have to accept that it could happen to them.

Men weren't so threatened by my experience in that sense, but I still hadn't known how Nick would react to the news. It wasn't as if he had a claim on me any longer, but Caroline had warned me. Some blokes behaved as if their girl had been unfaithful and was therefore damaged goods. These were the men who saw women as property, but then, in a situation like this, everyone you knew surprised you.

Nick, it turned out, *didn't* view women as property. Caroline might have been surprised, but I wasn't. He had many flaws, but chauvinist piggery wasn't one of them. Admittedly, this was a new line of thinking for me. When we lived together, Nick rarely tidied, and if he did, he tidied like a guest helping out around the house. Then, I'd called it sexist; with this new détente, I called it conditioning. Finally, I had the goodwill to try to understand him.

Outside my front door, we clutched each other. "Thank you for today, Nick, it was brilliant." The words came out clunkily, like chunks of Lego. What I had in mind was more poetic, but maybe that was the best place for it. As he hugged me, he murmured, "Special, special Holly, thank *you*." An unwelcome thought struck me as I watched us (I always did, these days, watch myself from a distance). Were we one of those drearily dysfunctional couples who could only thrive in a crisis? Everyday, humdrum life highlighting our failings, did we require a horrible drama to create the excitement our personalities lacked? Nick might have come in, but I stiffened in the hug and he backed off, blowing me a kiss as he hailed a cab.

Despite the cynic inside my head, I slept more soundly that night than in ages. Apart from the fogged conk-outs induced by glandular fever, I'd developed an allergy to sleeping. And I'd realized, over the last few months, that you can train yourself into insomnia. I needed the rest.

• • •

I woke up, groggy, at 8:45, but I drove to work smiling. There was something different about today. I stopped at traffic lights and it hit me. I was *humming*.

Five minutes in the office put a stop to that. The star of *Cat on a Hot Tin Roof* had broken his ankle. And, bizarrely, even though the part required the guy to *act* a broken ankle, the real thing precluded him from playing it.

"Not a fan of Method acting, then?" said Claw when Nige burst through the door and trumpeted the news.

The heir apparent rolled his eyes. "Like *that* hasn't been said a thousand times." He grinned and dropped to his knees. "Holly, dearest, pretty please, Holly, grant me an open-ended sabbatical as from today. Issy can fill in for me. This is fate, darling, it's Fate—I didn't trip him, I promise. I have to prepare for the role, attend rehearsal, perfect my lines, consider how to interpret the character, decide how precisely to blow every other sucker off the stage! Unfortunately, the bastard keeps his dressing room. But I'll get you and Claw free tickets, front row. You can even bring that ghastly friend of yours, Rachel—"

"We spend our *days* listening to you rattle on," said my ungrateful sister. "Now we've got to spend the evenings too?"

Nige blanked her, fixing me with moony eyes.

"Well," I said. "You're going to go whether I give permission or not, so I might as well be gracious. Of course you can have a sabbatical, you big twit. You're going to be a star!"

We all three nodded our glad amazement at fortune sticking out a leg to speed Nige on his journey to fame. Two seconds later he was gone.

Claw bit her lip. "B'locks. I'm actually going to miss him."

So was I. I'd gone through a phase of treating Nige with suspicion. Now I'd begun to recover my senses. I saw him for what he was—a good pal and great company. He cheered the entire office. Even Issy had thawed in his presence. (Claudia and I were amazed the day when

Nige expressed his boredom at needing the toilet, as it was down the end of the corridor. Issy, normally prudish, had confided that after her Caesarian she was displeased at having a catheter inserted, but to her surprise, "It was *remarkable.* You just don't feel the need to go— ever!" Nige had squealed, "Ohhhh, catheters are great! But society says no!") In his absence, I felt all three of us would wilt a little.

"Now what?" asked Claudia.

"We'll manage," I lied. "Get Issy in more often."

"Can we afford her?" said Claw. (Issy didn't let a little thing like family get in the way of income. She cherishes money, I suppose because growing up we never had much. Claw is the opposite—from a fiver to five grand, she spends frantically until it's all gone. It's as if she feels guilty about having it, as if any accumulation of wealth is an implied slight to our parents. She never extracts less than a hundred pounds from the cash machine, and squanders it at such a speed you'd think the notes were pure asbestos. I'm somewhere in between. I love buying for others, and I like buying for myself, but I don't have to.)

"Probably not." I glanced at a fresh sheet of office costs typed out by Nige and placed plonk in the center of my keyboard, presumably as a buttering-up ploy.

manning telephones
office space and facilities
sending questionnaires to callers
keeping database
organizing dates
writing letters, running copies
sorting date cards, liaising with members to organize
    second dates
collecting E-mails
organizing/running Date Nights
business development, e.g., Website
PR and coordinating journalists

Apparently, administration cost a breezy four hundred pounds per month, but then Nige hadn't listed his own pay, or Claudia's. Or mine, to be fair. *I* could take a pay cut. I wasn't exactly racking up bar bills at nightclubs or buying fur coats. That said, after my security binge Claudia had taken over liaising with our accountant, so I couldn't spend Girl Meets Boy's money even if I'd wanted to. Our number of weekly applications was still low, however, so I was mildly curious as to why, on my return to work, I found that the bank had backed off. When I'd mentioned this to Claudia, she'd said, in a sarcastic way, "Yeah, lucky that." Whatever she'd meant to imply, I hadn't pursued it.

"Could we hire a temp?" she said.

I wrinkled my nose. "The last one pilfered about a hundred quid's worth of stationery. And she never paid into the doughnut fund. We'll manage on our own."

"Right," said Claudia.

I peered at her. "You okay? You're supposed to be in love. You look gray, no offense."

She smiled weakly, showing tips of vampire teeth. "Period pain. Ouch."

I nodded. The phone rang and Claudia answered it. I realized I was still nodding and that my pulse was breaking records. With effort, I stopped jerking my head. A series of airless gasps passed for breathing. No matter how deeply I gulped, I couldn't seem to get oxygen to my lungs. I gripped the sides of the chair and heaved myself upright. I just about made it to the ladies' without falling flat. I splashed my face with cold water, stared bleakly into the mirror, and tried to remember.

When was the last time?

I've never been a great fan of periods. I know some people make a great deal of them, the entire family going out to celebrate their baby girl's first bleed. I can just imagine my father choking down a Bloody Mary in honor of the occasion. That said, Issy keeps a filed record of every date of every period she's ever had. Any week of the month she can tell you the exact day of her cycle. Should you need to know. Me, I have them and forget about them. I usually sense when one is due because I catch myself being more disagreeable than usual. But since Stuart, my disagreeable streak had stretched over three months, putting my period radar out of action. Think, Holly, when *was* the last time?

I must have had one since Stuart. I must have, because it would be too unfair if I hadn't. I raked through the trivia to see if a memory presented itself. But no. I'd check my diary, see if it sparked any associations. The truth was, I hadn't paid attention. After a Stuart, you don't want to pay attention to your body and its functions. You prefer to kid yourself that it's nothing to do with you. The more distance you can gain between your mind and it, the easier it is to minimalize the pain, until you could almost believe that it happened to someone else. If I'd bled continuously for three months, I hardly think it would have registered.

It couldn't be Stuart's. He'd worn a condom. But condoms split.

I skittered into the office, grabbed my bag, and skittered out again. I ran into the chemist and bought the first pregnancy testing kit I saw. I tried to look happy as I paid for it, in case the cashier formed any impertinent theories. Then I raced back to the office, dashed into the ladies', and peed on the wretched thing. What was it, blue square, blue circle? I knew the instructions, I didn't need to read them. What modern woman does at the age of thirty? I tried to look away, then look back, but I didn't have the self-control. As I stared, a faint blue line appeared and my heart peeled its skin in horror.

Speaking for myself, you're so used to false alarms, you never *truly* think that line will appear. So when it does you can't quite believe it. I broke the habit of a lifetime and sat down on a public toilet. (The lid was on, at least.) I didn't want to start mewling but a few wails bubbled out. It was plain that God had taken a dislike to me. An unfortunate enemy to make, considering how childish He is. ("You start something with *Me*, I'll finish it, see how you like a plague of locusts.")

If it was Stuart's I was getting rid of it, and send me to hell. My mind twitched to the flowers he'd sent me. I'd wanted to throw them out the window, but I'd placed them in water instead. They were *flowers*, not the person who bought them. And when Issy had told me to stop watering the houseplants to teach Nick the lesson of responsibility, I couldn't bring myself to let them die. You don't nurture something, then kill it. But this was different. But *how*? Was I putting an innocent to death to pay for Stuart's crime? It wouldn't have consciousness at this stage. It was a fetus. And I believed in choice. But I also remembered what Pamela Fidgett had said to Nick.

Nick had told her he felt he must have done something wrong for his mother to give him away. He must have been a bad, evil sort of baby for her to abandon him. Pamela had said, "I challenge you to look into any pram and pick out an 'evil' baby. How evil can a baby be?" She'd made Nick feel much better. But considering her words made me feel worse. Was it a blob or a baby at this stage? My choice. My choice, no one else's business. Jesus. What if it were Nick's? I scraped my hair out of my face and held my head in my hands, probably to prevent it from exploding. It was much more likely—even if I did blush at the fact there was a father shortlist.

I still had to remind myself that one of them hadn't *given* me a choice.

I stepped out of the ladies' and wandered slowly back to the office. It had to be Nick's. I didn't deserve for it to be Stuart's. What would Nick say when I told him? I wanted to get back with him, I had to admit it. It would be so cozy and safe—me, him, and a baby. Our own little family unit. He'd want that too, I knew he would. He needed me now, more than he did before. Now he'd appreciate me. A *baby*. Once you have one, you can't put it back. Then again, look at Nick's birth mother. He'd be thrilled, I was sure of it. By becoming parents ourselves, we'd be sloughing off all the crap that had gone before. Making a fresh start.

I didn't want to consider that Nick might not be thrilled to hear of his impending fatherhood. I tried not to remember that when Issy told Frank that she was pregnant, his reaction was to vacuum the entire house, in silence, for three hours. Not quite what Issy had been hoping for. But, I reassured myself, now Frank was a devoted dad, an outspoken champion of parenthood. If Nick was a little taken aback at first, he'd soon come around. I also tried not to remember that while Nick loved entertaining other people's children, he always returned from parties, slumped on the sofa, gestured around the room, and whispered, "Silence."

"You're the one who looks gray," said Claudia the second I walked in. (She likes to have the last word on insults.)

"I'm fine," I muttered. I could have done without this observation—when you're struggling to keep your house of cards from collapse, you don't appreciate so-called friends huffing and puffing. The tiny, ever-shrinking part of my brain devoted to realism suspected that Nick would be appalled beyond belief. Of course, I couldn't entertain such a possibility because then how would I cope? I was finding it hard enough to cope with my *own* doubts. It had been proved that I couldn't look after myself. How could I be trusted to look after a baby?

Recently, when I stroked Emily and she responded by rolling on her back and showing me her belly (quite the biggest compliment you can receive from a cat), I found myself looking forward to her death. I loved her so much, it seemed the safest option. I wanted her to have a happy life and die quickly, before anything horrible happened to her. I knew this was an odd line of reasoning. I also knew the fierce, consuming love that most babies inspire in their mothers and—judging from what I could feel about a cat—I worried about the terror it would bring. With the world in the state that it was, how could you dare to love another being so much that your life depended on it?

"I'm fine," I repeated.

"Good," replied Claudia, "because I've got something to tell you that will make you feel even finer."

Really. "Go on, then."

Claudia beamed. "We made a match. Sam and Bernard have resigned their membership."

My jaw dropped. (It's amazing how, when you're experiencing disbelief, that this actually happens.) "But," I squeaked, "how could they? God, they love Girl Meets Boy!"

Claudia's smile drooped. She looked confused. "Er, Hol. That's what members do when they find love. They resign their membership."

I could feel the fear rise. We *needed* people like Sam and

Bernard. I didn't care if Nige said they had radio faces. We needed their sweet natures. We needed their membership fees. And, despite my attempts to be normal, *I* still needed to keep everyone safely single. How could I run a dating agency if my instinct now opposed the very point of it?

"Claudia, do you know for certain that they've got together?"

"They rang within twenty minutes of each other. They were coy, but it was obvious."

I hardly heard her. I was sunk in gloom. I'd failed. I'd failed on every count. I'd botched my life good and proper. I'd trusted Stuart, the Big Bad Wolf. I'd ditched Nick, the Frog Prince. And I couldn't manage a business. You know, I bet the baby *wasn't* Nick's. And even if it was, he'd hate me for burdening him with a child. I might as well face it. He still was a child. And I was an idiot. An incompetent fool. Only *I* could end up being sued for damages by my own rapist.

Funny. Once upon a time I was a strong, confident woman. I was the do-it-herself princess who didn't *need* a prince. Now I had to have him to prop me up.

I sat down in my executive chair and crossed my legs. "Claudia," I said, "I'm going to give you first refusal. I'm selling Girl Meets Boy. I'm sure you'll understand. I've had enough."

CHAPTER 31

As Claudia started to say all the stuff you say to people who are poised on a window ledge, I decided to tell her about the pregnancy. Not because I wanted her to know, but because I didn't have the strength to engage in an argument with a clever person and I hoped it would shut her up. Having a kid was a marvelous excuse to jack in the business, even if it wasn't the real one. Now *her* mouth fell open.

"It's Nick's," I said before she could ask.

Most people would have cried "Congratulations!" but Claudia wasn't most people. "Are you *sure* it's his? When did you, uh? Shouldn't he take a paternity test? Or won't a gynecologist tell you how many weeks it is? And are you sure this is a good idea? Don't you need to spend a bit more time sorting your head out? Would you be having it for the right reasons? It shouldn't just be a distraction. Are you and Nick back together? Does he know yet?" She finished up with, "Well, if you *are* having a kid, all the more reason to stick with your business and make it work. You need money to raise a child."

Like lemon juice finds a paper cut, that was Claudia. I snapped my bag shut, dragged my coat off the back of the chair, and replied, "Ring Issy, ask her to cover. Find a temp. I don't care. If you want me, I'll be at home."

As I flounced from the office, Claudia yelled after me, "Fine, but I'm going to have to tell Issy about Stuart, because I can't keep up this charade any longer. I've run out of excuses for you."

I turned and screamed, "Tell her everything, see if I care. Tell Nige, tell Rachel, tell them all, let them speculate about how it was just a shag but it fucked me up anyway, I don't give a shit!"

I glimpsed Claudia framed in the doorway, shock on her pale face. Sun streamed in from the window, lighting the edges of her hair, a dark angel. "Holly," she said, and I had to strain to hear, "they are your real friends and they would *never* doubt you. Please have faith. Not everyone is as cruel and unkind as Stuart."

Claudia was as good as her word and told all three of them, because on Wednesday Rachel sent me flowers. White roses. I put them in a glass vase and stared at them. If your life is a pigsty, white roses in a glass vase are—superficially—the answer. The very fact there are white roses in a glass vase in your house creates the illusion that everything is under control. *Look,* they say, *I have the time, money, and peace of mind to purchase the beautiful and superfluous.* I tried to think what else they might say. White, the color of innocence. The card read "Dearest, precious Holly, I am so, so sorry."

Naturally, I was screening my calls, and I felt tragic doing it. She also rang, but I didn't pick up even though I knew I should thank her for the roses. I still felt rage toward her—she was almost definitely screwing my brother-in-law. I couldn't send *her* white roses. Nige rang too, sounding shaken. I wondered if he really was appalled or if he were acting. I've always wondered this about actors. If Tom made Nicole cry, how did he know it was for real? How did she know it was for real if he had a tantrum? Obviously with, say, Stallone, there wouldn't be a problem. Nige also wrote me a letter in velvety black ink on thick cream notepaper about what a special person I was, begging me not to let this destroy me.

Destroy? I thought, admiring his jagged calligraphy—like rows of daggers on the page. A bit overdramatic, wasn't it? It was one thing, *me* believing that I was doomed to poverty and misery. It was quite another thing, my friends agreeing with me. Issy actually came around, ringing the doorbell, then—when I didn't answer it—bursting into a storm of tears, walking in a small, furious circle, drying her eyes, and ringing again. I watched her with curiosity from the upstairs window. She was always aloof, our eldest sister, as if whatever Claudia and I got up to was child's play. Even her attitude to Girl Meets Boy had been coolly condescending. It surprised me that the Stuart thing would rouse her to emotion. She was so accustomed to maintaining a professional distance, and half her clients had been through far worse than I had (the proof being that they were all bonkers). Surely, to her, my little mishap was piffle.

I couldn't even bear to face Nick, although I was slightly peeved that he'd only rung once since our date. (I'd been too lackluster to return his call, and he hadn't called again.) He'd *have* to ring more when I told him the news. I spent three days thinking, I'm pregnant. Great! Oh shit. Great! Oh shit. Great! Oh shit . . . I found this new state extremely effective in overriding my other concerns. *You cop-out,* said a small voice from somewhere in my head, but I disallowed it. Pregnancy was my ticket to an easy life. *Are you crazy?* said the voice. It was, though. It would guarantee me Nick's adoration, and if Stuart did sue it would give me the sympathy vote in court. It would permit me to bail out of Girl Meets Boy with minimum hassle from friends and family. It would wipe me from the radar of sexual predators. It was the best mistake I'd ever made.

I also spent more time than is healthy scrutinizing my stomach in the mirror. Despite swearing that I wouldn't lose weight, I'd dropped at least two stone in the last few months. Nick was right, it *didn't* suit me. It was more the glandular fever than Stuart, but I still objected to it on principle. When Gloria rang the doorbell (she always rang these days, even though she had a key) in Gloria-code—*tring tring tring!*—I told her the house was spotless. Would she mind if we went food shopping instead?

"Why aren't you at work?"

I frowned at her sharp little face. "I have sick leave."

"You've *had* sick leave."

"Gloria," I said, wondering how she dared wear stonewashed drainpipe jeans and walk the streets, "I don't want to discuss it."

"When was the last time you went to the supermarket by yourself?"

"Why is this relevant?"

"When, Holly?"

"Jesus! I don't know! Three months ago, okay?"

She pushed her hair from her eyes. "Can I ask, did the police offer you counseling?"

I tutted. "Yeah, yeah, they recommended people."

"And did you take it up?"

"Oh bloody *hell*, Gloria, leave it. I don't have time. I'm sick to death of talking about it, thinking about it, it's over. I just want to be normal again."

"Right. And that's why you need me to chaperon you to Tesco."

"Just forget it, then!" I screeched.

I stamped down the garden path, jammed my keys into the ignition, and roared off to Marks & Spencer. (If I was going to face crowds, it would have to be a slow acclimatization. I assumed that the M&S food hall—more posh and more expensive than Tesco—would be frequented by a genteel class of customer who'd keep their distance. I was mistaken; they were like a pack of starving wolves.) The sweats began as I drove into the car park. It took me ten minutes to leave the car. I took a basket and started dumping fruit and vegetables in it. As I stared at the shelves, people hovered close behind me, forcing me to dart away, glaring. I lost sight of the doors and couldn't get a full breath. I had to heave so hard my lungs hurt. I trembled and wanted to run, but too bad, I had to feed the blob.

Forty-five minutes later I staggered up the garden path, the weight of the bags cutting into my fingers and stretching my arms at least a couple of inches. I could still feel my heart racing, but altogether the experience hadn't been as horrendous as my imagination had drawn it. Supermarket shopping was, I decided, *do-able*. It wasn't like the subway, where the black walls of suits closed in on you and there really was no escape. Gloria said nothing when she saw the bags. She kept scrubbing the oven, but I could sense a smug aura. Only after she left did I see the note on the table. It was an E-mail address, in Gloria's rather painful handwriting. She'd misspelled words like *cousin* and *recommend*. I stuck it in the nearest drawer. Gloria had had one triumph with me that day, two would be overdoing it.

I did, however, order a pregnancy book off Amazon. If I liked, there was little need ever to set foot outside the house again. I could get a job proofreading and—now that I considered it—didn't Tesco do home deliveries? If I boarded up my mailbox and disconnected the phone, Stuart could sue me all he liked, I'd know nothing about it. I spent the rest of the week lying in bed, reading the pregnancy book (apparently written for ten-year-olds), and wondering whether—if I had an "incompetent cervix"—there was a danger of the fetus falling out of my body and getting stuck down my pajama leg like a sock. I had a moment or two of weakness, when I itched to ring Claudia to see how Date Night had gone, but I held back.

Then, on Friday morning, she rang me. "Hol, pick up, I'm bored of this. If you don't, I'm telling Mum and Dad. You're freaking me out."

She'd called my bluff. I lifted the receiver. "Hello. It's me."

"Finally. Great, well, come on, open the door."

"What?"

"Open the door, I'm standing outside freezing my bollocks off."

I peered down from my lookout, and there she was, yapping into her cell. She was wearing a high ponytail and red mittens.

"Wait a sec." I scrambled downstairs in my pajamas. I'd been wearing them for the best part of five days. The house gleamed, and so did I (who wouldn't, averaging three baths daily), but my pajamas were about to disintegrate. I redialed. "Wait another sec."

I ran upstairs into my bedroom and dragged on some clothes. In my haste, I pulled on a pink sweater. I'd been boycotting any tone brighter than brown, but Claudia was rapping the knocker to the tune of—as far as I could tell—"Why Are We Waiting," so I thought rather than change I'd be wise to get downstairs fast.

I let her in.

"Ah, good, you're a bit fuller in the face. How are you feeling? Where's the cat?"

"Out socializing."

Claudia nodded her approval. She and Emily hadn't seen eye-to-eye ever since Claw had taken off her pink-and-black ponyskin mules (acquired in Paris) at the door and Emily had been sick in the left shoe. Claudia had discovered the crime, of course, by putting her foot in it. She disliked cats anyway, and such sabotage confirmed it.

"Can you lock the cat flap until I've gone?"

"No! How would *you* like to be locked out of your own home!"

"You're mental," replied Claudia, and tip-tapped into the lounge. What she didn't know was that the cat flap *had* been locked until a week before. No matter how long Emily had sat by the door, scraping plaintively at the cat flap or yowling through the night, I couldn't bring myself to let her out. I'd huddled under the covers and blocked out her cries. Yet another bone of contention between Gloria and myself. I'd come home more than once to find a neat pile of ironing and Emily at large. When I'd asked Gloria not to let the cat out, she'd replied, "Cats are meant to go outside. They're hunters, it's their reason for being. It's not fair of you to take your hang-ups out on Emily. You're as bad as those vegan idiots who feed their dogs on broccoli. Or their children for that matter."

I suppose it was Gloria who prompted me to let Emily out again. She continued to unlock the cat flap in my absence, and no feline tragedy occurred. Furthermore, I hated to see Emily miserable. I felt like her jailer. And finally, Emily did four consecutive poos on my Persian rug. I'm loath to give in to blackmail, but I'm afraid the fourth poo swayed it for me. I let her out and cordial relations were resumed.

Claudia rejected a cup of coffee and stood by the sofa rather than sit on it. To be honest, I was pleased to see her. Despite the adrenaline charge of novelty, I felt a restlessness that seemed alarmingly close to boredom. I didn't want to admit it, but by Thursday I'd missed the office. I was still resolved to give it all up—after such a song and dance it would have been weak to change my mind—yet I was slowly coming 'round to the idea that maybe I could leave the house occasionally. I could be a—oh what was it called when you did nothing under the guise of expertise? A consultant!

"Flying visit," said Claw. "To say that I've been considering your offer about Girl Meets Boy, and I think we should have a serious talk about it. If we don't act fast, the agency is going to go under— the finances are better but not exactly great, and the business as a whole needs direction. I suggest Sunday, at seven, at my place. I'll make cheese on toast. It'll be a proper business meeting."

Quite how cheese on toast made a proper business meeting, I didn't know. And her determination caused flutters in my stomach. (It's easy not to want something, so long as no one else wants it. Once someone voices interest, you presume you've made the mistake of your life.) But it was too late.

"Yeah, okay," I replied. "Sunday at seven it is. I'll dig out the paperwork."

Claudia nodded, a pert business nod, paused at the door, and granted me a regal wave. "Be punctual."

I was left standing, mouth open. Be *punctual*! Before I employed her she was unemployable! Of all the cheek!

Sunday, dot on seven, I rang Claudia's bell. (Having first called her from the car to announce my arrival—I refused to wait outside in the dark, alone, not even for five seconds.) Obligingly, it played the first few bars of "God Save the Queen." A visit to

Claudia's flat was like going back in time. It was a shrine to the fifties. Or the sixties. It wavered according to whatever junk she'd picked up that week in Brick Lane. You walked through a shower of pink door beads into a lounge dominated by a fake tigerskin carpet, deep red walls, and a cocktail bar—a garish silver homage to vinyl and Formica, with a pineapple ice bucket claiming pride of place. Fairy lights twinkled from the ceiling, and the walls were adorned with illuminated pictures of waterfalls that I'd only ever seen in Indian restaurants. As Nige once said, "Christ alive, it's me Great-aunt Mabel's house!"

Claw yanked open the door as I took my finger off the buzzer. "Change of plan," she said as I walked in. I gasped, "Oh my God!" and started laughing. There, sitting meekly on various yellow poufs, were Nige, Nick—ba-*boom!* God, he still had that effect on me—Manjit, Rachel, Issy, Camille, Sam, and Bernard. They were all clutching dubious-looking red drinks, each accessorized with a cocktail umbrella. Everyone jumped up and started *clapping.*

I turned to Claudia, wide-eyed. What were they clapping at me for? I wondered. Being raped? She shrugged, grinned, said, "Sorry, dahl, but there was *no way* we were gonna roll over and let you quit the business. There are a million reasons why you should stay, as Bernard will explain."

Bernard—last seen sitting alone in a French restaurant—cleared his throat. He'd done something to his hair and, blow me down, it was rather cute. Next to him, Sam twisted her hands together and stared at her big feet. Nick winked at me, and I blushed beet-red. Issy was just about boring through my head with a laser gaze, willing me to make eye contact. Rachel jammed a cigarette butt in a burgundy glass ashtray and smiled an apologetic smile. Manjit looked as if he wasn't quite sure why he was here. *No, no, yes, yes, yes, no.* How easy it was to tell who knew what.

"I wanted to voice the opinion," declared Bernard in a strong voice, "on behalf of us all, that you'd be highly unwise to resign from Girl Meets Boy." He glanced at Claw for reassurance. She nodded. "And these are some of the many reasons."

I stood there politely, waiting. I'd kill Claudia. This was excruciating. Bernard was unaccustomed to public speaking. "First, that

Glamour wants to do a three-page feature on you and the agency. Second, that all your members miss you. Third, that Nige gave you a massive plug on his breakfast television interview on Friday, and the phone has, according to your sisters, been ringing off the hook. And fourth, that thanks to you, I am about to marry the love of my life."

At which point, Sam—speaking for at least two of us, I'm sure—burst into tears.

CHAPTER 32

There was a silence. Manjit started clapping, then stopped. I realized that I was expected to break it.

"Bernard! Sam! That's wonderful," I said on cue. And it was. Their joy was proof, it blasted away uncertainty, it made me see that what I did was good. Then, in an unwelcome flash, it struck me that Bernard hadn't actually specified Sam. But no, she stuck out her left hand and on her third finger shone a rock the size of Gibraltar. "Amazing," I added, as an appropriate response was required. "Someone fetch me a magnifying glass."

Sam giggled. "My dear," she said, with the super-duper confidence of the newly engaged woman, "do you *need* one?"

All the females crowded around and cooed. All the males shuffled from foot to foot looking uncomfortable.

Claudia touched my arm. "Hol, no one's asking you to make a decision this minute. But maybe you'll consider the possibility of staying. Drink?"

I glanced at Nick. He wasn't looking at me anymore. "The biggest you've got."

She poured me a double vodka and tonic, which I gulped down

before realizing that it might pickle the fetus. I suppose I would have been peeved if everyone had just let me quit Girl Meets Boy without a squeak of protest. I smiled nervously around the room. I owed a lot of people explanations. After the struggle with Stuart in his office, I'd rung Manjit and said I no longer wanted self-defense classes. Unless I had a gun, I figured, there was no point. He wasn't used to arguing, so he didn't. I still felt rotten about it. Issy—the therapist with more issues than the whole of Hollywood stuck together—was plainly aggrieved that I hadn't confided in her, and would doubtless remain so until I sat in her office and unpeeled the layers of my soul like an onion. Nick would be wondering why I hadn't returned his call after our magical last date, and—oh God, the last thing he needed was another person letting him down. And Nige would be busting to discover how I felt, to ooze horror and sympathy, and to suck up all this precious material, in case he were ever called upon to play a victim.

Or maybe I was too harsh.

"Come and help me in the kitchen, Hol," said Claw. A spurious request, but I scurried after her. She shut the door. "Baby coming along nicely?" she inquired, like it was a cake. "You're not cross, are you?"

"Fine. No." I checked mentally, to see if I was lying. I wasn't. I tried a smile. It was glorious that Bernard and Sam were engaged. And Nige had mentioned *Glamour* wanting to do a piece but, in my gloom, I hadn't believed him. I sat down on an orange plastic chair. (Claudia's entire kitchen was orange, it was like being held captive by a tangerine.) "Was Nige really on breakfast TV?"

"Yup."

"Er, why?"

"He's an understudy catapulted to stardom. The play previewed on Wednesday night, and Nige surprised them all. He's actually a reasonable actor. I don't think the critics expected it. *I* didn't."

"That's fantastic! He's going to be insufferable. So . . . so what did he say about us?"

Claw smiled at the "us."

"He said his only regret about his 'big break' was that it dragged him away from his between-jobs job. Said 'Girl Meets Boy' about five hundred times. Droned on about drowning in young, gorgeous, successful singles. I think that's what did it. The magic words, 'Young, gorgeous, successful singles.' We had forty-seven calls, not all of them from nutters."

"No!"

"I swear."

I felt a tingle of excitement.

Claudia gripped my hands. "Listen, Hol. You're going through a rough time. You've had what I hope is the worst experience you'll ever have in your life. But it's *over*. The CPS not prosecuting—remember, Caroline calls them 'the Criminal Protection Service.' I understand, it must have been like being abused all over again. But you are a tough cookie. You *will* get through this. I'm not saying shove it under the carpet. What I am saying is don't let the injustice of it beat you. You have a choice. You have no power over what has happened to you, but you have every power over what happens to you next. When Manjit was depressed, yes, he took his pills, but mentally, he *fought* it and that's crucial. He says all therapy is, is intelligent listening, and you know I'll always be here to listen to you, as will Issy, as will Nick."

She took a deep breath. "And talking of Nick . . . ?"

"I haven't told him. I will."

I bit my lip. This was ludicrous, like a half-played game of Cluedo come to life. Most of the guests in the lounge had a secret. Nick was adopted. Claudia was gay. Rachel was having an affair with Frank. Issy had marriage problems (duh). Camille was sleeping with Claudia. I was being sued by my rapist. I was also pregnant with someone's child. Oprah, eat your heart out.

"Don't delay it too long," murmured Claw, peering into the oven with something like bemusement. "Do you know how many weeks it is yet?"

I shook my head. No, and I wasn't about to start counting. What if it wasn't the right number of weeks? I hadn't even been to a doctor, because he would tell me and I didn't want to know. I sniffed. "It smells delicious in here, Claw. You haven't been . . . *cooking*?"

"If I'd been cooking, Hol, you'd be dialing the emergency services, begging for the number of Taco Bell. Everyone else cooked.

The yellow thing in the oven is a posh fish pie, courtesy of Sam. Bernard has made vegetable lasagne. Camille made herb soup, which sounds weird but it's bloody delicious. Rachel provided the wine . . ."

Claudia paused so we could grin at each other. Occasionally I err in thinking that Rachel is no different from me, and then I remember that when she hosts a dinner party, she buys a crate of Beaujolais and puts our pitiful hodgepodge of bottles on the side, so that no guest has to suffer the indignity of drinking random booze.

"Issy made a salad, and two loaves of walnut bread from that breadmaker she's so embarrassingly proud of. I didn't trust her with anything else. Eden made fairy cakes. Manjit made lemon roast chicken—he said it was that or a signature dish entitled Blastyerarse Chili. Nige has been flouncing around the kitchen all afternoon creating potato skins and avocado and sour cream dips. And Nick rang Brookfields Junior School, presumably slept with a dinner lady, and got the recipe for chocolate-and-cornflake-goo squares. He was on the phone this morning complaining that the ingredients were cheap and nasty and he could make a far superior version if I let him improvise, but I told him don't be clever, this isn't about taste, it's about nostalgia. Do exactly what it says on the recipe."

I gazed at the orange floor tiles. Eventually I said, "Everyone made a real effort."

"Yeah, well. For some reason they like you."

I punched her on the arm. Don't tell *me* about not being able to express your feelings.

"Come on. Let's go back in. Your public awaits."

I looked longingly at my empty glass and marched back into the lounge.

Rachel was standing near the door, a vision in a purple sari, talking to Nige. He was dressed in his trademark white jeans and white shirt, and together they looked like an advert for Silk Cut. Except for the fact that they were both smoking Marlboros. Now he'd snatched fame in the West End, I guessed she thought he was worth speaking to. As for him, he lost no love on her, but I supposed he'd grant anyone an audience if the subject was Number One. I caught myself thinking these mean-spirited thoughts and felt ashamed.

These were my *friends*. They were here for *me*. Nige had probably skipped an at-home with Rupert Everett to attend, and there was a high chance Rach had turned down the grand old Duke of York. As for her affair with Frank, I didn't have concrete proof. There was such a thing as coincidence.

I kissed Nige on the cheek. "Congratulations, you clever boy. I'm not at all surprised. How does it feel?"

He held out his drink to Rach, who took it, and hugged me to him. "You, my love, are going nowhere," he husked into my ear. "You're going to turn the agency 'round, and it's going to be the biggest success. The best revenge is living well." He took my hand and kissed it, a theatrical gesture but it meant a lot. "Although if you want him beaten to a pulp, I do know people."

"Oh, do be quiet, Nigel," snapped Rachel. She passed him back his glass and sighed. "I simply couldn't feel any worse," she said finally, a very Rachel thing to say. "I think that once you tried to tell me and I brushed you off. I apologize. I hope you can forgive me. I suppose I . . . I didn't want to believe it. If I had to . . . well, I hope you're rallying. I can't imagine how you must feel. But, Holly"—you knew it was serious when Rachel didn't call you "babes"—"I know you'll come through. And I'm sorry I haven't been in touch much recently. I've been fraught with work and the move."

"The move?"

"Yes, babes, I'm attempting to move house. Exchanged last week. You knew that, babes, I told you."

If I did, I wasn't aware of it.

"I'm sorry," continued Rachel. "It's been *such* a mare. I've not been in contact with anyone—I've not been able to detach myself from the horror of the moment."

"What moment?" said Nige.

"*Any* moment. Each one has had me paralyzed with shock. The moment when my vendor decided to pull out after we'd agreed on a price because rival estate agents valued his property at forty thousand pounds more than I was paying. The moment when I realized that my lawyer was an incompetent fool and was refusing to pick up the phone to my buyer's lawyer because he didn't *like* him. Roland

Rat, the real estate agent on loan from hell. Oh, there were plenty of moments."

"Poor you," said Nige. "I'm sure Holly's heart bleeds."

Rachel frowned. So did I. I wished he hadn't said it. "Moving house is a sod," I said quickly. "I always look through the local paper's property section, and I'll think, Ooh, three quarters of a million for a three-bedroom house in Hampstead. Mm, okay, horrendous, but it's a nice area. And then, Jesus Christ, you realize it's a *flat*!"

"Absolutely," said Rachel, although the last time her family worried about money was probably when Henry VIII repossessed the monasteries. "The greed of people is astonishing. The entire process is frankly distasteful. And stamp duty. They might as well tax you for walking down the road."

"They do," said Issy, who had elbowed into our circle. She eyed me sternly and said in a voice that for her was soft. "*I* could have helped, you know."

Nige stared.

Pause.

"So I hear Frank is thinking of buying an E-type. How marvelous. They're super cars."

Slowly, Issy turned her gaze on Rach. Like a cat seeing a dog for the first time. "Who told you that?"

"Foooooood!" bellowed Claudia from across the room. "Rachel, come and do the wine." You never saw a woman of Rachel's girth move so fast.

Nige coughed. "I did," he said, brushing an imaginary speck of dust from the front of his white shirt. "Just now. Didn't Frank say? I bumped into him in the petrol station the other day. We discussed cars."

"I see," said Issy. "No, he didn't say."

I scrutinized her from under my eyelashes. She didn't look happy. I frowned at Nige. Nige drove a green Fiat Panda and I couldn't imagine he had the least interest in discussing it or indeed any car. But then he had no reason to lie for Rachel. He didn't even *like* Rachel. Yet there was no denying that Rach was behaving oddly. She was definitely on edge in front of Issy. Nige smiled, not a care. "Shall we eat?" he said, linking arms with Issy and myself.

I nodded. Give it up, Holly. Why should I play detective? Particularly when real-live uniformed detectives didn't seem able to catch criminals with all the evidence in the world. What made me think I could play Miss Marple?

I allowed Nige to pile my plate with fish pie, potato skins, and—in thoughtful deference to Issy—salad. My appetite was back. I seemed to be untouched by morning sickness. Pregnancy must suit me. I ate a potato skin smugly—this little thing inside me (the fetus, not the potato skin) made me feel special. I was a link in evolution's chain instead of a dead end. Of course, I reminded myself, it was early days. But I felt smug all the same. I *knew* this baby would survive. It was meant to be. It was my rescue remedy. I wouldn't allow myself to think anything else.

My elbow knocked Camille's as I scooped up a heap of vegetable lasagne to smother the salad. She smiled, shy. "Hi. How are you?"

I nodded, equally tongue-tied. "Fine. This is great. Thank you for helping."

"Pleasure. Claw was worried. She thought you might freak."

"I came close. But how can I not appreciate this?" I wondered if I should congratulate her officially for getting it on with my sister. "Good news about you and Claw," I blurted out. I just stopped short of adding "Well done!"

"Oh, oh, thank you." A faint color tinted Camille's pale cheeks. "I adore her. I hope you're feeling less traumatized about Stuart," she added.

I nodded dumbly. This conversation was like a gun going off accidentally. Panic was causing us to ricochet wildly, smashing convention after convention. Camille gulped her drink. "I'm sorry. Anything I say will sound trite. He's disgusting. He deserves life. I loathe him and I loathe working for him. But . . ." She lowered her voice. As she spoke quietly anyhow, I had to strain to hear. "It won't be for much longer. He's got it coming, Holly. I know it's still not ideal. But he'll be punished in some sense. It looks like probate will be granted soon. And then, he'll contact various authorities to release the funds and—depending on what he does with the deeds of the Paris apartment—then we'll know. Obviously, I can't report him to the Law Society yet, as he could still make out it's just an administrative slip. We need to see money that isn't his being placed into *his* account, and presumably, it won't be an account that's easy to trace. I need to speak to someone who can advise me what to do then, and how to do it. Someone who is an expert in law but a hundred percent trustworthy. You don't want to know how hard that is." She added quickly, "But it *will* be fine, I'm working on it."

"Working on what?" inquired Nick, who had wandered over. He was immaculate in cream chinos, a blue-and-white-striped shirt, and brown moccasins. In my humble opinion, he looked like an idiot. He'd always despised men who dressed like this—from Fulham central casting, because they didn't have an original bone in their porky bodies—and I wasn't sure what point he was trying to make. That he made my heart go *ting!* even in his Hugh Grant getup was alarming.

"Oh, nothing," said Camille.

"It's all right. He knows." I smiled at Nick. "Camille's working on trapping Stuart."

Nick scowled. His whole body tensed.

I touched his arm. "Don't let's talk about that now. This is lovely. I can't *believe* you got the recipe for the cornflake-and-chocolate-goo squares." I paused, then thought I'd chance it. "That has to be just about the most romantic thing you've ever done for me."

Camille faded tactfully into the distance.

Nick grabbed me by the hand and led me to a twinkly pink and green corner. "Holly," he said, taking my groaning plate and shoving it onto a thin shelf, where it tilted precariously. "I hate not being with you. I feel half dead without you."

My heart hammered. This was perfect.

He added, "I've grown up a lot in the past few months, I swear it. I know what I was like, an irresponsible baby. I don't blame you for ending our engagement, I really don't. Although"—the words spewed out violently—"Pamela Fidgett says that Lavinia and Michael are largely to blame. She says that they probably never came to terms with their own infertility, they wanted to pretend to everyone, me included, that I was their real child, so it's *their* fault that I . . . I've not been as sensible and responsible and as adult as I might have been, you see, because I was lied to and manipulated and kept in a certain place and not given the opportunity to come to terms with life as it really is, and no wonder I don't trust people, because if you can't trust your own parents, who *can* you trust?"

He paused for breath. "Oh," I wanted to say. "So, what, you didn't trust *me*?"

Was this the root of his brattish behavior? Keep it all light-hearted, everything a joke, because if you betray real emotion, show how strongly you *could* feel, how much you *might* care, you risk abandonment. But then, I couldn't help thinking there was a good chance that theory was bullshit, the coward's excuse. If he'd shown how much he cared, then we might still be together. It was the so-what act that had become a self-fulfilling prophecy. Hell, I didn't know. You could blame your parents for your dysfunction until you were ninety-three, under the guise that if it was their fault, poor lit-tle you were obliged to do nothing about it. Surely Nick had to own some responsibility for how he'd been with me? I looked at his angry face. It was the face of a hurt child.

I took a breath. God, how I loved him. And if you love some-one, you want the best for them. Which can mean confronting them with the unwanted truth. It was obvious to me that Nick needed a buffer to the wisdom of Pamela Fidgett. Because while Pamela Fidgett was undoubtedly correct in many of her assump-tions about Lavinia and Michael, she was also telling Nick exactly what he wished to hear. Everything she said got him off the hook for every misdemeanor he'd committed over the past three decades, from squelching his hand into his first birthday cake to smashing up my home printer with a bamboo stick following a me-chanical disagreement.

Then again, the consequence of telling someone you love the unwanted truth can be disastrous. They resent you as the bearer of unwelcome news, and hate you as a result. I would have been a fool to tell Nick my gut feelings. I needed to encourage this fantasy line of thought. It was in my best interest. Anyway, what did the thinking matter, it was the actual conclusion that counted, and Nick's con-clusion was that he felt half dead without me.

I smiled into his eyes and pulled him closer, until we stood there, chest to chest. "Nick," I whispered, in the tradition of many a blushing screen goddess to her devilishly dashing hero, "I'm going to have your baby."

CHAPTER 33

Other than Frank vacuuming the house for three hours in silence, I had no experience of how a man typically reacts on hearing that he's about to become a father. So when Nick laughed and said, "No, you're not!" I was unsure if this was normal.

"No, really, I am," I replied, the moony-eyed expression dying on my face.

"What, you're *pregnant*?"

"Yes!"

Nick glanced from side to side, as if searching for an escape route. "Are you sure," he added, "that you're not fantasizing?"

If humans really did swell with indignation, I'd have ballooned to twice my size. "Of course I'm not fantasizing. I took a test! There was a blue line in the round window!"

Nick blinked. "Round window or square window?"

I was beginning to lose my temper. "I don't know, whichever damn window it is says you're pregnant!"

Nick squeezed his forehead with two fingers. "Right, okay. Right. Right. And when . . . and when was it we . . . ?"

My eyes widened in disbelief. "When I came 'round to you that time after you found out you were adopted!" I said, my voice a high squeak.

He frowned, as if trying to remember. I wanted to hit him about the head. I think he sensed this, because he stretched the corners of his mouth apologetically and murmured, "I was in a bit of a state." He smiled. "You made me feel a lot better."

If this was meant to salve the ego, it didn't. What did he think I was, a hooker?

He swallowed. "And so you've not had any periods since?"

Jesus. Bring back the 1950s male. "Nick," I said, in the most patronizing tone I could muster, "considering that I am a reasonably intelligent person who got an *A* in biology, do you honestly think I'd be claiming to be pregnant if I was still"—I summoned a word that frightens men—"*menstruating?*"

"Okay." He sighed. "One more question. And don't take this the wrong way. After your terrible—"

I held up a hand to stop him. "If," I said icily, "you were going to inquire about Stuart, don't. He wore . . . protection, and"—I wondered how to sound dignified and condescending at the same time—"my cycle continued as normal. Now, if you'll excuse me."

I snatched my plate from almost certain doom and stomped off. "Now, if you'll excuse me" is PG moviespeak for "Fuck you," and Nick had watched enough cinematic pap to know that. As for my cycle continuing as normal, I was bluffing, but I was pretty sure it had. If I made myself think back (which took some forcing), I could almost picture the scene, a scramble of relief and disgust, the drab physicality of bleeding from your unmentionable. Forgive me, after what I'd suffered for it, that part of my anatomy was not a flower or a reproductive organ or anything beautiful, it was unmentionable, preferably nonexistent. At the same time, I felt a gratifying sense of a bloodletting, putting out the rubbish, getting rid of any last trace of Stuart. Had I imagined it or was it true?

It was true, I decided, shoveling cold vegetable lasagne down my throat. The memory crept back inch by inch, like a dog afraid of being hit. But when Manjit sauntered over for a chat, I could barely concentrate on what he was saying. How *dare* Nick not be delighted? I ignored him for the rest of the evening and made a show of being too full to try a cornflake-and-chocolate-goo square (even though I all but drooled at the sight of them). And it had all been going so well.

I was staggered. I'd wanted comfort. I tucked my hair behind my ears and slipped from the room. Upstairs, in Claudia's study, I dialed a number I knew by heart.

"Two-nine-six-three, hello?"

"S'me, Holly. I wondered . . . How would you and Dad like another grandchild?"

There was a silence. Then a gasp. And a roar of "Stanleeeeee!"

All in all, I painted a cozy little picture. Yes, Nick and I were expecting. We weren't *together* together, but it was early days, and we were both thrilled. Yes, he was looking after me. Yes, I was feeling tired. Yes, I was taking folic acid. No, I hadn't seen the doctor yet, but I would. We were only telling close family. Nick hadn't told Lavinia and Michael yet, but soon. Yes, we were very happy.

I crept downstairs a while later, snug in the warm glow of parental pride. See, *they* knew how to make me feel special. Strengthened by their love and joy, I told myself that Claudia was right. My survival, mental and physical, was up to me. If I wanted, the twin curses of Stuart and Nick could be rendered powerless. All I had to do was be strong and keep fighting. So I stopped trying to meet Nick's eye. And later that evening, as Claudia waved me off at the door, I yelled, "See you at work tomorrow, nine o'clock sharp."

Her shout of "Yay!" ensured a stiff victory smile on my face all the way home—even if it felt like it was tacked on with nails.

As it's presumed important to look the part, I set my alarm for seven and spent an hour trying to fashion myself into the common impression of a businesswoman. This was harder than it sounds. As we tended to dress for pleasure in my office, I had only one suit in my wardrobe, circa 1995. It was a gray weave, the skirt was neither here nor there—not tapered or flared but a dreary in-between— and the jacket ended abruptly at the waist. I did own a black pair of high-heeled shoes, but even though they were from a funky store, they had a Marks & Spencer–ish air about them. I'd slip them on and they'd fast-forward me to forty.

I gazed into the wardrobe, waiting for it to perform a miracle, and—a once-in-a-lifetime occurrence—it did. A bright pink cashmere sweater winked at me from where it was squashed between two pairs of jeans. I tugged it out. Soft and feminine (and I mean that only in the sense that a hetero man wouldn't be pleased to get it for Christmas) and smelling musty. I hadn't worn it for months. I felt too girly and weak in it. Crap! It wasn't the sweater that was girly and weak, it was *me*. Well, no longer. I pulled it on, squirted perfume to disguise the mustiness—I'm afraid Nick's hygiene habits had rubbed off—and teamed it with flared black corduroy jeans and a shiny pair of pointy pink patent-leather boots (a birthday present from Claudia, secured, as I recall, from a sex shop in L.A. and guaranteed to scare the life out of people).

Issy and Claw applauded as I tottered in. I rolled my eyes and sank into a chair. "You know," I said, "you really must stop clapping for me all the time. I'm beginning to feel like the Queen."

I brandished a greasy paper bag in their faces. "Monday morning celebration."

My sisters laughed, producing identical paper bags from various hiding places.

I smiled. "In the spirit of greed, I think I can manage three doughnuts."

"Capitalism at its most ruthless," said Claudia happily. Issy's agreement wasn't quite so heartfelt, but she ripped open a stack of vacuum-sealed paper plates and handed them around. "Oooh!" cried Claudia. "I'nt she posh!"

"We need coffee," exclaimed Issy. "I'll go."

Claw and I raised our eyebrows at each other in silent approval. "New leaf," mouthed Claudia. I beamed. Work! This was part of what made life meaningful—striving! What had I been thinking? Who could do without it?

The second Issy was out the door, Claudia said, "What's wrong?"

I told her about Nick's reaction. "I'm fine, though," I insisted. "I'm more than capable of managing without him. And—ta daaa!—I told Mum and Dad last night. They're thrilled."

"Oh my God, of course they are! Christ, they must be over the moon. What did they say? That must have been why Mum rang me this morning. I was on my way out so I didn't pick up. I'll ring her back right now. It's *so* exciting, I can't believe it! And don't worry about Nick. We'll all help you. One kid is a piece of cake. You can pick it up and carry it around in your pocket!"

"Yeah," I said, "I can be doing without two."

We laughed, and I refused to feel guilty. Yes, it was mature of Nick to offer to beg a favor from Michael on my behalf at a time when he was still furious and hurt and wanting to reject his adoptive parents. But this was, I decided, the exception that proves the rule. Nick was a kid. I tried to disapprove of him. What about the time he stumbled in drunk after a boys' night out and made himself a sandwich by tearing the wrapping off a pound of Brie and sticking it between two slices of bread. He hadn't even cut off the rind. I did my best to frown but smirked instead. The thought of it made me laugh. *Was* this childish, or was it merely high spirits? And what about the time he stood in front of the mirror and said "Candyman" five times? I'd screamed at him not to (you never know). That was irresponsible, wasn't it? Yes, but it was also fun. I remembered something Claw had said when we'd got engaged: "You're lucky, Hol. You're marrying a man who's going to make you laugh for the rest of your life."

She'd always liked Nick. I sighed and thanked her for the previous night. It had turned my head around. Made me realize that it was up to *me* to make myself laugh for the rest of my life. It seemed a bit of a tall order. Still. I could do it. "Great to see Nige looking so happy," I said to ward off another "What's wrong?"

"Oh yeah," said Claw.

"I thought he'd drop us the second he got a sniff of success, but he hasn't. He's a good bloke. He really cares about the agency."

"He cares about you, you daft cow. He despises most of the world, but if he respects you, he'll stick by you. He *is* a good bloke. You were very sweet to him when he split with Marylou, he's never forgotten that. He still mentions it. A lot of his friends sided with her, presumably because she's on the telly. Did he tell you the latest on that score? Suddenly, now he's star of the show, she wants to meet him for a cappy. I said the filthy girl! He said she meant a cappuccino. My God. She's even more of a thespian than he is! I'm surprised they stood each other as long as they did. How their egos fit in that two-bed flat! You know, technically, they're still married."

I pouted. "I hope he doesn't meet her for a cappy or anything else. She treated him horribly."

Claw shrugged. "Right now he's getting his adrenaline kicks from elsewhere. He shouldn't need her."

We were nodding sagely when Issy returned with a caffeine tower. "Okay," I said, wanting to do justice to their faith in me. "To business! And in the interest of not wasting time, I suggest we speak unashamedly with our mouths full."

Cue an enjoyable morning of discussing *Glamour* articles, filing applications, and spitting crumbs. What, I thought to myself, would you be doing, if not this? At 1:00 P.M., Claw and Issy both skedaddled (my sisters take their statutory rights extremely seriously). At 1:05, there was a knock on the door. Instinctively—and this doesn't say much for my instincts—I snatched up a pencil.

"Who is it?" I snarled, brandishing my weapon.

"Delivery for Holly Appleton," said a male voice that wasn't Stuart's. I opened the door an inch, still wielding the pencil. A young guy in sloppy jeans thrust a huge bouquet at me and fled.

"Thanks," I shouted after him, feeling sheepish. I sniffed the flowers. They were mostly red and purple, clashing beautifully. I opened the card, hands trembling. What would it say this time? *"See you in court"?* The message was in untidy handwriting as familiar to me as my own.

> *For the mother of my child, xx*
> *N.*

I squirmed, part pleasure, part embarrassment. You think you want old-style romance, but when it comes, it feels icky. Well, he'd changed his tune. My heart began a faster beat. This was a highly significant statement. On a level with "Britain is now at war with Germany." Well, not *quite*. What I mean is that those six words, to me, were life-changing. They spoke the difference between single parenthood and a cozy family unit.

Five seconds later the phone rang. "S'me!"

I practically purred. How would, for instance, Audrey Hepburn say it? "The father of my child"?

"Oh Christ—Hol—listen—you got the flowers, yeah?—I'm sorry—about last night—I'm thrilled—it's a blessing—it was a lot to take in—a lot, that's all—I wasn't expecting it—but I'm ecstatic—it's the best thing that's ever happened to me—the best thing—I've hardly slept—I'm so excited—really—a kid—our own baby—wow—it's Fate—it is—for it to happen now—it's got to be!"

I beamed down the phone. I couldn't have put it better myself. But Nick (breathless with delayed joy) hadn't finished.

"Hol—are you free tonight?—because I want you to come with me—I have a very special evening arranged—yeah?—please say yes—cancel whatever you've got on—dress up—not too dressy—but nice—special—I'll pick you up from home—okay?—seven, all right?—don't want to be late—a surprise—you'll never guess—okay, great—see you at seven—be ready—okay—love you—bye!"

I replaced the receiver, shaking my head in wonder. "Love you too," I said aloud. One thing for sure, I'd never be bored again. I rested my hand on my stomach. There was something restful about being pregnant. In a dim corner of my mind a thought loitered that I wasn't quite ready to welcome into the light. That I could stop trying with my happiness and concentrate on the baby's. All over the world, people used their offspring as a reason to stop making an effort. Stop going out. Stop looking after their appearance. Stop *bothering*. Because then they didn't have to think about their own failed lives. They could legitimately distract themselves with someone else's.

I'm not saying that's what I decided. But it was nice to have the option.

The afternoon dragged by, and I sent Claw and Issy home on the dot, creeping off myself moments later. Nick arrived bang on seven. He looked like he'd bathed in electricity. He gave my outfit a critical once-over. "Will I do?" I asked half indignantly.

He laughed and kissed me. Then he knelt and kissed my stomach. "I can feel a bulge!"

Bless his innocence. "I'm afraid that's just pudge," I said, lowering myself into his car. "In the last couple of weeks I've been stockpiling. So, are you going to tell me where we're going?"

Nick grinned at me from the driver's seat. "You kind of gave me the impetus to do it," he said. "This morning I called my birth mother."

"What! You spoke to her?"

He was off. "For an *hour*."

I thought to myself, That's nothing, *we've* spoken for three hours on the phone before.

"Pamela Fidgett warned me to be careful. She said she prefers to make initial contact, but I wanted it to be me. And it was great, Holly, great—amazing. Her voice—it was *creepily* familiar. She answered the phone. When I said it was me, she screamed."

Screamed? I thought. Burst into tears, surely?

"She wanted to see me straightaway. She said she always hoped I'd get in touch."

But you say that to a casual acquaintance.

"And she asked about my life—and she told me about hers—I have a half brother called Russell—he's twenty-three—he's in retail—she lost touch with my father—it was a fling—not that I mind—well—it would have been too much to hope for—I suppose—but her husband knows about me—he doesn't mind—but he's not in tonight anyway—Russell might be there, though—she works in a hairdresser's—A Cut Above the Rest—which is fine—I told her I work in the entertainment business—I didn't want her to be disappointed—she couldn't believe how smart I sounded—I told her about you—and the baby—she wanted to meet you both—"

"Nick," I yelped. "You're meeting your mother for the first t—"

"*Second* time, Holly. She gave birth to me. In a way we are intimately acquainted."

"Of course, yes, sorry. What I mean is, are you sure I won't be in the way? Won't you two want to be alone?"

"I want to have you there. You're *my* family."

I was beginning to understand his thinking and it didn't make me feel comfortable. We drove the rest of the way in silence, the excitement buzzing off him. He raced down narrow roads at forty, and I suspected that—even if he'd merely sat in his car peering at her darkened windows—this wasn't his first visit to his birth mother's home. He rolled to a quiet halt a few doors up from an unremarkable suburban row house. There was nothing to distinguish it from a thousand other houses in a thousand other streets.

"There," he said, pointing. He looked rapt. But he didn't move from his seat.

"When is she expecting you?"

I half imagined that he'd reply, "She's been expecting me for the last thirty years," but he said, "Seven forty-five."

We were very early. Nick stared at the house. So did I. I wanted to ask a lot of petty questions. Was she making us dinner? (Already, with half an inch of baby inside me, I suspected I was going to be the kind of mother who encouraged people to eat at gunpoint.) Why wasn't she gazing out of the window? *I* would have been. This had to go well. I glanced at my watch as the minutes ticked by. At a quarter to eight precisely, Nick checked his (immaculate) hair in the rearview mirror. I wondered why there weren't more lights on in the house. Was she trying to save money?

Nick unclicked his seat belt. He looked at me, pale as milk. "Ready?" he said.

CHAPTER **34**

We padded up the garden path and I felt like a bloodhound, sensitive to every detail. The uneven paving stones. The weeds run riot in the flower beds. The paint cracking off the squeaky gate. The grayed net curtains hung limply in the bald windows. I glanced at Nick. He had a glazed look, as if he was taking in none of it. Don't be such a snob, I told myself. Only one thing matters here.

He turned and grinned at me, awkwardly, and rang the bell. He stepped back. He held a sorry-looking bunch of flowers in front of him with both hands like a knight wielding a sword. I crossed my fingers. Please let her be wonderful. Why didn't she open the door *immediately*? What was she doing, playing it cool? This is not a time to play it cool, I growled inside my head as the door swung open. And there stood Nick's biological mother.

She looks old compared to Lavinia, was my first thought. And despite working at a hairdresser's (did she work at one or was she one? I couldn't recall), her hair was strange. It was different from her wedding picture: bobbed, brown, and fine. It was thin, to be exact, and had been sprayed into shape to give it the appearance of body. Her pale skin might have once been an asset but was now smoked and worried into wrinkles. It seemed as if she had tossed her makeup into the air and walked through it, as proper ladies are supposed to walk through their perfume. Despite all this, she was pretty, even if it was a faded prettiness. If you asked me, Nick's looks were more than a credit to her, they were a jackpot. Her eyes—brown, like his—didn't rest. They darted from him, through me, to him again. She fanned the air around her mouth, and I could smell the cigarettes from where I stood. And then she flung her arms around him.

Nick dropped the flowers on the porch as he hugged her. As she held him tight, I watched her face. She cried enough. And her eyes were squeezed shut. I guessed she was genuine. The two of them stayed fixed in that hug for ages. She kept wheezing something I couldn't quite catch. Then I realized it was the name *she* had given him. His name is Nick, I thought stiffly. But he didn't correct her. I assessed her clothing. A black-and-beige-patterned sweater with a round neck, the sort of item a great-aunt might pick up in Woolworth's. Flat black shoes and beige trousers, which emphasized her barrel shape. Nick really must have taken after his father.

I never used to make snap judgments about people, but that had changed. I decided she wasn't a relaxing person. She radiated tension. Nor was she what I'd call warm. I tried to separate her from the situation and surroundings. The ordinariness of her house wasn't in her favor, but then my parents' home was the definition of ordinary, and it had no effect on their aura of contentment. But maybe I was being defensive. She was ushering in Nick, never taking her eyes off him, touching his hair, his face. As for him, he didn't speak. Then he did an odd thing. He leaned in close to her neck and *sniffed* it. A dreamy look came over him and he sank his head in his hands. His whole body shook.

"Holly." He signaled, waving a hand vaguely in my direction. "My girlfriend. We're having a baby."

Mrs. Nick—well, that's how I thought of her—smiled vacantly and said, "Hello." Suddenly her smile took on strength and she added, "I'm going to be a grandmother!"

She led us through a dark corridor and into a kitchen. It was big but plainly hadn't been redecorated since the fifties. None too clean, either. If I let loose Gloria in here, her teeth would itch. "Sit down," cried Mrs. Nick, pressing her newfound son into a chair. She fumbled for her Lambert & Butler, stuck one between her lips, and waved the pack at us. "Smoke?" she said, making the cigarette in her mouth jump. We shook our heads, although I could sense Nick not wanting to refuse her anything.

"Tea, I'll make you tea. And there's cake, and biscuits, and bread, and pickled cucumbers, cheddar cheese . . ." She ransacked the fridge and cupboards as she spoke, the cigarette in her mouth bobbing up and down as she did so. Bit by bit, she piled the random edible contents of her kitchen onto the table in front of us. She reminded me of a dog digging a hole to find a bone, kicking the earth into a mound. I fought to keep my mouth in a smile. This is two-star treatment, why didn't you go shopping *specially*? I beamed cheesily at Nick, but he didn't notice. She clanked down plates and knives, and Nick tucked in immediately, although I noticed he chewed each mouthful of sandwich fifty times. I ate a slightly soft chocolate biscuit—I didn't feel like taking my chances with her cutlery.

"It's incredible, to see you"—he hesitated—"again."

Her eyes narrowed as if she didn't understand. "Again!" she cried finally. "Yes, incredible!"

She lit another cigarette as the old one smoldered. "It was different then," she blurted. "More of a stigma. I didn't know what to do. I was eighteen. Mum and Dad wanted me to go to secretarial school, make something of myself. You obeyed your parents in them days. It was difficult. I cried for weeks. It was a difficult time. Rumors went 'round, even though we kept it quiet. Everyone knew, pretended they didn't. I say it was only the swinging sixties if you swung but was careful about it, left no trace. I never finished secretarial school anyways. I met Malcolm, and he was happy to take me on. Mum said I couldn't afford to be choosy, not after. We're still together, though; he's stuck by me, and I've stuck by him. I've thought about you over the years, growing up, wondering how your life turned out, if it were for the best. It was difficult, as I say I cried a lot, but as Malcolm says, these things happen. It's no one's fault, you've got to get on, you can't brood on what might have been."

I sat through this whirlwind of self-justification and repressed emotion, my hands tucked under my sizable bottom to prevent them from slapping her face. What was it? Had she been bullied into believing this crap, or was she just . . . not that bright?

I glanced at Nick. "You cried," he repeated. "You thought about me. You didn't want to give me up. They made you."

"That's right," she gasped, shaking her head, rubbing her eyes. I rubbed mine too, the smoke was stinging them. "They made me. You do understand that, don't you? It was different in them days. You did what your parents told you. My father was a strict man, re-ligious strict."

Those days, I wanted to thunder. *Those* days! I shoveled another soft biscuit into my mouth to keep it occupied. And then I smiled and tried not to fidget while Nick and his birth mother talked. I no-ticed that she talked a lot about her life, *her* disappointments, less about his. She listened while he spoke, and she did ask questions, but she fidgeted and smoked as if to hurry him up. I couldn't tell what he was thinking. I can usually, but that evening I couldn't. Only that he seemed to be filtering the unwelcome information and clinging to the positive.

At ten thirty, her fidgeting took on a new urgency. "Malcolm'll be home soon. He's on the late shift. No earthly idea where Russell's got to. He said he'd be here. You never know with him, up to no good I expect. Ah, kids, what can you do, eh?" She laughed sadly.

You can set your children a good example, I thought. *That's* what you can do. No wonder Russell was a loser, with this limp lettuce leaf of a parent. God only knew what her husband was like. An eternal discontent, I imagined. A man who watched Rodney Dangerfield rant about wives and mothers-in-law and agreed. She was nervous of this Malcolm, didn't want Nick to be in her kitchen when he got home. Thank heaven that boy had been adopted, I thought, he'd have been wretched, stuck in this house, with these unimaginative people. They wouldn't have understood him, appreciated him. He would have been so *understimulated*.

I hardly dared look at him as we scurried up the garden path. "Here," she'd said as Nick had stumbled out. She'd snatched a green ceramic frog off the windowsill and pressed it into his hands. "Have this!" As though he'd asked for it. He didn't speak, started the car, still not a word. Halfway up the hill I could bear it no longer. "How . . . how did you think it went?" I whispered.

He nodded dumbly. "Incredible," he replied. "Indescribable." He touched the frog, which was resting in his lap, mussed his hair over his eyes. "Possibly the most amazing three hours of my life."

I stared at him, alert for the sarcasm of bitter disappointment. But no, not a trace. His face was aglow with beatific wonder. Already, this ineffectual little woman was seen as a lifeline. Oh, *shit*.

I invited him in, as there was no way I was letting him drive home alone in this post-alien-abduction state of mind. He allowed himself to be led into the kitchen. Gloria had been. I could only tell because she stuck cryptic Post-it notes here and there—"More Fantastik," that kind of thing. She'd propped a crisp white envelope addressed to me against the toaster. It must have been there when I'd come from work, but in my rush to scrub up for Nick I hadn't noticed it. I ripped it open without a thought. The officious typeface loomed from the page. I made a choking sound. It snapped Nick out of his trance.

"What?"

I flapped the paper at him in disbelief. "It's a writ from the High Court. Stuart *is* suing me for defamation." I felt self-control whoosh from me. Stuart sticking pins in my new airtight life. I crumpled the paper into a tight ball and screamed, "I haaaaate him! I fucking want him to die! How dare he do this to me, I hate him!" That was the gist, I screamed it over and over, screaming "Aaaaaaaaarrr" when I ran out of words. Nick jumped up and tried to calm me, but I batted him off. I was so angry I couldn't be touched. I was too angry to be scared. I screamed until I turned hoarse and then I curled over, raucous sobs tearing out of me. Nick grabbed hold of my hands and this time I let him. I felt myself slide toward madness, gibbering, "I'll kill him, I'm going to kill him. He's going to die, I mean it. I want to burn his house down."

This struck me as the perfect solution, and I stood up straight. "I'm going to burn his house down," I announced. I scowled at Nick, daring him to defy me. "I'm going to burn it down. *Now.*"

Nick mussed his hair over his eyes, then mussed it away again. He cleared his throat. "I see," he said in a normal voice. "And might I ask how you intend to do this?"

I glared back, defiant. "Yes. You might. I'm going to take the cans of lighter fluid I have in the understairs cupboard. And I'm going to take a match. And I'm going to drive my car to Stuart's house. I have the address, from his Girl Meets Boy membership application, and I'm going to wait until he's asleep. And then I'm going to break a window 'round the back, so no nosy neighbors can alert him, and set fire to his, I imagine, battered leather armchair from a junk shop."

I *despise* people who buy battered leather armchairs from junk shops. Why can't they get them new from Heal's and pay fifteen hundred quid like the rest of us?

"And then I'm going to retreat to my car, which will be parked across the street, and watch him die."

"Well," said Nick. "You seem to have it all worked out."

"I will do it," I said. "You think I won't, but I will."

"I don't think anything," he replied pleasantly. He watched as I rattled about in the understairs cupboard and retrieved two metal cans and my tool kit. I thundered upstairs, wrenched off my clothes, and changed into black trousers, a black sweater, and flat black shoes. I also found a black wool hat in my underwear drawer, so I took that too. "Checklist," I said loudly on returning to the kitchen. "Petrol, yes; matches, yes; address, yes; hammer, yes; dishcloth to muffle sound of smashing window, yes; car keys—"

I knew he'd try to stop me after the hammer bit, so when he opened his mouth, I gave him a cold stare.

"*I'll* drive."

I'd misheard. "What?"

"I said, I'll drive." He smiled sweetly.

I nearly dropped the hammer. "You *will?*"

"Hol," replied Nick à la Prince Charming bending his gracious majesty to fit Cinderella's dainty foot in her glass slipper, "it's the least I can do."

"Oh. Okay. Thanks." I mean, what do you say in such a situation?

Grudgingly, I fetched my coat and checked that the road map was in my bag.

"Have you planned a route?" inquired Nick. His refusal to disapprove was starting to annoy me.

"No."

"I think you should. After you've set fire to his house I suggest we make a quick getaway. I'm afraid watching him die is a luxury. You might be spotted. Have you checked the location for closed-circuit cameras?"

"*No.*" Jesus. Couldn't I carry out a simple bit of arson without Nick going all Magnum, PI? "Look, let's just go. It's half-past eleven."

"I reckon we should wait."

"Why?"

"Half-past eleven! It's the middle of the afternoon! Three A.M., when he'll be sound asleep, and the Mrs. Busybody across the road will be snoring in her hair net. That's the time to start a fire."

He was doing it on purpose. He thought the anger would dry up or I'd nod off on the couch. "All right," I said. "Three A.M. it is."

I caught his gaze. He had a glint in his eye that was vaguely familiar. What was it? Oh Lord—*sex*. Perhaps my ego is fragile, but I've never liked it when I suspect a lover has been warmed up, so to speak, by an outside influence. I prefer the credit to be all my own. Plainly, Nick was excitable from meeting his mother. Freud would have been jubilant. Me, I felt a little disgusted. If there was one pastime I wasn't in the mood for, sex was it. Since that rather significant lapse with Nick two months previous—of which the essential function was to prove to myself that I was normal—I'd cut off from carnality. Love, I could just about tolerate. As long as I didn't have to witness any of the touchy smoochy sticky kissy smacky chopsy gunky musky stuff that went with it.

I jumped up. "We'll have to do something to keep awake," I said briskly. "We'll watch"—what, in my fearsome arsenal of passion killers, could I pull from the bag?—"*Lord of the Rings.*"

I pried the DVD out of its case and, for the first time ever, blessed Issy's taste in birthday presents. Three long hours later an unsullied me and a very sullen Nick crept to the car. I'd put the hammer, the matches, and the fuel cans in a Selfridges bag, so as not to look suspicious. Nick drove in silence until we reached Stuart's road, a smug white row of tall, thin, yuppified town houses in an area so shabby, any tramp with sense would walk miles to avoid it.

I'd sat through *Lord of the Rings*, but it might as well have been a dead TV screen, because I'd registered none of it. The rage and hatred churned. All I could see was Stuart, plotting to sue me. Nick turned off the engine and my face contorted with viciousness. You're dead, Stuart Marshall, and I will laugh as you burn.

"Here we are," said Nick brightly. "Well. Better not hang around. It's my license plate they'll be running through the police computer. It won't take a genius."

I clicked open the car door. My head was screaming. Fuck. Stuart lived in a bloody *terrace*. How the hell was I meant to reach his back window? I'd have to climb over about ninety fences. I hesitated. Nick started whistling under his breath. I booted the door wide open with my foot and slid out of the car.

"Back in a minute," I said, and I walked into the road.

"Careful," screamed Nick, as a car zoomed out of the dark from nowhere, blasting its horn. I jumped back, trembling on jelly legs. Shit, *shit*. That reckless bastard must have woken the entire street. And he'd *seen* me. My heart thundered. I cringed, my breath fogging the sharp air, waiting for lights to appear in windows. I had no choice. I'd have to soak the cloth in lighter fuel, post it through his mailbox followed by a lit match, or ten. It wasn't ideal. How fast would the fire spread? Fast enough for Stuart to dial 911? I could feel a thousand eyes boring into me from every house. With potatoes for fingers, I wrestled the cloth, fuel, and matches from the bag—the damn rustling, bright yellow beacon of a Selfridges bag. Nick whirred down his window and stuck out a hand. I passed it to him. Then I looked left, right, and left again, and sauntered across the road. Head down, I padded past number seventeen, nineteen, twenty-one, twenty-three, until I stood in front of Stuart's shinily painted black door with its gold lion-head brass knocker. Evil, evil, evil—*flash!* I was bathed in a security light like the criminal I was. A squeak of fright escaped me and I staggered backward, dropping the cloth. I crouched to pick it up, fumbling, shaking. Then I dropped the matches. I sank, gasping, onto the pavement. Can't do it, can't do it. "I can't fucking do it," I gasped as Nick lifted me to my feet, gathered the incendiary devices, and supported me to the car.

"Can't do it, can't do it," I said, falling into the seat. Nick leaned in and hugged me. "I want him punished. I want everyone to know what he is, but I can't do it."

"I know, baby. I know, sweetheart."

Can't do it. I cried hard, hackingly, but barely making a noise. Nick, in his contorted position, half in, half out of the car, rocked me, kissed my head, and whispered, "There, there."

CHAPTER 35

Nick bundled me home and gave me a bath. There's something profoundly comforting about being washed by another person. I sat there limply while he smoothed the soap over my arms and legs, then gently rinsed it off and patted me dry with a towel. He helped me into my pajamas, kissed me on the forehead, and tucked me into bed. Then he sat beside me and held my hand until I fell asleep. My last thought before drifting into a dream was, Maybe I *will* talk to a counselor. Not Issy, though.

"Are you sure you're up to going to work?" demanded Nick when I marched into the kitchen fully dressed at 8:30 and beelined for the kettle.

"Absolutely," I replied, hiding my shock at finding him awake before eleven. "Anyway, we're short-staffed now that Nige has gone." I was keen to reestablish myself in his mind as *sane*. Visions of the previous evening kept flitting into my head and making me shudder. I hadn't been so mortified since trying to kiss my own father at age four. (I'd observed that everyone on TV kissed in that twisty way, why shouldn't we? My one saving grace was that I hadn't known about tongues.) "And thanks for humoring me last night. It was like a red mist came down. I feel a bit silly."

Nick looked surprised. "Don't. You did what you had to do. Thank *you* for coming with me to see my mother."

I smiled. I felt quite shy in front of him. And pleased that I was wearing mascara and that it wasn't too humid in the house. (I am only good-looking in a controlled environment.) "Pleasure," I said. "When do you think you'll be seeing her again? Coffee?"

"God, I don't know. I think I'll wait for her to ring me, she'll probably call this afternoon. I don't want to crowd her. I'm still overwhelmed. It still feels unreal. I've got a lot of things to think about."

"Of course." Taking advantage of his docile mood, I added, "Um. By the way. I told my parents about the *bébé*. I would have, mm, consulted you, but I . . . I . . . forgot."

Nick merely smiled. He wanted to know their reaction, but he also wanted to know that they wouldn't tell Lavinia and Michael. Yet. Relieved, I turned down his offer of a lift and drove to work, wondering. The crumpled writ was stuffed down in the bottom of my bag, but I was aware of it every second. It seemed that it wasn't only Stuart I was fighting, it was the High Court, the ancient imposing Gothic building itself, the entire British legal system—a dinosaur, *a monster*. I felt like a fly about to be crushed. Still, I had twenty-eight days to respond. Twenty-seven to block it out.

"Did you get yours?" cried Claudia as I walked into the office with our first hour's supply of caffeine.

"My what?"

"Invitation to Bernard and Sam's wedding!"

I snatched the cream envelope she was waving. "Lord. They're not hanging around. They must have had the registrar on standby. How lovely. God, I must ring her, congratulate her properly. It's fantastic."

Ms. Claudia Appleton plus one was cordially invited to the marriage of Mr. Bernard Murphy and Miss Samantha Dowden, and the date of this momentous event appeared to be the following *Sunday*. Claudia did finger sums. "I wonder how they managed to organize it so fast. He must have proposed on their first date, and she must have booked it all the next morning. Presumably she had the caterers on speed dial."

I giggled. "So. You're just jealous because if you want to marry Camille, the wedding will have to be in California with an Elvis impersonator who's just married a French poodle to a Doberman. Which, now I think of it, sounds a lot more fun than most weddings. Can I be flower girl?"

Claudia grinned. "I might ask the poodle. As for Bernard and Sam, neither of them are babies exactly. And some people don't feel complete without a marriage certificate in their hot little paw. I'm pleased for them."

"Me too."

"And I'm even more pleased for us."

"Us?"

"Well, sweetie, the *Glamour* journalist rang bright and early this morning, wanting to know 'if Girl Meets Boy had any marriages.' And as luck would have it, I was able to say, oh so casually, that, yeah, actually, we have one next week. She got all hot and bothered and wanted to know if she could attend it, so I put in a call to Sam—"

"You didn't."

"My dear, she was thrilled."

"You did tell her that if it goes in, everyone she's ever known will be gossiping about how she met her husband through a dating agency?"

"Hol. Whose side are you on? Yes I *did*, and Sam doesn't give a damn. She's found a husband, that is *all*. And she fancies the idea of having a professional magazine photographer present. That was her condition. That they give her a free set of snaps."

"Very cunning."

"And another thing. The *Glamour* journalist, Tabitha, wants to do a Date Night! Next Tuesday! This time, we're not going to screw up. I'm thinking of calling in a friend of mine, Karl, have you met Karl? To put her with. He's vee good-looking, vee charming, an artist, a painter. Odd, but in a nice way. Funny. Vee intelligent. Quite posh. Entertaining."

I frowned. "Are you sure that's wise? Haven't we got enough gorgeous men on our books? What about Xak?"

"It'll be fine. Karl's just a bonus, to balance things out. But yeah, we'll definitely put her with Xak. And there are a couple of new guys who I know will do it."

"New guys—"

"Yes, but don't worry, Issy's done her psychological profiling, they're all kosher. In fact, there are some real goodies."

"Great, wonderful. But actually, all I was going to say was, you'd better update me. Update me, get it?"

Claudia winced. "Sadly, yes."

A happy few hours plotting, and I felt that Stuart couldn't touch me. I had my life, and I liked it. My father rang to ask if I could come to Penge the following weekend so that he and Mum could "see the bump." Perhaps Nick would come too? But only if he—we had the time, no rush, no pressure, a quiet family tea, perhaps, just Issy and Claudia. He and Mum couldn't make this weekend. They were away in Bude, unfortunately, but surely we young people were busy anyway. They were *dying* to tell everyone—Leila, their friends at the Caravan Club—but were managing, *just*, to keep it secret. Nick rang midmorning and my happiness was complete. Well, 98 percent.

"How's my baby? Are the two of you free for lunch?"

"Could be," I said coyly. This was new. Flirting with Nick. A habit that had died a painful and lingering death two years earlier. How great to resurrect it. See! Our relationship was good now, it was really good.

"Excellent. I'll book somewhere nice. I want to ask you something. Pick you up at one-ish."

My easily flattered heart started pounding. First, Nick wasn't a booker. He didn't book restaurants, theater, cinema, even holidays. It was always "Let's turn up at the last minute and see." Of course, usually what we saw was a full house and no vacancies, so inevitably, *I'd* become entertainments officer for the relationship. That he had voluntarily decided to book somewhere "nice" was therefore of huge significance. I was no longer regarded as the old-pair-of-slippers girlfriend. I was a special person, to be impressed. Second, he wanted to ask me something, in delightful surroundings. This meant one of two things. A request for either marriage or money.

Would any man ask the same woman twice? Surely it depended on the circumstances, and both our circumstances had greatly changed since I'd ended our engagement. Now, we were in a position to value each other. I don't think we had before. And, if I was honest, now we *needed* each other more. We craved safety and stability, both of us felt too vulnerable alone. I was sure that he would propose. Partly because we'd been so emotionally intimate lately, and partly because even Nick would realize that to ask a woman for money at this stage in a liaison was grotesquely inappropriate.

Sitting in a cozy corner of a French/Vietnamese restaurant in Charlotte Street—one of my favorite streets in London—I silently awarded Nick ten out of ten. Wood decor (just the right shade, not dark enough to be gloomy, not light enough to be pine), polite, unobtrusive service from waiting staff with good hygiene, and a chic, restful yet romantic atmosphere. And the food looked delicious. I smiled at him over my menu. He smiled back. Would he wait until we'd eaten, or would he do it when our drinks arrived? I'd ordered a glass of champagne, and he'd said, "Why not?" and ordered another.

As the pretty waitress set our flutes down on the table, I fiddled with my napkin.

"How was work this morning?" inquired Nick.

"Good, actually. We've had a few new applications. I can see at least three promising matches. I can hardly wait till Tuesday. We've got this girl called Shannon, she's a nanny, and she's not been that popular in the past because she tends to grill people, but Nige had a chat with her and apparently she's softened. She's also gone on this personal improvement crusade, and Claw says she looks fantastic, 'plump and wholesome.' And she's a lovely person, very caring, and I *swear* she'll get on beautifully with this new man we've got called Archie. Claw says he's sexy, sleepy-eyed, bit scruffy, but very successful. He sells fitness equipment, except he always seems to have a cold or catarrh and he reeks constantly of Olbas Oil, and you just *know* they'll be drawn to each other. I can't wait to see it."

I drew breath. Nick took my hand and stroked the inside of my palm with his thumb. "I love how you are with these people. It makes me think what a great mum you'll be."

Three months ago I'm not sure I'd have seen this as a compliment. And three months ago I'm not sure Nick would have given this compliment. Now, I beamed all over my face. I waited for him to continue. This had to be it! After what he'd been through, Nick *had* to see being "a great mum" as the most precious talent in the world. Wanting to encourage him, I clinked my glass against his. "Thank you," I said. "And I'm sure you'll be a great dad."

His eyes boggled. He mussed his hair. "I really want to be. More than anything." Pause. "And that kind of brings me on to why I asked you here." He blushed. I felt a squirm of excitement travel the entire length of my torso. I assumed a receptive expression. Eyes narrowed—*soft*, not too starey or demanding. Gentle smile— not glaring or expectant. The kind of face to make a man think he could spend the rest of his life with this woman without excess grief or hassle. It absolutely went against every principle I ever had, but I'd recently concluded that principles were luxuries, most of which I couldn't afford.

I said in a low voice (not high or shrill), "You know you can ask me anything." I wondered if I should pull out the table to enable him to kneel by the side of it. Nick nodded. He placed his champagne glass to one side. "Gorgeous Holly, this may surprise you, but I wanted to ask if you would give me"—as he said these words, my brain finished his sentence dreamily . . . *your hand in marriage;* what a quaint, old-fashioned turn of phrase, and how unlike Nick!—"a job."

My Me-No-Trouble-Meester face cracked and shattered, and my voice emerged, its shrillest ever. "A *job*?"

Nick blinked in surprise at my harsh tone. I took a hasty gulp of champagne. It went down the wrong way and caused a serious coughing fit, by the end of which I was able to ape recovery. "Sorry," I said, forcing a smile. "You were saying?"

A job? A job! Come over all smoochy, then ask me for a job! "You have no idea about women!" I wanted to yell. "No bloody idea!" I felt insulted and tearful. I bit the inside of my lip hard and feigned polite interest. How could he *not* want to marry me? We were doing so well!

"I do want to keep doing children's parties. I like being Mr. Elephant, it's a laugh, but it's not especially lucrative. And what with—well, I took out a loan about a month ago and it's all gone. So, what you said about being short-staffed at Girl Meets Boy, I thought I could help out, not necessarily full-time if you can't afford it, but part-time. I thought I could expand your Website. I had ideas for it—I know you've been concerned about women's safety, for example, and I thought I could provide information on that. You know, interview the police, or women's groups, or whatever. It could really help the business grow. I realize it's probably a bit of a shock, me, lazy git, asking for work, but I . . . I don't want to be a *nothing*. I want to make something of my life professionally. I . . . I suppose that I have, I mean—I took it all for granted, and, of course, obviously, I don't anymore. I want my mother—my *real* mother, that is—to be proud of me. I want to achieve. And you too, of course. I want to be worthy of you, do my bit, if I'm going to be a dad. I want to be the best dad. I don't want to be some loser pissing about in an elephant costume. I want to be responsible, contribute. I want our son or daughter to respect me."

Once upon a time I would have shaved my head *and* my eyebrows to hear such a speech from Nick. But hearing it now, I felt an unexpected sweep of sadness. It was like hearing your child swear for the first time. I replied in a small voice, "I *like* that elephant costume."

Nick smiled tensely.

I sighed. "Yes. Yes, you can have a job. We do need someone to expand the Website. We've neglected it out of fear. You need to take romance seriously, though, you can't have a sneery attitude. Nige is cynical, but he was, believe it or not, devoted to the cause. We do need someone good to replace him. And it's not as easy as you might think."

Nick leaped up and kissed me across the table. "I'll work like you wouldn't believe, Hol. You won't regret it. And how could you *doubt* that I take romance seriously? I read the second half of *Captain Corelli's Mandarin*. I take it very seriously indeed!"

I huffed, in reluctant amusement, through my nose. "*Mandolin.* Shall we order?" I said.

Under cover of my crispy smoked chicken starter, I engaged in silent discussion with myself. Nick chatted on about his mother, only requiring the occasional nod from me. Real romantic relationships, I decided, were a world away from imagined ones. Years back, when I heard from Nige that he and Marylou knew they'd marry before he even asked her, I'd been appalled. I hadn't met Nick then, and still assumed that a proposal came out of the blue, causing the woman to choke on her drink and/or burst into tears. I didn't think you discussed it prior to the event, as you'd discuss what you were having for supper.

But now, with five years' experience, I knew better. In a truly great relationship, hardly any subject was out-of-bounds. You were confident of the other person's love. Of *course* you'd discuss marriage before the proposal, you trusted each other so you didn't have to play games. Games were for insecure people unable to distinguish between a lover and an opponent. Why should I play games with Nick? He knew me as well as I knew myself, and vice versa. So what if he'd asked me for a job instead of marriage? I knew he loved me, and that he hadn't proposed changed nothing. And, indeed, why should he ask? He'd asked the last time.

If anyone should be proposing, it was *me.*

"Nick," I said, cutting short a ramble about Russell and Malcolm. "Can I ask *you* a question?"

He nodded.

I rose from my seat, then knelt by the side of his. "Nick. Will you marry me?"

He didn't burst into tears or choke on his drink. He slid off his chair and knelt on the floor beside me. "Yeah," he said, "why the hell not?"

CHAPTER 36

Yeah, why the hell not?'" repeated Rachel. She exhaled a gray stream of smoke from her nostrils. "Hardly the stuff of fairy tales, is it, babes?"

I itched and wriggled in my burgundy silk. Not my choice—Sam and Bernard had asked me to be a bridesmaid. Rach had organized the wedding party, as no one else would do it at such short notice. I was touched at the honor conferred on me by the happy couple, but still reeling from "Yeah, why the hell not?" It didn't make me want to tell people. Also, Nick was wandering around with a face like a wet dishcloth, which didn't create the desired impression.

"No," I said. "This is, though. Doesn't Sam look gorgeous?"

Rachel brushed a crumb off a white tablecloth. "In a pearls-and-Prozac kind of way."

"Rach! Be nice for one second. If you'd only seen the ceremony. They looked about to blister with joy. He swung her around afterward and one of her shoes flew off and hit the registrar in the chest. Don't you look at them and think, Awwww!?"

I adjusted my puffy lace sleeve. It pinched the skin, cutting off the circulation and leaving a deep purple ring on my upper arm. Secretly, I suspected I was twenty years too old to be dressing as Alice in Wonderland, but Sam—a vision in sleek-cream designer satin—had apparently "fallen in love" with this scarlet eighties meringue, and I didn't wish to spoil her special day by whining.

"Haven't heard you say that in a while," said Rachel. "But no. I look at them and think, How jolly fortunate for both of you."

I wasn't entirely sure what she was implying and chose not to ask. This was a happy occasion, and I didn't want Rachel's cynicism clouding my enjoyment of it. I had other background worries to ignore. We were clustered in the garden of Bernard's famed cottage in "rural Devon," pretending not to feel the cold. The bride and groom were posing for photographs in front of the brook that bubbled through their picturesque grounds. The sky was a crisp blue, and despite the chill, it was a beautiful afternoon.

A pity, then, that I didn't feel too well. I had the sort of stomachache that drags down into your legs, pulling the life out of your whole body. I'd checked my pregnancy book, and it reassured me that it was normal to feel "periodlike pains" in the early months. I'd gained ten pounds in the last six weeks but couldn't tell if this was baby or blubber. I'd finally made it to my doctor, who had taken my word for it and referred me to my local hospital for a first scan. The appointment wasn't until the following week. I was eager to swell up so that Nick would stop trying to have sex with me.

Not that he'd pestered me recently. Since my proposal, the only physical affection he'd attempted was a brief kiss on the cheek. I knew why. His biological mother had rung him, a leisurely *three days* after their grand reunion, to say that she did want him to meet his half brother and stepfather, but Malcolm was snowed under at work and couldn't fix on a date for at least a fortnight. So she'd be in touch nearer the time, okay? Nick had suggested that she "didn't want to overwhelm" him, but it seemed to require all his willpower to believe this. I didn't think it sensible to argue.

I hadn't mentioned our engagement to him again. Nor had I told anyone except Rachel. I suspected Claudia might disapprove. And no doubt Issy would fix on some dubious subconscious motivation highly unflattering to both of us. My parents would be delighted, but I didn't want to waste this trump card. When I finally gained the courage to tell them about the rape, breaking the news of my engagement five seconds later would be a useful distraction tool. I was also dizzy with trying to remember who knew what about me. I was keen to trumpet around that I was pregnant (then everyone would *have* to be nice), but wanted to wait until the three-month scan confirmed that the fetus was healthy. This, I'd gleaned from Issy, was protocol.

Talking of Issy, the scowl on her face seemed to be permanent. She and Frank were, to the casual observer, a well-heeled couple sipping champagne and having a chat. To the noncasual observer—me—they were at war. Issy wore a cold smile, and when she spoke to her husband it was through clenched teeth. When Frank lurched to snatch a raw carrot from the tray, Issy placed a beautifully manicured hand on the pale gray sleeve of his expensive suit. Only I noticed how tightly she clutched his arm. As if to say, "You *dare* move one inch away from me. We *will* present a united front."

I glanced at Rachel. Then back to Frank. He caught my eye and gave me a nervous wave. Rachel saw and waved back. Frank glared. It was, as Issy might say, a microemotion—barely visible to the naked eye, gone so fast you might have imagined it. But I hadn't. My fist tightened around the stem of my wineglass.

"Is there something going on between you and Frank?"

The accusation had escaped. Rachel flicked her shiny hair. "What?"

I picked irritably at my sleeve. It was awkward but I had to continue. "Rach. You and Frank have been behaving *very* oddly, and I'm not the only one who suspects."

Rach turned her imperious bulk toward me. She was wearing a purple wool dress with (I hoped) fake ermine edging at the wrists and neck, which added to an already regal aura. "Holly," she replied in a soft tone, "when a person undergoes what you have, their trust in human nature is irreparably damaged, and rightly so. But that person then faces a crucial challenge. To learn to distinguish between friend and foe." She paused and drained her champagne. "I am your friend, Holly, and if that isn't apparent, I am exquisitely sad for both of us."

She swept off, treating me to a lavish back view of her purple UFO of a hat and leaving me open-mouthed. I lifted my heels, which were sinking into the lawn, and checked that Sam didn't need me to fluff out her veil or help her go to the toilet. She gave me the "okay" sign—surely the only person in the Western world still using this gesture without irony—so I blew her a kiss and turned back to Issy and Frank. I felt I should go over there, but I didn't want to. If Issy was in the mood I guessed she was, I'd be employed as pig in the middle of a feuding couple. This is when an unwitting third party is dragged into the fray as an ally.

I've done it myself and it's shameful. You're filled with temporary (or otherwise) loathing for your partner, but as it's socially unacceptable to smack him around the chops in public, you employ a helpless friend to assist you in a verbal attack.

Such as, "What do you think of Nick's vile aquamarine suit? I did tell him it was a bit *Top Man*, but you know how stubborn he is." A crime against friendship—not to mention against love—but some couples commit an even worse offense. Roping an innocent party into their *foreplay*. This is horrible. The hapless victim is forced to witness no end of drooling and pawing and to agree that, yes, Nickety-Nick does have "the juiciest butt" in those jeans. (Note. I never ever did this. I merely provide the example.)

Who knew? Maybe they were weathering a rough patch and any woman in the same room as Frank was a target for Issy's rage. Rach *was* a flirt, and that couldn't help. At least I'd confronted her. And been put in my place. And offended a friend. What more could I do?

"You all right, Hol? Want to sit down? After all, a lady in *your* condition."

Claudia had the grace to whisper this last bit and rubbed my back as she spoke. Camille hovered close by, beaming in a navy smock. I resented that she was obviously party to every single piece of personal information I'd shared with my younger sister over the past three months. If Claw confided in me, I'd never run home and blab it all to Nick. For a start, he wasn't always interested in the brand of minutia that I drooled over, and also, Claw had never said, "I'm going to tell you and Nick a secret." She'd said, "I'm going to tell *you* a secret." It was a matter of honor.

"I'm fine. Hasn't it been perfect?"

Claw and Camille nodded. "Tabitha from *Glamour* seems happy," said Claw. "She's been 'interviewing' Xak for ages. So sweet of Bernard and Sam to invite him. And great for us. Their photographer has taken about forty million snaps. He took a nice one of you, from the back."

I tried to look haughty—impossible in puffy burgundy. "A contradiction in terms, surely. How are you, Camille?"

Camille smiled and sank her chin into her neck, which I understood to mean "fine."

"I was hoping," she began in her soft voice, "that your friend Nige would be here. Claudia just reminded me he has a matinee today. This is going to sound ever so *Murder Mystery*, but I wanted to ask him a favor."

My mind boggled.

Camille looked uncomfortable. "You know that I found that information about your grandmother's Paris apartment in an unmarked file. The thing is—the unfortunate thing is—I snuck a look in the same drawer yesterday, and it's *gone*. I kept meaning to photocopy it, but Stuart is constantly in and out. I need to find it, and I know I will. Men never think of good hiding places. But I have to get him out of the office, and this is going to sound stupid, but Claw says that Nige is a great mimic, and I thought he might be able to entice Stuart out of the office for an entire afternoon."

Camille was looking increasingly sheepish, as well she might. Her idea was ridiculous. She'd ring Stuart's grandest client for a bogus query, tape the conversation, and play it to Nige. He'd imitate the client, ring Stuart, and demand an urgent meeting somewhere far-off. Stuart would rush out and Camille could search his office for incriminating evidence.

I stifled a sigh. Camille and Claudia had been reading too much Raymond Chandler. "Are you *sure* this is all necessary? Won't Stuart suspect?" I didn't want to be sued twice. "Maybe we should just leave it. I don't want you to get into trouble."

Claudia started jumping up and down on the spot, a habit she'd favored at age six when urging our father to buy her ice cream. "Holleeeee! Come *on*, it'll be fine. We need the proof of that document. Look, we'll ask Nige. I know he'd love to do it. Tell you what, we won't mention it again till it's done, so you don't have to worry. How's that?"

"Too late," I replied, looking at the muddy patch she'd created in Bernard's lawn. "I know. And I'm worried."

Ting! Ting! Ting! Bernard's best man—with the aid of a spoon and a glass—was requesting our attention. Glad for the distraction, I sank into a chair. I could barely see the bride and groom over the wedding cake, an austere white marzipan tower bang in the middle of the top table. Nick, who'd disappeared to make a phone call, dropped into a seat beside me. I smiled and he squeezed my hand. "They're a handsome couple," he whispered. "Great for the agency profile. And it's a classy wedding. Very *Glamour*-worthy." I could tell that he was trying to be cheerful and say the right thing.

"Definitely," I replied. "It's great for Girl Meets Boy. But really, the agency is nothing. I'm just thrilled that Bernard and Sam have found each other. And you're right, it *is* classy. Secretly, I'd imagined Bernard's country cottage to be one of those new Barratt Homes–type things, all nasty pink brick and yellow gravel drive. But this is so pretty, very Hansel and Gretel. And Rach has done a great job with the food, flowers, and music. She really is very good."

I was confused. I knew I'd always love Nick, but here I was showing all the symptoms of being *in* love with Nick. Well, almost all of them. All the contradictory signs were there. Feeling self-conscious in his presence one minute, deep peace the next. Bliss one second, then frustration. I felt lustful when he held my hand but—and this is where part of the confusion arose—no desire to take it further. Also, there was a sense of acceptance toward him. Before, I'd always been egging him on to be just a little bit better. Now, I felt I'd take him, no conditions. And this wasn't wholly to do with the sense that he'd finally matured. After all, in the "respect speech" he'd made in the restaurant, he'd let slip that he'd taken out some loan and squandered it. Once, I'd have pursed my lips. Now, I was of the attitude that we all have our flaws. Also, it hit me that I didn't want him to be *too* grown up.

And yet. If he had improved, *I* certainly hadn't. Perhaps this was why I suspected he was not exactly raring to tie the knot. Did he suspect my motives? I tried to stop my next thought, which was, *Should* he?

When I'd asked him, possibly. But now . . . today . . . increasingly . . . it no longer felt as if it were about needing him for *me*, because of my fears. It was about needing him for *him*, because he was wonderful.

We sat and listened as Bernard himself thanked us for coming, heaped praise on Sam to the extent that even Issy's eyes watered, and invited us to eat, drink, and be merry. Sam, to my pride—although what I had to be proud of I wasn't sure—also made a speech. There was no sign of the shy, eczema-covered girl forever hiding in baggy dungarees. Here was a pretty and confident woman with clear skin and a cheeky sense of humor. I'd suspected as much when I saw my bridesmaid dress.

After the speeches, everyone gorged on salad, quiche, and coronation chicken. (Rach had discussed it with Sam, who'd decided on a traditional/retro theme.) An elegant string quartet played while we stuffed ourselves, and I couldn't recall a more civilized afternoon. I was introduced to Sam's parents—her mother had cried all the way through the service and was still bursting into tears on sight of her daughter. Bernard's mother seemed to be made of sterner stuff, until I spied her fondly adjusting his bow tie. He indulged her with such good grace, I wanted to congratulate Sam on her choice of life partner.

I dabbed my eyes. I could have sat there and wept happy tears all evening, but Sam had asked me to browbeat guests onto the dance floor. Bernard had exacting taste in music, and after serious discussion with Rachel, had been persuaded to hire one of her favorite DJs. I'd feared Europop, but we were treated instead to Frank Sinatra, Burt Bacharach, Andy Williams, and other greats (I say vaguely, having zero knowledge of the other greats). Bernard's patio was transformed into a dance floor, and his fruit trees winked and twinkled with pink fairy lights as the sun set.

"Can I book you for the next dance, Holly?" boomed the groom, his red face oozing sweat and joy as he bent over me. "My wife is dancing with her father."

"I'd love to," I cried. "Bernard, this is such a great wedding." I jumped up and felt giddy. I suspected my dress created a backwash. "I'll just go and . . . Won't be a sec."

I left Nick chatting to Claudia and bustled upstairs to the bathroom. And there I was, planted on the lavatory like a large burgundy mushroom, and I saw a stain. Rust red, on my knickers. Quaking, I dabbed myself with toilet paper. A smear of blood. Oh God. Please, no. The pain in my stomach was mild, though. How could *that* be a miscarriage? And the blood—it wasn't gushing out in clods, it was just like a normal period. Calmly, trapped in a bad dream, I upturned my bag, found my phone, and rang Claw on her cell. The second she tapped on the door I became hysterical.

"Okay, keep calm. I'll drive you to hospital. I presume they have hospitals in Devon."

"No . . . no. Wait."

Claudia looked at me oddly. "Don't some people get bleeding in early pregnancy?"

"Yeah." I couldn't speak. I had a horrible feeling, the sickening sense I'd got myself into a situation it would be hell to get out of.

"Shall I call an ambulance? Holly, what's wrong? There's no time to muck about."

I hid my face in my hands. I knew why I'd done it, but what had I done? Claudia let me hide for a reasonable length of time, then pried my fingers from my eyes. "Hol?"

I looked up. "You know when you do a pregnancy test. You must have done?"

"In my misspent youth."

"And . . ." I forced my voice to audible level. "There's a line in the round window if you're pregnant, right?"

"I can't remember. I thought there was a line in both windows. Hol? *What?* What are you talking about?"

I cleared my throat. Better get it over with. "This isn't a miscarriage. This is the plain old time of the month."

Claudia said nothing. She looked grave.

"I lost fifteen pounds in a short time when I had glandular fever. And sudden weight loss can cause you to skip periods. I read about it . . . a few days ago. But I've gained most of the weight back in the past six weeks. So, I suppose . . . I . . . I wanted . . . It would have made an end to it, been so nice if Nick and . . . Shit, oh God, what will I . . . ?"

Claudia shook her head and sat down hard on the side of the bath. She looked as if she'd been struck dumb.

"I believed it at first, Claw. I really did. I really thought I was pregnant. And then I wondered but . . . I didn't want to go back. It seemed so possible. I postponed the doctor's appointment . . . I thought . . ."

I stared at Bernard's cork matting and thought, If you want it badly enough you can make it happen.

Not true.

Claudia stood up. "Here's a Tampax," she said. "We're going back to the party and you are going to dance with Bernard. And tomorrow, Holly, you are going to start sorting out the mess in your head. Reality doesn't suit any of us all of the time. Functional adults accept that. If you can't, you will not have a happy life and I mean that. Christ knows what you're going to tell Nick."

She marched out of the bathroom. I stared at the door. It suddenly banged open again, nearly causing me to fall in the toilet with fright. Claudia burst back in. Her face was brick-red.

"How *dare* you?" she screamed. "How fucking *dare* you do this! How could you do this, to yourself, to Nick, to me, to Mum and Dad? It's not just about you, you know! We're all affected! I've had it with you and your weird behavior! You're letting him win, you know that? Do you want Stuart to win? Do you want to help him screw up your life? I am *sick* of this. You don't fucking lie about things like babies, whatever you've been through. It's not the way, it's not healthy. It's fucking insane! So fucking stop it, okay, you're frightening me!"

I gazed after her as she slipped out of the bathroom, then pulled up my knickers.

CHAPTER 37

Claudia was mostly right. Reality doesn't suit all of us all of the time. And, yes, successful grown-ups do accept that. But if you ask me, their acceptance is a bit on the sporadic side. Why else, seven evenings out of seven, is a good quarter of the British adult population to be found chucking alcohol down its neck? We smoke, drink, take drugs—recreational or prescription, they all serve the same purpose. It's about softening the sharp edges of life. My softener of choice that Sunday night was vodka, lots of it.

Vodka enabled me to trip through the remainder of the wedding, dance with Bernard, fuss over Sam. And if I began to feel ropey at around 1:00, vomited discreetly in the lavatory without splashing my dress at 1:05, and conked out in the guest bedroom at 1:08, few people noticed or were bothered. The bride and groom had departed at midnight for the splendor of the Heathrow Hilton, and the nearest and dearest whom I hadn't offended were too wrapped up in their own concerns to wonder about me.

Monday was a different story. Bernard's parents, cottage-sitting for their son, insisted on preparing a lavish breakfast for all remaining guests and—if this wasn't cruel enough—watching us eat it. Out of the sheer goodness of my heart, I forced down a pale, glutinous heap of scrambled egg, then spent the drive back to London gulping repeatedly to prevent its reappearance. Happily, Nick presumed I was suffering from morning sickness. Which, in a manner of speaking, I was.

Prior to the bathroom scene, I'd agreed with Claudia that we'd award ourselves the morning off and reconvene at the office at 2:00 P.M. I'd been nervous about announcing the news of Nick's employment, but then, still in the mood to indulge me, she'd replied, "Fine by me. If it weren't for nepotism I'd be on the dole."

I'd been all ready to reassure her that Nick had recently discovered the work ethic and was still displaying the fervor of the newly converted, but it hadn't been necessary. Claudia had been curiously positive about welcoming Nick aboard. Maybe she could tell he'd grown up some. He'd hardly drunk at the wedding because, as he explained, "It's my first day at work tomorrow. There's no point having a hangover unless it's the weekend and you can actually enjoy it."

Issy wasn't due in until Tuesday, which I was glad of. Claudia had left with Camille late on Sunday night without saying good-bye. I could understand it. For those few months I'd convinced myself I was pregnant, I'd realized the extent to which an unborn baby belongs to *all* the family. Claudia might have had her reservations about my reasons for wanting a child, but her excitement had betrayed itself. I knew it took all her self-control not to stage a dawn raid on Baby Gap. I got the feeling that if it weren't for common courtesy, she'd have bent over my belly and yelled, "Hurry *up!*"

Nick's presence at work would prevent Claudia from physically attacking me, but I was sure she'd find a thousand subtle ways to communicate her displeasure. At least Issy wouldn't be there to sense the mood and start ferreting. Monday afternoon, I showed Nick his desk and talked him around the office, all the while thinking, When will I tell him? *When?* At ten past two, Claudia marched in with one coffee and a single doughnut. I was glad when my cell rang and I could busy myself fumbling in my bag. It made her iciness less apparent.

"Holly?" said a familiar silvery voice.

"Hel-lo!" I cried. "Wait a second. I'm in the office, bad reception. I'll take it outside." I jumped up and ran into the corridor. "Mrs. Mortimer? Sorry. You know Nick started work at the agency today? Oh. No. Of course. Sorry. Well, he has. Are you . . . bearing up? You're 'round the corner! Yes. Yes, no, that wouldn't be a problem. Although I have only just got back to the office, so it might have to be quick." Listen to *me*, I thought, giving the Mortimers orders! "But . . . yes. Yes, I know it well. Fine. I'll see you in five minutes."

I stuck my head around the office door, said, "Something's come up, I'll be about twenty minutes." Nick nodded, without shifting his gaze from his screen. Claudia sipped her coffee and ignored me. She was wearing her hair in a high ponytail that reeked of disapproval.

"Oh God," I said aloud to myself, clomping down the stairs. I ran across the road to Martha's Got Buns, where Mr. and Mrs. Mortimer sat in orange and white plastic seats at an orange table, each nursing a coffee and an untouched slice of what Rachel called "Vicky sponge." Boring, boring cake, it didn't deserve a nickname. Lavinia and Michael looked prosperous and miserable. Michael, in his City man's coat—long, thick, and navy—and Lavinia, immaculately attired, superbly preserved. They seemed lost here, and it made them all the more pathetic. It pained me to see such powerful people helpless.

Ever courteous, they rose to their feet and kissed me. I ordered a tea from Martha—I couldn't quite bring myself to order the Vicky sponge, even out of solidarity. Then I changed my mind. I didn't have to *eat* it, for god's sake.

"Holly," said Michael in his captain-of-industry voice. "We are so sorry to trouble you again. I know Lavinia has already spoken with you. But we are really"—he pronounced it *rarely*—"at our wits' end. He is still barely speaking to us, and even when he does deign to see us, he is so terribly distant. We feel as if we're losing him, our only son, and we can't bear it."

It jolted me, to hear a man like Michael own up to not being able to *bear* something. Throughout our five-year acquaintance, I'd assumed he was made of steel.

"Tell us," Lavinia inquired gently, "has he traced his"—a delicate pause—"original mother?"

I was about to obey and launch into the tale. Lavinia and Michael were unaccustomed to being refused information or assistance. I opened my mouth—both of them leaned toward me, eagerly pressing their well-tailored jackets against the greasy edge of the orange plastic table—and I shut it.

"I . . . it wouldn't be fair of me to say," I said eventually. "You really need to speak to him."

"But, Holly," rumbled Michael. "We can't get a damned word out of him."

I gulped my tea. The Mortimers followed suit and sipped their coffees. Lavinia's eyes were turning red and watery, a look which didn't complement her tan. I noticed a tremor in Michael's hands. This was hideous. To think that my parents were so intimidated by these people that on the two occasions my mother had dared to invite them to her humble abode, she'd spent four hours cleaning and another four hours apologizing for the "mess." The Mortimers were richer than our family, more successful, more established. But, I now realized, the emotional evolution of the Appletons was far superior.

I took a deep breath. And I told them.

Not about Nick's visit to his birth mother—that was not my story to tell—but about Nick's feelings, Pamela Fidgett's theories, the possibility that they had yet to come to terms with their (I squeezed the word out of my mouth like the last wretched inch of toothpaste from a tube) *infertility*. I suggested that Nick needed evidence of their contrition. That perhaps there was a friend they could speak to who could help them see the situation from a new perspective, someone whose opinion they respected. I squeezed my knees tight together, the cheek of me. Headcase, who ought to be seeking therapy herself, advising the Mortimers to seek it. Hilariously (and I use the word in its ironic, bitter sense), I quoted Issy, "The child is always a symptom of the parents."

I listened to myself dispensing wisdom to this elegant couple so much more mature and important than me, and I wouldn't have blamed Lavinia if she'd pressed her Vicky sponge into my face, but she didn't. The two of them sat, nodding, their eyes fixed on my yapping mouth. Their attention was addictive, and I had to force myself to stop talking. I glanced at the clock on Martha's wall.

"I hope all this isn't too much of a . . . a shock," I added. "I know it can't be pleasant to hear. But I'm almost certain that that's what Nick needs of you, and if you want him . . . back, I'm sure you'd be more than happy to try anything."

This seemed to galvanize them into agreement. They leaped up, hugged me, thanked me, boomed, "Yes, oh, yes, absolutely," and waved as I scurried back across the road to work. I didn't look back. Grant them *some* dignity.

I entered an altogether cheerier office. Claudia and Nick—

they'd always got on—were hee-heeing over an application form. Under *Do you have any talents?* the guy had written "I can lay lino." In response to *What's your greatest asset?* he'd scrawled "My MBA." Claudia even gave me a ghost of a smile.

Nick stood up. "Do you mind if I nip to the bank for five minutes, Hol? I'll be right back."

I couldn't believe he was being so correct as to ask my permission. This, the man who was so accustomed to doing as he pleased that on their first meeting he had no qualms about telling my parents of the thin walls in his rented studio flat, which unfortunately enabled us to hear his neighbors having sex. He'd told my mother that their efforts sounded like "a sea lion fixing a squeaky door."

"Of course you can go to the bank, Nick," I said, wondering if I and his many parents had, with our mistreatment, managed to break his spirit entirely. "You don't have to ask."

"Camille spoke to Nige," said Claudia, the second he was out of sight. "He's going to do it. Camille spoke to Stuart's client, recorded the conversation—which is illegal but bite me—and she's biking the tape to him this afternoon."

If ever a plan had "fiasco" written all over it in pink fluorescent marker pen, here it was. And she hadn't apologized for shouting at me. I covered my ears. "I told you, I don't want to know," I said. "This is *your* idea, it's nothing to do with me. And if Stuart catches Camille, she'd better have an excuse ready that's nothing to do with me."

Claudia shrugged. "Fine, fine, whatever." Her mood froze as fast as it had melted. "FYI," she added, "Nick told me about being adopted last night. Which makes what you've done to him about the phantom baby even more . . . inconsiderate."

She spun her chair around to face her computer. Her black hair flew as if she were a witch on a broomstick.

I gave her a covert V sign. It didn't feel like enough so I snarled, "I feel evil enough without your input. And FYI, Claudia, you are *not* an American, you are a British citizen living in London who happens to watch *Seinfeld* on Sky occasionally, so kindly refrain from using phrases like 'FYI' and 'bite me.'"

Claudia gave me the V sign back, over her head. Ten frosty

minutes of silence followed, then Nick sauntered in, whistling. "Everything okay?"

"I need to get some air," muttered my sister. She snatched up her cell—she could have saved herself trouble and had it surgically attached—and marched out. I wondered if she expected me to tell Nick about the fantasy baby then and there. I smiled at him. I could feel my face turning puce. Martha's Got Buns was, in retrospect, an unsafe place to stage a secret assignment. Nick could have gone to the bank five minutes earlier and caught us red-handed, the Vicky sponge in our mouths. As it was, I knew he suspected I'd been up to no good.

He beamed. "Guess what. She rang! While you were out!"

My heart flopped in relief. Maybe his birth mother wasn't a lost cause. "Oh, fantastic. What did she say?"

Nick mussed his hair. "Malcolm's had a shift changed, so he's now free next Wednesday night. And so's Russell. It's nine days away, which is a while, but sooner than I thought it was going to be. That's all right, isn't it? It doesn't clash with work?"

"It's fine. There *is* a second Date Night, but we'll get Issy along. Meeting your, mm, other family is far more important, obviously."

His face fell. "Oh. Bother. I was hoping that you'd come with me again. You being my future wife and the mother of my unborn child and all that." He grinned, dropped to his knees, held my hips, and put his ear against my stomach. "Hello, darling," he whispered. "Daddy loves you." I tried not to flinch.

"Well," I said, stroking his hair and wanting to groan aloud. "There'll be other times."

I closed my eyes. Everything would fall apart when I told him the truth. We'd be the only couple ever to cancel our engagement *twice*. And what would I tell my family? I didn't want to shame them more than I had but it seemed inevitable. I'd convinced myself of that baby. The phantom loss was a scalpel, scraping the flesh from my insides. There'd been a young woman nursing a newborn in Martha's earlier, and I hadn't been able to look at her. I didn't feel sorry for myself, though. You shun reality, it's like swinging a wrecking ball away from you. Soon enough, it'll swing right back and pulp you.

"Do you mind if we don't see each other tonight?" I blurted out. "I've got stuff to do around the house."

"What stuff? Cleaning? Why, where's Gloria? You mustn't overdo it, Hol. Not in your state. Why don't I come and help?"

This was unreal. For the last few years, my gripe with Nick had been the gripe of a million women (and men, I guess)—that our relationship was no longer the precious jewel of love, laughter, and mutual respect that it had been at the beginning. But even at the beginning—love, laughter, precious jewels, and mutual respect notwithstanding—Nick had never offered to *clean*.

"Thanks, but really, don't worry. I won't lift anything heavy. It's other stuff. Phone calls. You'll be bored out of your head. I actually feel like being by myself."

The truth, which gushed out in a rush, proved more acceptable than the blather about "stuff."

"No problem," he said. He gave my stomach one last rub. "I probably shouldn't grope the boss in the office, but it *is* my first day." He returned to his desk.

That evening I arrived home (a light awaiting me in every room, I'd resigned myself to an extra few hundred pounds on the electricity bill), went through my usual twenty-minute checking ritual—ensuring Emily wasn't lying dead in the garden, her brains bashed out by a passing thug, marching around the house with a bread knife yanking open doors to reassure myself that no intruders were crouching in wardrobes—and threw out the pregnancy book. Then I rang Gloria.

"Ah bloody 'ell, I've not forgotten to clean, have I?"

"What! No. No. You were only here a few days ago, it's still spotless, I'm living in clinical conditions. No. I'm calling about something else."

"Thank Christ for that. What?"

"You know. Your cousin. The one who . . . was raped. You gave me the title of a Website she found useful. I put it away and then I lost it. I wondered if you could give it to me again."

"Of *course*."

Gloria spelled out the name for me.

"Great. Thank you. And. Did you mention that there was a psychologist she spoke to?"

"Yeah. Yeah. His name's David Goldstein, hang on a sec." I

heard a scrummage, then Gloria was back on the phone. "He's NHS and private, ask your doctor to refer you."

I took down the number. "And he was . . . nice, was he?"

"Oh! Yes! He was wonderful. So kind. And understanding. You'll never be a good therapist if you're not a nice person. No matter how many certificates you have. She'd have been done for without him. I mean, she still takes the pills, but a much lower dose than what she did, and that would never have happened without his help. She'd seen a psychiatrist, and he'd given her antidepressants, but the dose was so mental she was in a constant fug. It was like being preserved in ice. But it was better than having to feel. Sometimes a load of feelings drops on you before you're ready for 'em. The drugs helped that way. But Dr. Goldstein was a godsend. She'd have gone 'round the twist if it weren't for him. So . . . you gonna get referred? Didn't the police give you Victim Support?"

"Yes, I am," I replied. "And yes they did. But I'd rather try the, you know, personal recommendation first. Thanks, Gloria."

I put down the phone and stood there for a while looking at it. The last thing I wanted to do was to follow in the Clouseau-ish steps of Claudia and Camille, but I suspected that Gloria wasn't entirely telling the truth about her cousin.

CHAPTER 38

I didn't call my doctor, I called my mother. I think everyone needs their mother. I hadn't told Nick, but after his adoption news I'd searched the Internet and ordered a book entitled *The Primal Wound*. I just wanted to understand how he felt a little more closely. Understanding is the key to forgiveness. Mostly.

The book cited an anecdote similar to a tale Nick had told me, having heard it from Pamela Fidgett. A grown woman, who knew she was adopted, breaking down at a time of stress and wailing in her bedroom, "I want my mummy." She'd never *met* her mummy—unless you count the nine months of gestation—and her adoptive mother was perfectly lovely. In truth, she hadn't a clue who this "mummy" was, if she was alive or dead, wouldn't have known her had they met in the street, but when this thirty-four-year-old's emotions were stripped raw, what emerged was the child crying, "I want my mummy."

It made me want to hug her. It also turned my stomach. Grow up, why don't you, and do without! No one wants to be reminded of their own weakness. But then, perhaps we all have the same weakness. Some just hide it better than others. Nige had a friend whose father had been in the Israeli army. Three of their unit were captured and tortured, and because they had their walkie-talkies with them, the friend's father heard his colleagues' last moments. "They were calling for their mothers," he'd said. "*Ima,* in Hebrew."

Ah, God, it was too horrible, I wished Nige hadn't told me. But again, it proved my suspicion, that at heart we are all children. We just play at being adults.

When I spoke to my mother that evening, maternal concern oozed warm and treacly from the receiver. She and Dad were *so* looking forward to being grandparents again. If we wanted the baby's room painted, Dad would be honored. I so badly wanted to tell her the truth, but my voice stalled. How did I begin to inflict that much pain? I'd more easily hurt a kitten than my parents, that's how vulnerable I felt them to be. They didn't seem to need their mothers, but I thought of them as childlike. I wanted to protect them.

I remembered when Nick's parents visited a few years back, the day after Boxing Day. My mother's friend Leila had dropped 'round and, with her usual lack of finesse, hogged the conversation.

The subject of literature had arisen, as Lavinia had received a vintage edition of the complete works of Tolstoy for Christmas, and good luck to her. Leila piped up in her Wiltshire accent—its softness was *entirely* unsuited to her brash personality, her fleshy pink face seemed to swell as she spoke—"Oh, Linda's a great reader, Lavinia. She'll get through a Danielle Steel in, like, ten minutes!"

I'd squirmed for my mother who—I wanted to shout in her defense—was just as likely to read John Steinbeck as Danielle Steel. Mrs. Mortimer had smiled and said, "Goodness," and my mother had smiled back. Not one other person in the room seemed bothered, but to me, my mother's smile revealed that she was too naive to know she was being patronized. I'd mentioned it to Nick afterward, and he'd snorted, "Do you think my mother is actually going to open *War and Peace*? Holly, she barely gets through the *Daily Mail*!"

In the end, talking to my mother that evening proved harsh comfort, rather in the way that Heinz cream of tomato soup is soothing in theory but stings the back of your throat. I'd lied to her unforgivably, and now her generous words bounced off me. Doesn't everyone want to be better than their parents? Isn't that the point of evolution? I was so much worse. But it had started with Stuart. Stuart was responsible for destroying all the good relationships I had.

The next day, I rang the doctor on the dot of nine and—in a rare breakout of luck—got an emergency appointment at half-past. I explained about Dr. Goldstein and said I'd go private. (I'd rather *he* got my money than Stuart.) My doctor, whose primary aim seems to be to get you out of his office in under six minutes (when apparently your official NHS allocation is seven), agreed to write a letter.

Not a moment too soon. At work, Issy and Nick were full of baby stories, gabbling happily about first smiles and breast pumps and different makes of stroller. Claudia kept silent, hurling me sour looks with the force and regularity of a putting machine. A padded envelope arrived from my parents, addressed to me. Inside was a pair of the tiniest socks you ever saw, pink and white. They could barely fit over my thumb. I slid them into my desk and scurried to the toilet to compose myself. Soon, I'd tell them. Soon. And the writ, remember? What are you going to do about that? Twenty-six days, *ages*. It was a relief to distract myself with the business of Girl Meets Boy.

"Is everything set for tonight?" I asked Claudia, smiling at a point beyond her left ear.

"Yes," she replied, addressing my right shoulder. "Debbie from *Glamour* is being put with Xak, this new guy, Jim—a real sweetie, no pretentions, chatty, relaxing to be with, according to Issy—my painter friend Karl—"

"Eh?" said Nick.

"He *is* single," replied Claudia. "It's not cheating, he is up for meeting women. *I* think it's a clever idea—he gets a few free dates, Girl Meets Yob gets the benefit of his good looks and sparkling personality. Well, bizarre personality."

"I've got friends who'd like to meet women."

"Yes, dear, and they can pay."

"What, even Manjit?"

"Manjit's not single!" said Claudia and I together.

"Nick," I added, "*that* is precisely the sort of trick that journalists like to write about. And Manjit can't keep a secret."

Nick stuck out his bottom lip. "Well, if you must know, Bo has requested a trial separation. *She* went on a date last night. With this awful, pompous, balding *meeja* bore who works for the BBC. He was wearing beige cords. I think it would be good for Manjit, he's been mooning around the house."

"A trial separation, and she goes on a date?" I spluttered. "Poor Manjit!"

"God, she's a cow," offered Claudia. "I wouldn't mind, but she's punching above her weight with Manjit anyway!"

"A trial separation," declared Issy, "is the emotionally constipated method of saying 'I'm not happy in this relationship.' It means she'd like to end the relationship but she lacks the courage to express herself honestly. This is a half-arsed precursor. Disgusting, cowardly, selfish! Weak people who manipulate their innocent partners like that make me *sick*!"

"Of *course* Manjit can come tonight, we'd love to have him," I said, trying not to mind that Issy's passion had caused her to accidentally spit on my hand. "Tell him it'll be fun."

"Should we risk putting him with Debbie?" said Claudia.

"He'll be as good as gold," cried Nick. "I'll tell him to talk about Bo in the past tense. It'll be good practice for him."

"Hm," I said.

I was still saying "hm" when Manjit arrived at the Date Night wearing a beige suit. Then I saw him tug at his pink-and-blue tie—any tighter it would have choked him—and my stern heart melted.

"Oh, crikey," I said to Nick. "He is *so* adorable. Go and tell him he doesn't need to wear a tie. Or jacket. Unless he wants to."

"You tell him," said Nick. "He was looking forward to seeing you."

I lolloped over. "Hello, you. Would you like a drink?"

Manjit smiled his beautiful smile. "All right. Sorry, how are you? Yeah, go on, then. A pint of lager, I mean, glass of white, please."

"Manjit. You can have whatever you like. Would you like a lager?"

He paused. "Yeah, go on, you twisted my arm. How's the self-defense going, then? Practicing on Nick, are ya?"

I made a face. "Not lately. But you're the best teacher, really excellent."

Manjit dipped his head. "Ta, Hol. Thanks. Thanks a lot."

"I'm sorry to hear it's not going so well with Bo," I lied. "How are you doing?"

Manjit rubbed the back of his neck. "Ah, you know. Bit shell-shocked. That's what she wants, though, I can't stop her. What you see is what you get with Bo. She's . . . feisty."

The word *selfish* almost popped out of my mouth. I handed him his lager.

Manjit sighed. "This geezer. I think he was scared of me. I think he thought I was going to beat him up. Like I'd do a thing like that! I think he was taking her to have tea—dinner I mean—at his house. Nothing dodgy, I don't think. He's writing a documentary for Radio Four on the Czech Republic, he wanted her opinion. He's also writing a novel. When he said that, I said, That's brilliant, what, like *High Fidelity*? and his nostrils went all big and he goes—I can't do his voice but he sounded a bit like a girl—he goes, '*My* work is rather more profound than that male *Bridget Jones* crap, "Gary snogged Julie. Oh, Tracey, he's such a good kisser, better than Steve!" ' And then he and Bo both laughed. I don't think he'd read Nick Hornby, he's not like that at all. But I didn't say nothing. I didn't want to embarrass him in front of Bo. It's not fair."

"That was very thoughtful of you," I replied. "Especially in the face of such bad manners. This guy—what's his name?"

"Lance."

"*Lance?* Blimey. Lance has obviously been badly brought up."

"I think he thought I was a bit of a scummer. He lives in Islington. Bo says he's very left-wing. I think he thought my hair was too short, like I was a bit rough, you know, National Front-y."

"Mm," I said. "That's common. British Asians joining the NF. What a prat."

"You reckon?" Manjit looked hopeful.

I grasped his shoulders. "Listen to me. Forget Lance, forget Bo. She doesn't deserve you. I know you . . . I know you're very fond of her, but if you don't mind me saying, I think she's acted unfairly. So just enjoy yourself tonight and don't feel guilty. All it is, is a bit of chat, lighthearted, nothing heavy. Personally, I think the women here will swoon over you, you are—and I'd say this in front of Nick—bloody gorgeous. You are what they call a catch."

I stopped short of saying he was too good for Bo. Manjit laughed—he was that one in a million man who was God's gift but couldn't see it. All right, that one in twenty million. But I was spot on. He got two friendship ticks and two date ticks. Georgina—trainee solicitor, part-time model, and full-time flirt—didn't take her panda eyes off him once. All through the break, he talked and she *stared* at him, mouth half open, ready to laugh. When I'd come to tell her their date time was up, she'd pulled an unattractive face. As it was, she'd dragged her chair around the coffee table and just about sat in his lap. She'd even switched off her cell.

She had competition, however, from a new member called Verity. Verity was half-Chinese, a research scientist, and wore her shiny black hair in two "sticky-out" plaits. She was as slender as a reed with impossibly smooth skin, and I got the distinct impression that Georgina wanted to slap her. Verity certainly came across as a man's woman—preferably, Manjit's woman—but when you talked to her she was friendly and chatty. She giggled at everything Manjit said, and she made him laugh, too. I didn't hear him once say, "Sorry." I felt she was far better suited to him than fun-buster Bo.

We'd put Debbie from *Glamour* with Xak for her last date—if her behavior at Bernard and Sam's wedding was anything to go by, I thought she'd appreciate it, and she did. She posed for the photographs eagerly enough. Afterward, when she interviewed me, Xak stood bashful guard nearby, his floppy blond hair hiding his blushes. She kept darting glances at him, but even so, *"Manjit,"* she said. "I did like Manjit. He was plain lovely. The kind of bloke you want to introduce to your sister." I could tell she meant it or she'd have referred to him as "Number Three." (Our members do this alarmingly often, even if they like someone.) Debbie grinned at me slyly. "Whereas Xak's the kind of bloke you want to keep for yourself. Holly, don't look so nervous. It's been fantastic. Much better than I'd thought, to be honest. This is going to be a *great* piece."

The rest of the week was notable for only two reasons. The first was that Manjit dumped Bo. Apparently, she had a habit of kicking him in bed if he snored. Or grunted. Or breathed too heavily. Or rolled over. Or tugged the duvet. On average, Manjit received eight kicks per night. They'd been together for three years, two months, and seventeen days. Three times three hundred and sixty-five, plus sixty-one, plus seventeen, minus the three nights Bo had spent with Lance, times eight, equaled nine thousand, three hundred and sixty kicks.

Well, on his return from Girl Meets Boy, Bo was in a foul mood. (Despite the "trial separation," they still slept in the same bed, unless Bo chose to go missing.) That night, Manjit dropped off into a contented sleep, let out a snuffle, and Bo attempted the nine thousand, three hundred and sixty-first kick. Nick and I like to think it was the admiration he'd received from all the women at the agency—that maybe their friendliness highlighted Bo's disrespect and gave him confidence—but Manjit felt the kick, started awake, and realized he'd had enough. He snatched up his pillow, smacked it down hard on the bed, and yelled, "Remember that kick, because that was the last time you *ever* kick me. This ain't love, Bo, it's boot camp, and I've 'ad it, you're 'istory!"

To everyone's delight, Bo was inconsolable.

The second thing was that on Friday morning Dr. Goldstein's office called. He had a waiting list, but there'd been a cancellation. If it was convenient, he could see me on Tuesday at five fifteen.

CHAPTER 39

My main worry was that Dr. Goldstein would think I was a nut. I asked Issy if therapists ever entertained such unorthodox thoughts about their clients, and she said, "God, yes! At least a quarter of mine are totally mad. They're loons. Crazy. Mental. Insane. Bonkers. Barking. Gaga. Round the—"

"All right, Isabella," I said. "I get the picture." I felt I'd encouraged her to be unprofessional and been duly punished. "God, yes!" was not the answer I'd been hoping for. She should have refused to discuss the people in her care, even in the abstract. I hoped Dr. Goldstein wasn't so easily led.

Tuesday at five, I rang the polished bell of a green door on Harley Street. I wondered if the builders on the scaffolding across the street thought I was a nut. I'd tried to dress sane (no haute couture or hats with earflaps), but then look at Hannibal Lecter, so well turned out. I announced myself to the receptionist—I wondered if she thought I was a nut—who pointed me to the waiting room. By then, I was weary of trying to appear in peak mental condition. The two people already sitting in the waiting room were probably also nuts, so it hardly mattered.

The waiting room had green-and-beige armchairs scattered around its edges and a grand oak table in its center. The magazines on display were of an altogether finer quality than on the NHS. Current, pristine issues of *Tatler, Country Life, Harpers & Queen,* broadsheet newspapers. In my doctor's waiting room a few days before, I'd picked over an ancient, torn edition of *Woman & Home*. Now I divided my time surreptitiously assessing the man in the corner reading the *Daily Telegraph*—obsessive-compulsive? manic-depressive? borderline personality disorder?—and considering the practicalities of moving to a Prominent 17th-Century County Property in Montgomeryshire, or a Barn Conversion Dating Back to the 19th Century in Kent (Tunbridge Wells about six miles).

Then a tall man with curly brown hair and a smiley face appeared at the door and said, "Ms. Appleton?"

I jumped up, and he shook my hand. "I'm David Goldstein. How are you?"

A trick question, surely.

"I'm all right," I replied, deciding that, in the circumstances, "fine" was the wrong answer. I didn't want him to think, Yeah, really!

Dr. Goldstein led me into a large, airy office and showed me to a comfortable chair. This small courtesy was enough to bring a lump to my throat. There were a lot of fat books squeezed onto bookshelves and even more in towering piles on the floor. This reminded me of something Nige once said, when I asked if he was breeding a library on his lounge floor. "I like piles of books. They remind me of how intelligent I am." I wondered if Dr. Goldstein thought that too. I noticed that his secretary was right next door, sitting like a large squirrel in what appeared to be a cubbyhole, and that he'd left his own door ajar. This struck me as thoughtful and made me feel safe. I gulped. He had a box of tissues on his desk too, like Issy. I hoped Kleenex gave therapists a discount.

The tip of my nose must have turned pink, because Dr. Goldstein asked if I'd like a glass of water. I nodded, and he sprang up to ask his secretary to bring one. I sipped the cool water and tried not to cry. Dr. Goldstein looked concerned, which made it impossible. Then he said gently, "What's the problem?"

A great woolly tangle of anxieties tumbled out.

The rape . . . I have had a few problems but I feel I'm getting through them . . . I hadn't told my parents because I didn't want to upset them . . . There are a few things I've done that are now con-

cerning me . . . the fantasy baby . . . My sister had been so supportive but now she was angry . . . My fiancé would end it when he found
out . . . I'd so wanted to begin again . . . I feel frightened at the state
of mind I'm in, out of control . . . The CPS believed him, not me . . .
and now he's suing me . . . I do have fun but I feel as if there's no
heart in it . . . I'm better than I was but I am so *not good* . . . I don't
like how I am . . . The fear that everyone is Stuart and the world is
full of evil . . .

I blew my nose. If he could make sense of that lot, he was worth
what he charged. I was too ashamed to make eye contact so I
looked everywhere but at him. But there was very little to fix on. No
photographs of his family, no school pictures of kids with gappy
grins. Reluctantly, I met his gaze.

Dr. Goldstein paused. "You're worried," he said, "that the
trauma is still unresolved and influencing your thinking, your behavior, and your understanding of yourself in relation to the world
around you."

I nodded. He clasped his hands in front of him on his desk,
which was neither too small nor too suspiciously big. I supposed a
therapist couldn't have his patients think he was compensating. His
nails were neat and not bitten—the nails of an untroubled mind.

"Okay. It sounds to me as though you've adopted a defensive
posture, Holly. You've invested all your emotional energy in something that's distracting. This stems from unresolved feelings surrounding the trauma. You've not really processed the rape
experience, you've not fully come to terms with it. Which is why
you're wanting to create a new life in terms of motherhood. In a
sense, it would have given you many gains. You would have been
able to avoid sex, stay in more legitimately—there would have been
a social sanctioning of behaviors that get you off the hook."

I listened, wide-eyed and wet-nosed. It was, I thought, amazing
that I could walk into a room and tell a stranger my deepest, weirdest
secrets, the terrible essence of my fucked-upness, and that he
wouldn't make an embarrassed face and say in a silly voice, "*Interesting.*" You could acclimatize quickly, though. It was like visiting a gynecologist. A middle-aged man in a suit foraging wrist-deep in one's

vagina—a brief second of mortification, then you think, Ach, seen one, seen 'em all. It's an *EastEnders* repeat for him, it's only *skin*.

Dr. Goldstein smiled and added, "We have to help you get a better understanding of that trauma, to use the technical jargon, to process it."

I nodded. I liked the way he talked to me as if I wasn't an idiot. Mind you, as I'd spoken, he'd taken notes. I couldn't see what he'd written, which, for all I knew, was "What a fruit bat."

"Can I ask what came into your mind when you started crying just then after mentioning Stuart? Were there any pictures in your mind? Any thoughts?"

I hesitated. A small part of me was tempted to lie to make myself sound good. But there were cheaper ways of showing off and better ways of wasting my time.

The thoughts and pictures in my mind were inexplicable. "I was twelve and forced to take part in this miserable youth-club treasure hunt, because my mum's friend Leila ran it and both my sisters refused to go. I had no friends there, and I remember trying to be friendly about this stupid clue 'M07S' to some of the teenagers. I said, 'I can't think what M07S means,' and they laughed at me in a mean way. It turned out to be the sign on the road—SLOW."

I fully expected Dr. Goldstein to roar heartily with laughter, but he scribbled and said, "What would it feel like to be twelve and alone and laughed at by other children?"

"It was horrible. Humiliating. I felt they were laughing at me because *I* was slow. When I think of Stuart, I am that twelve-year-old, I haven't progressed. It's the . . . the being stupid and helpless, taken for a fool. It makes me feel worthless. And I thought I'd grown out of that. Until I met Stuart I was pretty pleased with myself."

"Why is feeling helpless such a bad thing?" said Dr. Goldstein. "I know that sounds like a silly question."

I crumpled my tissue and reached for another. This was *proper* therapy! "I don't like being helpless or out of control," I whispered. "It makes me panic. I don't trust other people to take care of me. I need to take care of myself. So if I'm out of control, I feel that something terrible will happen. And—*snivel*—something terrible *did* happen."

"Mm-hm. So, if you can't control things, that kind of automatically means that something bad will happen. Right. And within that is the idea that you can't trust people."

Having your feeble state of mind played back to you can make you feel foolish. But this was reassuring. It clarified my fears, popped them into boxes.

"Yes. I used to trust people. I used to be very trusting. But after this, I've found it hard. I feel that everyone is like Stuart, and the world is a horrible world full of cruel people. It's really affected how I live my life."

Dr. Goldstein leaned forward. I hoped this meant he thought I was of psychological interest. "Holly, you've had something bad happen to you, and so you see the world as a far more dangerous place than it actually is. It's what we call elevated risk assessment. But this is a consequence that we can explore in a later session. The first thing we need to do is find out what that experience meant to you."

Gloom descended. I saw myself, sitting there, unable to get on with my life. My unhealthy state of mind wasn't tangible, not like a broken leg, so it was hard to feel justified spending wads of cash on a brain doctor. A part of me felt I should be able to get *on*. I couldn't get away from the nasty suspicion that talking about myself to a person who I financially rewarded for not running away was a luxury. It was like having a massage, an indulgence that makes you feel better, but you won't die without it. There was no immediate danger, the bulk of my unhappiness belonged to my past. So why was I still in bits?

"This is what I'd like to do," said Dr. Goldstein. "I want you to relax, close your eyes, and talk through the experience in a very, very detailed, structured way. I'm going to ask you questions. You see, when a traumatic memory has not been processed, it does influence behavior, and that behavior is not in your interest, by your own admission. What we need to do is help you to come to terms with it, and this is the theory. If you go over it a certain number of times when you're in a relaxed state, it has a beneficial effect. The memory can be packed away, and you learn that you don't have to avoid these emotions, that they won't destroy you or kill you, that they're just bad feelings that you can come to terms with. At the end of the session you'll feel stronger, in fact. It's really building your confidence to manage your own mind."

What an appalling idea. I said in a small voice, "The last time I talked about it, with Caroline, the policewoman, I had a panic attack." My heart juddered. That terrifying sensation of lacking the apparatus to breathe, the hideous conviction your lungs had shriveled to the size of two kidney beans.

Dr. Goldstein fixed me with his kindest eyes. "Right now, Holly," he said, "your thinking is 'I can't deal with it, it's too much.' You avoid it, and because you avoid it, you never test out your capacity to cope with the trauma. By getting you to stay with it, I'm *skilling* you. Nothing terrible will happen. The memory is frightening, but you're safe now. It will be very emotional, you will cry, and yes, you may have a panic attack, but I'll make sure you breathe properly. And at end of the session you'll get up and walk out. You'll realize you can cope, you can deal with it. Whereas, if you avoid things to do with the experience, you never provide yourself with the opportunity to learn that you are more resilient than you think."

I bit my lip. I realized with a start that Dr. Goldstein was treating me like an adult. A capable, intelligent adult. All this time I'd deluded myself that it would be a relief to be treated like a child—shrugging off responsibility, letting others take care of you—when, in fact, being treated like a child at the age of thirty can only ever be infuriating and insulting. This was greatly preferable. "What sort of questions would you ask?"

Dr. Goldstein's smile was apologetic. "Questions that will make the rape experience as vivid as possible. That way, we access your emotions, which you can then deal with. So, questions like, Where was his hand at that point? What did it feel like? Go through the experience like a film in slow motion in your mind—and *pause*. Okay, what can you see? Can you feel anything on your skin? How hot is it? Can you smell anything? What can you hear?"

I stared at him. "I thought you were a nice man," I said. "You're a monster."

He tapped his pen, smiling down at his desk. "I don't do this with every client," he replied. "Only the ones who I feel understand the theory and can cope with it."

Oh, he was clever.

"All righty," I said. (Because if you say "all righty" about something, how bad can it be?) "We'll do it."

CHAPTER 40

When rabbiting on about understanding and forgiveness, it never occurred to me that the same principle might apply to myself. I've always been harder on myself than on others. I presumed that if I wasn't, I'd never get anywhere. I didn't realize that the opposite is also true. If you don't tolerate error in your life, you eventually wilt in the heat of your own self-loathing.

"Rape can happen to *anyone*," Dr. Goldstein had said.

I floated through the next day, serene. It was as if the worries swarming my brain like ants on sugar had been sprayed with repellent. I certainly felt that Fate, God, Kramer—some higher power—was trying to tell me something.

For instance, Issy was excitable because the previous night she'd nearly been mugged. She'd visited a girlfriend in a rough area, and at twelve the friend had seen her to her car. She'd just locked herself in when four men appeared from nowhere. Three white skinheads, one black guy wearing a hat. The hat guy tapped on her car window and said, " 'Scuse me, love." Issy was about to buzz down the window, but her girlfriend reappeared at the passenger door—for solidarity? protection?—Issy had let her in, and he'd run away. She'd stared after him as the pale soles of his shoes shrank into the distance, and the other men—were they even with him?—melted into the night.

"I am so stupid," said Issy again and again. She kept rolling her eyes in dismay, her usual sheen of confidence rumpled. "I thought, He wants to ask me something, what if it's important? I felt so rude and racist *not* opening the window. I only didn't because I was so flustered I forgot where the button was. I can't believe I was so slow-witted. What did I *think* four scruffy strange men slinking out of a basketball court wanted at midnight from a woman in a silver Mercedes?"

Nick and Claudia—shaken by this new, frail version of Issy—were full of kindly reproaches. "You learned a lesson," said Nick. "In future just remember that no stranger has any business asking you *anything*. And you did do the right thing, even if your instinct wasn't as quick as you might have liked. No harm was done, there'll be no different future because of this. So don't obsess."

I gazed at him, covertly, from behind my coffee mug. He was a kind man.

"You mustn't think of yourself as a victim," added Claudia. "In that sort of situation, you must think of yourself as a survivor, using whatever you have to help you. And what did you have?"

"I could have beeped the horn."

"Exactly. Well done!"

"Yes," wailed Issy, "but I only thought of that now, because you asked me!"

Nick squeezed her arm. "It would be ironic," he said, "if you thought badly of yourself for not wanting to think the worst of people."

It can happen to anyone.

I was cleaning my teeth before bed, after another boisterous Date Night, when the phone rang. In the mind-set of ready-for-anything, I snatched it up.

"It's me," said a dull voice. "Are you awake? Can I come 'round?"

"Nick. Of course. What's wrong?"

I was addressing dead air.

My heart thundered. Nick hadn't attended work that night because he was meeting his birth mother, Malcolm, and Russell. The chosen venue for this momentous occasion was a McDonald's near Malcolm's office. I'd bitten back the comment, "Well, that will make it really special." I hadn't wanted to pursue my bad feeling about it.

When the bell rang, I peered through the fisheye, put down the knife, and heaved open the door. Nick stood there, white and drawn. He looked like a vampire's leftovers. He stumbled into my arms, and I hugged him silently. He was cold, from outside. I let him hang on for as long as he wanted, until his skin was warmed by mine. I took him by the hand and led him into the kitchen. Then I made him a hot chocolate with milk. He sat at the table, fingers curled around the mug, staring sightlessly at the wall, shivering in bursts. He's in shock, I realized. I pulled Emily's blanket out of her basket and placed it over his knees. She hopped on his lap and he raised a thin smile.

Waiting for him to speak, I remembered something he'd once said: "I prefer excitement to contentment." He'd thrown it at me during a row over money. He'd rather slit his throat, he'd declared, than save for a new kitchen. The very *thought* of it made him shudder. He wanted to live in Rome, winter in Zermatt, spend the New Year in Barbados, meet thrilling people, do glamorous things, not save for kitchens. He made me feel like a dullard, and I'd repeated his claim to Rachel, who—like any good friend—pronounced it "a rotten, suspicious statement."

"Does the sweet thing not realize that contented people can *also* be excited?" she'd drawled, killing a match and taking the first glorious drag of nicotine. "To need constant excitement, babes, it's an escape, a fix. It suggests a person who is unhappy in life and unreconciled to reality."

With dread I'd thought, Was that Nick?

It wasn't now.

"They were so sodding *unfriendly*," he blurted out. "I'd bought him this plastic dancing Elvis for his dashboard as a hello present—it twirls and jiggles as you drive—and Russell goes, 'What the fuck would I want with that?' He's my half brother, and there was . . . nothing. It was like he *hated* me. He looks nothing like me, he's really weird. I don't know what you call it—arrested development? He's twenty-three and he's like a baby. Belligerent. Dressed in black, head to foot, and he smelled, like he hadn't washed. He picked his nose *openly*. Our mother said his room's all black too, and he collects knives. He doesn't look at you when he's talking to you, but mostly he doesn't talk, he grunts. He ate with his mouth open and laughed at how I speak. He kept snorting to himself and—get this—we're halfway through eating and Blockbuster rings him on his cell phone to tell him what videos they've just got in! And I thought I was a loser. There's no way he's got a job. And even my mother was acting weird—Holly, she ate a Big Mac while smoking *and* chewing gum. She flattens the gum and stores it above her two front teeth. I went to hug her and she went stiff, it was like hugging a waxwork. She hardly said anything to me. I don't know if she's nervous of Malcolm or what. I'd taken my camera to get a picture of us all together, and in the end I didn't even get it out of my rucksack. You know when you feel something just isn't appropriate? It felt too . . . expensive. They'd think I was showing off. I just wanted a photo of me and my real mum—"

His voice cracked. Bolt upright on his lap, Emily purred and kneaded, her eyes wide with adoration. Cats have a reputation for being selfish, but in my experience they show sympathy—well, polite curiosity, at least—when people are upset. Nick wrapped his arms around her solid little body and kissed her head.

"And Malcolm's a psycho. Ker-*ist*. He just *sat* there, his arms folded, staring at me. Like he was about to challenge me to a fist-fight! Even when he was eating his Party Meal, he looked at me menacingly while he chewed. His nose is so red it's almost purple, with huge pores. There's practically more pore than skin. I wanted to stare back, but I didn't dare. And I insisted on paying—I mean, it was McDonald's, please—and now I think that was a bad idea. Malcolm thought I was trying to get one up on him. "I'nt you flush," he said. Like I was flashing my money around. I mean, Hol, you know what I'm like—*what* money? And even their clothes were different from mine in a noticeable and awkward way. I felt like Little Lord Fucking Fauntleroy in my stupid blazer and brogues. I mean, what did I think I was doing, dressing like Dad—Michael? Michael, I mean," he added.

He swigged his not-so-hot chocolate. "And *then* my mum looks at her watch—she's got this Casio digital watch, the kind you had when you were thirteen—and she goes, 'Malcy, did you want to watch the snooker on Sky?' Hol, I didn't know people still *played* snooker on television. So he goes, 'Yeah, we should make a move.' And they all scuffled out. They didn't say even thank you for the food. Not that I care about that, but—"

"She didn't say good-bye to you?"

"No, she did. But hurriedly. Malcolm and Russell were halfway out the door. I said, 'Can I call you?' and she says in this ratty voice, 'Look, I'll be in touch, okay?' As if I was some kind of phone pest."

He shook his head in disbelief. "What's happened. It's too much. My head is about to burst. You hope, Hol. You imagine. You never think it won't turn out right. You're so used to that warm feeling as the credits roll, you get complacent. I feel like I've messed up, like I'm this big blundering mistake no one wants. Like Frankenstein's monster. I have no one. *No* family. I'm an orphan. I don't fit in anywhere. I feel hollow. I can't believe I feel this isolated. I feel like I had the chance to have a family and I blew it."

He paused. "At least I have you two."

I clutched my stomach, aghast.

His phone rang and he fumbled for it, animated with hope. Then his face sagged. "What does *she* want?" he muttered. "It's the fifth time she's called today." He jammed the phone back in his pocket.

My conscience went hysterical. *You have no right*, it scolded. *You put a stop to this now.*

Okay, I bargained. I will. But first things first.

I got up and poured myself a glass of water. I felt like a strong person. I'd been convinced Stuart had raped me because I was weak. Dr. Goldstein had said that, in fact, many rapists targeted women who were strong and successful, because these were the sort of women they dreamed of dominating.

I could do this. No more lying. To anyone. Including Nick, my parents, and myself.

I sat down and cleared my throat. "Was that Lavinia?"

A terse nod.

"Listen, Nick," I began. Emily chose this moment to yawn so widely her head just about vanished in a vast expanse of throat. Her stress levels, I thought enviously, were remarkably low. "Nick, I have two confessions to make, and neither of them are going to please you. One, in fact, is very bad news."

He frowned. "Go on."

I clenched my fists in my lap. "Okay. First. I've been in . . . *communication* with Lavinia and Michael."

"What!"

"*Wait,* will you? Let me explain. The truth is, they love you deeply, and they're devastated that you're so hostile to them. I saw them a few days ago and they both look terrible. You must have noticed. It's as if their lives have stopped dead, as if they're frozen in grief. They can't function. You're everything to them, really."

His face was already scarlet. You think this is bad? Save it, I thought.

"You saw them behind my back?"

"Yes. Once, Lavinia came 'round here by herself, and then they both came to the office. They were desperate. But listen. They wanted to know what they could do—"

"They've done enough."

"They're both contrite. Ready to do anything to show how sorry they are. I told them what Pamela Fidgett said, about the infertility, and the lying to you, and effectively keeping you a child by not telling you the truth, and betraying your trust and—"

"You said all that?"

"Yes."

I waited for a response, but he was silent. Then he blurted out, "What did they say?"

"They hadn't realized. They honestly thought they were doing the right thing, and they were horrified to hear how you felt. But they didn't argue. They accepted full blame. They didn't try to wriggle out of anything. Even the stuff about not coming to terms with infertility. I suggested they might need to speak to a friend or even a counselor—"

"Get off!"

"No, I did. And they accepted that. They're desperate, Nick. They've probably had about ten sessions by now. You know, Issy tried to explain this to me once, about the love you have for your children. She said, 'If you were in a plane and you had to jump out to save your partner, you—well, he—probably would. Of course, you'd make a big deal about what a sacrifice it was first, make sure they appreciated it. But if it was to save your children, there'd be no question. You'd die for them in a second.' I suppose I understood it, because I'm sure Mum and Dad would willingly die for me, Claw, or Issy. And Issy said that if anything ever happened to Eden, she and Frank would commit suicide. She was quite matter-of-fact about it. But . . . it's not often that you see that degree of devotion played out in front of your eyes. I saw it with Michael and Lavinia."

Nick was screwing his face up. Finally he spoke. "Okay. Okay."

He stopped. He pinched the bridge of his nose and tried again. "Okay. Know that I am *very* surprised at you for seeing them when you knew I could hardly bear to myself, but"—he paused, as if searching for precisely the right words—"I see why you did it. I can imagine they didn't offer you much choice. I . . . I *suppose* you did the right thing. You didn't tell them about my birth mother?"

"No." His reaction was roughly fifteen million times more moderate than I'd feared. So far, so good. But not for long.

"So . . . was that the bad news?"

I hesitated. Would it be wise to hold his hand, maintain some kind of physical contact as I told him? Would he be soothed or enraged?

"No," I said. "That wasn't the bad news."

How *could* it be? I thought. What is a "real parent" anyway? In my opinion, Lavinia and Michael were Nick's real parents. They'd raised him and loved him. His blood mother was merely the vessel.

"No," I said. "The bad news is going to be very difficult for you. Incredibly difficult." I paused. "And I can only ask you to try and understand the contributing factors to why I—well, 'did it' is the wrong phrase. Why it happened—"

"Jesus, what is it? Just tell me!"

"We're not having a baby."

A flicker in his eyes, nothing more. "I don't understand." His voice trembled. "What do you mean?"

He stood up, tipping Emily from his lap and knocking over his chair.

"I made a mistake. I thought I was pregnant. I hoped I was. I did the test. I didn't read the instructions properly. I'm not pregnant, Nick. I'm so sorry."

"But . . . your stomach was growing . . ."

"I'd put on weight."

"You'd not had periods."

"I'd lost weight."

"But"—now he was shouting—"I was going to be a dad! This . . . we . . . we were having a family! This was our new family! How could you make a mistake like that? How stupid are you?"

I opened my mouth to quote Dr. Goldstein on "massive avoidance," but my attempt was drowned out by Nick yelling. Emily crouched in the corner of the kitchen and stared at him.

"Christ! I've got nothing now! Do you realize that? Nothing!" His voice sank to a hiss. "Everything I have gets taken away from me. I lose everything. I so wanted . . . a brand-new . . . This was going to be the first blood relative that I got to . . . *keep*. Oh God, I feel sick. You . . . stupid, thoughtless, careless . . . I've been reading *baby care* books." He shuffled in his bag, yanked out what looked like an illustrated manual, and hurled it across the room. It landed by the dishwasher. "I was planning my life around this. This baby was going to save my life! I'm just . . ." He stumbled over the chair leg, then kicked it. I flinched.

"No point in marrying now, is there?"

Although I'd expected this, it still felt like a punch to the throat. It shocked me, because I realized that alone, we weren't enough for each other. In which case, it was better that the baby *was* a figment of my imagination. No child deserves to be born with the burden of keeping its parents together.

Nick was stamping toward the front door. I scurried after him. He snapped it open.

"You've ruined my life," he announced grandly before slamming it in my face.

My heart seemed to rupture with the violence of a burst tire, its flayed shreds sharp and black in my chest. But sure, that was just me indulging my runaway imagination. When the doorbell rang, almost immediately I was able to open it as if I was fine.

Nick stood there, fists clenched. "I'm sorry for shouting," he said. "I understand, a bit, why you did it. I understand that you might have needed to do it. What with all you were . . . are going through. And I feel really, really sorry for you. I can see how you . . . might have needed this baby too . . . more than me even." He paused. "But I must be a terrible person. Because I don't think I can forgive you."

CHAPTER 41

I trust the outfit is falling apart without me?" cooed Nige, batting his eyelashes. We were having a breakfast meeting, a meeting I normally object to on principle, as the business detracts from the eating. My attitude to employers is, Don't patronize me with a bowl of Frosties, we're all grown-ups here. Just call that meeting what it is: unpaid overtime that cuts into your beauty sleep. But Nige had rung at seven that morning demanding to see me, and after the woe of the previous night I felt I could do with the fun company.

"We're scraping by," I said, tearing at a chocolate croissant. "So, star boy, when can we come and see you?"

Nige groaned. He was wearing yellow sunglasses and a white fake-fur coat and looked less like an actor than a pimp. "All in good time. But give me *a moment*. And don't expect front-row seats. Yeah, yeah, I know that's what I said, but I was lying. I'll probably stick you in the gods. There's nothing more disconcerting than being grinned at from three yards by people you know. Not," he added hastily, "that you're a grinner, darling, but a single disaster makes you wary. Marylou fell asleep during the press showing of *The Cherry Orchard* and snored. I suspect she did it to put me in my place, but it shook my performance. Mind you, my mate Jonas—he does mainly fringe and panto—walked on once and this voice in the audience booms, 'Oh no, not him again. He's terrible!' We thesps are a highly sensitive breed. We must protect our fragilities where we can."

"We must," I replied, smiling.

Nige wedged the greater half of an iced currant bun into his mouth—"surprisingly low-fat, darling, muffins are *heinous* in comparison"—and grew serious. "Look," he said. "I don't mean to go behind Claw's back—well, actually I do—but I did her that favor. I mimicked the client, I fooled Stuart. According to Camille, he hared out the office at speed. I presume she found what she was looking for in his files. I haven't spoken to her yet. But, Hol. I've got a bad feeling about this. What I did was illegal. If Stuart *is* defrauding your parents and it goes to court, we could all be in trouble. And I'm not talking about me being outed as a criminal on page seven of *News of the World*. I know less than nothing about law, but if his defense finds out how Camille got the evidence, wouldn't that make the case invalid?"

I lifted my hands. "Nige. I have no idea." I picked at the crumbs on my plate. The quaint decor of Patisserie Valerie was intended to encourage a higher standard of etiquette than Martha's Got Buns, but I was too jittery to care. "I'm sorry they got you involved. To be honest, I don't know what's going on, but I'm pretty certain it'll end in disaster. When did you speak to Stuart? Yesterday? Wednesday. Wednesday *is* yesterday. Well, the thing is, Claudia's furious with me—oh, too silly to go into. She's not really telling me anything and I don't feel like asking."

"*I* could ask."

I looked at Nige's eager face.

"Nige. Just don't. It's too risky, the whole thing. And it's complicated, more so than Claudia thinks." I paused. I had to tell someone, if only to receive the reassurance that friends so will-ingly give when it's not their problem. "Stuart's suing me. For defa-mation."

"What!" screeched Nige. Every head in Patisserie Valerie turned in its crisply starched white collar. "What?" he repeated, this time in a whisper.

I wormed in my seat. "I know, I know. I got a writ. So far I've done the adult thing and ignored it. I had twenty-eight days to reply. Only a week or so down."

"Darling, you have to consult a lawyer. It's outrageous. What a load of crap. God, he's scum."

"I don't *know* any lawyers. Well, Nick's father, Michael. But."

"What?"

"Nick offered, I declined—I wasn't ready for him to know. Now I suppose I am, but I don't feel I can ask him without Nick's per-mission, and Nick is in a, mm, bit of a huff with me at the moment."

"Balls," said Nige rudely. "Nick doesn't know the meaning of huff! If he knew you wanted Michael's advice on this, he'd ask him. Oh, come on, the man dotes on you—there's not many blokes who'd take out a loan and stick it into their *ex*-girlfriend's faltering business . . . Aaaaahhh, you didn't know." Nige groaned like a dying horse, causing heads to swivel again. I spluttered my cup of coffee all over the table, but by then the clientele had cricks in their necks and didn't bother looking.

"You're joking."

"Yes," said Nige hopefully. "Ah Christ. He said he owed you after five years of squandering your cash. But please don't let on you know. Claw'll kill me. Are you rabid?"

I thought for a second. Should I be? On behalf of feminism, if nothing else? But I wasn't. I was touched to my soul. And the bastard was right. All those copies of *What Hi-fi?*—damn right he owed me!

I shook my head and slapped a twenty on the table. (Nige might have taken over from the star, but he was still being paid his under-study's wage.) "I won't say anything. Although I will say that only Nick could take out a loan to save my business, then take a job at that business to repay the loan!" I shook my head again. "Lunatic!

I'd better get to work, and you, I'm sure, have to get back to bed. It's sweet of you to worry about the writ, but don't. I will sort it out."

Nige was frowning as he received his kiss.

Thursday and Friday in the office were a struggle in roughly the same way that World War II was a struggle. Claudia didn't say whether or not Camille had found the incriminating evidence. She seemed to be in such a foul temper I didn't want to provoke her by asking. Nick was equally discomfiting to be around. Every time I attempted to send him a fond glance, he ignored it. The two of them sat in front of their screens tapping in silence. If they had to speak on the phone, they'd force civility, but a scowl would settle the second the call ended. When Issy asked if Nick had done anything nice recently, he replied, "I watched Michael J. Fox in *Teen Wolf*."

This ended the conversation. At one point, Issy and I took refuge at Martha's.

"What*ever* is going on?" murmured Issy, sipping at her tea. "It's so hostile in there."

She paused, so did I. "Actually," she said, "don't ask me how, but I know what's going on with Nick."

I started. "You do? How? He didn't tell you, did he?"

Issy merely raised her neatly plucked eyebrows, referring me to her last statement. "What's Claudia's problem?"

If Issy doesn't want to tell you something, you could pin her to the ceiling by her earlobes, she wouldn't breathe a word. I filed my interest in Nick, took a breath, and related the baby saga. By then I'd honed the tale down to three minutes. "I feel terrible, letting the family down like this. I'm sorry, Izz. I know you were looking forward to a cousin for Eden. But before you say anything," I added, "I'm in analysis, whatever you call it. I'm going to break it to Mum and Dad this weekend." I stopped. "I don't know if Claudia's more angry about the nonexistence of the baby or the nonexistence of my sanity."

I expected harsh words from Issy—she'd never held back in the past—but instead she covered my hands with hers.

"Ah, Holly," she said. "I'm so sorry. But truthfully, I'm not that surprised. You experienced the ultimate disempowerment. Control was taken away from you in the most brutal manner. Rape is not about sex, it's about power. The emotional consequences can last a lifetime. You are doing *so* well, but it was never going to be a breeze. All your mind was doing was trying to help you cope. You wanted a baby to fast-forward over what has happened to you. It *would* have been the perfect excuse not to process the trauma, motherhood would have been your priority, enabling you to pretend that Stuart never happened. But then, you would have just been storing up pain for later on."

She squeezed my hand, extremely hard. "Denial is a defense mechanism, Hol, and all defense mechanisms work by distorting the truth. They try to protect us from the truth, in this case by diverting attention to someone else. The danger is that we become out of touch with reality. We relate to the world and the people around us falsely. Eventually, something happens to puncture our defense."

She muttered something I didn't catch.

"Pardon?" I said.

"Nothing."

I peered at her. What she said made sense to me, and it was a relief to hear it. I'd never thought that having a psychologist in the family was useful. I'd have swapped her for a good old-fashioned doctor any day, but now I was purring with gratitude. Instead of analyzing my behavior in the unflattering and frankly alarming light that was her habit, she'd claimed to understand me. And when you think you might be teetering on lunacy's edge, the peace afforded by an expert—or rather, *two* experts—saying "No, no, perfectly normal!" cannot be underestimated. I suddenly felt quite bouncy, but Issy's empathy seemed to fade.

A faint tremor around her mouth.

"What, Izz?"

She gulped. Shook her head, huffed through her nose. "Here I am," she said, "preaching to you about denial. When I'm the worst offender I know." She smiled weakly. "Denial. Off the record, I recommend it. What idiot would embrace awareness when the closer you get, the more anxious and miserable you become?"

She'd lost me. I thought I was keeping up, I was mistaken. It was the same feeling I got when attempting to read Don DeLillo.

Issy stabbed at her rock cake with her knife. "Frank's having an affair. I've been kidding myself that he isn't for months now. I can't do it anymore." She threw down the knife, crumpled her napkin, dabbed at her eyes. "Sorry. I hate to make a scene."

It was my turn to squeeze *her* hand. Rachel. I knew it. "Issy, that's terrible. I'm so sorry. Is there . . . Do you know for sure? You haven't, er, caught him in the act, er, have you?"

She shook her head. "Phone calls to the same number. Mysterious late nights. Unexplained disappearances from work in the middle of the day. But it's more than that. It's his attitude toward me."

"Cold?"

"No! Extra loving! Guilt!" she hissed. She lifted her gaze to mine. "I know who it is." Her voice turned shrill.

My mouth was dry.

"Your friend Rachel."

To her credit, Issy managed not to emphasize "your."

"Oh God," I whispered. The irony was, Rachel considered herself a good friend of mine and yet at the same time was capable of betraying me and my whole family with a clear conscience. She didn't have the same social ties as other people. I'll always remember remarking on her room at college. All the students, myself included, feverishly covered every inch of their walls with posters of Marilyn Monroe, James Dean, *Taxi Driver*, the usual. Rachel's walls remained bare. "I don't," she said when I questioned her, "feel the need to externalize my personality for the benefit of others."

"Oh, Issy."

"I found her card in his pocket. It's *her* number he's been calling. The other night he came home with lipstick on his cheek!"

This was indefensible. I tried, feebly, to defend it. "Thing is, Issy, that anyone who comes into contact with Rachel comes away with lipstick on their cheek. No one ever tells you and you spend the whole day looking like something out of *Risky Business*."

Issy bristled. "Yes, Sherlock, but ask yourself what was he *doing* with her in the first place? At least do me the courtesy of allowing me my pain. If you minimize it, or disbelieve me, you make it worse."

"Sorry," I said, chastened. "Of course. What are you going to do?"

"Don't breathe a word to that slut friend of yours. I plan to confront him. It's our tenth anniversary soon. I'll do it then. He'll book somewhere glamorous, exclusive, and expensive for dinner, and I intend to stand up, in front of London's snootiest, and throw the vintage champagne in his bastard two-timing face."

It was reassuring to see how the expert in human behavior was so much more refined in resolving relationship conflict than the rest of us. Issy and I dragged our heels back to the office, dreaming of Saturday.

Saturday arrived, although it damn well took its time. My mother rang at ten thirty ("I worry about waking you up otherwise") to check if it was still convenient for me to visit. No doubt Claudia had received an identical call.

This is ridiculous, I thought, and dialed Claudia's number. "Hi, it's me," I said. "Just so you know, I told Nick the truth—as you might have guessed from his demeanor at work. The engagement is off, obviously."

"*Hi*, you," she cried. "I know. He said. I'm sorry."

"I'm sorry too."

We giggled.

"Do you want to drive to M and D's together?" I asked.

"Defo. What time?"

"One?"

"I'll pick you up."

I sighed with relief. Claw was the most aggressive driver I knew, and the journey was bound to take a year off my life, but at least she and I were friends again. Nick, though, was going to be harder. That morning, I'd picked up the book he'd thrown across the room. *The Social Baby.* It contained a series of photographs of a baby moments after birth, showing how it was fascinated by its mother's face and intolerant of any interruption (the midwife, picking it up to be weighed; the father, stroking its brow). Further pictures showed it reacting to the sound of its mother's voice, straining eagerly in the direction of the sound. And in an illustrated experiment, another newborn had a pad placed on either side of it. One smelled of its mother, the other of a stranger. Even when the pads were switched, the baby turned toward the pad that smelled of its mother, focusing on it 73 percent of the time.

I'd slammed shut *The Social Baby*.

Oh, Nick. What must he have felt, reading that? To think of yourself, new to the world, wanting your mother, *knowing* your mother, reaching for her, getting a stranger. To feel scared and alone, and yet to have no understanding of why. To hope and hope and hope, until that hope slowly ebbs away.

I decided to take whatever he threw at me (books, blame . . .). I had to show him that, despite our shaky past, I *would* stand by him. He could push me, but this time I wouldn't go. Someone in his life had to stay. I wanted him to see this. Even if our relationship was over, I could be his friend. The world owed him *that*.

"So today's the day," said Claudia, as we checked on our food supplies. (A barrel of Minstrels, left over from a cinema visit, four cans of Coke. We were traveling light.) My stomach lurched. I presumed she was referring to the fact that, in roughly two hours, I'd be breaking the baby news to my heartbroken parents.

"Yes," I said. "It's going to be a complete nightmare."

Claw gave me a foul look as she turned into the traffic. "Thanks for your support, Hol. That really—fuck off you fucking wanker, you drive a fucking Lada for fuck's sake—helps my confidence."

"*Your*— Oh no! Sorry, sorry. I thought you meant about the baby. You're going to tell them you're gay?"

She laughed grimly. "Yes. What, you were planning to announce the nonexistence—piss off, yeah, yeah, give me the finger, stick it up your arse, you imbecile—of their grandchild? Jesus. What did they do to deserve us? I hope the accumulated shocks— hello? *beeeeeeeeeeeeeeeeeeep!* no, no, *you* don't have to use your signals, you're above the law, obviously, you arsehole twat—aren't too much for them. If either Mum or Dad drops dead of a heart attack in the next few days, we'll have to toss a coin—Jesus, hog the road why don't you in your gas-guzzling Land Rover, why not cut to the fucking chase and drive around town in a Chieftain tank—for whose fault it is."

"Well, don't hold back, Claw," I said. "The most important thing is, you say what's on your mind."

She laughed, her features reverting to glumness the second her mouth shut. "Camille couldn't find the stuff," she blurted. "But it's okay. I'm just going to have to tell Mum what we suspect—Jesus, do you want to come any closer up my arse, fuck you, you fucking fuck, yeah, emergency stop, that'll teach you, *beeeeeeeeeeeeeeeeeeeeeeeeeeeep* to you, too. The evidence is still there. The Paris apartment exists, and Stuart's made sure *they* don't know about it. That's dodgy enough." She paused. "So, another cheery revelation—yeah, flash me, would you, stupid bitch, fuck off and die. It'll be a while before M and D ask us to stay again."

"About Stuart. Would you—" she began after a short silence.

"No. Not yet."

Claudia lifted a hand and nodded her agreement. For a split second she was the image of reason.

"Fair enough," she said, hooting and gesturing at a defenseless meathead in a white van. "In the rotten stinking circumstances, fair enough."

CHAPTER 42

Our parents sat huddled on their khaki-green velveteen sofa, their hands clutching their knees. Claudia and I were all but pinching ourselves. If we weren't mistaken, my mother had just said, in a clear tinkly voice, "As long as you're happy, dear. I must say, we *had* suspected, for ever so long in fact."

And my father had chipped in, "We're delighted that you finally decided to tell us, Claudia. We felt it was important not to push you. She'll let us know in her own time, when she's good and ready, that's what we told ourselves. Isn't that right, Linda?"

My mother nodded and stood up. "Well *done*, darling," she said, bending to hug Claudia. My father followed.

"But . . . how did you . . . ?" croaked Claw.

"Darling, after this long we *do* know our own children. We might not ring every day, but we think about you constantly. Stanley, would you, dear?" she added. Obediently, he trotted into the kitchen. My mother smiled. "So. Is there anyone special at the moment?"

Claudia indicated that there was. I think she was too surprised to speak.

"That's wonderful! What's her name? What does she do? And when do we meet her?"

Our love for our children is unconditional, Mum once told Leila, who was gossiping about a friend's daughter who'd married out of the religion and was duly cut off by her parents. All the same, it was one thing to say it. Easy to make such grand declarations when she hadn't yet been tested. Claudia hadn't even been a *proper* vampire. She'd just liked the black clothes. She'd resigned at the first suggestion of blood-drinking. And she'd only been caught shoplifting once. Issy's grades had been consistently brilliant. I'd tried smoking and failed. Our parents had had it easy!

But now they were showing more grit than I'd given them credit for. They'd sailed over the first fence with ease. Still, would they have the mental strength to complete the course? I tuned back in.

Claw and my mother appeared to be discussing lesbian friends of my parents. Mum volunteered once a week at her local infant school, helping children learn to read. Janice was deputy head, and they'd started chatting. The chats had grown into coffee breaks until Mum—and Dad—had been invited to Janice's for Saturday tea. Janice and her partner, Brigid, had been together for thirty-six years. They'd met at Oxford, and in those days homosexuality was taboo, so they'd had to conduct their relationship in secrecy. Now, of course, young lesbians were fortunate that society was so much more accepting, although Janice kept her orientation hidden from the parents as, unfortunately, some ignorant people confused being gay with pedophilia. There was no point in inviting trouble. Mum thought it was shocking, that people could do that.

"*You* haven't had any offensive comments, have you, dear?" she asked.

"God, no, Mum. I've had more hassle off bull dykes in lesbian bars for looking girlie."

My mother sipped her tea. *Au courant* though she was, I think this lost her slightly. Claudia caught my gaze and widened her eyes. I smiled and shrugged. "So, Mum," I said—I couldn't resist—"what do you and Dad and Janice and Brigid talk about?"

"Literature and caravanning," replied my mother. It emerged that Brigid and Mum had hit it off immediately, when Mum shook Brigid's hand and cried, "What cold hands! You must make wonderful pastry!" Brigid and Janice were members of a book club, and Mum and Dad had joined. "So far, we've discussed *Angela's Ashes*, *The Corrections*, and, oh, a host of others," said my mother, dunking a biscuit in her tea and losing half of it. "It's so pleasant. And makes a nice change from television. I've never really warmed to television. Everyone takes it in turns to bring food. I was nervous about saying what I thought, but everyone is so *interested*, aren't they, Stanley?"

Dad nodded. "Janice and Brigid have been thinking of buying a caravan, so I've been advising them. They were wondering about a secondhand Honda Romahome. It was reasonably priced, but I had reservations about it suiting their requirements."

"They respect his opinion," added my mother.

Intriguing and incredible though this exchange was, my attention drifted. I realized that I couldn't stand my parents not knowing about the rape for one more minute. The secret was straining at my chest, about to burst every button off my cardigan. Much as I struggled with the knowledge, what had occurred with Stuart was now a part of who I was. It had changed me as a person and there was no going back. It was essential for my peace of mind that Mum and Dad *knew* the real me. Until then I was a stranger sitting before them. I saw Claudia who—having revealed an essential part of *her* identity to two of the people in our lives who mattered most—looked more happy and relaxed than she'd done in a long while.

I considered what Dr. Goldstein had said in our second session, squeezed in at the crack of dawn on Friday morning. At the risk of sounding like a big fat cliché, we'd discussed my parents. Why, I'd asked Dr. Goldstein—who despite his knack of reducing me to rivers of tears on sight was fast becoming my own personal Oracle—was I so scared of telling them about Stuart?

I could remember his reply just about word for word.

"It sounds like an Americanism, but there is such a thing as the inner child. Part of you permanently wants the approval of parent figures, and to be looked after by them. Even when you become an adult, there is a part of you that wants to be cuddled in a primitive way, which, of course, is a resonance from early childhood. As it is not socially acceptable to adopt an infantile role with one's parents, that kind of parenting is encouraged in other ways—adult children receive material presents from their parents and help. But there's a part of you that wants to be cuddled, nurtured, told it's all right. To retreat into your mother's bosom and feel secure. You want that naive and very primitive security that often can only be felt as a child in the presence of a stable parent figure. So, Holly, there is a primitive pressure to disclose your experience . . . You are looking for something that perhaps you won't get, but still, the desire to get it is there and never fails. In your heart of hearts you still want your parents to do the job properly, to behave like Mum and Dad, even if they adamantly refuse to . . . There's always a little version of you, wanting Mum and Dad to love you in an idealized way. You're always carrying that needy child within you. So there's a fear of punishment, a fear they won't deliver, or they'll deliver the wrong thing."

But, I'd exclaimed in great excitement, my parents *do* deliver. They're not so big on the material gifts, but their emotional support is unconditional. They'll be horrified and devastated, but now that you say all that, I'm sure they wouldn't be disappointed in me, and they certainly wouldn't punish me.

I thought of Nige. Not so long ago his father had peered at an old family photograph, pointed at Nige, age eighteen, and said in all seriousness, "Who's *that?*" Perhaps I'd underestimated my parents. Under-*used* them, even. It was wrong to expect the whole world to parent you—and anyway, I felt I'd grown out of that at last—but apparently, it was entirely natural to want your parents to parent you, if you were thirty, forty, or fifty. Only now did I appreciate how beautifully they'd done their jobs—and would still do them, if only I gave them the chance.

Dr. Goldstein had looked amused. I thought, He really enjoys his job. *Awwww!*

"Holly," he said, "supposing you tell your parents and they behave in the right way. What's the cost of that? Zero. What's the benefit? Huge. On balance of probabilities, what do you want to do and what have you got to lose?"

And yet, I was still hesitant. Gloria's cousin had told her sister about her rape. Her sister had replied, "Why can't you just admit you like sex?"

Then she'd told her mother but, after her sister's mind-blowing response, had struggled to find the words. "I was raped" is almost impossible to say. Her mother had snapped, "Either you were or you weren't."

What *did* I have to lose? While such inhumanity was beyond my mother, I didn't want her to, in the shock of the moment, blurt something ill-advised for which I could never then forgive her. Nor did I want my father to think he was ineffectual. Late in life, he seemed to be finally stumbling upon the self-confidence that most of us acquire in our thirties. I presumed it was a delicate process— sort of like glassblowing—and I didn't want to jolt him. From what I could tell, in such situations men always feel they should have *done* something. Quite what my father could have accomplished from Penge, I'm not sure. Though if his thinking was anything like Nick's, it would have involved telepathy, pants over his trousers, and a big red cape.

I stared at them both, cozy on their shabby sofa in their shabby home. As ever, they looked content. God, they loved each other. It was low-key, but it emanated from them in waves, even in the way they sat beside each other. Over the years they'd adapted to the other like two rosebushes planted on the same spot gradually entwine. If my mother said "Would you, dear?" my father made tea. Some people might prefer to shoot themselves than live such a life, but *I* felt that if Nick truly valued excitement over happiness he was insane.

Little did my parents know their coziness was about to be torn away by the gray gusting might of the cruel world. But then, why did I persist in seeing them as tiny acorns instead of mighty oaks? You needed strength of mind to be at peace in this world. You required cast-iron self-belief. When every powerful voice in the twenty-first century coaxed you to need cars and clothes and mansions and millions to be content, my parents were immune to it all because they had each other, and *us*. Not only was *I* more resilient than I'd presumed, my parents were too.

"Mum, Dad," I said, in a much louder voice than I'd planned on, "I also have something to tell you, but I have to warn you it's upsetting. I'm fine—well, I'm recovering, and I don't want you to worry, but . . ."

I trailed off. Claudia quietly left the room. My parents looked terrified.

"I was sexually assaulted."

I couldn't believe I'd said "sexually" in front of my father. "Raped," I added, "technically speaking."

I hoped that "technically," being as it was an unemotional, matter-of-fact sort of word, would soften the blow.

"It was quite a while ago now. Three months."

Time, the Great Healer. Although privately, I thought he was a quack.

"Not by a stranger. By someone I knew."

I hoped my parents weren't intelligent enough to realize that one wasn't necessarily worse than the other.

"In my house. Not on the street or anything."

I *think* I was trying to make it sound more civilized.

"I reported it to the police, who were very kind."

I knew my mother would appreciate that. She treats any child under forty who visits the house as she'd want *her* children to be treated.

"Unfortunately, the Crown Prosecution Service decided not to prosecute. The detective inspector from CID said they often don't."

You see if a man as important as a detective inspector from CID said it, it couldn't be my fault.

"He didn't hurt me, more than he . . . needed to. As these things go, it wasn't a . . . a *bad* rape."

"All rapes are bad," said my father, and burst into tears. It's a terrible thing to see your own father cry. I wouldn't wish it on my worst enemy. Except Stuart. My mother was crying too. "My baby," she sobbed. "Oh God," she choked, "my poor baby."

She ran across the room, stumbling past the coffee table, knocking a full cup of tea onto the yellow carpet, and wrapped her arms around me, rocking me. My father was suddenly there beside her, one hand on my shoulder, the other on hers. He stood there, numb, shaking his head. The tears ran down his cheeks, and he gave my mother's shoulder a squeeze before lifting his hand to hide his eyes.

I didn't want to cry, but they were making me.

CHAPTER 43

Telling my parents about the phantom baby was a mere scatter of rain in a great pool of grief. Their distress about the rape was so palpable it felt like a living thing. The loss of an idea couldn't hurt them in the same way. I'm not saying it didn't hurt them. They'd lost a future, hopes, and dreams. They had already invested love and emotion in a child who didn't exist. But to my surprise, they understood the *why* instantly and chose to focus on the child who did exist. I didn't have to explain, much. Perhaps they were relieved I hadn't done anything worse.

"No harm done," said my mother, when I tried to apologize about the lack of grandchild. Except she muttered it again and again, which inclined me to disbelieve her. My father held my hand as if I were five. I could see him choking down his rage like he choked down my mother's brussels sprouts at Christmas. I don't think I'd ever seen him angry. Actually, that's not true. Once, he put down the phone on a business associate and said the word *cunt.* I remember being shocked to the core of my fourteen-year-old soul, so grossly appalled I barely knew what face to make.

Anger is part of grief, indeed anger *is* grief. Much of my father's anger was directed at Stuart. I think he and Mum found it incredible that a fellow human could be so free of morality. They were breathless at his insolence. Claudia and I recognized their disgust at having employed him (even though *we* were to blame for hiding his crime against the family) and we both rushed to reassure them. Claw was so eager to recount the ingenious tale of the fraudster trap, her words tumbled over each other. When, eventually, she finished, there was silence.

I glanced at Claw. Her eyes gleamed, but there was a hardness to them. I realized she needed my parents to gasp, "Why, Claudia, that's brilliant. We'll report him to the Law Society and now he'll go to prison, and we'll all live happily ever after, and our fair daughter Holly will be avenged by our own hands!"

Finally my mother spoke. "But, dear," she said in a bewildered voice. "We *know* about the Paris apartment. It *was* on the final list of assets. Perhaps Camille saw an earlier copy. I know there was so much paperwork to do in regard to the flat that it had its own file. Perhaps that was why the misunderstanding occurred. I'm afraid . . . oh dear, I'm so sorry to disappoint you. All your work . . . I'm very much afraid that as a solicitor, Stuart's actions were entirely aboveboard. And, even if he *was* tempted to try anything, he knew Henry Flaherty was keeping a close eye—he's retired from the law, but we've known him for so long he's more of a friend. He's ever so fond of your father."

I guessed my mother had seen the look on Claudia's face and was scared to stop talking.

I wasn't so bothered. To me, the idea of reporting Stuart to another gang of bureaucrats, gathering and giving evidence, involving my poor parents—it was all too much. This was not about forgiveness—I would never forgive Stuart. Why should I? But if I had learned one thing, it was that I had to concentrate on *me*, not him. You can't always wreak the perfect revenge on your enemies, and if you're unable to accept that fact you endanger your health. The bitterness corrodes your life. Now, I'm convinced that your revenge on the people who wrong you is the certainty of their deep unhappiness, because I believe *that* is the root of evil.

Claudia ran out the room.

Mum put her head in her hands, but briefly. When she removed them her eyes were dry. She addressed my father. "I had to tell her the truth."

He touched her knee.

"Holly," she said.

I shook my head to indicate that I was untouched by the news. "That was Claudia's baby," I was about to say, but thought better of it.

"You know, you *will* be okay," declared my mother, as if it were a fact. A bold statement, but, I realized, the right one. She and Dad still believed in me.

"We've been speaking to Michael and Lavinia," she added abruptly. "They've been ringing a lot. Poor Nick."

I wondered if this uncharacteristic indiscretion was to save me from the burden of further confessions.

"Oh right. So I suppose you can guess," I blurted out, "that Nick and I are off again."

Not even a twitch.

"In the circumstances," said my mother gently, "it's not a surprise."

My father placed a hand on my back. "We love Nick dearly," he said. "But we would hate to see you two marry for the wrong reasons. And from what we can gather, Nick has a list of wrong reasons as long as his arm, and who could blame him. His head must be spinning like a top. Not that he doesn't love you, he *certainly* loves you, Holly, with all his heart. But now is probably not the right time. For him or for you."

I tried to bristle at this fairy-wing touch of parental guidance, but truly, I couldn't find fault.

"I better go and see how Claudia is," I said. I reckoned until I'd soothed her no crockery was safe. I found her sobbing in the garden. I glanced back at the house and saw our parents standing at the sink window—not even pretending to do the washing up—gazing out at us. They looked small and sad, but determined. God, I'd read them wrong. I thought of the little things I'd despised—yes, *despised*—them for. Because you can love and loathe at the same time. I'd despised them for their delight in the cheap home-shopping catalogues that came with the *Mirror,* full of items such as the Portable Urinal, the Roll and Store Your Jigsaw, Outdoor Tap Jackets, and the Sensor Owl ("I hoot and turn my head as soon as someone approaches").

I'd despised them for rejecting our offer of an exotic holiday and choosing to celebrate their thirty-fifth anniversary at the Braunton Beach Hotel in North Devon (a parochial, British four-star affair with the air and ambience of a prison—the prices of a luxury retreat in the Caribbean, chintzy sea-view rooms reserved for guests staying a week or longer, nonrefundable deposit of one hundred and fifty pounds, a charge of 33 percent if a holiday was canceled, no dogs, no fun, no children on the dance floor, only one child per person, golliwog postcards in the "boutique," foul food in the restaurant, and the four-star kitchen's interpretation of a banana milk shake, a blend of milk and yellow syrup).

I'd despised them for all the wrong reasons. I'd confused modest needs with small-mindedness. In my heart of hearts I didn't regard my parents as classy, an error that merely revealed my own small-mindedness. My parents might have been middle-aged in their ways, but they were also wise, and, in their own manner, sophisticated. Not once that day had they shaken their fists at the ceiling and bleated, "Why *us*?" I presumed their thinking to be, Why *not* us? I wondered if any of the great philosophers—or even some of the mediocre ones—came from Penge.

I watched Claudia kick at the compost heap.

"Don't do that, Claw, you'll probably dislodge a dead rabbit."

She laugh-sniffled. (A beloved pet, Concorde Ears, had been accorded the finest of funeral ceremonies by my father at this very spot. Claudia, age ten, had worn a black veil.)

Then she burst into a fresh round of tears. I could barely hear what she was saying—so clogged were the words with mucus and rage—but I got the gist. She'd so wanted to *do* something to punish Stuart. She felt so guilty about what had happened. She was the one who'd encouraged me to go on a date with him. She'd so wanted to make it up to me. She felt terrible, she thought about it every day. It would have been so *just*, she couldn't believe he was going to get away with it. If only he'd been defrauding our parents, there would have been a way of getting back at him. There had to be, it wasn't fair otherwise.

I hugged her shaking shoulders and she fell against me. She was wearing a taupe knitted top, and the wool was scratchy. "Oh Holly," she cried, "I am so sorry for you. It's a tragedy, a tragedy."

We stood in silence, and I closed my eyes.

The garden smelled fresh. There were fat pink blossoms on the trees, and the sky was a cool blue. An airplane droned above us, the noise of its engines echoing in the crisp air of late spring. I sighed. Since I was very young, I'd prided myself on knowing if it was a sunny day without drawing the curtains, because every airplane drone echoed across the sky. I hadn't a clue why, but if it was gray or rainy the sound was different.

"Claudia," I whispered. "Please don't think that. It isn't a tragedy. A tragedy ends in disaster. This isn't the end. It's a fresh beginning."

Claudia opened her eyes and pushed me away. "What, you *really* believe that? How can you *say* that? How can you turn such a terrible trauma into something positive? It's a travesty."

"Claw, of course I'm not turning it into something positive. It will always be . . . what it was. What I mean is, I don't need Stuart punished in order to lead a happy life. I don't forgive him, I don't think that's necessary. But I have to give myself permission to live well, not take my cue from *him*. It happened, and there's nothing I can do to *un*happen it. But I can try to accept it, file it, and go forward. I won't say I'm trying to learn lessons from the thing itself—

I don't think being victim of a crime teaches you anything of value. I don't think suffering teaches you anything that you couldn't have learned in a pleasant, civilized alternative way. But my reactions to the whole experience and afterward have taught me a lot about me, some of which can be improved on. I hope to be happier as a result of the knowledge."

Claudia shot me the weirdest look.

"Well," I said, "*you're* the one who told me to go to a therapist."

Her mouth dropped open.

"Yeah," I added, "but before you say anything, only *some* of this is down to him. He's very good, but most of it is *me*."

Claudia smeared the tears across her face with her bare arm. Her mascara remained at its station. She is one of those rare women who can look good on a beach. "I'm amazed," she said, finally. "No, not amazed. I'm in awe. If you can go through what you did and come to *that* conclusion, well, Holly, you're something special. I'm grateful. I thank God that you have the strength and courage . . . to only be a *little* screwy. To come out of it and still have optimism."

"Thanks. A little screwy is perfect. Except you don't believe in God."

"This moment now, I do. Just don't ask me again in five minutes."

I pulled gently on her ponytail, a traditional sign of affection, and together we went back inside.

We both stayed the night. My old room was a muted version of its young self—the bright pink walls vandalized with Walt Disney stickers screamed that it had once belonged to a child, but all the toys and teddies had been tidied away, making it a respectable guest bedroom. I opened a purple wardrobe door, though, and stacked neatly inside were the novels of my youth. I pulled out *The Secret Garden*, jumped into bed, and clicked on the reading light. For some reason, when my mother knocked with a mug of hot chocolate, I hid the book under the covers. I think I fell asleep in the middle of reading it, because when I woke in the morning, it had been placed on the bedside table—a Beatrix Potter bookmark keeping my place—and the empty mug had been removed.

I lay back against the pillows, closed my eyes again, and listened to an airplane's drone echo lazily across the sky.

CHAPTER 44

Before Claudia and I left for London, my father suggested that he and I go for a walk. We walked, and I waited for him to speak. But he didn't, and I realized he was waiting for *me* to speak. That was the thing about my father. The average person, if you confide a problem, will rush to give their opinion like a small child running into the road. When often, all you want them to do is listen. Listening is the most generous kind of support.

For a long time I didn't know what to say. Eventually I said, "I didn't want it to have happened because I was too trusting, I didn't want it to have happened because of *me*."

My father continued to walk beside me, his thin gray hair wisping in the breeze. "The criminal is responsible for the crime. That's why criminals are sent to prison, not their victims."

I smiled.

He added, "He'd have probably done it anyway, whatever you'd done. If not you, another woman."

"I know," I said. "I know."

I slipped my arm into my father's. The only other thing he said on the walk was, "When you have children, Holly, you never relax again. You are forced to care about the state of the world. Your dearest wish as a parent is to protect your babies. You're terrified to let them go, because you cannot stand for them to experience pain, yet you know that a life without pain is impossible. Feeling pain is the price of loving, the price of living. You paid a terrible price, Holly. But don't shut out life because of him."

Taking Dad's advice literally, I persuaded Claudia to let *me* drive home. We nibbled on my mother's rock cakes (fairy cakes according to the recipe, but strictly speaking all my mother's cakes were rock cakes) and discussed the visit. I suspect we were high on relief and sugar.

"I can't believe," said Claw, "that half of that actually happened. I feel about a stone lighter."

"Me too."

"Most of the time I don't think of them as people."

"I know. Just Mum and Dad."

"They were . . . good about Stuart, weren't they? They weren't shocked in the wrong way."

"No, they were brilliant. I am slowly coming 'round to having healthy beliefs about it all—but it's much easier to maintain belief in your healthy beliefs when your parents do too. Parents are so powerful, and I don't know that ours realize that."

"I think they do. That's what makes them better than most other parents. They're so gentle with us. I could never have imagined, in a million years, Mum and Dad attending secret lesbian lunches. I have friends who swear they'll *never* come out to their parents because they know the response will be too painful to bear. But this was more like six of one, half a dozen of the other. My God, they're practically fag hags!"

I bent over the steering wheel laughing. "You're right. They pretty much came out to *us*!"

Claw clutched her head. "Jesus. I've had a revolting thought. Hol, do you think . . . do you think there's a remote possibility that our parents are funky?"

"Next thing you'll be suggesting they still have sex."

"Oh stop it. *Gross!*" screamed Claudia. "Oh no, they can't do! Holly Appleton, you know very well they've only done it three times, once for each of us." Pause. "I mean, it runs in the family. Look at Granny."

The sad truth is that our mother's mother (she of the "an apple tree will grow inside you") had a strict Victorian upbringing and didn't know that sex led to pregnancy. She thought sex was one thing and babies were another, that your body produced them when it was ready. And, when she *did* fall pregnant with Auntie Rose, she didn't realize from which orifice the baby would emerge. "She thought," boomed Auntie Rose, "that when the time came the doctor would make a neat little slit in her side."

The wonder of it was, she had two children.

Claudia and I sniggered, for a moment teenagers again. She was in a rush to see Camille, so she declined my offer of coffee. As I walked to the door, it opened. I squeaked before I remembered.

"Gloria! Oh, thanks for feeding Emily, sorry it was last minute. Were her injections okay?"

Gloria scowled. "Like givin' Satan a measles jab."

I made an apologetic face on behalf of my cat. "Sorry. Do you want to come in for a sec?"

Gloria lifted her wrist on which there was no watch. "Can't. Busy."

She looked tired, and paler than normal. Her tomboyish clothes and porcelain skin made her seem young and fragile. I suppose I wanted to cheer her up.

"I've seen Dr. Goldstein, by the way. Twice. He's brilliant. He's helping me to see things in perspective. Thank your cousin for recommending him."

I gave her an encouraging smile, but she drooped. "Yeah," she said, scuffing her sneakers on the doorstep. "He's good. But then some of us aren't so fucked in the head as others." She gazed at the ground, letting her fringe fall over her eyes. "Then it's easy for a shrink to be brilliant." She raised her head and stared at me. "Some of us have outside support. Their friends and family believe them. They don't say shit like 'Yeah, he's a bastard, Glor, but it was *your* fault.'"

"No, I—"

"Then it's like swimming the Channel with a lead weight tied to yer neck."

I was lost for words. I'd never seen her like this. Bitter. She was always so cheerful.

She dragged a fist across her eyes. "Run out of pills. Forgot to send in my repeat prescription, didn't I?" She laughed, a horrible hard laugh. "Be fine tomorrow, though. Right as rain."

"Gloria, please, won't you come in for a bit and sit down?"

I stepped toward her with an arm outstretched, but she shook her head and pushed me away, her small hand leaving a throbbing imprint on my chest. She turned to go. Then she stopped, her shoulders sagged. "If you can make sense of it, then." She faced me. "There *is* no making sense of it, though, is there? You've been straight with me, Hol, so I reckon I owe y—"

She tugged at her polo neck, and my breath caught. A jagged white scar cut across the pale flesh of her throat. I shook my head, my eyes hot with tears. And for the second time in two days I found myself with a bawling woman in my arms. I rubbed her back and told her she owed me nothing, she didn't have to say anything. A minute in, she ended the hug. She spat a strand of long hair out of her mouth. "It's enough," she said, "that you understand." She granted me a thin smile and hurried to her car.

I felt shaken. I'd had a suspicion, but now that it was confirmed it was as if I'd been digging about in someone else's laundry. I didn't know why, after a bad experience, some people merely survived while others learned to thrive. Was it to do with the severity of the experience itself or the personality, even the age, of the victim? Was recovery linked to the people around you? If this was even a possibility, and I was certain of it, I'd make an effort to see Gloria more often. For my sake, as well as hers.

Our exchange had altered the mood, and when the phone rang I pounced on it.

"Where have you been?" demanded Issy. It was a delight to hear her bossy voice.

"M and D's."

"Of course. Silly me. Eden, darling, what have you—*noooo! stop that!* naughty girl! Really bad! Oh my God. The artist will just have to paint over it. Frank will just have to track him down."

"Issy?"

"Sorry. I don't believe this. You know my ten-thousand-pound painting, *Sky and Sea, the Maldives*? By that very edgy, very now, very expensive artist, what'sisname?"

"Mm."

How could I forget. This work of art dominated their open-plan lounge, truly a showpiece. It was a ten-foot-square canvas, the lower half painted a deep blue, the upper half a pale blue. While some (Claudia) might call this pretentious, it was actually a restful, beautiful painting. You could feel the faint breeze in the skeins of cloud in the sky, lose yourself in the haze of the horizon, feel the sun on your face, and hear the rush of the waves.

"Eden just took a black marker pen and drew a boat on it."

I tried to sound sympathetic. The best I could come up with was, "You sound very calm, considering."

"Only because Michael and Lavinia Mortimer are sitting in my kitchen."

"What! Why?"

"Normally, I couldn't tell you, I'd be breaking all sorts of rules, but as you, apparently, were the one who said 'get thee to a couch,' they're happy for you to know that they decided to come to *me*. Anyway, the reason I rang is that Michael wanted to talk to you—something legal, he says, bring the letter?—and I thought you might as well come 'round here. Eden's dying to see you, although mainly because she expects a gift. No confectionary, though. At least three of her little friends suffer from ADHD, *plainly* because their parents constantly give them sweets to shut them up. Of course, *I* only have to put Mozart on the stereo and Eden goes as quiet as a mouse—she remembers it from when she was in the womb."

God, people who have children are smug.

"How about I bring her some new marker pens?" I said sweetly, and put the phone down. I sank into a chair. I was elderly, I tell you, elderly. Once you pass thirty you can't cope with more than one late night and an hour's excitement in a weekend without chemical assistance. Michael could only be referring to the writ, which was still radiating hatred and poison from the bottom of my bag. I'd wanted to discuss it with Dr. Goldstein, but each session was only fifty minutes and we hadn't had enough time. As it was, I spoke twice as fast as normal to get my money's worth.

I was telling myself that I wouldn't have ignored it until the twenty-eight days were up and I was hauled off to the stocks when a thought occurred. Nick. *Nick* must have told Michael about the writ, because how else would he know? With my fabulous powers of detection, I came to two conclusions: Nige had told Nick that it was okay to tell Michael, and even though he'd broken off the engagement, Nick couldn't hate me that much. My mouth curled into a smile. I galloped upstairs, showered, changed, and applied lipstick. Then I smacked my chops at myself in the mirror and bared my teeth. As Nick would say (about me, rather than himself), "I'm Woman—outta my way!"

I sped downstairs, locked up, hopped in the car, and sped to Issy's. It was only as I rang the doorbell that I realized I hadn't performed my usual trick of ringing as I parked the car, so that I didn't have to spend one half of a second loitering like prey on the porch, ripe for ambush by evil men who were, doubtless, lurking in bushes. I cheered myself with the thought that any man who could successfully hide behind one of Issy's lavender plants had to be no taller than a Ken doll, so if he tried to attack me I could step on him. I was congratulating myself on actually believing me when Eden opened the door.

No sign of Frank.

"Mummy's gone to bed, she's got a migraine," she announced.

"Oh dear," I said, and tried to edge past her. Her hands were always sticky, like she'd rinsed them in marmalade. "Happy Sunday. It's a sketch pad."

Eden shot my gift a derisory glance. "That's not a present, that's *paper*. Sandy gives us that free at kindergarten."

"Then I'll keep it," I replied. "Move, please."

I scurried into the lounge. Michael was perched on a beige minimalist sofa—Issy had had it specially commissioned by a well-known designer to fit the room. He looked highly uncomfortable, like a dog sitting on his squeaky toy. But happy. Michael rose to his feet and Lavinia swept in from the kitchen, bearing a tray of tea and biscuits. I noticed Issy had left out her antique bone china for them to make use of. (This was on a par with lending out her husband.)

Lavinia looked radiant. "Isabella was feeling poorly," she whispered. "I'm afraid listening to us rather wore her out."

I nodded at the defaced painting. "I doubt it was entirely your fault."

For the first time in our acquaintance, Lavinia giggled. I'd only ever heard her laugh, always an elegant sound. This was schoolgirl-ish. "Holly, we are so obliged to you," she exclaimed. "We've seen Isabella a handful of times on an informal basis, more of a chat than anything else, but it has been ever so informative. Quite revelatory. With the benefit of hindsight, I feel ashamed for being quite so . . . *dense* where Nick was concerned. We were dreadfully shortsighted, it's no wonder he reacted as he did. When we were able to see the situation from his point of view, we were appalled. But we didn't want him to think we had consulted Isabella for show. She suggested we write him a letter but then"—her voice lifted with joy—"*he* telephoned us. His attitude had changed completely. He was willing to . . . build bridges. He'd spoken to you, Holly. It was thanks to you. The three of us are having supper at Simpson's tomorrow night."

Michael smiled at me, a grave, paternal smile, full of concern. "He also had a word with me about a legal matter with which you required assistance." He glanced at his wife who, so beautifully mannered as she was, took the hint and retreated to the kitchen. A little lump in my chest, I realized neither Michael nor Nick had told Lavinia *what* the legal matter was, and that—unlike a normal human being—she had accepted my right to privacy without question. Of course, everyone wants to be respected, but when you have had respect torn away from you, you are especially grateful to those who see it as your due.

Michael took my hand and held it. His hands were warm and dry. "Holly," he said, "I regard you as the daughter I never had." He pressed his left hand to his heart. "I'm so deeply sorry."

I nodded. He didn't need to say anything more. "Thank you," I said. I fished the dog-eared summons out of my bag. "I can't say what a relief it is to have you look at this," I added.

Michael studied it for three seconds, his bushy black eyebrows beetling together. His face turned redder and redder, and he burst out, "This is garbage!"

I breathed in.

"What a load of old bollocks! I'll apply to have it struck out tomorrow. He didn't write to your solicitor before taking action, did he?"

"I don't *have* a solicitor."

"*I'm* your solicitor! He didn't write to me, which is protocol. The court would take a very dim view. There's a penalty for this. All he's done is popped down to court, filled in an application, and no doubt served it himself. Stuck it through your mailbox, did he? What a pile of nonsense! What a bloody fool! He has to show that you reported him to the police out of malice, which is notoriously difficult to prove. And he's a solicitor! Good God, he must be one of the worst! A disgrace to the profession, as well as to humanity! If only he'd consulted a colleague—they would have told him not to start this case."

The feeling was like shrugging off a heavy coat. I stared at him. "So . . . it's okay, is it?"

Michael waved the summons in the air. "I beg you. Do not give this piece of wastepaper another moment's thought. I'll deal with it tomorrow morning, and that will be the end of it. He was trying to bully you, Holly, nothing more."

I closed my eyes. "Michael, thank you *so* much. I . . . the relief, the peace of mind." Words failed me, so I gave him a hug. As I drew away, I noticed I'd ruffled his hair. For a second I wondered if I'd been too familiar—the Mortimers weren't given to lavish displays of affection—but he looked as pleased as punch.

CHAPTER 45

Along with tennis, the Buddhist concept of detachment is a skill I've never quite mastered. How can you detach from something that matters to you? People who refuse to worry about things that are out of their control astound me. Are they mad? Of course, you should worry about things you can't control—they're the things most likely to go wrong!

Another problem I had with the concept of detachment, Buddhist or otherwise, was that you couldn't pretend. When Issy was pregnant with Eden, she refused to buy even one baby-related item until a week before her due date (when Frank was dispatched with a long, fearsome list), as she didn't want to tempt Fate. Now, as long as she didn't sneak a diaper pail into the house under cover of darkness, Fate could *see* that Issy had kept her half of the bargain. The concept of detachment is trickier, because even a thought can break the deal.

I was so accustomed to attaching, willy-nilly, to everyone and everything that I barely noticed I was making progress. Only when I got the call did I realize that I'd been obsessing less about Stuart. He was no longer the monstrous shadow that loomed from all sides, caging me in, whichever way I turned. He was simply a bad man who had done a bad thing. He did not possess the terrible omnipotence I'd given him. He did not have the power to destroy my life.

"Holly, is that you? It's Caroline. Constable Caroline Keats, from the CSU."

If there's one talent I *do* have, it's remembering names and faces. (There was a boy in my junior school called Attar, and when I saw him in Oxford Street twenty years later I recognized him instantly. But I didn't say hello, he would have thought I was strange.)

"*Caroline!* I knew it was you, how are you?"

"I'm fine, love, fine. How are you doing?"

"Really well, thanks. Everything is . . . not bad. I'm doing fine."

"Listen, love. I thought I'd put in a call. I can't tell you too much—data protection and all that—but last night we nicked someone you know. Stuart Marshall. For a similar offense."

I choked on air. "Oh God. Oh God." For one second, I was jubilant. And then. "The woman, is she—"

"As I said, love, this is off the record. I can't tell you any more."

"Yes, of course. Oh, but can I tell my solicitor? Stuart's trying to sue me for defamation."

"Christ. Not the sharpest tool in the box, is he? Of course, love. Now you take care."

I smiled. "You too. Thanks, Caroline."

I rang Michael and left a message on his cell. Then I had a bubble bath. Sometimes (at the risk of encouraging lazy journalism on women's pages everywhere) a bubble bath is the only answer.

The following day Claudia and I were as two rays of sunshine struggling against a pair of storm clouds. Though she denied it, Issy was in a foul mood. (Proven when I said, "I love your top, where did you get it?" and she snapped, "Harley Street.") When I thanked Nick for speaking to his dad for me, he replied ungraciously, "Yeah, well, whatcha gonna do?"

I didn't press it with Nick. Despite the fact I'd done him a grave injustice, he'd behaved decently. In fact, he kept behaving decently. If he didn't watch out it would become a habit. I was particularly moved that he'd gone into debt to save my business without telling me. The equivalent, I felt, of a celeb giving to charity without singing about it from hill and dale. So I felt he was entitled to play the martyr. Despite a silly, mischievous streak, Nick *was* the loveliest person I knew.

My all-time favorite photograph was of Nick, age one, face like thunder, tipping his birthday cake onto the floor. At age two he managed to climb up his aunt's chimney, get stuck, and *fall asleep,* prompting a police search.

As an adult, he'd only changed in that the mischief and silliness was premeditated. In the second year of our relationship, we'd gone to Italy and—despite Michael and Lavinia's offer of the Umbria house—stayed in a crumbling hotel on Lake Garda. I was reading by the pool when Nick called, "Holly!" As I looked, he dived at the deep end with a towel billowing from his head à la Superman's cape. It was daft but it made me—and a middle-aged German on the next lounge chair—collapse into giggles. I also have a photo of Nick on all fours with two bananas protruding from his mouth pretending to be a walrus. No reason.

Once, we'd visited Issy when Eden's rather prim friends, Chloe and Victoria, were over to play. Chloe and Victoria had refused to eat the salmon that Issy had lovingly stuck in the microwave. Until Nick explained that this salmon was special—it was moon salmon. Then they wolfed it. Two weeks later, Nick starred as Mr. Elephant at Eden's fourth birthday, and Chloe and Victoria told him off. Their mummy had said there was no such thing as moon salmon. "Tell your mummy," replied Nick, "that what she knows about moon salmon could be written on the back of a postage stamp."

Then, I'd wondered if it was irresponsible to lie to children. But now I saw it as glorious, feeding their minds. Poor Chloe and Victoria, to have such a dull mummy. She couldn't bear to allow them the fantasy of moon salmon lest one day they mentioned it in their geography A-level and failed to get into Cambridge. Lucky Holly, to have such a fun fiancé, for whom the world would never be gray because life would always be lit by the brilliance of his imagination.

Well, I no longer had the fun fiancé, but maybe one day I'd meet a nice sensible banker who'd provide me with what really mattered—a BMW and ensuring I got my tax returns in on time.

Could I be happy with a man who was less in love with life than Nick? A man who didn't look at the eat-by date on his box of Weetabix and cry, "Best before January third, twenty thirty-one! Twenty *thirty-one*! Right! I'm putting this cereal packet in the loft, and on January the second, I'm going to complain. 'Hello! I'd like to speak to the chairman—if he's still alive!' . . . 'Did you keep them in a cool, dark—' "

I sniggered to myself, then huffed over to my desk, scrolling down the morning's E-mails. I mustn't rewrite history. For the last few years of our engagement, Nick *had* been a shit, there was no denying it. It was one thing to have a gorgeous sense of creativity, to be finely attuned to your inner child. It was quite another to let that inner child out to run amok. Along with the delights of banana walruses and moon salmon had gone the irritations of sink teabags, back-of-the-sofa socks (and other debris), red bills—a feast of selfishness, goddammit.

Based on the evidence, I'd made the right decision for then. If only I'd known six months back that a *challenge* would improve him. That he would lose the worst of his brattishness and retain his cheekiness. That he would become more considerate. But then, isn't that always the case? You rid yourself of a frog, only for him to become a prince the minute he escapes your jurisdiction.

"Holly," said Claudia, whose pink blusher defined her mood. "Guess what. Debbie just called. Debbie from *Glamour*. She wanted to tell us that she and Xak are madly in luuurrvve, and so he's leaving Girl Meets Boy. She says very sorry for pinching one of our clients, but she's going to make up for it in publicity terms with the feature. So hooray, no?"

"Yes." I reengaged with the present. "Yes, hooray!"

Claudia hummed to herself as she tapped the keyboard. I'd called her the previous night to tell her about Stuart's arrest. I hadn't wanted her or Camille to feel wretched about the failure of the Clouseau plan for a second longer than necessary. Occasionally, life works out. She, in turn, told me that she'd called M and D to check they were okay, and Mum couldn't come to the phone because—said Dad—she was in the bath. But Claw could hear her in the background and she was hysterical. Claudia reckoned it was delayed shock. Dad had asked Claw how was Holly *really*, did she think there was anything they could do? Claudia had told them simply, "Listen, be there if she needs you."

I felt bad for my parents, but not as bad as I thought I'd feel.

The phone shrilled. "Hello?"

"Hol? Yeah, sorry, it's Manjit."

"He*llo*! How are yoou?"

You know you're pleased to hear from someone when you find yourself elongating all your O's.

"Yeah, fine, fine. Listen. I was thinking about joining the club. As a paying member. What with me being single and that. That bird, girl, sorry, woman, Verity, she's not left or anything, has she?"

"Manjit," I said. "Would you like to go on a date with Verity?"

Manjit did a what-an-outlandish-suggestion laugh.

"Tell you what. Why don't I give Verity your cell, and if she wants to call you, which I'm sure she does, she will. Then the two hundred quid you save on membership, you can spend on a posh dinner and a 'Pussy, Cock, Ass, Tit, Beaver' shirt."

"Yeah?" Manjit sounded overwhelmed. "That shirt of Nick's was the business. Do you reckon they still sell 'em? If you're sure. I don't wanna do you out of any wedge."

"Pah. Don't insult me."

"What? Right, yeah then. That'd be sweet. Thanks, Hol. Thanks very much."

"Don't mention it, sweetie-pea. Your wish is my command."

I plunked down the receiver, feeling fairy-godmotherish. It felt good to do good again.

Issy stamped out of the office, banging the door. I presumed she'd overheard our conversation. I knew that money mattered to her but surely, after all he'd endured with Bo, she couldn't begrudge Manjit this tiny favor? I followed the noise of slamming doors and traced her to the toilet.

"Izz, are you okay?"

"No."

"What's wrong?"

"Oh, nothing, except Frank and I are probably getting *divorced*."

"What?"

"Yet again, my husband rings our house—when he *knows* I am at this *office*—to leave a message that he'll be working late tonight, and I am sick to bloody death of it. I will not be taken for a fool. I am not a woman to be cheated on, and when my solicitors have finished with him and he's living in a basement bedsit in . . . in . . . in *Basildon*"—Issy burst from the toilet, shaking with all the emotion that the image of one's unfaithful spouse ruing the day in a Basildon basement bedsit can prompt—"the bastard will realize that!"

She glared at me.

Rachel.

I'd had enough. And today, I was the all-powerful Oz.

"Issy. Go home. Take the day off. Just don't do anything rash like listen to The Smiths and—"

"The who?"

"Never mind. Just take the day off and enjoy it. You've been working very hard, and you were fantastic with the Mortimers. So have a break and, for the moment, hold off the litigators. You never know. I'm not saying I don't believe you, but until you catch him with his trousers down, there is always the possibility you could be mistaken. Tonight I am going to find Rachel and have a word."

I wasn't kidding. The shards of my life were slowly beginning to piece themselves together, and I raged at Rachel's destructive influence. Not, of course, that *she* was wholly to blame. She was single. Morally speaking, she was free to seduce any man she pleased. Most of the guilt lay with Frank, a husband and a father who should have known better.

At 5:05, I rang Rachel's PA, a spectacularly dim girl named Abigail. Every time I saw her I was intrigued that a woman in her early twenties could dress like a fifty-year-old. Pearls. Headbands. Twinsets. Tweed. She hung out in Chelsea (although she lived in the rougher part of Earl's Court) and got notoriously drunk at least four times a week. Despite this, she was a person who took life— and a lot of antiquated society rules like positions of forks on tables—extremely seriously. While this made her a good PA, it also made her gullible.

I explained that I was meeting up with an old pal of Rachel's (who I'd decided was named Horace and trained officers at Sandhurst) and that we wanted to surprise her.

"What an absolutely jolly idea!" cried Abigail. "Hang on a mo', I'll check the diary."

It emerged that Rachel had a "business meeting" in a hotel bar on Monmouth Street in Covent Garden at 7:00.

I was wondering if Abigail would suspect if I pressed for an identity, when she volunteered that the client's name was Frank Ellis-Willis.

I clapped my hand over my mouth. It was true!

"Thanks *ever* so, Abi," I trilled, attempting to ingratiate by speaking her native tongue. "Now don't breathe a word to Rach about Horace—it'll be a super surprise!"

At 6:45, I slipped on a pair of pink sunglasses, wiggled my toes in their white boots (having taken the necessity for disguise as an opportunity to shop), and marched into the bar area of the chosen hotel. The decor was spartan—stained wood floors and furniture, a vase of white lilies, and little else. I slid into a dark corner, hid behind a menu, and, because it seemed appropriate, ordered a double scotch. It was disgusting, cost nine quid, and made me choke. I rubbed my throat in a pointless attempt to ease the burning sensation and wondered what the hell I thought I was doing.

And then she walked in.

She shrugged off her red shawl, and I felt a low growl at the back of my throat. *That* was not business-meeting attire. It was rip-this-off-and-ravish-me wear. It was a spit for the dress Monroe wore to be photographed above the air vent, except black. And I'd bet my family's life on it, those weren't tights. They were stockings.

When Frank sauntered in, I could hardly bear to look. He lifted her hand as if to say, "Stand up and give me a twirl," which she did. They laughed and he kissed her cheek. Boiling with rage, I drained the rest of my scotch and turned purple as I attempted to choke silently. It then occurred that at this point my plan stopped dead. They were chatting over bar snacks. I could hardly march up to them when I had no more evidence than a bowl of peanuts and shout, *"Ho!"*

I ordered another nine-quid scotch, and suddenly my brain had a power surge. What I'd said to Issy was true. Until Frank was caught with his trousers down, she . . . we *could* be mistaken. But whoa there, Sherlock, this was a hotel. They must have rented a room! My lip curled. Lilies and shawls notwithstanding, this was nothing less than seedy. Well, fine. I'd show them seedy. I necked my third and fourth scotches and slammed down a crisp twenty.

As I crept out of the bar, they were intent in conversation, and Rach had out her Events Planner, a big red tome in which she detailed all her bookings. What, pray, was she doing—scheduling their next tryst? I hoped Frank realized she saw him and his dick as a business proposition. I snuck around the corner and sized up the reception staff. Then I waited until the officious-looking blonde was busy on a call, the fifty-year-old Basil Fawlty clone had trundled out of sight, and the green teenager from the Scilly Isles (or so I guessed) was free.

I rang the hotel from outside the main door of the lobby, imperious and irate, because I was meeting a hotel guest, Rachel Fotherington, in her room, had been given the wrong number, and had consequently burst in on an elderly Swiss couple in flagrante. How *dare* you!

"Madam, I am terribly sorry. It's room number fifteen, I do apologize."

"Thank you," I purred. "*Hic!* You're very kind."

Oh *ho*. Oh no.

Issy would be devastated. In her way, she loved him. My mind boggled that he could *do* this to her. To me, cheating on your partner is like scrambling an egg. There is no going back. Even if they never find out, *you* know what you've done, and the sanctity of your relationship is violated forever. I decided that Frank was *not* going to do this to her. He was not a man who wanted to live in a basement bedsit in Basildon, and so he'd be, I reckoned, easy to persuade.

I staggered down the road to find a disposable camera. My plan was, snap 'em at it, then—on pain of showing Issy the pictures—force Frank never to see Rachel again *and* have him deny everything. As for Rachel herself, I'd threaten to send the pictures to the *Telegraph*. She didn't care about her own reputation, but I knew she'd hate to embarrass her family. I was impressed with myself. What a brilliant plan! (In my defense, by this point I could hardly stand, which might have had some bearing on my judgment.)

It took me a full hour to find a place that disposed distolable cameras. I mean, that sold disposable cameras. Dishgraceful. Thish ish a capital shitty. I deshided to have a quick drink in a pub—"double shcotch, no rocksh"—before returning to the hotel. They'd drink, they'd eat, they'd get to the room at, what, ten? He wouldn't shtay out too late. He washn't that kind of guy.

I loitered outside the hotel until reception was unattended, then wobbled into a lift. Room fifteen was on the second floor. *Ping!* said the lift. I hastily unwrapped the camera and tiptoed along the white-walled corridor. Room fifteen was at the end. I held my breath as I put my ear to the cool wood. *Groaning*. Horrible! I could do without hearing the noise Rachel made at the point of orgasm. It was just the thing my brain would replay to creep me out.

I braced myself. Damn. What if the door was locked? I'd have to knock. The photo wouldn't be as incriminating, but it would do. Slowly, I twisted the handle. Then I raised the camera to eye level, hurled open the door, and pressed the trigger.

Rachel screamed.

The flash didn't go off.

I tripped over a shoe.

Nige covered his erection with the sheet, peered over the edge of the bed at me, sprawled on the floor, and said, "Holly Appleton, you foul pervert!"

CHAPTER 46

As my nose swelled to twice its size, Rachel lit a cigarette and explained. Nige, who seemed alarmingly free and easy about me seeing him naked, sat cross-legged and ordered roast chicken on room service. I no longer felt drunk. The alcohol seemed to desert my body with the speed of a family fleeing a house on fire. Nige passed me a cold can of Coke from the minibar to hold to my face to numb the pain. I felt stupid enough, so I drank it.

"Babes, you really have shown yourself up. I told you there was nothing going on with Frank. Give me *some* credit. He's married to your sister! I wouldn't touch him if he begged me, which, incidentally, he hasn't and wouldn't. What were you planning, a spot of blackmail?"

I glared at her. She still managed to look composed, despite being a victim of coitus interruptus and unbrushed hair.

"You're still not in the clear, *lovey*," I said in a screech. "Earlier tonight you were canoodling with Frank in the hotel bar. And you've had a succession of secret meetings and phone calls with him. Issy is going out of her mind. She's distraught. She's considering divorce. What do you say to that? And does Nige know about this? What are you running here, a brothel?"

Rachel tugged her white hotel bathrobe around her chunky body and laughed. "You're a very silly girl," she said. "You won't give up, will you? For the last time, Frank and I are *not* having an affair. I am sworn to secrecy, so if I'm struck down, *you* are to blame. Frank and I are organizing a surprise tenth-anniversary party for Issy, to take place two weeks next Saturday. A stiffy—first-class, *bien sûr*—is scheduled to drop through your mailbox tomorrow morning. There are two hundred and fifty guests. He is holding it at the Ritz, and he is the most . . . *particular* client, so it has required a mountain of organization. He has wanted to oversee every detail, he has specified an exact shade of pink for the sugar roses on the chocolate cake, he has requested a certain band and listed, in order, every song he wishes them to play—and considering what they charge, should he require it, they'll sing 'Humpty Dumpty Sat on a Wall.' "

Rachel paused to suck the remains of life from her cigarette.

"Babes. Never in the history of party planning have I ever seen a man so ridiculously in love with his wife. Certainly not after a decade of imprisonment—a slip, forgive me—wedded bliss. Alas, he's tediously insisted on keeping it a secret, while having no aptitude for deception whatsoever. Well, frankly—ha-ha—I've had enough. *I* suggest you trot home and spill the beans to big sis, otherwise the party will be ruined anyhow. Issy will be so deeply entrenched in months of envy and suspicion she'll be unable to make the mental transition to beloved wife. And if she does—although men never understand this—she'll be so deeply peeved at being denied the chance to look twenty by spending thousands on dresses, lipo, detox, Botox, and so on, for the benefit of her audience, that she'll spend the entire night feeling fat and sulking."

There was a loud rap on the door.

"Enter!" called Nige.

A penguin-suited waiter wheeled in a trolley on which gleamed a bosom of silver domes and started to fussily arrange knives, forks, and plates on a table by the window. Oh, don't worry, I wanted to say, just leave it, we'll sort it, thank you *so* much, have a fiver, urk, lady muck, a fellow human being in a servant situation, implies I'm better than you, who do you think you are, no, no, can't deal with it . . .

"Babes," said Rachel, addressing Nige, "there's some shrapnel in my bag. Tip the man. Please"—raising her voice as if the waiter was an idiot and deaf to boot—"return in half an hour to clear the table. Nothing like a chicken carcass to stink out a room. Thank you."

I shrank in my seat and attempted an apologetic glance at the guy. He pocketed the change and leered at me in—at the risk of sounding as bad as Rachel—an impertinent manner. Ah, he thought we'd had a threesome. I stopped feeling embarrassed for him and started feeling embarrassed for me. The second he'd gone I took it out on Rachel.

"Jesus Christ," I spluttered. "Well, thank God. But you didn't exactly help the situation. You kept dropping clangers about Frank buying a new car or doing this or that—if the party was a secret, what was Issy *meant* to think? You can deny it, but I think you've enjoyed making mischief."

"Babes, I am a friendly, tactile person who likes my clients to feel at ease. That's all there is to it, it's hardly a crime. If Issy insists on suspecting her husband of foul play when he clearly worships the ground she walks on, I am not responsible."

Rachel stopped talking. Not, I felt, because she'd said all she wanted, but because she was busy hacking into the roast chicken.

"Want some?" asked Nige, opening his mouth for Rach to drop a strand of chicken into it.

If I hadn't been hunched on a chair keeping as still as possible in an effort to keep the throbbing in my nose under control, I would have stamped my foot. Instead I squeaked, "And how *dare* you make out you're so innocent—you too, Nigel—when you've been sneaking around behind everyone's backs for months and months, pretending to hate each other when all the time you were conducting an illicit affai—"

"We *did* hate each other," said Nige in a hurt voice.

"I disliked him intensely," added Rach, fondling his thigh. "For years I thought he was a common little thing with no taste or class, didn't I, babes?"

Nige nodded and curled a lock of Rach's hair around his

chicken-greasy fingers. "Absolutely. And I thought she was too posh and grubby to be believed."

"She *is* too posh and grubby to be believed!" I roared.

Nige and Rach smiled gooily.

"So when did you change your minds?"

"We had a huge row at the Girl Meets Boy party at Nige's club over whether Tom Cruise was gay or straight and ended up kissing."

"Oh, well," I said. "Now it all makes sense."

"Darling, *don't* be miffed," said Nige. "Rachey was such a saucy little minx that—"

"Please. Spare me. I already know far more than I want to about your sex life."

"For which you only have yourself to blame," said Rach.

"*You* told me you were dating a married man, Rachel! You misled me on purpose."

"Babes, I said married*ish*. Which describes Nigely-Widgely perfectly."

I looked accusingly at Nige.

He smiled his best media smile—a pity, because it was wasted on me *and* he had lettuce in his teeth.

"Darling angel Holly, Marylou is trouble and if she knew I was head over heels with Rachey, she'd never agree to a divorce. Since *Cat on a Hot Tin Roof* she has shown alarming signs of wanting to hang on to me. So you see, our need for secrecy."

"Secrecy, balls!" I yelled. "You're just a shameless pair of drama queens who get a thrill out of room service. Oh God, you're rotten. I can't believe it, you've caused no end of trouble. You . . ." Against my better judgment I started to smile. Then laugh. Which hurt my nose.

"So how's your love life?" said Nige. Instantly, he looked embarrassed. I flinched. I'd had enough of being handled with care, I was ready to be normal again. I wanted my friends to be able to pose that great conversational nonentity without fear of the terrible chain reaction they might be sparking in my head. Even though my love life was, for the record, shit.

Nige must have read my thoughts. "No, no." He gasped, "I didn't mean it like *that*, what I meant was, I can't believe I asked you, *anyone*, such an elderly aunt of a question. Please tell me that finding Rachey won't turn me into a bore. It's the duty of an actor to live life as deeply as possible. More to the point, I need to be quirky and interesting, the papers don't quote you otherwise."

Reassured, I beamed at him. "It's not great. But I'm fine. I'm still reeling from getting unengaged twice to the same man. I think I could do with a break."

Nige flapped his arms. "Someone pull the plug, I'm drowning in bullshit. Holly, sweetheart. I know you and I know when you're lying. Confess all to Uncle Nige." He adopted a thick French accent. "Yeu steel leuve heem!"

I sucked in my cheeks. "Of course I still love him. All I'm saying is that now is not the right time. Not for him, especially. He can hardly bear to look at me. Tricky when we work in the same office and I'm his boss."

Rachel snorted. "Babes, *I* could have told you that was a mistake on a par with white-tie. What were you thinking?"

"I was thinking that your precious darling Niggle, or whatever hideous name you've thought up for him, had abandoned me to be a West End starlet and who the hell was I going to get to replace him."

Rachel lit a cigarette in lieu of a putdown.

Nige shook his head. "Is matching people even Nick's thing?" he asked hopefully.

I shook my head. "Not really. He's done a beautiful job of the Website, but not the day-to-day dealing with clients, nurturing them, deciding who they'd like, stroking their egos, managing them on Date Nights. It requires concentration, dedication."

"Oh, stop," lied Nige eagerly, "my head will swell."

"Well, it *does* require concentration. Patience. It's a lot of sitting still. And Nick isn't fabulous at sitting still. He's too creative. Darling," I added, for fear of seeming precious.

"I hope he's still doing his Mr. Elephant work."

I sighed. "Well, Rach, that's the thing. He's put it on hold. And I know I used to nag him about it, about it not being a *vocation*—"

"Shame on you, babes, it was what he loved doing and he was superb at it. The brats doted on him."

"Yes, I know, shame on me!" I snapped. "But what am I going to do about it? Sack him so he's forced to go back to entertaining four-year-olds? I don't want to do anything to destabilize him."

"No, babes," said Rach, who had either missed the sarcasm or chosen to ignore it, "don't sack him. That wouldn't be clever."

I must have been single for too long, because this (as far as I could see) perfectly innocuous statement elicited a passionate kiss from Nige. Love was so *inexplicable*. Who could tell what fanned the flames? The trigger was unique for each one of the zillions of people living on this earth. Sometimes, I doubted I was in the right job.

I got to my feet and wobbled to the door. "I'm exhausted. And horribly aware that I broke up the party. I'm going to leave you two to . . . it." I grinned and left.

My only other mission that night (thank goodness) was to ring Issy and break the glorious news that her marriage was in rude health. I explained about the no-longer-a-surprise anniversary party and there was a long silence. Then, in a very cross voice, she exclaimed, "The stupid arse!"

I held the phone a distance from my ear and gazed at it. Issy's language was famously clean and free of slang.

"What a bloody idiot!" she continued. "What an utter fool! The *agony* I've gone through, the misery, the dread of spiteful rumors spreading 'round the Montessori! Good God, I came this close to instructing my lawyers! Another twenty-four hours, I'd have cut up his Savile Row suits and roasted our wedding album in the Aga! As it is, I've already keyed his car. He thought it was the eleven-year-olds from the estate." Pause. "Holly, I am astonished. Astonished, and speechless—lost for words! Ten years of marriage, an entire decade! Does the man not know me? I *hate* surprises, they put one at such a disadvantage. My God, Saskia from the health club would have been there, all diamonds and nails and VPL, positively *gloating*."

I knew she shook her head in disgust at this point, because I heard her earrings jangle. "Has he *no* idea about women?" she cried. "Doesn't he realize we have to prepare for a social event as a soldier prepares for battle? Unbelievable. And I'll bet he and that Rachel woman—she needn't think *she's* off the hook, she's got that sly, mistressy look about her—have invited people I've been carefully snubbing for years. Then they'll refuse and feel they've got one up on me, the imbecile. It's too exasperating!"

Issy laughed in a witchy way. I think she was slightly hysterical. With relief, I hoped.

"He meant well," I said meekly. "And Rachel is obsessed with Nige. I'm sorry to say I saw the evidence for myself. Come on, Issy. Five minutes ago you were convinced your marriage was over. You've *got* to be grateful, surely?"

"My God, what a bore!" she declared, as if I hadn't spoken. "I've been the Queen of Mean for months on end. Now I have to execute a full and dramatic U-turn! Awkward and humiliating."

"What's awkward and humiliating?" I couldn't see the problem.

"Being nice to your husband after months of being horrid to him!" she screeched. "You can't snap out of the habit just like that. For crying out loud, now I've got to be *loving*. I don't have the energy. I'll have to fake it and hope that in the end it comes naturally. Mind you, I've hoped that before."

Issy laughed, but I refused to collude. She hesitated.

"The silly sausage."

Progress, I suppose.

"Oooh," she simpered. "I wonder what I'll wear?"

CHAPTER 47

Two days later Nick resigned. I wasn't sorry. We'd had two superb Date Nights, no thanks to him. I'd spotted him chatting to one of our new girls, Sian. She had a face that would look washed out after a month in the Caribbean—think Hepburn meets *Trainspotting*—but her complexion was chalkier than ever. I sidled up, and to my despair, he was discussing hemorrhoids in graphic detail. (Thanks to his Esso station diet, he'd suffered all through college.) "They *itch*," he told her. "You want to drag your bum along the ground like a dog!" Couldn't he tell Sian was nervous, reserved, not a hemorrhoids kind of gal? I'd steered him away before she threw up her cosmopolitan.

Now, he sat opposite me in Martha's, mussing his hair. I'd suspected mischief was afoot when he'd asked if I fancied going for a cup of tea. All recent communication between us had been on a need-to-know basis. As he spoke, I wondered if there was a blues soundtrack playing in his head. That happens when a relationship ends. You're so used to talking to your lover on an almost subliminal level that when you split and the shorthand of intimacy is no longer acceptable, you feel the full weight of your loss. Now there is no one in the world, you think, who prefers *me*. You think that even if he was a nightmare and you ended it.

"I'm leaving you, Hol," he said, looking up from a heavy mug of brown tea. He made it sound friendly. "Rach has offered me a job."

I crumbled my scone and tried not to show relief. I smiled into his eyes. I've always wondered if it's *really* possible to see hurt in the eyes themselves. Surely, any pain is betrayed by the surrounding features. The skin beneath was dark, with a slight puffiness to it. He was tired, I decided, that was all.

"She wants to extend her party business. Cater for children as well as adults. It would be great for me. With Rach, I could offer the whole package—food, as well as entertainment, venue, theme, decor—if they needed it. Parents"—he grinned—"are always knackered. Mostly, they want the easy option. And the cheapest. This way, we'd be able to offer them a good deal." With effort, he wiped the grin. "I'm sorry, Hol. I'll work my notice—"

"Nah. Don't worry. You go when you like. You've done a lovely job on the Website, it's already attracting quite a few new clients." Good Lord, listen to me speaking like a computer salesman. That's what comes from disengaging brain from heart. *Nick*, went the internal soundtrack, *look at you so cool and in control. You don't need me anymore, do you? You're finally getting yourself together. Once, you told me I made your life. Not "I made your life complete," just "I made your life." Which meant so much more. And once, I told you it was over and you were desolate. How do you travel such a long emotional distance in such a short time?*

"Rach has offered you a good deal, hasn't she?"

Nick smiled. "Oh, Hol," he said *fondly*. "You always did baby me. Of course she has. Very generous. Shares in the company even. I wouldn't take anything less. I'm not an idiot."

I didn't baby you. Well, not that much. And if I did, it wasn't my fault. Not totally. Some of the time you behaved like a baby. So I was forced to treat you like one. I hope your mind doesn't select just the bad memories. We had so much fun. There was a lot of happiness in our relationship. What about when we moved into our new house, and halfway through the day you dragged me out of the kitchen, out onto the porch, and carried me over the threshold in front of the whistling removal men . . .

"Nick, that's not what I meant."

I felt hurt.

He placed a hand over mine and stroked it. Excitement crackled briefly. Stupid Holly. What would Issy call me? A silly sausage. A light-as-air phrase that was cruel at heart because it denied a person's emotions and reduced them to a clown.

"Ah, Hol, I know you didn't. I'm sorry. You only do it because you care, and that's a lovely thing."

I ate a bit of scone and tried to look nonchalant. It never does to be seen to care too much. Certainly not with a former boyfriend eager to explore fresh pastures. I decided to change the subject. To hint, perhaps, that he wasn't made of steel, because he seemed to need reminding. But that wasn't the only reason. He was right. I did care.

"Tell me, how are things with your birth mother?"

Nick scratched at the table with a fingernail. "She's been in touch. Suggested a day, a time, a place to meet, all sorts of conditions, if Malcolm was working. I said it wasn't convenient—which was the truth, I was going to the football with Manjit—so she went all sullen and said she'd call back. I'm still waiting."

He caught my expression and shook his head. "Don't look so fierce, Hol. You don't have to fight my battles for me. I'm fine with it. Well, not *fine,* it hurts like fuck, but well, you try to be rational rather than emotional. If I wanted I could torture myself about all kinds of stuff that's not my fault. And you were right. Lavinia and Michael *do* love me, and as far as I'm concerned *they* are my real parents. I love them, I fit with them. All that crap I said before, it wasn't true."

He paused, blinked.

"They made a big mistake, but their intentions were honorable, and they really do regret it. And I respect them for that. We have a way to go with trust and all that, but I know we'll get there. I don't feel angry with them anymore. I don't even feel angry with my birth mother. I feel sorry for her. I think she's a woman too afraid to commit to anyone or anything. I tell myself that's her problem, not mine. It's not personal, how could it be? She never knew me, *me.*"

He took a sip of murky tea and stared into it.

"You have hopes. After they told me, I dreamed about her. Every fifty-something woman on the street, I'd think, Are *you* her, are *you* her? I couldn't sleep for wondering where she was, what she was doing, did she think about me. It was hard not to imagine a grown-up fairy princess. In my head she was a cross between Glinda, the white witch, and Olivia Newton-John. And then I met her. *Boof!* It's hard to give up your dreams, Hol. No one wants to do that. It brings you closer to death."

"Oh, Nick."

"I'm fine." He smiled. "I wanted to change her life. I wanted to walk back into her life, and I wanted her to be awestruck, lovestruck. I wanted to see what we had in common. Did we laugh the same way? I wanted to go on picnics with her for chrissake, watch her eat. I wanted her to be besotted, to follow me around like a puppy, to be desperate to get to know me. I wanted to tell her every stupid little thing about me, things she *should* have known, like when my first tooth fell out and I swallowed it, how I played a pirate in the school play and smuggled in a real knife, the time I got a haircut like Luke Skywalker. But she didn't ask, she wasn't bothered. She had no idea who I was, and no real interest in finding out. She had her life, her family. She didn't need a new addition, she didn't know what the hell to do with me. She'd never tried to trace *me.* She made me feel foolish for *wanting.*"

"Nick," I whispered. "That's so sad, I'm so sorry."

"Don't be," he replied. He seemed to mean it. His gaze was direct. "You can't force someone to change their nature. Think of all the bad parents out there. My biological mother isn't the only one. There are millions of them! All useless in different ways. I'm lucky in that I have Lavinia and Michael, who aren't perfect, but who love me and are, deep down, *good.* I have their adoration, their approval, their never-ending interest, the fact that however little I've achieved they've remained impressed by me. How many children—well, you know what I mean—have that? You know what Lavinia showed me the other day? A snowball I'd brought into the house when I was nine. She'd kept it in the freezer. It was the size of a cannonball! That taught me something. I was happy before I met my birth mother. I don't need her to be complete, that's what I realize."

"You're being amazingly mature about all this."

Nick smiled. "Did Manjit tell you I put my fist through Bo's glass door the other week? Then fell to the floor and howled like a baby? *And* left a large bloodstain on her white carpet. Believe me, I have not been mature. Sometimes you look at your friends and envy them. You feel futile, and I mean that in the most literal sense. As if there's no point to you. Some days are dark as hell. And I'm not sure the worst is over. The grief comes in waves. But gradually you—*I,* I should say—I accept it, accept her for what she is."

He broke off a piece of my poor, decimated scone and squashed it flat on the plate, pressing it into a dirty yellow dough with his thumb.

"If I chose, I could stay in that place forever, being that wounded, abandoned, resentful kid, waiting for his mother to rescue him. But isn't that where every sad, damaged, unpleasant adult is stuck? Acting out their childhood disappointments, replaying them, chasing away every chance of happiness because once, an age ago, someone hurt them. So they refuse to let anyone close again and insist on living mean, meager, miserable lives, punishing themselves for—what? *Nothing.* Someone else's crime. It's senseless. No fucking way is that going to be me."

He grinned his old sloppy smile, the smile that could weaken my knees. "I'm stronger than that, I'm a big boy now, *baby!*"

The next time I saw him was at Isabella and Frank's anniversary party. And he did look different, older. He was dressed smartly in a suit, but a rather *modish* one—if that word doesn't make me sound about sixty-five. There was color in his cheeks. He had a pen tucked behind his ear and was in animated conversation with Rach. Always a fan of his cooking, she'd asked him to try out as catering manager. Add this to his other role as Mr. Elephant and she was paying him—as she'd told me with her usual indiscretion— "a fuck-off salary." I didn't want to think about who exactly was being told to fuck off here.

I was glad I'd made an effort for the party. I was back to my normal weight, it was good to feel substantial again. I was wearing a red Grace Kelly–ish cocktail dress and pink mules. Even now, when I watch *The Wizard of Oz* (which tends to be every other Christmas but feels like every second month), I itch to own Dorothy's ruby slippers. My pink shoes are a modern, funkier approximation— skinnier, higher heels, open toes, and an elegant band of hot-pink fake crocodile skin. Now that I've described them, they couldn't be more different, but their aura is identical. You could wish for anything and get it in those shoes.

My first thought on seeing the ballroom was that Frank had a grudge against minimalism. If the central chandelier were to fall on anyone's head they'd be crushed to the thickness of a wafer. I made a mental note never to pass beneath it. There were monster displays of flowers everywhere, big, fat, ostentatious blooms, and so many it was as if we had been transported to the rain forest. The pink lilies I recognized, and I breathed in their cheap, heady scent—the others I steered clear of, they looked red and ferocious, as if they might try and take a bite out of you when your back was turned.

In a corner lit by—what would you call these things, fire cones?—a man in a stripey hat was handing out pink cotton candy with whirly gestures like a magician performing a trick. I accepted a stick, because it suited the decadent atmosphere and matched my shoes. Nige appeared—a dead ringer (he hoped) for Jay Gatsby—clutching a bowl of champagne and swiped a wisp of fluffy cloud without asking.

"Can money buy you love?" he murmured. "That is the question."

"Hamlet never said that," I replied. "Anyway, glad as I am to see you, who invited you? Surely your girlfriend wouldn't abuse her position?"

"That entirely depends on which position she's in," said Nige, adding a Sid James cackle in case I was too pure of mind to get the joke. "No. Frank invited everyone, darling. Look at Sam and Bernard over there lowering the tone—village High Street *fash-ee-own* ahoy. The trouble is, when people like Sam and Bernard invite you to their wedding, you become embroiled in a ceaseless round of counterinvitations that—unless you can qualify for a witness protection program—dog you for the rest of your lives. Talking of unwanted invites, my new D-grade celebrity seems to be working wonders. I'm *so* popular, Hol. My old tutor rang my agent last week—*simpering*, he said she was. Having been perfectly content to ignore my existence for twelve years, she's suddenly gasping for me to attend some lecturey dinnery thing at the college. I suspect her to be motived by money, rather than by sudden recall of my super personality. Academics obviously don't know how much stage actors get paid."

I shook my head. "Aren't people embarrassed to be so openly shallow?"

Nige grinned. "Why should they be? Without the lubricant of insincerity, society would grind to a halt. Bernard! Samantha! Two of my favorites, what an absolute *treat*! Kiss kiss!"—said with not the slightest attempt to perform the action. "Samantha, a vision, where did you get that dress. I must have one! Bernard, old chap, how the devil are you?! What! Orange juice? Good Lord, am I the only alcoholic here?"

I left him to it and went to say hi to Claw and Camille. Camille was wearing a floaty, khaki-green dress that went surprisingly well with the butterfly tattoo on her upper arm. I knew she was looking for a new job—having resigned when the firm dithered over moving her to another position—and I was wondering whether she'd fit in at Girl Meets Boy. I decided to say nothing before discussing it with Claudia. After all, my recent experiments with nepotism had not been a success, best to let Claw make the choice.

"M and D are all right, aren't they?" said Claw as I approached.

I glanced over to where our parents were gazing at a huge ice sculpture of two cautiously entwined figures—presumably Frank and Isabella, but easily mistaken for Mr. and Mrs. Shrek. Mum and Dad, in their 1974 wear, looked underdressed amid all the sequins and beaded designer flounce of the other guests (who, sartorially, were years ahead—1982 at least). They were holding their champagne bowls a wary distance from their bodies, as if they were cell phones.

"Aw, they're fine," I said. "Just a bit stunned at Frank's . . . style. Have you introduced Camille yet?"

"Yes." Camille grinned, squinting at Claw. "That's why she's asking if they look okay."

I widened my eyes. "How was it?"

Camille and Claw glanced at each other and, without any visible change in expression, glowed with joy. I felt a great sense of relief. Not because the meeting had plainly been a success, but because my little sister was so thoroughly in love, and her love was so obviously reciprocated with such an honest and open heart.

Claw had always been restless, jumpy, shifting from one phase, trend, job, to the next, and no matter how vivacious and witty she seemed, you always sensed her dissatisfaction simmering below the surface. Now, I saw, she had found a destiny that suited her, and it showed. Her fidgetiness had been replaced with a mood of calm. (That said, the vampire teeth were as sharp as ever, and her dress sense remained the same, which I found reassuring. The day I see Claudia and she isn't wearing an item that makes you blink is the day I'll start to worry.)

Smiling around the room, I spotted Frank and Issy. I don't think Issy had told Frank his cover was blown—she'd certainly fluttered her lashes and arranged her mouth into a neat O when we'd all jumped out from behind the flowers yelling "Surpriiiiise!" Even Nige had rated her performance. And now, they were standing in the center of the dance floor, just out of range—I was pleased to note—of the killer chandelier, and Issy was resting her head on his shoulder. I was proud of her (she was two inches taller than him, so it was a generous concession). Eden was stealing pink sugar roses off the cake and squashing them in her Hello Kitty purse, but I think Issy had spent just enough on her dress not to mind.

I slipped out of the room, passing a famous rock star who should have died of shame at the fact he was playing at such an event, and after a good five minutes trekking down corridors, found the exit to a central courtyard. It was quiet and pretty, with jasmine tumbling down the brickwork, more Paris than London. I sat on a wooden bench and closed my eyes. This was a triumph in itself. A month ago I'd only dare close my eyes when there were two Banham locks, three bolted doors, and a large kitchen knife between me and the open air. I felt the breeze on my skin and breathed deeply, sinking my shoulders and trying to relax.

I could be cynical about Frank and Issy's anniversary party, but there was no denying it was a room shimmering with hope. Some had already found happiness, others tentatively reached toward it. I counted myself somewhere in the middle. Perhaps, if I wanted to make progress, I'd have to make some tough decisions. Well, one. Nick had talked several times about selling the house but done nothing about it. I was loath to—partly because moving house is a monstrous affair (you're at the mercy of other people's incompetence), but mostly because it would, in the most concrete way possible, signal the end of Nick and me.

"Still trying to tan your eyelids?"

And there he stood, watching me. I laughed. A private joke. Me, on every holiday, determined to tan my eyelids (because, after all, it's the small achievements that make life such a blast). It had never worked. Without sunscreen they went bright red and peeled, and I looked like a salamander. With sunscreen they swelled up and I looked as if I'd been crying for a week.

I shaded my eyes from the gentle evening sun and gazed at Nick. His smile faded. "Ah," he said, "don't. I know what you're going to say." He sighed. "You're going to be sensible and suggest we sell the house."

CHAPTER 48

Nick was jostling gobbets of chicken around the pan as if he was trying to get them to leave a nightclub.

" 'All it needs is a lick of paint,' " he growled. "How dare she. They weren't even interested. All they wanted was a poke around. I feel as if I've been defiled!"

I watched him bully the dinner and flapped shut my copy of *Elle Deco*. I had to agree. "The house has been on the market for two weeks and already we're stressed," I said.

"And why is every estate agent in the world called Jeremy? I can't wait for all of these people to be out of my life. I've been patronized by four idiots in *one* day!"

I could tell by his voice that the chicken was suffering. So was I. I'd asked Nick to be present when people came to view the house after it became clear that our estate agent was more than happy to disappear to the pub and send me 'round an ax murderer who hadn't even bothered to put his house on the market.

Nick and I were being civilized about it—hence the dinner— but it was proving hard to spend time with him. I kept thinking that in a few years he'd be doing this with some other woman, whipping up dinner, while she sat at her oak table (made of reclaimed wood salvaged from the banks of the Thames), flicking through *Elle Deco* (although not in the catatonic state of depression that I did—it would be a friend's copy, all her stuff would be "flea-market finds"). She'd have wacky pictures of the Queen and Jesus tacked up around the place and everyone would think how cool she was. I didn't know who she was, but I wanted to kill her.

I was holding my breath for Nick to drop into conversation the name of a girl or the word *we*. He hadn't yet, but I wasn't complacent. He wouldn't be short of offers. Women liked Nick. There is a time, after a love affair ends, when you feel proprietary. Even when your ex presents with a new squeeze, you cling to a sense of superiority. Yes, you silly little thing, with your low-slung trousers and pierced belly button and media training, you may have snogged in a nightclub, shagged back at your Camden-ethnicky pad, then trolled out your thruppenceworth on the meaning of life. That, dear, does not a relationship make.

I could cling to my scorn for a few months. Yes, but you don't have what *we had*. I know more about him than you ever will. Issy once told me that after nine years of marriage, and being a mother, she had no patience with people who got engaged and were excited about it. "It's so *babyish*," she'd said. Being engaged myself at that point, I couldn't empathize, but I would happily apply her logic to the potential new-girlfriend situation. And yet.

What if the "we need to talk" with Ms. Pierced Belly Button never came? What if the years rolled on, and Nick developed a taste for, oh what, *floor cushions*, and they moved into a loft apartment in Hoxton, or worse, went traveling for a year to Africa and New Zealand? My ascendancy would be slowly erased, it would count for less and less, until I was barely an acquaintance. And if they ever sent me a Christmas card it would be one of those pointedly insulting We Are Family photos of their kids in fancy dress and signed by *her* from both of them. I boiled with rage as I considered the magnitude of the affront. Why—to quote her devoted husband—she might as well have sent me a poo in a parcel. And he, the smug bastard, had done nothing to stop her!

I stood up, scraping my chair. "I don't *want* any chicken!" I shouted. "It's for people too stupid to know what they really like to eat!" Then, feeling blushy about having repeated something I'd heard a chef say on *Ready Steady Cook* in a desperate attempt to be mass-audience controversial, I thundered up the stairs, ran into our—my my *my*, why couldn't I get that into my head?—bedroom, and banged the door.

I heard footsteps on the landing. Nick bawled, "Holly! I'm confiscating *Elle Deco*! It's not good for you! You always get like this when you read it! I'm throwing it away! Right! I'm going down-stairs! I'm in the kitchen! I'm placing my foot on the trash pedal! The lid is up! The magazine is going, going . . . It's gone! Good-bye, *Elle Deco*! I'm sorry, she cannot cope with you"—he raised his voice—"even though I always tell her every house in that evil publi-cation is a film set and does she not think that when the owners know *Elle Deco* are coming 'round they scoot off to Notting Hill to buy antique chandeliers and Venetian mirrors, and get the stain on the ceiling painted over, and stuff all their junk from IKEA in the cellar, and lock the baby in the attic, and light twenty Diptyque can-dles to mask the smell of cooking oil and old diapers and wet dog, and light every gas ring on the stove to try to raise the temperature in the house above freezing because ripping up the carpets to re-veal all those marvelous wooden floorboards has turned it into a miserable drafty icebox . . . Holly? You listening to me?"

"No I'm not!" I roared. "Eat the chicken and go!"

"Fine," said Nick, losing patience. "Grumpy cow." He certainly paid more attention to what I said these days. He ate the chicken and went. When I crept down to the kitchen to see if he'd left me any, the pan was scrubbed and resting on the draining board and the fridge was bare and smelled of ripe cheese (not in a good way). Emily was sitting on the windowsill looking well fed and washing her face with a paw. I ate twelve slices of toast while staring at the wall with a sour expression and wondering if piercing your belly button hurt.

I t's out, it's out!" shrieked Claudia when I got into work one day.

"What?" I said. "Who? Don't tell me. Tom. Penelope was a beard, I'm head over heels with Russell—ooh he's such a scamp and so outspoken. I'm putting him on a diet and we're eloping to Canberra, romance capital of th—"

"Shush, you're not funny. The *Glamour* feature!"

I snatched the magazine she was waving. Claudia sank to her knees and kowtowed to an imaginary Tabitha. Four minutes later and I was down there with her, kowtowing to Xak and making a mental note to get the office carpet cleaned.

Tabitha had written what I can only describe as the dream feature. It was funny, self-deprecating, sweetly cynical about dating agencies, and bashfully charming about ours. Well, it would have to be. Seeing as she was announcing her engagement to Xak in print. Best of all, there was a photo. She looked sparky and fun, he looked good enough to eat. He'd also been kind enough to give his fiancée an exclusive. All the women he'd met at Girl Meets Boy were sexy, clever, a laugh—filthily eligible, in fact—but then he'd seen Tabitha taking notes in shorthand and nearly expired with desire.

" 'Filthily eligible,' what a delicious phrase, the little Rent-a-quote."

Claw, forgetting her orientation for a moment, rained kisses on Xak's dolly face, leaving red lipstick prints on the page. "I love you, I worship you, angel boy! I praise the day you walked through our door. I bless the unlikely fact you find shorthand sexy. May you make Tabitha the happiest woman alive, and if you ever divorce, please let it be in fifty years' time when she's retired and arthritic and can't write about it!"

As if on cue the phone rang.

"A thought," I said, reaching for the receiver. "It's a women's mag. What if *only* women apply?"

Claw frowned. "Then we'll have to invite a reporter down from *GQ* to even out the odds. Or *Esquire*. Or *FHM*. Or start up our own men's magazine. Pick up already!"

I picked. "Hello, Girl Meets Boy, how can I help you?"

"Yeah," said a male voice. "Um. The dating agency, right? I saw this thing about you? In my flatmate's copy of *Glamour*? She'd left it lying around? On the kitchen table? I had to move it to, um, read *Newsweek*? And I caught a glimpse of the article? Thought it sounded a laugh?"

After twenty-seven such calls—give or take a few ums and ers—I realized that Britain's young single men are voracious readers of women's magazines, forever leafing through them in a feverish hunt for rogue nipples (*Loaded* and other publications where female full-frontal nudity is compulsory presumably don't hold the same sly appeal). In comparison, we had eighteen calls from women.

"And that," crowed Claudia, vampire teeth glinting, "isn't counting all the queries via E-mail and the hits on the Website."

She looked around the scruffy paper-ridden office. I followed her gaze. It had that generic office look—a gray aura, buzzy white-strip lighting, messiness even when it was tidy, hard-wearing furniture. "Hol," she said, "we should do this place up a bit. Paint it hot pink and azure blue . . . and have a hardwood floor put down instead of this manky hide-a-million-stains carpet. It's not a *crèche*, for god's sake, how many stains are we expected to make? I've only dropped my coffee once. And I make it a rule never to drop food. This is only a tiny room, it won't cost much. *We* can do the painting. I think we need to do something to mark the fact that business is on the up. And not just because of the *Glamour* piece. It's been improving steadily month on month—after that awful series of blips. We're really doing very well."

I was pleased. It's certainly good, I thought, to have at least one portion of your life sorted out. Rather like a child dividing peas, potato, and chicken into separate sections on their plate, I retained a habit of dividing my life into compartments. (Except at five years of age I'd gone a step further than most children. I used to remove all the black currants in my Ski yogurt—after cleaning them in my mouth—and line them up on the table for afterward.) When Claudia forced me to analyze how I felt about my achievements, I realized that I'd dragged whatever neurosis lay behind the yogurt custom with me into adulthood.

I couldn't even discuss it with Dr. Goldstein. Over the last few months we'd had ten sessions. By session nine, I'd been scratching around for dilemmas to maintain his interest. He hadn't felled my bugbears with a big stick, one by one, as they ran at me; it wasn't that simple. But he was able to help me understand how a person who doesn't want to deal with a problem can invest all their energies in a distraction. I liked talking to him. He was the opposite of a god in that he turned wine into water. (Not so flashy, but a life essential rather than an extra.) And I think he liked talking to me—it wouldn't have worked otherwise. After our chats I felt the same intense satisfaction you get from popping bubble wrap. I could have gone on seeing him, except it was like a love affair—you know in your heart when it's over. I walked out of his office for the last time, quaking. Now I was on my own. But, I consoled myself, aren't we all?

"Yes," I said. "We are doing well. And you're right. We should paint the office blue and pink."

The more I considered it, the more I loved the idea of such a color scheme. It reminded me of a Walt Disney book I'd had when I was young. The illustration of Sleeping Beauty's castle had been a rush of hot pink and azure blue, to signify the spell cast by the kind fairy godmothers to save our princess from death and send her into a slumber that would last a hundred years.

Although, I had to concede, that spell was in no way the perfect solution. Sleeping Beauty's parents would die long before she awoke, *and*—snooze of the century or not—until they did, it would be like having a daughter in a coma. I felt quite strongly that the king and queen's feelings had been clumsily overlooked by the well-meaning fairy godmothers. And the poor girl was at the mercy of being woken by a handsome prince. It was quite a gamble.

I was about to tell Claudia all this when the phone rang. Presuming it was new male client number twenty-eight, I answered with a trill. "Girl Meets Boy! How can I help you?"

There was an embarrassed cough, so I knew instantly it was the estate agent. He was curiously priggish. "Jeremy. We have an offer on your house. From Mr. and Mrs. Piddington. And"—dramatic pause, perhaps to illustrate his brilliance, my luck, and the imbecility of the Piddingtons—"it's the asking price. I've spoken to Nick, and he's happy, but he wanted me to check with you. You'll wanna accept, right?"

For a moment I couldn't speak. Perhaps, had Nick and I painted the house hot pink and azure blue, *our* love story would have ended differently. Mr. and Mrs. Piddington would have been less likely to offer the asking price, that was for sure. I swallowed. I was being ridiculous. Ten hours with a shrink and I was subjecting the Dulux color collection to psychoanalysis. What nonsense.

We'd paint the walls of Girl Meets Boy hot pink and azure blue because they matched the theme of our business. There would be more pink than blue, just in case anyone argued that. Like Sleeping Beauty, our princesses had placed their lives on hold in the hope of being rescued by princes. If there was more pink than blue, then we could argue it was just as likely to be the other way around.

But listen to me. Why was I so defensive? Once I'd been proud, brazen even, about the goals of Girl Meets Boy. I'd never thought it was shameful to join a dating agency, to want to find love so badly you'd pay a firm to find it for you. Love, I'd declare to anyone who would listen, was the meaning of life. After we are dead, all that remains is love. A big house, a powerful job—poor comforts if you lead a loveless existence. It was your duty to yourself to do everything in your power to ensure that you found love. And I *still* believed that, with all my heart.

So why was I suddenly coy?

The truth. I'd always been confident that I would find love without anyone's help. That was what distinguished me from my clients. Because, I'd always *had* love. From my family, from Nick. Now, I was staring a future of singledom dead in the face. There was no guarantee that I'd find a prince—a prince, a pauper, who cared, so long as he was my soul mate?—or that he'd find me.

Now, I was the same as them. And when I thought about this, I saw that I'd always treated the members of Girl Meets Boy as children. Little people who couldn't look after themselves. I'd nurtured them, fussed over them, loved them. I'd felt compassion, empathy even, and I *thought* I'd respected them, and yet . . . I had never regarded them as equals. But now—in a shock of cold understanding—suddenly I did.

I found my voice.

"Jeremy?" I said. "Accept the offer on the house."

CHAPTER 49

"A week from next Saturday is Nige's last night," said Claw, singing over the babble of Capital Gold. "I was thinking of taking M and D. Evening at the theater and all that. Do you want to come?"

I sat back on my heels and rubbed my aching shoulder. The first half hour of painting a wall is a thrill. Then—hot pink or no—it becomes mind-numbingly dull. Not as dull, however, as a Saturday night in front of the TV.

In the last year of our relationship, Nick and I had spent an alarming number of our Saturday nights in this way. It would have been fine if we'd nipped to the bedroom between *Blind Date* and *Inspector Frost* and ravished each other, but we didn't. Now I was single, there was no question of any ravishing (unless I ravished myself, which took three minutes and was about as satisfying as a lettuce salad), and this felt nearly as bad. If I plot my way through more than one evening a week via television programs, I get the sense of my life draining away. Partner or not.

"Yes, I'd love to."

"Good," replied Claw, "because they keep hinting about getting together. They worry about you, you know."

I knew. After I'd told them about Stuart, my normally unpushy parents had become *clingy*. I'd mentioned it to Issy, who said she'd only seen this behavior once before—when Eden was born. Dad had taken to ringing me every night at ten, to see "how things were." *I* would then be obliged to talk. *He* would listen, in complete silence, with not so much as a "Really?" or an "Mm-hmm" to encourage me, and I'd keep thinking that either he or the line was dead. I love my father, but he has no idea how to conduct a decent telephone conversation. As Woody Allen once said about being sent flowers, "The onus is all on the receiver."

Mum was as bad. She'd ring at 8:00 A.M. and wake me up. A flurry of "how are you feeling"s would ensue. Then, because I always felt rotten at eight in the morning, I wouldn't sound as chipper as her mental barometer required, and she'd start to panic and fall into a mailing frenzy. One week I received: a fat series of clippings from the *Guardian* women's page on Rohypnol, serial rapists, and other jolly tales, each sentient phrase dotted with a pink fluorescent asterisk; a rape alarm and a can of hairspray; a huge bottle of vitamin pills and *The SAS Urban Survival Handbook;* a pink T-shirt nightie from M&S (presumably, to kill any man's sexual urge on sight). Because my mother didn't wish to "intrude," she never sent any notes with these parcels, so it was like having a stalker.

Parental pressure was only alleviated by a call from Michael Mortimer, three days after the offer on the house. "Good news, Holly," he barked. "The case Caroline Keats rang you about? The CPS have seen sense and brought charges against that swine, Marshall."

If Michael Mortimer hadn't been Michael Mortimer I would have screamed. Instead I said, "They have?"

"And you can rest assured that their decision to prosecute was partly down to you."

"It *was?*"

"Certainly. The police report would have mentioned that there had been a previous allegation."

I paused, to see if he wanted to say anything else, but Michael was not a man who wasted words.

"Is there," I ventured, "a date?"

Michael said there was and mentioned which court. I scribbled it in my diary.

"Do you plan to attend?"

"I'm not sure," I replied.

"Think carefully, Holly," he said, his tone soft.

I nodded at the phone. It would be wonderful to watch justice being done. But what if justice *wasn't* done? If I attended his trial, would I be letting Stuart back into my head? I was doing so well.

After ruling my inner life for so long, he was receding to a dot in my mind's eye. And *I'd* made him recede. A tormentor rarely recedes of their own accord. I decided to wait till nearer the time and see how I felt.

"How's Nick?" I said, to change the subject.

New life entered Michael's voice. "Marvelous. Bit of a shock to the system, having the son and heir back at home . . . but marvelous. When the exchange on your house goes through, he'll start looking for a flat. What are your plans, my dear?"

"I suppose I'll be looking for a flat too."

I'd been putting it off. The thought of going back to a flat after living in a house made my heart sink. If your toilet stopped flushing, twenty-seven faceless people might be responsible, and you'd have to put in fourteen calls to the alcoholic porter (who, you suspected, spied on you with one hand on his binoculars, the other on his willy). The porter would, in turn, put in a call to the managing agents, who were like the worst sort of strict parents, rules coming out of their ears, no sense of humor, always wanting money off you. Ten days later, your toilet might be fixed.

"Pity," said Michael.

I tried not to think about the pity of Nick and me, and to concentrate on the pleasing fact of Stuart's prosecution. I rang Claudia, Issy, and my parents, told them the good news. And I hoped that Stuart's parents knew and were ashamed of him. *My* parents, who had had less occasion to study the British justice system than I had, were delighted. In the following weeks, they adjusted their fussing to second gear. The parcels and phone calls became less frequent.

"Claw," I said. "Shall we invite Issy and Frank too? They'd love to see *Cat on a Hot Tin Roof.* Or at least they'd love to say that they'd seen it. We could invite Rach as well—she's probably already going, but it would be nice to all go together."

"It would be worth having Rach along just so I can hear her say, 'Would anyone like a can of Diet Coke?' " said Claw. (Rach spoke so smartly, she pronounced it "Cake.") She grinned. "You're thinking safety in numbers, aren't you?" She had a smear of azure blue across her cheek and a blob of hot pink in her hair, and she still looked glamorous. Like a woman in an advert. Whereas I looked like a woman who had been painting a wall.

"I'm being sociable, Claudia," I replied, laughing.

She hesitated. "Tell you what, I'll ask Mum and Dad if they want to invite some friends too. Then we can all descend on Nige in a great big rowdy group, and if M and D have friends with them, they'll have to restrain any urge to mollycoddle their middle child. How about that?"

"Perfect."

I looked at the clock: 11:27. "Tea break?"

Claw carefully laid her paintbrush across the top of the tin. "Hol! You'd make the worst sort of decorator! Tea break every five minutes, skiving off for your nan's funeral every second day. If it was down to you the quickest job would take a month."

I prayed she'd submit to my plaintive expression, and she did. "Oh, go on, then. I'll carry on, you go back to sitting on your arse."

Trying not to smirk, I removed my overalls and skipped to the ladies' to wash the emulsion off my hands. I sat at my desk and tore at the first of the morning's pile of applications—most of which were addressed to me—with relief.

My gaze settled halfway down the page.

Describe your perfect night in. "Naomi Campbell and Claudia Schiffer coming 'round in nurse's uniforms to run me a nice hot bath, cook me dinner, and make me feel special before tucking me into bed and kissing me good night . . ."

I scrutinized the accompanying photo. A pale thin guy with glasses, dressed in a toga. Or rather, a sheet masquerading as a toga. Jim Dillon his name was.

Under *Bad habits,* he'd written "I squeeze the toothpaste from the top."

Under *Your greatest asset,* he'd put "My creativity."

I doubt it, I thought. Then I turned the page and saw that under *Talents* he'd scrawled "Wooing women."

I took it back.

Jim Dillon seemed fine, if average. Average jokes, average looks, average desires. "A man"—to quote Jane Austen—"whom any woman, not fastidious, might like."

I felt a curiously personal sense of disappointment. Try harder, I wanted to say. Be funnier. But then, Holly, I told myself, we aren't looking for a match for you. There are plenty—well, a few—women who would find *your* ideal man a nightmare. And Mr. Dillon charming. I put his letter aside and opened the next envelope.

Describe your perfect night in. "A nice meal, a cuddle on the sofa. More cuddling. Unless it's a night in with my mates."

I smiled at the page. Flicked to the photo. Oof. Maybe it was a bad photo.

Dislikes. "People who use the word 'lush.' Women who describe themselves as 'bubbly.' "

I smiled again. Flicked to the photo again. This was supposed to be an agency for the cute, and this man had a cute mind. I was certain it was a bad photo. It was taken in a booth, and he had deep-set eyes—the stark lighting made him look like a criminal.

Under *Talents,* he'd put "Hell, yes."

Under *Do you smoke?* he'd written "As if my life depended on it."

I tipped back in my chair and surveyed Claudia's work. Why was I tense about being single when there were men like this out there?

I zipped through a few more applications.

"How's it going there?" said Claw, as I ripped open the last envelope.

"Good," I replied. "We've got some good people."

I scanned the final letter. This one certainly rated himself. He'd printed the application form off our Website—thank you, Nick—and the typing under *Talents* took up half a page.

"I am an enigmatic figure," it began, "often seen scaling walls and saving whales. I write award-winning sonnets. I can peel an avocado using only the toes of my right foot. I know the precise location of every item in the supermarket. I wow women worldwide with my lyrical and sensuous oboe playing. I sleep once a week, and when I sleep, I sleep standing up. I can chat in Latin. I don't perspire. Governments beg me to solve their problems; often, I refuse. I have swum with dolphins and spoken with Elvis . . ."

Reluctant as I was to stop reading, I had to. The millisecond it took to flip over to the photo stretched to an hour. And—there *was* no photo. I felt irked. How dare you? How dare you be so funny,

clever, and—look at this man, Jim Dillon, this is what you should as-
pire to!—*implicitly* gorgeous and not provide visual corroboration. I
shuffled the pages clumsily, searching for a contact number. Then I
took a deep breath and placed his application on the desk in front
of me. What was I doing? My engagement was barely cold in its
grave! Oh, but this man. What a *jewel*. He'd seduced me in two minutes via remote control. I shivered to think what he might do in person. Then, said my conscience sternly, you should do your job and
introduce him to the legions of trusting women who have coughed
up two hundred pounds for you to find them love. You ought to be
ashamed, plotting to skim off the cream for yourself!

But, I argued. I *get* this man. I get his sense of humor, the way
he thinks.

Look what happened with Stuart.

Please. That was uncalled for.

I sighed. I could only hope he only went for skinny six-foot
blondes. Then I'd be saved from myself. I crumpled the paper in
my haste to find what he'd said under *Your ideal woman*.

"Caring, clever, serious, crazy, funny, sarcastic, attractive but not
interested that she is, compassionate, tactile, romantic, sexy. A
woman who inspires and excites me. A woman with whom I will
enjoy growing old, but with whom I can act like a toddler if I wish.
A woman who, whenever I see her, takes my breath away with her
incredible beauty, inside and out. A woman who is at peace with
herself, who will let me be myself . . ."

"Mm grrff!"

Claudia looked up. "You all right, Hol?"

"Paint fumes," I sniffed.

I scanned the top of the page. The fool hadn't put his name in
the box. I felt, I imagined, like the Prince on realizing that Cinders
had fled.

Heart thumping, I flicked to the bottom of the second page.
There was his name. I read it, twice, and blinked.

"Nick Mortimer."

CHAPTER 50

When Issy and Frank bought their first mansion, it was exactly what they wanted. Five bedrooms, large garden, an impressive address. And they paid for the privilege. Of course they did. I presumed that Issy, triumphant in her stately new home, would be glad to stop reading all the highly embellished details of inferior properties for sale in the local rag. But no. She continued to scrutinize the section from cover to cover. And I realized she was comparing—to see how well they'd done on price. If she saw the mirage of a bargain basement, it would ruin her day. I saw it as resisting happiness. And what is the point in that?

When I read Nick's name, signed in his usual scrawl, I was furious. What? Did he want me to pimp for him? I felt tricked. And hurt, as if he was laying out his wares, parading his freedom in front of me but not *for* me. I was about to jump up and bleat to Claudia when something stopped me. (I got as far as jerking in my chair.) I could take this the wrong way, assume the very worst. Or . . .

I snatched at the envelope. He had addressed it to *me*. Where was my sense of optimism? Come to that, where was my sense? The old Holly was forever being teased by Nick for her sunshine outlook on the world. Now, I was more cautious. But green shoots of the old me were growing amid the rubble and I couldn't help wondering how thin the line between caution and idiocy. Like most of us, I'd been knocked about a bit by life and yet I realized my instinct was—*still was*—to think the best of people. I didn't want to be like Issy, stubborn against the chance of happiness. I wanted this to be a love letter.

So maybe it was.

I rang Rachel. "You will, of course," I said, "be attending your darling's last night of glory?"

"Babes," she replied. "Every night I attend to Nige is a night of glory, hah!" Faced with silence, she simmered down. "Oh, babes, silly me, you mean his *play!*"

Why hadn't I guessed those two were made for each other? They were frightful in exactly the same way.

"I do, and the plan is that we all go. Me, Claw, Camille, Issy, Frank, my parents. You."

"I'm not sure I like being tacked on the end of a list, babes," she replied in a jovial manner that I had no time for.

"Ha-ha funny. Well, you're not. I want you to tack Nick on the end of it."

"Why?"

That was the trouble with Rachel. I think it ran in her family. They rarely performed to expectation. They were posh and rich and yet Mummy and Daddy dressed like tramps. They were thoroughbred English yet seemed to have lost the national trait of reserve around the time Drake sent the Armada packing.

"I'm not sure yet. I just want you to invite him. In fact, I demand it."

Rachel's gravelly voice came rasping down the phone like a nail file being scraped. "Babes, you aren't going to do anything tacky like ask him to marry you in front of the entire audience, are you?"

I blushed to the *bone.*

"Oh, bloody hell, Rachel. Yes, I *was* going to, actually!" I could hardly get the words out. I hate when you have a secret and people guess it. It's so rude. And it makes you look so unoriginal.

"I think we can do better," she said.

We?

For once in my life, I decided to do the girl thing and prepare for my proposal. I even had a facial. It was as bad as I remembered—at various points the mortician—sorry, beautician—tried to choke me in steam, then suffocate me under a tissue. A succession of creams were patted on and patted off and the torture was interminable. As a finale she tapped all over my face with her fingertips as if trying to unlock a secret doorway. I tried to look grateful but my reflex thought was This is bullshit.

By the time Saturday came, despite the hydrated skin, I was constipated with fear. My parents had chosen to invite Lavinia and Michael. Nige and Rach were in on the plan—by necessity—but this only made me more uptight. And the plan? Having rejected the "tackiness" of proposing to Nick in front of a huge audience, we'd decided that I'd wait for everyone to disperse after the show. Claudia, Camille, Issy, Frank, Nick, and both sets of parents would remain in their seats, having been told that Nige was going to grandly descend from backstage and chaperon them to the aftershow party. Then the curtain would rise, I'd appear and pop the question.

It could, of course, end in disaster, with Nick shouting "No!" and running out of the auditorium. Secretly, I thought it would have been rather romantic to have proposed in front of a huge crowd of people I didn't know. Romance is only tacky to those not emotionally involved in it. If the feeling behind the action is genuine, heart-shaped balloons and giant teddy bears are the most beautiful gestures in the world. Of course, if Nick *did* shout "No!" and run out of the auditorium, I'd look a fool, but that's also a part of romance—running the risk of looking a fool because love is all and you'd do anything for it.

Nige summoned me to his dressing room just before curtain-up, to "run through the plan."

"I look at you," I said, "and I feel I should have worn more makeup."

The painted one laughed and fluttered his eyelashes. He was surrounded by good-luck cards and bottles of champagne and bouquets of flowers, and he was in his element. A familiar red shawl draped across the window hid the dead pigeon.

"You look divine, sweetheart. So you know what to do? The *second* the curtain falls, Peggy, the utter dear"—the ninety-three-year-old usher who had led me to Nige's dressing room—"will be waiting for you. She'll lead you to backstage left. Then you walk to center stage, wait for the curtain to rise, and then give our Nick the fright— sorry—the night of his life!"

I nodded. Nige looked pleased with himself. He reminded me of a squirrel I once saw in our garden holding a chunk of honey cake as big as his torso.

A bell rang.

"Now, be off with you! And don't *any* of you dare try to catch my eye!"

I didn't dare wish him luck in case the show was a disaster and he blamed me for jinxing it, so I scuttled out. The faithful Peggy was waiting to lead me back to my seat. There was an excited murmur and a few superior glances—the blue velvet curtain rose as I sat down. Toward the front of the auditorium, a couple were receiving equally baleful looks, having arrived late. To add insult, the woman was wearing a hat inappropriate for theater: it sprouted purple feathers like a fountain, obscuring the view of a great fan of seats behind her. Rach and Nick. Typical.

"How was he?" mouthed my mother, fanning her face with the program. She'd had her hair "done" for the theater. It was almost as high as Rachel's hat. My father clutched a bag of Maltesers and beamed at the thought of his own daughter, friend to the stars.

"Fine," I mouthed back. "Not nervous at all."

Which was more than I could say for me. The play was excellent, apparently. I registered none of it. I was too busy staring at the back of Nick's head. He turned to whisper to Rachel once or twice, and I could sense tension. What did *he* have to be tense about? He sauntered over in the interval to say hello and look handsome, and he barely made eye contact with me. I found myself shaking with terror and lust. But this was *good*, I told myself. By the time most people proposed, desire had slowed to a trickle. Not so long ago, I felt as if my sex drive had been hacked out by the root. And now, I wanted Nick so badly my insides were ooze.

"Nick's looking, er, relaxed," I ventured to Lavinia.

"Do you think?" she replied in her crisp manner. "I'm so glad. *I* thought he seemed preoccupied."

Wrong answer. I turned to Claw, who was sitting on my left. "Nice of Nick to come over, wasn't it?"

She swigged her Coke. "It would have been rude of him *not* to. I don't think he wanted to, though. I think Rachel made him. I watched him speaking to Mum and Dad, and he looked as if he had a porcupine in his pants."

I fell back in my seat, grateful that the lights dimmed at that moment so she couldn't see my expression. Maybe it *wasn't* a love letter. I had made a serious effort not to doubt Nick or myself. But I had an innate prejudice against people who didn't doubt themselves. People who don't doubt themselves tend to be mediocre. Then again, people who don't doubt themselves also tend to get annoyingly far in life. If the possibility of failure doesn't cross your mind, you don't fear it. And it's mostly fear that stops us from fulfilling our dreams.

As the final curtain fell, I sprang from my seat, muttering "Toilet" as I barged past Claw and Camille. It wasn't a lie, terror is as effective as prunes. I checked my face in the mirror. There was no color to it. I applied another coat of lipstick and sighed—it's amazing what lipstick does to the most unpromising of faces. I straightened my skirt. I wasn't exactly wearing "safe" clothes. Teetering heels, when I was tall enough without them. And the red Grace Kelly dress. I told myself I didn't care. People *should* dress up to go to the theater. It's about eking the most from life. I always think of Claw, biting into a peach on a dreary February day and exclaiming, "Oh, it's like being in Spain!" The same afternoon, she'd booked a trip to Barcelona. I loved that.

Peggy was waiting for me at the end of row V. She was a slow walker. I wondered how old she was and if she enjoyed her job. I wouldn't want *my* grandmother to be working at the age of what, seventy? Happily she was dead, so it wasn't an issue. I wanted to gabble, "Guess what, I'm going to propose onstage to my ex-boyfriend!" but I had a hunch Peggy would be unimpressed. Nige had sworn she was "an utter dear," but I suspected actors said that of the foulest of people. I'm not suggesting that Peggy was anything but sweet, yet she certainly appeared to be taking her time. I was sure there was a quicker route to the stage; we seemed to be going via Peru.

"There you go," she said suddenly, and vanished. I started. The stage—surprisingly small when you were *on* it—was deserted. It looked dirty. The cast must have taken their bows and adjourned to their dressing rooms. It was spookily quiet. I felt like a girl in a Scooby Doo cartoon, standing in an abandoned warehouse, the man from the fairground preparing to spring. I tiptoed to center stage, as Nige had instructed. My legs were hot and heavy. I could have peeked through the curtain to check if family and friends and Mr. Right Now Please I'm Tired of Messing About were all present and correct, but there was a good chance I'd faint at the sight of them, so I didn't.

I smoothed my hair. Any moment now, Nige would raise the curtain. Christ, what if he'd forgotten? I cleared my throat, and a gray silent creature with huge ears and an alienlike funnel instead of a nose wafted into view from stage right.

"Arrgh!" I gasped, clutching my heart. As well I might. It was Nick. Or rather, I *hoped* it was Nick, making a surprise appearance as Mr. Elephant. I was mute with shock. For half a second.

"Nick? Is that you? What—what are *you* doing here?"

Mr. Elephant reached to his neck and removed his head.

Small comfort that underneath, Nick looked as horrified to see me as I looked to see him. His mouth fell open. "Me? What are *you* doing here? You're supposed to be sitting in your seat!"

My complexion turned as hot and as red as my dress. "No, I'm not! God, now you've ruined everything!" I was furious. What a bodge. "Oh, what's the point!"

I glared at him, and he glared back. It didn't help that anger made him beautiful, despite the furry gray body and tail. His jaw was tight, which emphasized the sharp line of his cheekbones. He raked a hand through his hair.

"You," he said—holding Mr. Elephant's head underneath one arm in the style of an Elizabethan ghost—"are the most infuriating woman. You don't ever bloody do what you're *meant* to!"

"Meant to?" I shrieked. "What, so you're saying that women are *meant* to stay in their seats?" (Admittedly, I was interpreting freely, but I sensed an undertone insulting to the sisterhood.) "You . . . you *twit*! And you're too thin for an elephant!"

As I yelled *"twit"* I whapped him around the arm with my dinky pink evening bag. (Actually a child's bag from a toy shop, faux velvet boasting an embroidered princess on its side with real blond wool hair, for the distinctly *non*royal sum of £12.99.) The curtain rose during the attack, and everyone started laughing. Nick and I slowly turned. *Everyone.* Not just Rach and Claw and Camille and Mum and Dad and Lavinia and Michael. The entire audience. Not one person—and there were hundreds of them—had left their seat. They must have been huddled in silence for the last ten minutes, gulping back their giggles.

"Christ!" I squeaked. I waved at the sea of faces, uncertain what else to do. There was a smatter of clapping. I laughed. Then I frowned. Nick grabbed my hand. The clapping got louder.

"No," he said. "*You're* the twit."

"Kiss her!" roared a voice. It took a moment for the refined theater audience to mutate into a football crowd. "Kiss her, kiss her, kiss her!" they shouted.

Nick raised an eyebrow.

"You don't have to," I said sulkily.

He gave my arm a little shake. "I came up here to propose to you, Holly."

"What! Me too."

A smile lit his face.

"But Rachel said—"

"But Nige said—"

Nick tugged me a little nearer. The audience cheered.

"Nige and Rach," I whispered. "This is *their* idea of a joke. I'm going to kill them."

Nick tilted his head. "Won't you kiss me first?"

I wrinkled my nose. Nodded toward the full house. "What about *them*? It's embarrassing."

Nick grinned. "Presumably, when we were both being needlessly led around backstage in circles, *someone*—Rach, I'll bet—promised them a laugh if they hung around and kept quiet.

So"—he shot me a coy look from under his girl's eyelashes—"the least they deserve is a small kiss."

I blushed. He placed Mr. Elephant's head on the stage floor beside us. I pulled him closer, breathed in the scent of him. The tension, uncertainty, and fear dissolved. It was like bathing in a waterfall after a long arduous trek through the desert. Oh Nick. If there was nothing more to life than this, it would be enough. I stroked Mr. Elephant's furry behind and wondered how I ever thought I could do without either of them. We spend so much of our existence striving for a better tomorrow that we can fail to notice the best time of our lives is *now*—the only moment you can enjoy for sure. I hugged my happiness to me. I touched his hair. He traced my waist to my hip, and the world shone like sunlight on water.

We were the perfect match.

I cupped my hand to my mouth. And I said, "I love you, Nick, so much. I don't even *want* to be engaged a third time, I'm useless at it. I just want to be with you."

He nodded. Spoke into my ear, "I love you. Not, I love you too. 'Too' is too much of an *extra* for how much I love you."

We kissed. The small kiss grew into a big kiss. And even though we walked off the stage to continue our kissing in private (neither of us were entirely comfortable about using tongues in front of our parents), we got a standing ovation.

Nick twined his fingers with mine, a promise of forever. "See, Hol," he said. "Even the most cynical audience can't resist a happy ending."